ON THE COMP

On the Company's Service

Service

Ellis K. Meacham
(with map by Samuel H. Bryant)

CORONET BOOKS
Hodder Paperbacks Ltd., London

Copyright © 1971 by Ellis K. Meacham
First published by Little, Brown and
Company 1971
First published in Great Britain by
Hodder and Stoughton Ltd, 1972
Coronet edition 1973

Printed and bound in Great Britain for
Coronet Books,
Hodder Paperbacks Ltd,
St. Paul's House, Warwick Lane,
London, EC4P 4AH
by Hazell Watson & Viney Ltd,
Aylesbury, Bucks

ISBN 0 340 17828 0

To Kirby & Kay
Jere & Linda

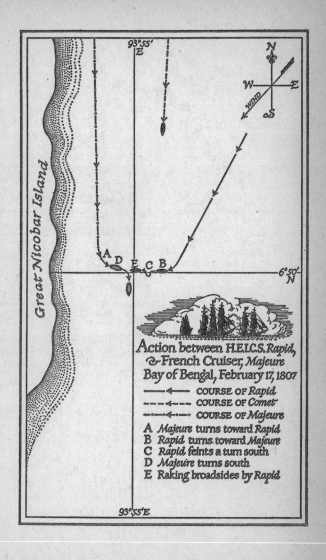

N

W   E

WIND

S

93°55'
E

6°50'
N

Great Nicobar Island

A
D
E
C
B

93°55' E

Action between H.E.I.C.S. *Rapid,*
& French Cruiser, *Majeure*
Bay of Bengal, February 17, 1807

———◄——— COURSE OF *Rapid*
——◄—— COURSE OF *Comet*
——◄—— COURSE OF *Majeure*

A   *Majeure* turns toward *Rapid*
B   *Rapid* turns toward *Majeure*
C   *Rapid* feints a turn south
D   *Majeure* turns south
E   Raking broadsides by *Rapid*

PART I

OFFICER IN TACTICAL COMMAND

CHAPTER ONE

Irritation welled up, tightening his throat. Merewether stole a glance at Commodore Land beside him, and saw the heightened color in his cheeks. The proposition did not sit well with Land either, he decided. Sir George Barlow, Acting Governor-General of India, sat across the table in icy composure, eyes fixed upon the speaker.

". . . And, of course, the Admiral anticipates that the Marine will take part in the combined operations against Mauritius and Java later this year. High time, he says, that the Royal Navy had a look at your state of readiness. Give you a chance to make up shortcomings," concluded Foreman, Admiral Pellew's Flag Captain, settling back in his chair with a bland expression. Beside him, Captain Wolfe sat quietly with a faint smile on his face.

Only a week ago, Wolfe had been first lieutenant in *Apollo*, thirty-six guns, when the Admiralty pouch from London by way of the Overland Mail, the Persian Gulf, Bombay Castle and *Rapid* had brought the news that he was posted captain. There was no command available, but evidently the energetic Sir Edward Pellew did not intend that he should be idle meanwhile.

"Your Excellency . . ." began Commodore Land.

"It's unusual," broke in Sir George, ignoring Land. "There should, of course, be the closest relationship and cooperation between the Navy and the Marine; each has the same ultimate objective : destruction of the enemy. I'll not argue the point with Sir Edward, but it must be understood that Commodore Merewether is under the orders of the Governor-General, the Company and Commandant of the Marine, and responsible solely to them."

"Certainly, Your Excellency," replied Captain Foreman easily.

9

"I am sure Wolfe here clearly understands that he is no more than an observer. I might say that Admiral Pellew expressed the highest regard for Commodore Merewether's abilities. It may well be that we shall learn a bit from him."

The irritation persisted in spite of the fair words of Foreman. Merewether reached into his memory for the term Lady Caroline Austen had used in conversation last night: sophistry, he recalled. He had tracked down its definition this noon in the library of the Calcutta Club. There was some motive here lying beneath the surface, he was convinced.

"Very well," said Sir George briskly. "It's settled then : Wolfe, his midshipman aide, and one servant. You have suitable accommodations, Merewether?"

"Yes, Your Excellency." It meant evicting Larkin from the supercargo's cabin in *Rapid*, and moving each junior officer to less comfortable quarters, but this was only an incident of the service. The irritation subsided a little as the discipline of a lifetime at sea asserted itself, but suspicion lingered. The capture of the privateer schooner last July, and the prominent part played by *Rapid* in the taking of a French frigate, must have brought home to the Royal Navy that the Bengal Squadron of the Bombay Marine would be a force to reckon with.

Sir George stood up in dismissal, and Merewether marched out with the rest to the anteroom where Locksley, the secretary, presided. Wolfe approached him with the same half smile upon his face.

"Ah, Commodore, we'll get along famously, I am sure. I am a man of simple tastes, but I do like my wine cellar along. Is there an empty room where I may store it under lock and key?" Wolfe was almost the same height as Merewether, but slighter in body, with unwinking blue eyes, blond hair and curling side-whiskers, and the self-confident air of one whose complete acceptance by any group is assured. Up close, the fair complexion was marred by a number of tiny purple veins visible under the skin along each side of the high-arched nose. Merewether decided he was about his own age and wondered fleetingly if the man were a heavy drinker.

Larkin's pigeons had sickened and died during the voyage to

China last fall, and the extra bosun's locker was empty. "Yes, of course," he told Wolfe, thinking of the small supply of wines and spirits that he must replenish for himself, though he did not anticipate many occasions this cruise when such luxuries would be necessary.

"Thank you. And how did you acquire that extraordinary scar on your face?"

The scar was nearly two years old, and Merewether was unmindful of its existence, except when it became irritated and caused difficulty in shaving. It was an honorable scar, and his fellow officers in the Marine either knew its origin or made discreet inquiry of others. He was not self-conscious, but the bald question from an officer he had not seen until an hour ago brought annoyance flushing up.

"Repelling boarders," he said, turning away.

It was only a moment before he regained his poise. It was ridiculous to let a tactless question upset him, particularly when this captain would be his guest aboard ship for an indefinite period.

"And do you require a boat, Captain?" he forced himself to ask.

"I was about to inquire as to that," said Wolfe, still with the half smile. "I'm the guest of Captain Flournoy ashore, and if you can send a boat and working party of, oh say eight in round figures at noon tomorrow, I'll have my furniture and baggage ready to move."

"Very well, Captain," said Merewether, thinking of the sea chest that held his worldly belongings. "I expect to weigh on the ebb day after tomorrow."

"Quite," said Wolfe.

Merewether joined Commodore Land to emerge into the blinding afternoon sun of Calcutta and mount the dockyard tonga. In three minutes, they had circled the square and pulled up beside Velloso's public house. In the cool, dim interior, they found a table, and the white-haired proprietor brought London gin and lemons. Each took a swallow, and Land set down his glass with a thump.

"God damned whippersnappers!" he exploded. "We've shaken them up, taken prize money out of their pockets, and now they want to find out how! No more than a spying mission and then an after-the-fact report." He shook his head, black eyes snapping. "I thought Sir George would give them short shrift, but he wants a foot in each camp, what with the political situation so tight."

Merewether felt the gin take effect, expanding through his body, and relaxed a bit. He finished the glass, bit into the lemon, and signaled Velloso. He could not afford to let the patronizing smile and arrogant manner of a junior Royal Navy captain upset him. He was solely responsible for the mission of the Bengal Squadron of the Bombay Marine.

Land tasted the second glass, then continued his remarks, damning the Royal Navy and spineless politicians who held high office. Merewether fixed himself in an attitude of rapt attention, but let his thoughts wander. This was the last day of 1806, and tomorrow would be his twenty-ninth birthday. A year ago he had been a first lieutenant in London, full of anxieties as to his prospects for promotion at the New Year's meeting of the Court of Directors of the Honourable East India Company, the new full-dress uniform sponged and pressed, hanging ready for his appearance before the session. The promotion to captain had been only the first event in a year of movement, culminating in his acquittal early this month of charges of violating the laws of China before a Court of Inquiry at Bombay, and the loss to another of the woman he had convinced himself he loved. The thought of Flora Dean inevitably brought to mind Lady Caroline Austen, niece of Sir George, a woman of poise and beauty, but so reserved that he had had difficulty making conversation with her on the three occasions they had been thrown together. Possibly the watch party for the new year tonight would thaw her.

Merewether became aware that Land had ceased his tirade and had asked a question. "Certainly, sir, right here." He unbuckled the oilskin-lined portfolio and handed over the commission to form the Bengal Squadron, engrossed on parchment with its seals and ribbons, to Land, who scanned it briefly.

"Now, Merewether, I hope you are aware that this commission

gives you a broad command to achieve a single objective: Sweep clear the Bay of Bengal and its approaches of the enemy. How you accomplish this result is your affair. I hope you've given the matter some thought."

"Yes, sir," replied Merewether anxiously, reaching for the dozen sheets of foolscap in the portfolio on which he had drafted his tentative operational orders.

"Not now," interrupted Land. "I haven't the foggiest idea at the moment of where to start, other than that report, nearly two months old, from Mister Ross in the Cocos Islands. I take it you'll hold a council of war with your captains before you leave?" He handed back the commission.

"Yes, sir, tomorrow afternoon in *Rapid*. I hope you can be present."

"No, I'm invited elsewhere, but I'll be on board before you weigh anchor."

Merewether looked again at the commission. Some nameless clerk at Bombay Castle had made the instrument a work of art with his elaborate penmanship. He ran his eye down it for the fortieth time since he had received it.

COMMODORE'S COMMISSION

To Percival Merewether, Esq., Captain in the Bombay Marine, Greeting—

Whereas open hostilities have taken place between our Sovereign Lord, the King, and the French and Batavian Republics, and whereas we, the said United Company, are duly authorized and empowered by virtue of divers charters in that behalf given and granted unto us by the predecessors of our said Sovereign Lord, King of Great Britain, France and Ireland, to raise and maintain forces and armies, both by sea and land, and to appoint such and so many Generals, Commanders and other officers as we shall see fit for the purpose of encountering and resisting by force of arms all and every the enemy and enemies of our Sovereign Lord, the King, and ourselves, and the said enemies, and every of them, their ship's armour, ammunition and other goods, to invade and destroy in such manner as in and by the said Charters is provided, mentioned and contained. Now, we, the said

United Company, in consideration of the premises, and reposing especial trust and confidence in your good conduct, loyalty and courage, do by these presents, and under and by virtue of the Royal Charter aforesaid, and all other powers in us vested, constitute and appoint you, Percival Merewether, Esq., Captain in the Bombay Marine, to be during the hostilities aforesaid, and during our pleasure, and the pleasure of the Governor-General in Council, COMMODORE. . . .

There followed admonitions and directions of obedience to his orders addressed to all other commanders, officers and warrant officers of the Bombay Ships, Naval and Marine Service, an order to destroy or capture all forces of the French or Batavian Republics in the Bay of Bengal, and a brief conclusion. It was signed and sealed by Commodore Sir John Waldron, Commandant of the Marine, Sir James Campbell, Superintendent of the Marine, and endorsed, "Approved," by the Governor-General and Council, under the Common Seal.

Beyond the formal language, to Merewether, the commission contained but a single order: Sweep clear the Bay of Bengal of the enemy. The manner and means of accomplishing this was left entirely to his discretion. He thought of the books he had labored through the past week, accounts of naval operations, strategy and tactics, which shed little light on how to find an elusive enemy in an area of almost a million square miles of open sea. Suddenly, the meaning and implications of a "broad command" came home to him with all its frightening responsibilities. He tucked the commission back into the portfolio, buckled it, drained his glass and followed Commodore Land out to the tonga.

The watch party was at the town mansion of a high official in the Company. He was uncertain of his host's exact title, but Sir George and Lady Barlow, other members of the Council, and two justices of the High Court of Judicature, with their wives, were among the glittering throng when he arrived. This was not one of the formal events of Calcutta society, there was no announcement of the arrival of guests, but they were quietly greeted, identified, and ushered into the drawing room where servants presided over punch bowls containing real ice. The new title of Commodore opened doors, Merewether cynically concluded, taking a cup of punch.

A little later, he found himself paying his respects to Sir George and Lady Barlow, and soon after found himself in the company of Lady Caroline, striving to find some subject that would penetrate her reserve. He was on his third attempt, when out of the corner of his eye, he saw the blue coat and gold lace of the Royal Navy approaching.

"Ah there, Merewether. Delightful occasion."

There was no escape. He turned and made the introduction. "Lady Caroline, may I present Captain Wolfe?" The captain made a deep bow.

"Enchanted," he said. "I had no idea such beauty had found its way to Calcutta!"

Lady Caroline blushed and stammered in response, her reserve penetrated, and Merewether could see that Wolfe had made an impression upon her in a moment that he had not during several hours. The man's color was high, his speech eloquent, and he soon led her away toward the ballroom where musicians were playing.

Merewether cursed his inability to make the light conversation and witty remarks that had flowed so easily from the lips of Wolfe. He went back for more punch, and then found himself cornered by the host, a portly gentleman with a vast concern for the price of cotton cloth and the wages demanded by seamen serving in East Indiamen. By the time he had extricated himself from this affair, it was midnight, the New Year was welcomed in with a medley of toasts, and supper was announced.

Lingering beside the door, Merewether watched the group coming from the ballroom, mostly the younger set in high spirits, giggling and chattering. Finally, Lady Caroline emerged, chin high and spots of color in her cheeks. Wolfe beside her, smiling and turning toward her at each step to make some remark. She came across the floor at a determined pace, took Merewether's arm, inclined her head slightly to Wolfe, and led the way toward the dining room where the buffet was laid.

As he turned, he saw Wolfe make an elaborate bow, and heard him say, "Au 'voir, you beautiful minx." Lady Caroline gave no indication that she heard, but proceeded swiftly to the verandah where Sir George and Lady Barlow had gathered with the host and hostess. Even with the aid of the sparkling wines, Merewether could obtain little response from her. She barely picked at the repast until she saw Merewether finished, then whispered to him.

"Can you take me home?"

"Certainly," he replied. "If you wish." She stood up, moved around the table, and whispered in the ear of Lady Barlow, who appeared startled, looked hard at Merewether, and then nodded. Lady Caroline took her leave of the host and hostesss, as did Merewether.

"Take the barouche, and send it back," said Sir George in an undertone.

The ride to the palace was quiet, Merewether puzzled at the turn of events and unable to think of anything to say, Lady Caroline sitting rigidly against the arm of the seat. The gates swung open, the guard saluted, and the Indian watchman ushered them into the entrance hall.

"I know you must want to get back," she said quickly. "I'll not detain you, and thank you for an introduction to a cad!" She turned, and started through the door at the end of the hall.

Merewether was astounded, he had no idea of what was behind this remarkable statement.

"Wait. . ." he called, and she hesitated in the doorway. "I don't understand," he continued lamely. "Have I offended you?"

She was weeping, Merewether could see now, tears trickling down her cheeks and shoulders heaving. He advanced cautiously, holding out his hands, to find them seized, and her head pressed against his chest as she sobbed. He waited, holding her hands, for the paroxysm to subside, then led her into the sitting room behind the door, and applied his handkerchief until the tears were dried. She sat down, and Merewether took a chair opposite, still unable to fathom the reason for her distress, or the meaning of the accusation she had hurled at him.

After a space, she lifted her face, composure restored, and said in a low voice, "It's hard to be a young widow, especially after you come out of mourning. People misunderstand you. Men think you're fair game for their schemes, that all they need do is beckon to have you fall into bed. . . ."

Merewether had heard vaguely that Lady Caroline's late husband had died at Trafalgar last year, but on the two previous occasions he had been in her company, he had given the matter no thought, and certainly had not considered the fact of widowhood to be an overt invitation to solicit a casual liaison.

She continued, "That horrible man—Captain Wolfe?—made a most explicit and insulting proposal to me tonight, and then laughed at me!" Merewether wondered for a moment if it were the proposal or the laugh that had so upset her. "Did you tell him I was widowed?" she demanded.

"Why, no!" he replied, a little nettled. "I never saw the man before this, or rather, yesterday afternoon." The implications of his roles as the one making an unwelcome introduction, and now as a prospective champion, began to sink in. Gad, was he under some chivalrous obligation here? The man had provoked irritation yesterday afternoon with his patronizing half smile and tactless question, but he would be in close association with him for an indefinite period at sea. Was he under an obligation of honor to this woman he had only seen a few times before to go back and call out Wolfe? Lady Caroline resolved the dilemma.

"I'm sorry I made such a scene," she said, standing up and stretching out her hand. "It was not your fault; you could not know his character. Now you must go back to the party. And thank you for your understanding."

Merewether protested, but she was firm, and he took his departure. The barouche had long since gone back to await the Governor-General; he had no desire to return to the affair himself and walked back to the dockyard. He was still debating what he should have done—had she decided he was a poltroon, and let him off? Nonsense, he decided as he signaled Hamlyn from the gig not to pipe the side.

In his cabin, he pulled off the full-dress uniform and saw Sangh, his steward, hang it away in a locker.

"Gin . . . No, a pot of tea, please, Sangh, and I'll not require anything further."

It was seven bells into the midwatch, but he felt compelled to read and edit again the draft of his operational order upon which his whole future might depend. It would be copied off in the morning, then distributed to his captains, the Governor-General and the Marine. The brief conversation with Land yesterday afternoon had brought home again to him the tremendous responsibilities he bore for the success or failure of the operation. He weighed each paragraph, seeking weakness, amending and emending, until at the tenth page, he found the tea cold, his eyes not focusing, and blew out the lamp to fall across the brass bed. As he lay back, the curious events of the evening crossed his mind again. Could Lady Caroline be the kind of female whose desire to be the center of attention caused her to provoke conflict among her admirers? Her subsequent conduct did not confirm the fact, but Merewether resolved that he would be cautious.

CHAPTER TWO

By noon, all departments in *Rapid* had reported ready for departure tomorrow, and the port watch had left for a last liberty in Calcutta until sunset. Mister Midshipman Hamlyn, Mister Davis, the purser, and Webster, a taciturn middle-aged seaman who refused to disclose the sources of his education, had made the fair copies of the order. Merewether reread and signed them, then took the gig to the dockyard to meet MacLellan, who had been his first lieutenant a year ago, and go on to the Calcutta Club for lunch this New Year's Day.

"You can't guess what day this is, Mac," Merewether said as the waitress set Scots whisky and gin before them.

"Your birthday?" said MacLellan, raising his glass and looking for confirmation. "Many happy returns, and a muckle more of them!" The big Scots officer glowed with goodwill as he drank the toast. "I only wish I were going with you, Captain, on this sweep."

"And I too. With you as my chief of staff, I'd have no worries. And now, what's the news of Calcutta?"

He was back on board by six bells of the afternoon watch, the charts of the Bay of Bengal and its approaches tacked on the bulkhead, looking at them blindly as though by sufficient concentration he might divine the location of the French cruisers. Within the hour, Morison of *Tiger* arrived with his officers. MacRae was not far behind, informing Merewether that only yesterday had he felt this state of readiness in *Comet* sufficient to commission her. He led the group aft and stood aside as they went below to the cabin. He heard the watch hail and saw the launch coming alongside the port gangway, her gunwales almost awash.

Wolfe came up the ladder to the squeal of the boatswain's pipe, followed by a midshipman—Kinney was the name in the orders—and Merewether greeted him. "Welcome aboard, Captain, and do you require more hands?"

"Yes, a responsible warrant officer to check my manifest and stow my cellar, and some artisans to set up the furniture in my cabin. My servant, Dyer, will be present to show them where."

"Very well, Mister Davis will see to the stowage of the cellar, and the carpenter will send his mates to set up your furniture. I regret I am detained at the moment by the necessity of presenting my plan of operation to my commanders." Merewether turned to go below.

"Your plan of operation?" said Wolfe. "Well, now, I should be present for that."

"The officers are in my cabin," Merewether agreed, "and you are welcome."

The assemblage stood up as he entered, the first recognition of his new rank. "At ease, gentlemen," he told them, and took his seat behind the desk. He had only had time to say a few platitudes when Wolfe came in.

"Captain Wolfe of the Royal Navy, gentlemen," he told them. "May I present Captains Morison and MacRae of the Marine." Wolfe bowed stiffly twice. "And their officers . . ." He managed the names of all but the third lieutenant in *Tiger*. "And my officers, Lieutenants Larkin, MacCamy and Dobbs, Doctor Buttram and Mister Hamlyn." The assemblage crowded even the spacious cabin in *Rapid*. Wolfe took the chair pushed forward by Sangh, as all took seats or stood pressed against the bulkheads.

For the first time in his life, Merewether felt a twinge of stage fright. He looked at the outline of his order for fully half a minute, then began in a nervous voice the introduction he had learned by rote.

"Gentlemen, our mission is to sweep clear the Bay of Bengal and its approaches of the enemy. As you know, the mouth of the bay is a thousand miles south of here, and more than a thousand miles wide. It is obviously impossible for a single squadron to cover this vast area, and equally obvious that this is not necessary. We need not concern ourselves, for instance, with the Coromandel Coast or the eastern shores of India. . . ."

"And why not, Commodore?" Wolfe sat staring at him with the half smile on his lips.

Knocked off stride, Merewether stammered. "Why, this season . . . the northeast monsoon makes it a lee shore; there are no harbors sheltered from the east; and the underwriters refuse to insure vessels calling at ports on that coast from October to April, so there is no shipping."

Wolfe stared at him a moment more, then said, "Quite. I think it a valuable item of information for these officers. Pray proceed."

Annoyance almost choked him, as Merewether wondered for a moment if he dared go back to Sir George and inform him that this officer was personally obnoxious and must be replaced. It would be a confession of weakness, he decided instantly. He tried to pick up the lost thread of his presentation.

"So, gentlemen, we do not attempt the impossible, but concentrate upon the probable, seeking our enemy in the customary shipping lanes for this season." Out of the corner of his eye, he saw Wolfe about to speak again and hurried on, ignoring him. "A ship approaching from the south, Mauritius for example, has the choice of trying to beat almost into the eye of the wind at great expense of labor and matériel, or of running close-hauled far enough east that she can then come about and sail back to her destination." He picked up the ruler from his desk and pointed to a cluster of islands on the chart in nearly fifteen degrees south latitude. "Mister Ross, who has plantations in the Cocos Islands, has reported that four French ships landed there and took on water and citrus fruits six weeks ago. They departed eastwardly, I suspect to go about and proceed northwestwardly along the coast of Sumatra, then cross the shipping lanes into the Strait of Malacca." He paused and took a swallow of water from the glass on his desk.

"And why just at that point?" asked Wolfe suddenly.

Merewether got the mouthful down without strangling. "Small end of the horn. Nearly all shipping is westbound this season, from China and the Indies," he managed. "Four smaller ships are reported overdue from Amboyna and the Celebes. The China convoy came through under escort last month, and the commodore reported two sightings just west of the Strait, a brig and a large schooner, but they did not attack. He had one India-man straggler, of which we have no report."

He looked Wolfe in the eye. He had attempted to describe the situation and evaluate the meager intelligence upon which he had based the operation in enough detail so that these officers would have a vivid mental picture of the entire affair. Even young Hamlyn there might find himself called upon to act in an emergency without time for consultation with higher authority.

"A Royal Navy sloop came through the Strait three weeks ago and never sighted a sail," said Wolfe. "The Captain was offering ten pounds for any sighting that proved to be French, too." He smiled at Merewether, then looked away at the chart on the bulkhead.

"Now, gentlemen," said Merewether after a pause to recover his equanimity. "I propose this disposition: First Captain Morison in *Tiger* will take station a hundred miles southeast of the Sandheads and maintain a patrol across the shipping lanes to Calcutta. This is a most important assignment, as we know four ships have been captured in this area in the past year," he concluded in haste, seeing disappointment in Morison's thin, intense face. It was unfortunate that his command was one of the slow, slab-sided, top-heavy brigs—floating coffins, the Marine called them—designed with a shallow draft and heavy armament to penetrate tidal estuaries and rivers. He must have an anchor point upon which he could rely, he justified himself, and with *Tiger*'s poor windward sailing qualities, her ten twenty-four-pounder carronades were more valuable athwart the shipping lanes leading to Calcutta.

"Second, *Comet* and *Rapid* will follow the usual route south-eastward to the Strait, looking in at Rangoon and the Gulf of Martaban, investigating the Bentinck Channel and offshore islands along the way, and then calling at Penang. If no contact is made, and lacking intelligence at Penang, we shall sail westward through the Nicobar Islands towards Ceylon. If all this turns up nothing, we start over. Now, Morison, do not spare your questions or comments. You'll have your turn too, MacRae." He settled back, ready to defend or amend the plan.

Morison looked at the chart a moment and cleared his throat. Then Wolfe said, "Why not just the reverse, Commodore, run down to Ceylon, and beat back to the Strait. That way, you might very well intercept both the cruisers and their prizes." He sat back with an air of triumph.

This was one question for which Merewether was completely prepared. He had had the same thought and laboriously analyzed the alternatives during the past week, before settling on his operational order. "Captain, your suggestion has considerable merit, and I confess I considered it at length before making a decision. I decided against it for these reasons: First, I think a prize, once clear of Sumatra with a fair wind, would unhesitatingly turn south. It would be purely fortuitous if we happened to intercept. Second, we would waste the time sailing south through waters that are untraveled at this season, and then face a long beat to windward. Third, by following the shipping lanes southeast, we show the flag, protect the shipping en route to Calcutta, and have the chance of picking up intelligence. Fourth, and most important, privateers will undoubtedly station themselves where they may intercept the maximum amount of traffic, and that is at the approaches to the Strait and off the Sandheads." Merewether paused. "And now your comments, Morison."

"I'm in full agreement, except I'd like a more active assignment," he said in his deep voice.

"And MacRae?"

"Oh, in the narrow seas, sir, that's where the prizes are, and the French should be close by."

"Then, unless there is objection from higher authority, this will be our initial order." He saw Sangh peer in through the door. Time to set up refreshments and call an end to the council. "One more thing. Doctor Buttram will call upon you early in the forenoon watch tomorrow to examine crews and inspect ships for any symptoms of pestilence or infestation." Merewether stood up, signaling the end of the meeting. He saw Wolfe approach, face wreathed in smiles.

"Well, Commodore, did I overplay my part as Devil's Advocate?"

"Devil's . . . ?" began Merewether. "Oh, I see." Perhaps, he thought, the man was instructed to play such a part and certainly his questions had elicited amplification of the bases for the order that might indeed be valuable to the junior officers. His irritation melted, and he smiled back at Wolfe. "They certainly were searching questions, Captain, almost the same as those I asked myself in reaching the decision. And now, gentlemen, a toast!"

They were halfway through the buffet when Sangh brought the note to him. Amid the jovial conversation, no one noticed; and Merewether broke the seal and read the single line.

"See me in my quarters tonight at your early convenience." There was a stylistic cypher below that he recognized as the initial *B*. He slid the note into his breast pocket and addressed himself again to the ham. His conscience was reasonably clear, but he found himself gobbling his food and forced himself to eat deliberately, joining in the conversation until raisins, cheese and port had been served. He saw MacRae and Morison over the side, then called away the gig.

There was little delay while the dockyard tonga was sent for; the courtesy title "Commodore" worked wonders here too, Merewether noted. In a few minutes he was ushered into the library where Sir George sat before a stack of documents.

"Evening, Merewether," growled Sir George. "I have not seen a copy of your operation order as yet."

"No, Your Excellency, it will be over in the morning, but I can . . ."

"Never mind, that was not the matter I wished to see you about." Sir George paused and looked a little self-conscious. "Lady Barlow was concerned, and I must say I am curious. What happened last night to send Caroline home so early?"

"I don't really know, Your Excellency," Merewether began, trying to think of some way to avoid the blunt question.

"Lady Barlow gathered that something passed between Caroline and that captain—Wolfe—that upset her."

"There could have. I admit I introduced Captain Wolfe to her," said Merewether carefully. "He took her off to dance, and I did not see them again until she rejoined me to go in to supper."

"And what reason did she give you for leaving?"

"Sir—Your Excellency—she said, 'Thank you for an introduction to a cad,' and then said something about people misunderstanding a young widow."

"And what did you understand from that?"

"I concluded that Wolfe had said something, made some remark to Lady Caroline that was distasteful to her. I tried to inquire further, but she said it was not my fault and dismissed me."

"Aha!" said Barlow. "I begin to understand. Wolfe, I've heard, has some reputation in the fleet as a rake, though he's married to a daughter of one of the Admiralty Commissioners. Well, Lady Barlow and I want no scandal; a few remarks by a man in his cups, with no overt action, does not justify a call to the field of honor."

Barlow sat staring into the middle distance for a moment. "I confess, however, the man did not appeal to me. Do you want me to veto his appointment as observer in the Bengal Squadron?"

The proposal caught Merewether by surprise. He thought of yesterday's tactless question, the condescending air, the distress of Lady Caroline last night, the rude interrogation as to the bases of his operational order this afternoon, and then the sincere smile and half apology for playing the part of "Devil's Advocate." The man evidently had ability and understanding of naval affairs. And too, he could not condemn Wolfe for an alcoholically inspired proposition to a beautiful, unattached woman—he had transgressed in that direction himself—and one never knew whether such a proposal could be considered an insult, or accepted as a compliment. The warm smile of this afternoon out-weighed the other factors.

"Your Excellency, the man appears able, he gave an excellent critique of my plan this afternoon, and there would be delay and possibly hard feelings on the part of Admiral Pellew and others."

Sir George, head down, considered for a moment, then looked up keenly at Merewether. "I think you would rather I do just that, but you have this damnable sense of fair play. Well, I'll take no action. I only hope you do not regret your decision." He shook his head. "And now, I'm sure, you'll want to say farewell to Lady Barlow and Lady Caroline."

There were more raisins, cheese, sweetmeats, port and conversation. It was midnight before he escaped, uncomfortably aware that some matter, he hoped it was not still the affair of the night before, was troubling Sir George.

CHAPTER THREE

The trip down the Hooghly was uneventful. Off the Sand-heads, as the pilots were dropped, Merewether took the opportunity to shift his flag into *Comet*. He had no doubts of MacRae's ability to command, but with a patchwork crew and strange officers, he wished to see for himself her state of readiness and sailing qualities. There followed two strenuous days and nights of general exercises, both internal and tactical. The ships sailed in formation, executing maneuvers in obedience to the arbitrary signals; they rigged pumps and dragged hoses to the scenes of imaginary fires; they cleared for action, launched boats, rescued men overboard, towed and were towed, strung hammock nettings, and repelled boarders.

At noon the second day, *Rapid* put over a target raft, and the ships came about in turn, firing their batteries until the canvas targets were shredded. Merewether winced at the cost, but he was using up old powder and letting the new men hear the broadsides speak. *Comet* came last in the line on the final passage, her starboard gun crews anxiously training and sighting the five eighteen-pounders, and the two long-nine pivot guns that had been added to her battery at Calcutta.

"Fire!" roared Dillon, MacRae's first lieutenant, and flame spouted from the side. The ship heeled to port as smoke blotted out the target.

From their perch in the lee shrouds, Merewether and MacRae saw a cloud of splinters fly up, and the entire target raft vanished.

"Well done!" shouted Merewether. "I think you are ready, Captain."

"I think as much myself," said MacRae with one of his infrequent smiles. Merewether felt a sense of elation. He knew *Rapid* was ready, was sure Morison and *Tiger* could be depended on, and now MacRae had whipped *Comet* into an efficient ship. This mission would not fail!

After declining a drink with MacRae, Merewether went back to *Rapid* in the first dogwatch. As he came over the side, and the shrill boatswain's pipe ceased its squealing just as his pennant reached the peak, he saw that Larkin's usually impassive face was livid, his pale blue eyes blazing.

"What is it, Larkin?" he asked.

The tall American was silent for a moment, looked aft, and then said bluntly, "That captain, he's drunk!" He paused, looking hard at Merewether, and continued, "Been drunk, sir, ever since you left the ship." He hesitated a moment, then said in a quivering voice, "And this morning he tried to assume command of the ship from me!"

"What!"

"Yes, sir, and he's challenged me to a duel. Considering his condition, I refused the honor."

"Quite right, and now let us see this gentleman." He started aft.

"He's in your cabin, sir, more convenient for service from the pantry, he said."

"Well, I'm damned! Now, signal the squadron to get underway, line ahead; *Rapid* is guide, course southeast, a half east; shielded stern lanterns to be rigged on guide and second ship."

Merewether waited while Larkin passed the word to MacCamy

and Hamlyn, and then wrote the order on the slate, as the flag hoist was two-blocked.

The setting sun illuminated the cabin through the stern windows, revealing the figure in full uniform sprawled across the brass bed on the rumpled coverlet. On his desk, a tray held a dark bottle, its neck red with the broken wax seal of a vintage sack, but the crystal wineglass was on the surface of the desk amid a whole congregation of white circles etched into the varnished finish. In the corner of the cabin, the small figure of Sangh perched on the edge of a chair. His gorge rose at the sight, but he forced himself to be civil.

"Good evening, Captain." The figure moved, rolled into a sitting position, then unsteadily stood up, the vacant eyes focusing finally on him. "May we assist you to your quarters?"

"What? God damn your eyes, don't patronize me, you Bombay lubber!" Wolfe picked up the half-full glass, drained it, and dropped it to shatter on the desk top.

"You are not yourself, Captain," said Merewether, though the blood was pounding in his ears. "We wish only to assist you in your disorder, and I'll have Doctor Buttram wait on you."

"Wait on me!" mimicked Wolfe. He stepped forward and slapped Merewether's left cheek with his open hand. "I'll wait on you on the field of honor, if a bastard such as you knows what that means!"

Merewether's fist was clenched and he half stepped forward, with the instinct of the lower deck and the boatswain's mate from which he had risen, to strike down this man and his unforgivable insults. He managed to restrain himself.

"I excuse you. You're not responsible," he said thickly. "Mister Larkin, will you assist the captain to his quarters, and then ask Doctor Buttram to wait on him."

Wolfe stood rocking on his feet. "Not responsible . . ." he said. "You excuse me . . ." He seemed almost to become sober, but Larkin did not hesitate; he snapped Wolfe's arm up behind his back and propelled him through the door. Merewether stood bemused, as Sangh, clucking in dismay, began to pick up the fragments of glass on the desk top. Was it too late to go back to the Sandheads and transfer this captain to the pilot lugger?

Half an hour later, Buttram knocked and entered. "Well, sir, I've given the captain something to make him sleep and enough purgatives to keep him busy the next two days. Larkin has put his padlock back on the cellar and here's the key. Not much more I can do now."

"Thank you, Doctor." The elation of an hour ago had been replaced by depression. Was this an omen for the operation?

After daylight the next morning, *Tiger* hoisted a signal, "Request permission to carry out orders." Merewether came on deck wrapped in his old boat cloak against the morning chill. By dead reckoning, the squadron was a hundred and thirty-five miles southeast of the Sandheads, and in position to maintain a patrol across the trade routes. It was as good a point as any to part company with the brig.

"Affirmative, and good luck," he told Hamlyn. "And be sure you get our position from Mister Dobbs to enter in the log."

The signal soared up, and he watched *Tiger*'s hoist come down, then saw her wear about and head southwest, already shortening sail, on the first leg of an interminable succession of courses, reaches and tacks. She must claw back, close-hauled, northwardly, then go about southeastwardly to close the triangle and hold her position here. Merewether commiserated with Morison, but there was as much chance for action here as in any other area of the Bay of Bengal.

Merewether came back to the cabin to eat the poached egg on toast, with ham on the side, that Sangh served him, and drink a second cup of tea. Only three days out of port, there was still fresh food. The events of last night seemed unreal as a dream as he settled into the routine at sea. Even the white rings, etched by wine into the surface of his desk, had vanished, the lemon odor of polish still in the air. He permitted himself only a brief thought of Wolfe. Pray God, with no wine there would be no repetition.

Two days later, Midshipman Kinney appeared in his cabin. "Sir, Captain Wolfe requests permission to call upon you." The dark young man appeared sheepishly nervous.

"Why, certainly," Merewether told him, surprised. "At the captain's convenience."

A half hour later, Wolfe entered the cabin in full-dress uniform, cocked hat under his left arm, but not wearing his sword. He was pale, and there was a noticeable tremor in his hands.

"Yes, Captain?"

"Sir, I hardly know how to commence," said Wolfe in a high, strained voice. "I can only say I am miserably ashamed of myself, and I beg your pardon for my inexcusable conduct. It will not happen again, sir." Wolfe remained stiffly at attention before the desk.

Merewether felt a wave of compassion wash over him. It required moral courage for this officer to abase himself and make the apology. His conduct had bordered on mutiny and certainly had been unbecoming an officer and gentleman, but Merewether could testify from personal experience as to the insidious effects of wine. He decided to accept the apology and forget the incident.

"Very well, Captain. I accept your apology, and the matter is closed."

The two ships made a weary beat to windward through Preparis North Channel toward the shallow Gulf of Martaban, sailing at the limits of visual signal range, even with the oversize flags Merewether had had the sailmaker run up, so as to cover the maximum area. They spoke two country ships, but their masters could furnish no intelligence. Finally, they came to anchor in eight fathoms off the mouth of the Rangoon River, and Larkin took the cutter in to the pilot station, with Sangh as an interpreter. Four hours later, he was back with nothing to report.

"The Master Pilot says nine small vessels have called in the past fortnight, but none have seen a thing. Looks as though the Frogs may have gone back south, sir."

"Hard to believe," grumbled Merewether. "Unless they caught that straggler Indiaman and are content with a four-way split in prize money." He contained his disappointment and signaled the squadron under way. Could Wolfe have been right? Should he have followed the reverse of his course in the initial sweep? He could not be sure, but all logic had pointed to the eastern sector of the Bay of Bengal as the better hunting ground. So far, the mission was a failure.

The squadron headed a point east of south, looking in at the myriad islands of the Mergui Archipelago along the west coast of the Malay Peninsula, sending boat crews in to land and reconnoiter the bays and sounds to the east, but with no real expectation of finding the French hiding among them. In three weeks, they spoke a Norwegian barque, an American brig, and half a dozen Indian or Burmese dhows, none of whom had any information. Finally in the approach to the Strait of Malacca, it came home to Merewether that even these narrow waters, "the small end of the funnel," as he had so glibly termed them on the chart, encompassed thousands of square miles of empty ocean.

"Well, Captain, it has been a water haul thus far," he told Wolfe at dinner that night. It was the second time he had invited the captain to dine with him since the apology, and he had found him pleasant and entertaining each time. Tonight, Midshipmen Hamlyn and Kinney were also guests, each yet a little wary of the other and not anxious to be noticed by their seniors.

"Quite," replied Wolfe. "A needle in a haystack." He smiled and continued, "There is a great deal of chance in everything at sea. A mile east or west, and you might sail right by the plate fleet, let alone a pair of fast schooners. What are your plans now?"

Merewether hesitated a moment. He had made the decision two days ago in a brief conference with MacRae, hove to off Similan Island, and there was no reason to conceal it from anyone on board, though he was uncomfortably aware that Wolfe was keeping a private log.

"We are now at seven degrees, five minutes north, ninety-seven degrees, ten minutes east. I think we may as well call at George Town on Penang and see what news the Governor has there."

"Quite. And now, Captain, if you'll excuse us, I have a splitting headache." The men withdrew, and Merewether went on deck to give Larkin the new course, and signal it to MacRae.

Rapid sighted lights on Penang just after midnight two days later, but lay off until dawn to make the approach to the anchorage between the island and mainland in daylight. They picked up the pilot, a retired master's mate from the Royal Navy, who spoke in thick Devonshire as he looked aloft at the broad pennant.

"Only four ships present," he said pleasantly. "American, Norwegian and Swedish, and His Majesty's sloop *Argus,* but she's out of commission. There'll be no salutes for your flag, Commodore."

"Just as well, save powder," responded Merewether, thinking sourly that unless he had more success in the future, it was unlikely that his flag would ever receive a salute.

They managed to work in to the anchorage, catching a favorable slant of wind, and heading for the Company dock. Half a mile south, off what must be the dockyard, he saw a sloop at anchor, barges carrying shear legs moored to either side. She carried a mizzenmast, but no fore- or mainmast.

"That's *Argus,* twenty-two, Captain Richard Ackroyd, Royal Navy, Commodore," volunteered the pilot. "She was caught in a typhoon last October east of Bintan, lost her foremast and sprung her mainmast. Not a stick of timber fit to make a spar in this place! The Navy had to send to Rangoon to find enough pine, and they're just now ready to step the new masts with those shear legs."

Merewether remembered his own ordeal with a typhoon last fall in the China Sea, and though he had lost his mizzen royal mast, the others had survived. With such scarcity of suitable timber down here, he hoped he would not require replacements. *Comet* and *Rapid* came to anchor off the Company dock at four bells in the forenoon watch, and half an hour later, he was at Government House inquiring for Governor Dundas.

"Not here," said the clerk at the desk in the outer office. "And who might you be?"

"Merewether, commanding the Bengal Squadron of the Marine," he replied. "Then I'll speak with the First Secretary, please."

"Mister Pearson is sick. The Assistant Secretary, Mister Thomas Stamford Raffles, is acting." The clerk sniffed and said, "Two ships would not seem to be much of a squadron."

"The balance of my command is cruising elsewhere," said Merewether, a little stung by the cheeky attitude of this clerk. Announce me, please, to your Mister Raffles."

"Your name?" demanded the clerk, and departed toward the inner office.

In a moment, he was back. "Come in, sir."

Merewether entered a large dimly lighted office to find a young man behind a long table covered with papers. He was younger than Merewether by several years, it appeared. As the man stood up, an ornate gold watch chain, hung with seals, stretched across his unbuttoned waistcoat, made a musical jingle.

"Tom Raffles, Commodore," he said, extending his hand. "I seem to be holding the fort alone today. Have a chair. We had word of your appointment to the Bengal Squadron but did not expect to see you here so soon."

The man was handsome, dark hair over wide-set gray eyes, and had an easy smile. He wore an elaborately ruffled shirt under the waistcoat, with a neckpiece of scarlet tied about the high collar. In spite of the foppish attire, Merewether found himself liking the young man immediately. He exuded an aura of wisdom beyond his years, coupled with the energy to act upon a decision. He sat down and came to the point.

"Sir, we have made a sweep from the Sandheads southeast along the shipping lanes this past month, but have neither seen nor heard anything of the four privateers we have reason to believe are operating in the area. Would you have any later information?"

Raffles looked at him directly over interlaced fingers delicately supporting his chin. "No, Commodore. I received the information forwarded by Mister Ross in the Cocos Islands last month, but no ship calling here has reported any further sightings. We had a single Indiaman pass two weeks ago, already reported as a straggler from the China convoy, but she did not stop here. Of course, nearly all shipping has been westbound at this season of the year, and the French would be stationed west of the Strait to intercept."

"Of course. But I hoped some of your local trade might have heard something; even a rumor would be helpful."

"No ..." commenced Raffles, then paused. "Only thing, Commodore, not over an hour ago, a native farmer from something over fifty miles northwest of here brought in a load of chickens and told the Port Captain he had seen a column of smoke rising from one of the offshore islands that is not regularly inhabited, and he wondered who might be on it."

"Can you get this farmer back?"

"Probably." Raffles rang a bell on the desk, and the clerk came in.

"Menzies, see if you can get the Port Captain to bring in that Malay who made the report this morning about smoke from the island."

"Yes, sir," said the man, and started sulkily out.

"Afternoon will be time enough," Raffles called after him, and explained, "I'm due at home for lunch in a quarter hour, and you shall be my guest."

With the sense of failure hanging over him, Merewether was anxious for intelligence, even this scrap about a column of smoke from an uninhabited island. He would have gone to the Port Captain himself in the interests of time. He opened his mouth.

"No protests, Commodore," interposed Raffles. "You are losing no time, and I wish you to meet my darling wife. Shall we go?" He rose, took a handsome coat and hat from a rack beside the door, and put them on, then buttoned his waistcoat. "Have to keep up appearances even in the tropics, Commodore." He led the way out into the blinding sunlight where a barouche waited.

It was only a short ride to the house of Mister Raffles, set on a hill west of George Town among bright flowers and blooming shrubs, but Merewether was glad to reach this cooler refuge from the noonday heat. A servant took his hat, and he followed Raffles into a sitting room where a punkah swung rhythmically from the ceiling and kept the air in motion. A woman sat in a wicker chair, a sewing basket beside her and a partly embroidered square of cloth hanging on the chair arm. She stood up, and Raffles kissed her unselfconsciously.

"Livie, this is Commodore Merewether of the Bombay Marine. My wife, Olivia, Commodore."

33

Merewether bowed and straightened up to meet her direct gaze. "I am delighted Tom brought you, Commodore. It is very dull here most of the time." She spoke in a husky, caressing voice, somewhat at variance with her slender figure. Her hair and eyes were dark, and her mobile features indicated a woman of spirit; but, Merewether saw with some surprise, she must have been nearly ten years older than Raffles.

"I hope I am not intruding, ma'am."

"Not at all. This is such a dull place," she said again, and cut her expressive eyes toward Raffles and back to Merewether.

"Pays well, though, dear, and the chances for promotion are excellent," said Raffles with his easy smile.

"Oh. And how is poor Mister Pearson this morning?"

"No better, I'm afraid. ... A drink and a bit of lunch, Commodore?"

A Malay girl brought a tray of squat glasses filled with a cool, brownish liquid that gave off a slight aroma of rum.

"A Straits Cooler, Commodore," explained Mrs. Raffles. "Cold tea, lime and coconut juice, a dash of bitters, and just a touch of rum for your constitution. Tom invented it."

The concoction was tart and delicious, and they soon went in to lunch. This was an intelligent and attractive couple, Merewether decided, taking his seat. The luncheon was enlivened by a continuous flow of conversation between Raffles and his wife; apparently she was fully informed as to every detail of the government of this small, new Presidency, and her comments were shrewd. He found his mission soon discussed and disposed of as Raffles began to talk of the future of the Company's trade out here.

"This location has not been very successful thus far," explained Raffles. "I've been here nearly two years, but the trade has not increased. It is not a convenient port of call; the anchorage is exposed at either end; the Strait here is much too wide to be controlled by anything less than a squadron; and all we have is one disabled sloop at present."

"And the climate is most enervating," broke in Mrs. Raffles.

"True, but this is in the tropics, my dear. Calcutta is not much better."

"At least, there is more social activity . . . the Governor-General and Council," she said sharply.

Raffles smiled, and she smiled back at him. "We have enough for my taste here," he said. Merewether felt comfortably relaxed, enjoying the interchange between this pair, but he was ready to leave.

"You've been on east through the Strait, Commodore?"

"Yes, most recently last fall."

"Did you ever stop at a tiny native village, Singapore, on the mainland, almost at the eastern end of the Strait?'

"Why, no, I don't think I even knew there was one."

"I went down there last fall. Took passage on a country ship and looked over the whole area. The Company and Crown both need a better post than this to command the Strait. That place has the finest harbor I've seen out here, and the channel there is narrow enough to control with a single ship. I'm surprised the Dutch or Portuguese or French haven't already colonized it.

" . . . No siesta today, my dear. The Commodore is anxious to learn why an island is smoking." Raffles rose, kissed her, and led the way out after Merewether had expressed his thanks to this vibrant woman for the luncheon.

Back at Government House, they found the clerk's desk vacant, but a small Malay was sitting on the bench at the door, and a paunchy officer in the uniform of a sailing master in the Marine, his empty right sleeve pinned to the jacket, was waiting.

"Commodore Merewether, may I present Mister Johnson, our Port Captain." Johnson touched his hat with his left hand. "Come." Raffles stood aside as Johnson, the Malay and Merewether preceded him into the chamber.

"I speak the language," said Raffles in an aside, as he hung his coat and hat on the rack, then unbuttoned the waistcoat and took his seat. The Malay remained standing before the desk, head down and hands clasped together before him. A sheathed kris was thrust into a substantial leather belt about his waist. He looked, Merewether thought suddenly, for all the world like one of the Atjenese pirates he had captured last year off the Andaman Islands.

Raffles wasted no time, speaking at once. The man straight-

35

ened up, unclasped his hands, replied, listened, then spoke several rapid sentences with gestures. Raffles turned to Merewether.

"This man lives a hundred miles north of here on the mainland. He and his party paddled down here to George Town to trade chickens for iron. As near as I can understand, they passed this group of islands about here." Raffles rose, and stepped over to the chart on the wall, pointing to a cluster of dots. "They are uninhabited, he says, no fresh water except at this time of the year. There was a column of smoke rising up, and he thought there might be a crew of Atjenese pirates around, so they kept on." He came back to his chair.

"He saw nothing, no ships?" pressed Merewether.

Raffles spoke again to the Malay. "No, he says. They were afraid, and paddled as hard as they could. Not much help, I'm afraid, but on your way back, you might take a look." He paused. "Thank you, Johnson," he said, and then added something unintelligible to the Malay.

"Thank you, Johnson," echoed Merewether. "I'm happy you saw fit to report what this man told you." In his own mind, he had written this matter off, as he already had the entire voyage to Penang. It was not out of his way to look in on the islands on his way northwestward, however and it had been a pleasant interlude to meet young Raffles and his charming wife.

He turned back to face Raffles across the table. "I'm most obliged to you, sir, and thank you again for the luncheon."

"You are welcome, Commodore, and please, would you say nothing of my mention of Singapore today?"

Merewether was about to go out when Menzies, the sullen clerk, came in. "Captain Ackroyd again, sir," he told Raffles.

"Oh, Merewether, wait a moment. You should meet your opposite number in the Royal Navy here."

In a moment an officer entered, saying in a high, carrying voice, "Damn these dockyard jacklegs, Raffles! Now MacDonald says he has to refit the base of the mainmast. Some damn fool measured the step an inch too much!"

Raffles smiled at him. "Well, Captain," he said, "it is far better than if they had measured an inch too little. You can always take off a bit, but it is hard to add to a piece of timber." He turned to Merewether. "May I present Captain Richard Ackroyd, Commodore Merewether of the Honourable Company's Bombay Marine, commanding the Bengal Squadron." The two officers bowed and murmured.

Ackroyd almost instantly returned to the attack. "Now, Raffles, will you tell that confounded churl MacDonald to keep his men at work, no more four-hour siestas, until those masts are fitted and set up! They marched off again as soon as the noon gun fired today, and those shear-leg barges are rubbing my sides bare!"

Ackroyd was a small, wiry man, with black curly hair, glittering slate-gray eyes, sharp nose and a cruel, protruding mouth. He interrupted Raffles' attempted explanation, saying with a mirthless smile. "You hear the platitudes these politicians mouth, Commodore? Another two weeks, at best, before I am in commission again, and you'll have snapped up all the prize money by then!"

"Well, Captain, if I am as successful the next two weeks as I have been for the past month, you've lost nothing."

"What? A water haul so far?" Ackroyd smiled again, "That makes me feel better. Lord knows, I need the money, and I've been four months here at the mercy of these John Company idlers."

The man grated on Merewether, and he made his excuses, leaving Raffles to continue his discussion with Ackroyd. He was halfway out to *Rapid* in the gig when he realized that the pall of depression that had enveloped him since that awful afternoon last month had lifted. Perhaps it had been that delightful Raffles pair, or the mood, like a low fever, had simply worn itself out; in any event, the sense of frustration was gone, and he was sanguine again. He ordered the coxswain to steer for *Comet,* and went aboard to acquaint MacRae with the situation. He had learned next to nothing here at Penang, but he was in good spirits as he gave the orders to get under way.

CHAPTER FOUR

It was less than an hour to dawn when the lookout hailed the deck.

"Where away?" roared Dobbs.

"Broad on the starboard beam, sir. Looks like a fire."

Merewether was in his canvas chair against the weather rail, unable to sleep while the squadron sailed these narrow seas. He could see nothing from the deck and did not expect he could see anything more of value from the maintop. There had to be a fire to make the smoke the Malay had reported, and he was happy the particular atoll was now identified.

"Signal *Comet* to heave to," he told Dobbs. "And get a bearing on that fire." The ships had only the simplest system of night signals; three flashes of the dark lantern, three times repeated, and *Comet*'s profile astern altered in the night glass. Satisfied that the consort had understood and obeyed, Dobbs brought *Rapid* into the wind, and she lay to, rolling in the long swell, canvas slatting, yards creaking, and blocks squealing as lines slackened and tightened. With the steady pressure of the northeast breeze, both ships were drifting to leeward; but Merewether did not intend to approach the islands any closer until after daylight.

"Mister Dobbs, would you be kind enough to send for Gunny?" The Marine detachments in both ships had participated in the general drills last month, but here was a heaven-sent opportunity for a realistic amphibious exercise under the command of the jemadar, the senior noncommissioned *Sepoy* Marine officer present.

"Yes, sah?" The erect figure was now visible against the increasing light to the east.

"We have a report of a fire on that island, Gunny. I wish to embark the landing force, together with that of *Comet,* and make a reconnaissance. I don't expect we'll find more than a pair of frightened fishermen, but it should be a useful exercise."

"Aye aye, sah. Full kit, sah?"

Forty pounds of equipment, in addition to the musket, should make the exercise realistic enough, Merewether decided. "We may have time to fire a few rounds at targets, too."

It was almost light enough for *Comet* to read a flag hoist now. He wrote out the message and handed it to Dobbs. "And pass the word to the gunner to mount that four-pounder boat gun in the launch, with both round shot and canister." It was also an opportunity to try a new piece of equipment acquired last month at Bombay Castle. He saw Hamlyn, junior officer of the watch, coming aft. "You are boat officer in the launch, Hamlyn." High time the boy had a taste of responsibility.

The cheerful mood that had come over him yesterday afternoon persisted, as Merewether went below to eat the breakfast laid out by Sangh and then pull on the oiled landing-force boots. His sword and the pair of double-barreled pistols he had taken from Abercrombie last year were laid out on the bed, but he decided not to encumber himself with them. Another thought occurred to him. It was only common courtesy to invite Wolfe and Kinney to go along for the exercise, and he stepped around to Wolfe's room to proffer the invitation.

By six bells in the morning watch, the ships had beaten in to an anchorage two miles off the atoll in eight fathoms, and both had their launches in the water. Through the glass, Merewether could see a sand spit toward the south end of the island and the faintest intimation of smoke still rising behind the trees near the center of the island. It was less than three-quarters of a mile in length, he estimated. A number of coconut palms rose in the center, which indicated there would not be too much undergrowth to impede a party making its way across the island. There was a narrow beach opposite the palm grove and no coral visible off shore.

The marines embarked in their orderly fashion. Totten, the gunner's mate, and his three seamen-strikers, already clustered about the gun in the bow, with shot rack and copper boat magazine beside them. Wolfe appeared on the deck coatless, sword belted on, and a blue kerchief knotted about his head in lieu of a hat. Kinney was at his side, dirk at his hip. They went into the boat, and Merewether timed the rise of the launch, then dropped from the ladder into the stern.

"Shove off!" Hamlyn told the coxswain. "Give way." The boat pulled away from the ship and converged on the launch carrying *Comet*'s landing force.

Merewether picked up his speaking trumpet. "Dillon, land on the south spit, and send your party north. This party will cross the center to meet you!" This might be no more than a drill, but the men were high-spirited and in dead earnest, as the two boats pulled away on diverging courses.

Half an hour later, Merewether's boat approached a moderate surf. The beach was littered with broken lumps of coral. "Drop your stern anchor," he told Hamlyn. "Pull on in, but make sure your stern hook keeps that line taut." Though the surf was nominal on this leeward side of the island, the stern anchor would keep the launch bow on, her gun covering the landing force, and prevent her broaching in a much heavier sea. This bit of knowledge, like the rest of the exercise, would be valuable to a young officer. It was only a moment before the keel scraped, and the bow hook went over the side hauling the painter over his shoulder to the beach.

The marines disembarked in knee-deep water, reached the narrow strand, and formed up. Scouts slanted off right and left, and the senior private soldier in each eight-man squad took his position at the point, musket held at port arms. Merewether came ashore, his boots sloshing full of water, followed closely by Wolfe and Kenney. He paused to bend each leg up behind him and empty the boots, seeing the erect figure of Gunny beside his bugler disappearing into the trees between the right and center squad, the Naique, his second in command, between the center and left.

The first shot was clearly from a musket, as was the next, ten seconds later. They were followed by the sharper report of a pistol. The sounds came from a quarter mile away, across the island, not from the marine detachment, still visible less than a hundred yards from the beach. Merewether balanced on one leg as the last of the water drained from his boot. Something was going on here!

"Hamlyn, take the launch around the north point and down the east side," he shouted out to the boat. "Totten, load your gun

40

with solid shot, canister on top, and look lively!" The bow hook was already trotting into the water, coiling the painter as he went, and the seaman in the stern was hauling in on the anchor cable as the crew backed oars.

Merewether turned to follow the marines through the grove and saw Wolfe already far ahead of him to the right, Kinney trailing after him. He noticed that Wolfe appeared to limp as he hurried along and started to shout for him to wait, then decided no use and followed after the troops.

He came up with Gunny just as he could see sunlight glinting on the water through the tree trunks. Wolfe had disappeared from sight somewhere to the right. Another two hundred yards, and they could see the beach bordering a small cove, no more than an indentation in the shore of the island. The point men halted, muskets held crosswise overhead, to check the squads, as the scouts reconnoitered. Merewether and Gunny came forward and saw what looked like an enormous rabbit hutch built of driftwood on the beach about the exposed ribs of a wrecked dhow. Sand had been heaped against the barrier, and piled to form a sort of platform at either side on which fires still smoldered. The crude redoubt was occupied, he realized, as he saw a flash of movement, and the barrel of a musket protruding.

Two hundred yards up the beach, the Malay version of a bugaloo was moored, stern just outside the breakers, and opposite it was a group of ten or twelve natives, lounging in shallow pits dug in the sand behind driftwood thrust into the sand to form a kind of fence.

"Sah," said Gunny in a low voice. "I think there are Europeans in that fort." He looked left and right to his Naiques and made a signal. The men almost instantly went through the loading drill, each man extracting a cartridge from the box, biting off the bullet, pouring powder down the barrel, and ramming home ball and wad, then priming the lock. "I shall send two squads to the left and . . ."

There was a flash of white shirt to the right through the trees, just opposite a patch of undergrowth fifty yards south of the fort. Wolfe came leaping across the dozen yards that separated the scrub from the grove, sword in hand. Four Malays, brandishing krises, exploded from the patch, and Wolfe caught one, driving his sword clean through the Malay's back. The others started to run southwardly, and Wolfe pursued them down the beach. Then a second Malay turned suddenly, swinging his kris. Wolfe parried the stroke without effort, and his riposte drove the blade through the man's body.

Gunny uttered a harsh expletive, and Merewether said, "Damnation!"

The men in the pits raced for the bugaloo through the surf, as the marines went forward at the double. They were out of effective musket range, and the entire operation had been blown sky-high by Wolfe's impetuous action.

At the edge of the grove, the squads halted, took aim, and fired a volley. There was no apparent effect. The Malays had scrambled into the small vessel and had sweeps going as their stone anchor came in. They were going to get clean away!

Merewether stood with Gunny on the beach, watching the bugaloo pull off, its sail now going up in jerks, as it headed north. Even a party of a dozen Malay pirates was better than a water haul, he thought sourly, turning to go toward the driftwood stronghold.

"Wait!" Gunny shaded his eyes, then pointed north. "The launch!"

Coming into view around the end of the island was the boat, her oars rhythmically rising and falling like the wings of a monstrous bird. The launch altered course to intercept the bugaloo, and Merewether could see Totten and his crew standing beside the gun in the bow. The bugaloo swung to starboard in an instinctive effort to escape, then her helmsman realized the launch was the swifter of the two and changed course to port to ram and destroy the smaller vessel.

"Hold her bow on!" Merewether shouted uselessly. He could see Hamlyn standing in the stern beside the coxswain, his gaze intent upon the approaching bugaloo.

"Fire, oh fire!" prayed Merewether aloud.

The launch, fifty yards from the bow of a vessel three times her size, suddenly sheared to starboard, and was off the port bow of the clumsier native boat before it could turn. Totten and his strikers slewed the gun about, stood aside, and fired, the sullen report sounding muffled here on the beach.

A canister of eighty musket balls on top of a round shot, even though fired from a four-pounder boat gun, was deadly at that range. The charge swept diagonally across the deck, from foremast to tiller, striking down almost half the Malays manning sweeps in the waist and killing the steersman. The launch came rowing around in a circle astern, Totten ramming home another charge, then fired again across the stern quarter, forward. The sweeps had ceased to move, and the bugaloo, no hand at her tiller, came into the wind, rolling in the swell.

Hamlyn brought the launch along the starboard side and pointed the gun into the vessel. The midshipman swung over the side, dirk in one hand, pistol in the other, followed by bow hook and stern hook. In a few minutes, the launch had the bugaloo in tow. Hamlyn, at her tiller, brought her back to be anchored again just outside the breakers.

Merewether turned to find Dillon, first lieutenant in *Comet,* panting at his side. "Didn't know there was such a hurry, Commodore," he gasped. His party of marines was drawn up on the beach south of the rabbit hutch, holding two Malay prisoners.

"Nor I," Merewether told him. "Now, can you put two squads of marines in that bugaloo, and bring her around to the squadron. Midshipman Hamlyn is prize master."

Merewether headed for the driftwood fort, passing by the embers of the fire. Inside the curious structure were a number of European men and one woman. Captain Wolfe was already there, his sword in hand and still bloody on the blade. Somehow, he had managed to get a picturesque smear of blood on his cheek and another across the breast of his white shirt.

"Who's in command here?" demanded Merewether.

A stocky, middle-aged man with gray side-whiskers, wearing the buff breeches of the maritime service and a soiled white shirt, stepped forward, still holding a pistol.

"I am. Captain James Forehand, lately commander of the Indiaman *Duchy of Lancaster,* captured two weeks ago by the French and marooned here since."

43

"Two weeks? You must have been captured almost in sight of Penang."

"Right off there," confirmed the captain, pointing west across the island. "About five miles. We had a crew of lascars; only my four mates and these warrant officers were Europeans. The lascars ran below, and we could not get a gun laid or fired." He shook his head.

That was the trouble with lascar crews, Merewether thought, fairly competent as seamen, but they would not fight, at least not for the Company. Their employment in Indiamen was discouraged, but low wages and the cheap rations they subsisted on were an inducement to many owners.

"What type of ship took you?" inquired Merewether.

"A brig, ten guns, I counted. The French put a prize crew aboard, but the lascars agreed to go on and work the ship. So long as they get their rations, they don't care who commands the ship."

"Who is the woman, and how many have you here?" asked Merewether, looking about.

"Sixteen, including the surgeon, and my wife, of course."

The woman was leaning against the parapet a dozen feet away, a half-grown black kitten cuddled against her bosom. She was dimpling and smiling at Captain Wolfe, as he leaned on his blood-stained sword, its point negligently thrust into the sand, speaking to her in a low voice that did not carry. She was young, no more than eighteen or twenty, with a heart-shaped, empty, pretty face. Merewether thought for a moment that Wolfe was cradle-robbing, but no more so than this grizzled captain who had married the child. Oh well, none of his business, he decided, and turned back to Forehand.

"And how long have those Malays been here?"

"Two days, a little more. They came at dawn day before yesterday, I think. We had only the two muskets the French left us, a horn of powder, and a bag of small shot for hunting. I had a brace of pistols in my chest. We winged two or three of them the first morning, then they just sat down and waited for us to run out of water. Almost did at that." The captain pushed a water breaker with his foot, and it rolled easily with only a gurgle. "We kept fires going at each side of our shelter at night to prevent surprise, but I'm sure they had made up their minds to rush us this morning. Just before you appeared, four of them ran into those bushes over there where your man found them. I think they had only a pair or so of muskets themselves, though they all carried krises."

"Are you ready to move aboard," Merewether asked, "and how much baggage do you have?"

"That French commander was a real gentleman. He let us take our chests and my wife's trunks." He pointed to the chests stacked along the side of the fort forming part of the rude barricade.

"And how does it happen your wife is along on a China cruise, Captain?" Merewether was genuinely curious. It was not unheard of, by any means, for a captain to bring his wife on a voyage, but it was seldom done in these last few years of war all around the world.

"Why, Lucy was a passenger, coming out to live with her brother at Madras, both parents dead. I had lost my wife last year, so we decided to marry at Johanna."

"Very well. I'll give you a working party to help load your gear." Merewether went on to other duties, seeing in passing Wolfe bowing over Lucy's hand, kissing it in the French fashion, then vaulting easily over the barrier to saunter, still with that slight limp, down to the boat.

Two hours later, the squadron was under way back toward Penang, the bugaloo under tow by *Rapid*. To the mortification of Prize Master Hamlyn, he could not make the cranky vessel with its fiber sails hold a course that would conform with that of the squadron. However, the boy had reacted today with courage and judgment when confronted with a sudden emergency, and Merewether took pleasure in mentioning his services, together with those of Totten, in the report he wrote during the first dogwatch. To Wolfe's exploit, he devoted a single line. He had just signed and sealed the report, with the intention of leaving it with Raffles tomorrow morning for forwarding, when Buttram knocked and entered. Behind him, Merewether saw another figure. "Captain, this is Doctor Keese, surgeon in the Company's Service, and lately serving in the *Duchy of Lancaster*."

Keese was a man past middle age with blond hair faded gray and a lined, good-humored face. Merewether remembered vaguely seeing him in the hutch on the beach this morning, but now he wore a coat and held his hat correctly under his arm, bowing at the introduction.

"Be seated, gentlemen," invited Merewether with a smile. "I've just finished mentioning Doctor Buttram in my report for the excellent manner in which he removed that Malay's mangled arm today." In all truth, the doctor had spent a full afternoon treating the men in the bugaloo who had suffered wounds from the launch's boat gun. "If you have your report ready, Doctor, I'll append it to mine."

"Yes, sir, ready a little later," said Buttram easily. "But Doctor Keese here gave me a hand this afternoon, and he has some information I think will interest you."

Merewether looked inquiringly at Keese, who looked back with keen blue eyes. "Yes, Captain, but I heard you called 'Commodore' today too."

"Only a courtesy title," Merewether told him. "The doctor here refuses to promote me, and I do not mind. Go ahead."

The surgeon smiled briefly, then said bluntly, "Sir, I have reason to believe the *Duchy of Lancaster* may be a pest ship by now, and adrift or anchored not too far away."

"Pest ship?"

"Yes, sir. Typhoid, or it might be typhus, or even contagious brain fever—the early symptoms are much the same. I had diagnosed three cases among the lascars the morning we were captured." The surgeon sat back, then continued, "Captain Forehand is not an easy man to advise. 'Keep 'em for'ard,' he says, and in an hour we were taken. I'd guess nearly the whole damn crew could be down by now, considering the water we took on at the Anambas Islands last month."

"Water?" Merewether knew that impure water was often blamed for sickness, and the closer to civilization the source from which it was drawn, the more often it seemed to spawn a fatal disease, however clear and sparkling it came from the stream.

"Yes, sir," said Keese. "We were knocked about by a typhoon in the South China Sea, and the next thing we knew, the boatswain reported he was pumping fresh water from the bilges. Of course, the casks were stove, and we took on fresh water from that island. It was clear and running, but I could see the smoke of a village upstream. Captain said he had watered there before and it was all right. Fortunately, the casks serving our mess aft were sound, and none of the new water was used."

"How serious is this?"

"The fact is," Keese went on, "some of those lascars have been drinking worse water than that all their lives. Some few of them will take sick, like the ones I saw, but it's not them I'm worried about, it's the French prize crew. Water that will make a lascar sick will kill a white man, and the lascars know nothing of navigation. That is why I think the ship may be adrift or anchored by now not too far away."

It was circumstantial enough, Merewether thought—another matter to keep in mind, which, however, did not solve his problem of where to find the French cruisers. "Your party is clean, I trust? Well, thank you, Doctor, I shall bear the matter in mind, and after we clear Penang tomorrow, we'll keep a sharp lookout for the ship." Merewether went on deck to write his night orders to be signaled to *Comet* before dark.

It had been a long day, with some mild exertion, and Merewether lay down across the bed. It seemed only a moment before the messenger knocked. He rose, slid into his shoes, decided he did not need the boat cloak, and started on deck. Larkin had reluctantly surrendered his room to Captain Forehand and his wife, but it was only for tonight, Merewether justified himself. The night lantern was burning dimly in the passage as he made his way to the companionway and started up the ladder. He had reached the deck and paused for a moment for his eyes to adjust to the darkness when there was a crash below, followed by a succession of piercing screams.

He swung down the ladder and beheld Lucy, her shift clutched well above her knees, running along the passage toward him, emitting a shriek at every step. Close behind her was Forehand, in drawers and shirt, bellowing, his face contorted with rage. The girl reached Merewether and agilely dodged behind him to reach the ladder.

"Here, now, Captain, shear off!" Merewether cried, pushing Forehand away. "What's going on here?" He fended off two more clumsy rushes, as the girl perched on the ladder, ready to climb on deck, or jump and run again.

Forehand came to a standstill, then mopped sweat from his brow and dabbed with his sleeve at his eyes. Merewether saw that the man was weeping. Down the passage, he caught a flicker of movement, and the door of Wolfe's cabin closed with a click.

"You promised!" Forehand suddenly shouted. "After I forgave you for that supercargo at Macao!"

"Pooh," said the girl. "It was nothing. You don't pleasure me. All you want is to get me with child. You have no thought how I feel!"

"You whore!" Forehand moved forward again. Merewether pushed him back.

"Now, I don't understand all this," Merewether commenced. "But I must be on deck."

"I understand only too well!" Forehand started to the supercargo's cabin and kicked at the door. It opened almost instantly, and there stood Wolfe in a blue silk dressing gown.

"You swine!" shouted Forehand, and swung his fist at the taller man.

Wolfe blocked the blow easily and shoved the man away. "My seconds will wait on you in the morning," he told Forehand. "You are a witness, Commodore, I am the injured party."

"Injured party!" screamed Forehand. "After I find my wife naked in your cabin!"

"Enough." The entire tawdry scene caused Merewether's stomach to revolt. "Young lady, you will go into your quarters and bolt the door. You, sir," he told Forehand, "get your clothing and wait in my cabin. As for you, Wolfe, remain in your room. I shall post a guard in the passage to see that these orders are carried out. Now, move!"

"Merewether, this is an affair of honor . . ."

"Not in my ship, sir!" Merewether reached behind Wolfe and took the handle of the door as the man, faced flushed with rage, stepped back, and the door closed on him. Forehand stood a moment, then hurried into Larkin's cabin.

The girl came down from her perch on the ladder, pulled at her shift, and smoothed it over her hips, preening herself with a downcast smile, then clasped her bare arms about her breasts. Merewether looked at her a moment. There was no mistaking the invitation. She was willing to play the harlot for him this night, as well as for Wolfe, and the thought disgusted him.

"Now, get in that cabin, Mrs. Forehand, as soon as your husband is out. And bolt the door." As though summoned, Forehand came out, buckling his belt. His tears had dried, and he stared straight ahead with a strained expression.

They watched Forehand out of sight, and Lucy stepped into the room. "I'll be waiting," she whispered, then closed the door. Merewether felt a flush of heat in his face in spite of his revulsion. She was certainly a whore, he thought, but damned pretty with it. Merewether climbed the ladder.

On deck, he verified the squadron's position, ordered the signal given *Comet* to heave to until daylight, and remained to see the maneuver accomplished. Only then did he think of posting his watchman below. He hesitated, doubting the necessity now, almost an hour after the affair, then decided not to and went below.

Forehand was not in the cabin, nor was he in the officers' head, or the pantry where Sangh slept on his pallet. Hell's bells! Had the man gone on deck? Yet Merewether was sure he would have seen him. And there was no access to officers' country aft below decks from the forward compartments in this ex-slave ship. The only explanation must be that Forehand had rejoined his wife and somehow made peace with the wench.

He hesitated a moment more, not wanting to rekindle the affair of an hour ago, then reluctantly decided he must make sure Forehand was back with his wife. Out in the passage, he knocked on the door. No response. He knocked again and tried the handle. It was locked or bolted, or both. These were solidly constructed rooms, not the flimsy partitions and curtains put up in a man-o'-war or Indiaman to form cabins designed to be knocked down when the ship was cleared for action. He heard a click and saw Wolfe peering through the crack of his door.

"Have you seen Forehand?" demanded Merewether.

"Not since you closed this door on my nose."

Merewether went up the companion ladder and called to MacCamy, "Send the carpenter aft with tools to open a door." He came back to stand outside the door. Wolfe, in dressing gown and slippers, joined him after a moment.

"I can't imagine where that fellow got such an idea," said Wolfe suddenly. "I never touched the woman." Neither made any reference to the earlier order for Wolfe to remain in his room.

Finally, the carpenter came down the companionway, hammer, long-nosed pincers and a jimmy in hand. He tried the door handle, held his lantern to the keyhole, and then pushed the pincers gingerly in. He took a firm grip and rotated the pincers. There was a click, and he tried the handle again.

"Damned thing is bolted," he said. "Have to jimmy it after all, but we won't break the lock now." He pushed the bent steel blade between the door and jamb, moved it up and down, and then pushed the handle sharply. There was a screech of metal suddenly withdrawn from oak, and the door opened part way. The carpenter shoved again, forcing the door back against some obstacle, and brought his lantern up.

"Good God! He's hanged hisself."

Merewether slid through the partially open door behind the carpenter. In the yellow light of the lantern, Forehand's empurpled face swung from a line knotted about his neck and through a ring bolt in the overhead, his toes less than six inches from the deck. A small stool lay overturned beside him, but Merewether's gaze was fixed on the bed. Across it, head hanging over the near edge, was Lucy Forehand, still in her shift, eyes staring wide from a face suffused with blood, and dark bruises about her neck.

He turned to catch Forehand's body as the carpenter slashed his knife through the line and helped ease him to the deck.

"Call Doctor Buttram, please," he told Wolfe. He turned back and found the carpenter with his ear pressed to Forehand's chest.

"Can't hear nothing," he said, standing up.

It was only a moment before Buttram burst in, medical kit in hand.

The examination was brief. Forehand and his wife were both dead, she by manual strangulation, he by hanging.

"Murder and suicide?" wondered Buttram. "What brought this on?" Merewether shook his head, and they straightened the girl on the bed, laid Forehand beside her, and covered them with a single sheet. There was a rustle of movement behind a gown hanging against the bulkhead, and Merewether reached down to grasp the half-grown cat by the nape of the neck. He handed the kitten out the door to Sangh without comment before turning the key in the lock.

"Thank you, Mister Svenson," he told the carpenter. "Good night, Wolfe." Merewether led Buttram into his cabin. "We are in the territorial waters of Penang, and this will be a matter for the Governor and coroner," he reminded Buttram, as they wrote their reports.

It was an unpleasant thought that came to Merewether midway through the composition. The girl had been vain, foolish and amoral, but she had not deserved death in this fashion. He, in all innocence, might well be responsible for her murder. As he remembered events, he had told her to go in the cabin and lock the door. But, once the door had closed, he could not remember the click of lock or thump of bolt. He suddenly realized that she had left the door unlocked, expecting him to visit her, while Forehand remained incarcerated in the cabin. It was all conjecture, of course, but the conviction remained. He bore a share of the guilt for her death, both in the failure to station a guard and his failure to disavow any intention of visiting her. Gloom descended upon him.

It was three more days of waiting in the stifling heat of the anchorage at Penang before the Governor and his coroner were satisfied. There were the burials, and then a chest and trunk to be inventoried and sealed. They found a marriage certificate dated last June signed by the chaplain in another Indiaman, and a hand-written will, in which Forehand mentioned nine children by two previous marriages. All these items had to be shipped back to London, to the ship's husband of the *Duchy of Lancaster* at an address in Marylebone High Street.

Merewether found young Raffles a tower of strength in dealing with the legal niceties of the affair. He had edited Merewether's bald report of the events of that horrible morning, and without changing or omitting a single fact, put it in such form that it satisfied the hair-splitting coroner and his six-man jury. After the verdict came in, death by murder of Lucy Forehand at the hands of Andrew Forehand, and death by his own hand of Andrew Forehand, Raffles intercepted Merewether and insisted that he come to dinner. It was too late in the day to get under way by now, so he pushed back his gnawing anxiety to get on with the interrupted mission of the Bengal Squadron and accepted.

There were two other couples and an unattached woman at the informal affair. Raffles' wife was sparkling, in her element. There was a Major Anderson, commanding the garrison, and a Mister Winningham, one of the Company's agents, who had ambitions to go back to England and stand for Parliament from his district in Surrey. Their wives were pretty and lively, and with the unattached woman, Mrs. Hartley, a slender, attractive widow, kept up an entertaining exchange of gossip and wit with Mrs. Raffles.

There came a pause in the conversation, and Mrs. Anderson said brightly, "It *was* in your ship that girl was murdered? Is it true that it was because of the attentions of an officer to her?"

"Neither me nor any officer of mine!" Merewether replied instantly. He looked to Raffles, who came to his rescue.

"There was no such evidence at the inquest," Raffles said smoothly. "We'll never learn the man's motive; it was a May and December marriage, you know." He turned the topic of conversation into other fields.

There had been evidence of the quarrel, and the accusation of Wolfe by Forehand, but any contact with the woman Wolfe had categorically denied, attributing the matter to an unfounded, insane jealousy on the part of the husband. The coroner had ordered the reference to him by the dead man stricken from the record, so Raffles was technically correct, but there must be a hundred rumors flying about in George Town tonight.

After three London gins, Merewether felt himself relax into good humor again, forgetting his ordeal with the law. As the party went in to dinner, Mrs. Raffles paused beside him a moment.

"Be a dear," she whispered, "and be especially attentive to Kate Hartley. She is a lonely woman." Merewether nodded, a little puzzled, and went in. He found the woman charming.

After dinner, he pretended to smoke a cigar with Raffles, Anderson and Winningham over a beaker of brandy, and then rejoined the ladies to stumble through an evening of whist. The affair did not break up until an hour after midnight.

The other two couples had departed, and Merewether was preparing to take his leave with thanks for the entertainment when he detected a sort of wordless message exchanged between Mrs. Raffles and Mrs. Hartley. A question had been asked and answered, he surmised.

"It's only the next house down the lane, Commodore," said Mrs. Raffles. "On your way to the landing, I'd be most obliged if you would see Kate to her house."

At this point, the gig's crew waiting at the landing had probably drunk their fill of rum from the public house a stone's throw away and were asleep anyway. It was barely a hundred yards, but Mrs. Hartley seized his hand, and he felt her tremble as he led her across uneven turf to her door, where a sleepy Malay servant let her in.

"Oh, come in, Commodore, the evening is young. A brandy . . ."

She had wept a little afterward in mortification and apologized for her unbridled display of passion. It was almost daylight when he pulled on his clothing and crept out. She was a lonely woman, he justified her, still full of life and deprived of a husband in her prime. Yet he had the feeling that he had been used. In the cold light of dawn, that wordless interchange between Olivia Raffles and Kate Hartley last night was perfectly intelligible. Entirely unaware at the time, Merewether realized that during the evening he had been vetted and passed like a prize bull. Kate had decided she wanted him, and Olivia had forthwith procured the assignation. His thoughts wandered for a moment to Lady Caroline. Was it possible that Wolfe had been correct in his assumption there? The thought unaccountably made him uncomfortable as he came down to the landing.

CHAPTER FIVE

Two days later, the squadron cleared the northern tip of Sumatra. One of those dots over there on the horizon was Pulo Rondo, where he had burned Abercrombie's pirate stronghold last May. The son of Abercrombie came to mind, probably now living in some Indian village, being reared as a native, his English heritage forgotten. The thought of the child still troubled him, but he told himself again it was none of his affair. He turned and paced the weather side of the quarterdeck, considering a change in his operation order, to head south in the hope of overtaking or intercepting a prize or cruiser, but immediately concluded that his original plan was sound. He signaled *Comet* to change course to north-northwest, intending to look in on the Nicobar Islands before heading for Ceylon.

It was just after the first watch had been called and already dark, with *Rapid* laboring along in a moderate swell, close-hauled, under reduced sail, when Sangh made his grisly discovery. Coming down the companionway ladder, Merewether saw the small figure kneeling on the deck in the passage. He thought for a moment that something had been spilled, what with the motion of the ship, and that the steward was wiping it up. Then he saw black fur and the cord still about the kitten's neck.

"Sahib, the cat has been hanged!" Its neck was stretched, and there were drops of blood glistening on the cat's throat where it had torn at the noose with its claws in a final frenzy.

"Where was it?"

Sangh pointed silently to the handle of the door behind which Forehand and his wife had died, tears in his eyes. Merewether stepped over to look and saw scratches on the woodwork below it and a few specks of blood.

"Well, I'm damned! I passed this way half an hour ago. Who's below now?"

Sangh did not reply, merely inclining his head and shifting his sad eyes toward the supercargo's cabin.

"Oh." Merewether paused. There was nothing he could do, no proof, and even if there had been, who would take seriously the execution of a kitten? It had been an appealing little animal, affectionate and playful, and he had granted Sangh's request to keep it, but there were many people who simply could not abide cats. He felt regret for the small life that had been so cruelly extinguished, but it was no cause for an inquiry.

"I'm sorry, Sangh, he was a nice little fellow. Best drop him over the side and forget the matter. And then, will you ask Doctor Buttram to come in at his convenience?" He went on in to his cabin.

Buttram came in a quarter hour later, red in the face and indignant. "What a monstrous thing!" he exploded.

"No," said Merewether. "Common enough. Did you ever see a pack of boys tie two cats together by their tails and hang them over a branch? This was gentle by comparison."

"It's still the act of a diseased mind!"

"Perhaps, but that's not what I wanted to discuss with you. This Doctor Keese, is he a competent surgeon?"

"Yes. A bit old-fashioned and opinionated, but that's to be expected at his age. He was a surgeon in a line regiment under Cornwallis in the American War and then came back to establish a practice in Plymouth. When his wife died and his children had left, he sold his practice and signed on with the Company. Why, he is fifty-five, if he's a day, and this is his first voyage out here!"

"He is qualified then?"

"Certainly. Why do you ask, Captain?"

"It seems," said Merewether, "at the last minute—I was ashore at Mister Raffles' house—he decided he wanted a fling in the Bombay Marine and MacRae took him in as a volunteer. If you recommend him, I'll authorize issuance of an acting warrant as assistant surgeon. I can't make him senior to you, of course."

Buttram laughed shortly. "I don't think rank will be of much concern to Keese. He'll go his own way, but he is entirely qualified as a medical officer." He hesitated, then looked searchingly at Merewether. "And now, let me hark back to another matter. . . . It is a very delicate subject, entirely confidential, sir, and perhaps you'll not want me to go further. This man Wolfe—"

"I don't know what you are going to say," Merewether said, "so continue."

Buttram put the tips of his fingers together and looked at the overhead. "Of course, I spent a time as part of my medical education observing the inmates of Bedlam. There is no valid explanation of the causes of madness, not much more than the old superstition that such persons are possessed by demons. We do know that some diseases of the body, such as syphilis, cause lesions or damage to the brain and ultimately affect the mind. But I've dissected the brain of a howling lunatic, and it was no different from that of a healthy man."

"I have an idea of what you are leading up to, Doctor."

"I admit five or six weeks is a very short period of observation," continued Buttram slowly. "But I have had more contact with Wolfe than you have, sir. I made it a point to cultivate him after that first outburst, and I've played chess with him nearly every afternoon since . . ." He took his fingers apart, and looked directly at Merewether.

"Sir, it is as though there were two men inhabiting the same body. He's a competitor, and I admit he wins at chess more often than he loses; but when he does lose, there's pure murderous hate looking out from his eyes. Oh, he restrains it well enough, but having seen it displayed when his control was overcome by wine, I suspect the depth of the mania that exists in him. . . ."

"Just a moment, Doctor," demanded Merewether. "Are you telling me the man's insane?"

"Not certifiably, sir. That is what I have been trying to explain. It would be simple enough if he had obvious delusions, or the gibbering and ranting symptoms of the typical madman. I have read in translation some of the notes on the theories of two Frenchmen, Mesmer and Pinel, but medicine knows very little of those matters yet. I do not believe a physician or surgeon is qualified to make any sort of a diagnosis of a mania of the kind I suspect in Wolfe. I limit my opinion to the observation that this man is dangerous. I think he has two natures, one that he customarily exhibits to his associates and another that lurks beneath, awaiting an opportunity to leap out and seize control. It has done so twice now."

"Twice?"

"Yes, sir. The second time was last week when he made the senseless attack on the Malays."

"How about the night Forehand killed his wife?"

"Possibly. When I saw him he was under control, and of course, you have no proof as to the cat, though there seems to be a sort of symbolism in hanging it on the door of the room where the murder and suicide occurred."

"You realize," said Merewether, "that if Wolfe learned you had made these statements, he could have you cast in damages for slander?"

"Of course, and I trust your discretion implicitly, sir. I only wish you to be on your guard," replied Buttram, rising. "If you'll excuse me, sir . . ."

"Wait. What is your opinion of Keese's surmise that a pestilence may have overtaken the Indiaman?"

"No opinion, sir. I'm sure Keese knows typhoid symptoms when he sees them, and it can be most deadly, especially to Europeans out here."

It had been an interesting conversation. The concept of two minds, one sane, the other mad, inhabiting the same body was novel. Yet, Merewether had encountered numbers of people in his life whose duplicity was hidden behind a façade of honesty or chastity or loyalty. These common traits were not the same as the thing Buttram envisioned, he concluded, and put the matter aside. He needed no medical advice to be on his guard against Wolfe.

By noon the next day, Merewether had the mountains of Great

Nicobar in sight off the starboard bow. There were few anchorages on either side of the archipelago, but in this season a vessel would seek shelter from the northeast monsoon on the western side, and that was where he intended to look. *Comet* was nearly four miles abeam to starboard, and Merewether asked Dobbs whether an alteration of course would be necessary for her to weather the southern tip of the island, with the wind steady out of the northeast.

"No, sir," said Dobbs, looking out toward *Comet*. "She'll clear it by . . . Aha! he's signaling!" He picked up the glass and swung into the mizzen shrouds.

"Sail bearing north-northeast," he shouted down.

Merewether conjured up a mental picture of the situation. With *Comet*'s true bearing northeast of *Rapid*, four miles distant, the target must be northeast and by east from his present position, which would put it eight or ten miles off the eastern shore of Great Nicobar. His train of thought was interrupted by another shout from Dobbs.

"Signals: Two sails in sight!"

"Acknowledge," Merewether told the signal quartermaster and harked back to the problem of interception.

It was an awkward situation. *Comet*, with her windward sailing qualities, and four-mile advantage to the northeast of *Rapid*, might be barely able to hold a course to intercept the ships. But it would be foolish thus to divide his force and make piecemeal attacks upon what could be superior forces. And too, if the targets decided to avoid a fight, they could go about and escape through St. George's Channel between Great Nicobar and Little Nicobar, to make a long stern chase of it. *Rapid* effectively blocked escape to the southwest, but it was essential that *Comet* gain the weather gauge in order to counter any maneuver the enemy—and he suddenly knew in his bones it was the enemy—might attempt.

He picked up the slate to write his message and was momentarily distracted by the passing of a shining, close-shaven pate. He realized that it was Midshipman Kinney, but did not pause in his composition of the message. There was no arbitrary signal for this order, and it must be spelled out as economically as possible: "Take weather gauge. Flag sails north."

He watched the hoists go up and down, each acknowledged by *Comet*, then saw her profile change as she went about and settled on a reach that would give her the easting necessary to put her to windward of the targets. As for *Rapid*, there was a weary period of working her to the northeast, with the necessity of going about every few minutes as she clawed her way into the eye of the wind in a succession of tacks. Merewether fretted inwardly, but he compelled himself to preserve an appearance of calm while Mac-Camy worked the ship. It was more than an hour and *Comet* had disappeared to the east before Hamlyn hailed from the maintop.

"What course?" Merewether shouted back, unable to wait for MacCamy's leisurely inquiry.

"Looks bows on, near south, sir. Two ships in line ahead."

Two ships sailing in line ahead suggested men-o'-war, rather than free and easy privateers.

"Both are square-rigged, but the second ship's sails are brailed up," shouted down Hamlyn.

What in hell? Merewether picked up the glass and started forward. The thing did not add up: two ships in line ahead, the second ship not under sail. He stopped dead. It was so simple he had overlooked the solution. The second ship must be under tow! He went up the mainmast and then to perch on the royal yard. It was difficult to find those specks in the field of the glass with the continuous motion of the ship, but once he had located them, he held them. The leading ship was close-hauled on the port tack, and the following ship indeed had her sails brailed up. Even as he watched, she altered course to starboard, the intervals between her masts widening, then yawed back to port. There must be no one at her helm! Merewether heard MacCamy's command to go about and scrambled out of the way for the maneuver.

By the time *Rapid* had settled on the port tack, he had reached a tentative conclusion: The ship under tow must be the *Duchy of Lancaster*, her crew stricken by disease, and the towing ship would have to be the French brig that had captured her. He could see the logic of the matter. Once dragged south of the

Nicobars, there was unlimited sea room where the prize might drift until such time as the captor considered it safe to board the valuable ship again. He found the target again in his glass.

It was only a few minutes before the brig altered shape, wearing around to head northwest. The other ship remained in place. Evidently the tow had been cast off as *Rapid* was sighted, and with the appearance of a ship-rigged vessel, the privateer was making a run for St. George's Channel. Merewether prayed that MacRae had had time to sail back westward far enough to intercept. He clung to his perch, trying to sort out the situation. At least, he could retake the pest ship, for what it was worth, but he had no chance of overtaking the brig. He descended to the deck.

Half an hour later, there was another shout from Hamlyn. "Deck there, brig's hauled her wind!"

Merewether went into the rigging again. *Rapid* was on the port tack on a reach eastward. From the maintop, he could see the brig coming south, all sail set, with the wind on her quarter. Evidently, her commander had sighted *Comet* and decided there was a better chance of escape in this direction, rather than trying to outsail the schooner through narrow waters to the north. He heard MacCamy give the preliminary order to go about.

"Belay that!" he shouted down. A little more easting and the brig could not double back on him as that frigate had done last summer, leaving only a long stern chase. He had no doubt that *Rapid* had the heels of any brig, but it was hard to wait through those dragging minutes as her topsails became visible, until the bearing satisfied him.

"Wear ship!" he shouted down. "Hands to the braces. Port your helm." Merewether reached the quarterdeck in time to give the final orders to the helm, as the ship wore about almost before the wind. "Ease your helm. Meet her. Course south-southwest and by west," he told the quartermaster. "And send the hands to quarters, Mister MacCamy."

"Sail ho!" came the hail from the masthead. "It's *Comet,* due north."

Well, the thing had worked out. He had the Frenchman pinned against a lee shore, both his ships holding the weather gauge. The privateer could escape now only through the gross incompetence of Merewether or MacRae, or by overwhelming one or both of his ships, or by blind luck. He looked out to see her, now hull up, every sail set, a bone in her teeth, driving south. Five miles astern he could see the Indiaman rolling aimlessly in the swell. It would be some hours yet before she drifted onto soundings off Great Nicobar, but in any event, the first responsibility under Merewether's commission was to destroy or capture that cruiser. He heard the batteries reporting, and Dobbs, officer of the deck at quarters, touched his hat and reported all stations manned and ready. Hoses were strung out, buckets filled with water, sand spread on deck, slow matches burning in tubs beside the guns, pikes and cutlasses in the racks abaft each mast, and the marine detachment deployed on forecastle, poop and in the tops, their muskets glinting in the late afternoon sun.

"Come a point to port," Merewether told the helmsman. The bearing of the Frenchman was almost steady, the ships on collision courses for a point not too far southwest. He looked aft. *Comet* was now visible from the deck, under a tower of canvas. MacRae had positioned her exactly to cut off any escape northwardly, and it was *Rapid*'s sole responsibility to bring the cruiser to bay.

The scene assumed a dreamlike quality, with Wolfe on deck, sword belted on, wearing his cocked hat, eyes sparkling, the butts of pistols protruding from the pockets of his coat, still apparently favoring his left leg. Merewether looked about. No sign of Kinney now, but he was sure he had seen him, scalp shaved clean, only a bit ago. A shout brought his attention back to the brig. She had broken a flag, the tricolor, of course.

"Hoist our colors," he told Dobbs. "And signal, 'Engage the enemy.' " There was really no necessity for the signal, but it went into the log.

It was less than two miles now, and high time the guns were loaded and run out. A nod to Larkin, and the deck burst into activity. Merewether focused the glass on the brig and saw that her ports were also open and guns run out. He could not identify their caliber, but he counted six. The sun was well down to the west, outlining the mountains of Great Nicobar, and her southern tip was less than five miles ahead. He was cutting things damned fine!

"Try a ranging shot, Mister Larkin," he called forward.

The blond hair flashed as Larkin bent over the forward pivot, setting the sights on the long nine-pounder. He stood aside, gauged the pitch of the ship, and pulled the lanyard. The spiteful report blasted out, and Merewether strained his eyes for a sign of the fall of shot. There was a spout off the port bow of the target.

"Short, and a little to the left," he called, and Larkin waved in acknowledgment.

When Merewether looked back at the brig, she was turning toward him, seeking to cross his bow. It was a bold maneuver: there was no profit for a privateer to engage a ship of war. But the French captain had realized that *Rapid* would intercept within minutes and decided to force the issue with a chance of success. *Comet* was three miles astern, and coming fast, but she would not be in time to help here. The brig was now close-hauled, thrashing through the swells, but *Rapid* would forereach on her in a moment and lose the advantage of the weather gauge. He was conscious of Wolfe shouting something at him, but the words were lost in the sound of the second shot from the pivot gun. He hesitated the fraction of a moment it took to observe the shot, and saw splinters fly from the forecastle of the brig. Nothing crippling, he thought, turning to the helm.

"Hands to the braces," he told Dobbs. "Wear ship. Port your helm." The ship swung about to the reciprocal of the course of the privateer, but still to windward, as the hands tailed on to the braces. "Steady as you go, nothing to the left!" The enemy was half a mile ahead, only a point on the port bow. "Keep the hands at the braces."

That French captain had precipitated a situation with several alternatives, and a wrong choice here might mean disaster. The man was holding on resolutely, Merewether thought, looking through the glass. If the brig held her course, *Rapid* might turn across her bow for a raking broadside, or continuing on course for an almost muzzle-to-muzzle exchange. If he turned south, and the brig held on, *Rapid* would in turn be raked from the stern and would lose the weather gauge without a chance for revenge. The Frenchman had his hands at the braces, too, ready to play the game of bluff and artful dodger with *Rapid*.

"Wear ship!" shouted Merewether. "Starboard your helm." He waited a moment for the effect. The brig had reacted like lightning to the first movement of the ship and was swinging to the south.

"Midships! Meet her!" he shouted to the quartermaster. "Belay, as you were!" he told Dobbs, and the yards were trimmed back as *Rapid* continued on course.

The feint had succeeded. The side of the cruiser erupted in flame, but the guns, hastily laid in a ship turning across a moderate swell, managed only one hit forward.

"Come two points to port," he told the helm. "Stand by!" he shouted to MacCamy commanding the port battery. "Fire as your guns bear!" *Rapid* was drawing across the defenseless stern of the brig less than half a cable's length away. Merewether could read the name picked out in gilt: *Majeure*.

The huge twenty-four-pound forward carronade was the first gun to fire, striking through the stern lights, followed by the whole battery. A hundred and two pounds of iron balls smashing lengthwise through a wooden ship was devastating, but Merewether had no time to consider the matter. The powder smoke was rolling down toward the brig, blotting out sight of her, but over it he could see her masts widening; she was still wearing about to starboard! In a moment she would be in a position to repay the broadside with vengeance.

"Starboard helm. Wear ship!" *Rapid* came about alertly to port, to cross the stern of the Frenchman again, with the starboard battery standing ready. Two shots were fired from the privateer, one striking home about midships. Merewether waved to Larkin, and the shots crashed out from bow to stern in succession, as Larkin came running down the battery, to end on the quarterdeck. Every shot took effect, it appeared. Dobbs shouted at him, pointing out over the port quarter. *Comet* was sweeping across his stern, guns run out and ready to fire into the French ship. He saw the tricolor come down, but it was too late to stop the broadside *Comet* sent into her.

The enemy came up into the wind, black smoke now pouring

63

from her shattered stern lights. *Rapid* and *Comet* hove to on either side of the prize, guns run out to cover her.

"Away fire party! Away marines!" roared Dobbs.

The boatswain and his party were manhandling the portable pump into the launch, then throwing lengths of canvas hose, buckets, axes and crowbars into the boat, even as it was being hoisted from its cradle. The men had no intention of being cheated of prize money by fire. The cutter was half full of sea water to serve as a ready reservoir on deck. Her coxswain had pulled both plugs, and water was still pouring from her bottom as she rose in turn to be lowered into the water, the coxswain now hammering the plugs home again in frantic haste.

Larkin and the boatswain were rowing double-time for the prize, even as *Comet's* launch was pulling toward the other side. The marines, under Gunny, embarked in the second boat in disciplined haste, Hamlyn, awaiting Wolfe, fairly dancing with impatience in her stern. Merewether saw the fire party swarm up the side of the brig, then lay hoses aft as the pump was rigged. It was only a few minutes before the smoke had turned white, then diminished to invisibility, as *Comet's* party joined the action. The marines were formed up across the waist and on the forecastle, their muskets at the ready.

Merewether was suddenly so weary he could hardly stand. The sun was now behind the mountains of Great Nicobar, and darkness would not be far behind at this season. He wished desperately for a moment to have a glass of gin, but put the thought aside to deal with the situation. The carpenter was reporting that *Rapid* had been hulled twice above the waterline. There was no immediate danger, and repairs were under way. He signaled *Comet* to provide her share of the prize crew, Dillon, her first lieutenant, to be master. He called Whitfield, the senior boatswain's mate, informed him that he was acting boatswain, second in command, told him to pick eight steady men to help man the brig, and to tell Gunny to leave five marines each from *Comet* and *Rapid,* with a Naique in command, as a guard. The launch, bringing back the fire party, was alongside, the men taking far longer to unload their gear than they had to load it.

Buttram appeared before him in the gathering dusk, his bare arms and shirt spotted with blood.

"Sir, we have a passenger mortally wounded and five men with slighter wounds, all by splinters."

"Passenger?" asked Merewether, puzzled.

"That's what I would call him. Young Kinney . . . He was on the main deck when the second shot struck. A four-foot piece of oak went right through his belly. No chance at all, he's unconscious, a blessing, but I expect he will expire within the hour." The young surgeon shook his head, "A very pleasant lad. He endured a great deal without complaint. Well. I'll discuss the matter later. And now, what about that pest ship?"

Merewether jumped, and then strove to dissemble. He had completely forgotten the *Duchy of Lancaster,* adrift on a lee shore some miles north. He saw Boatswain Tompkins hovering in the background, and sought to gain time.

"Yes?"

"Sir, the Frenchie is not disabled, the standing and running rigging is in good shape. Her cabin is a bit scorched, a shot hit the lamp and scattered oil; that's all the fire was." He paused, a middle-aged, crag-faced seaman from Preston, near Liverpool, who had first gone to sea in the Royal Navy, then in the slave trade, before he was drafted into the Bombay Marine. He continued with an air of wonder, "Sir, every shot went clean through that ship, and never touched a man! Three broadsides, and not a drop of blood. Who'd believe it?"

"She's secured, I hope?"

"Yes, sir. Them marines run everybody on deck, and there's no fight in them."

"Very well, Mister Tompkins, I've sent Whitfield, and eight leading seamen for the prize crew. And now, that Indiaman that's adrift north of here, we've got to get her under tow, or anchored safely. Leave the boats in the water, and I'll require a crew when we come up with her." Merewether cut his eyes at Buttram in the gloom, daring him to say anything. Tompkins touched his hat and went forward.

Merewether turned to Buttram again. "How much danger is there from infection, assuming that ship is infested with fever?"

"Well, Captain, a party boarding her should carry its own food and water, and avoid contact with the sick, of course. All human excrement should be disposed of, the living quarters and galleys flushed out and disinfected. I have a formula I can make up for that with supplies on board. It might help to fumigate the ship with brimstone, as well. I can't predict the chances, of course, but if a man stays clean, avoids direct contact, and consumes uncontaminated food and water, he should escape infection. But the party must remain in quarantine for at least two weeks after the last exposure."

Merewether turned the matter over in his mind. Any party he put on board would be lost to him for the balance of the operation, and he certainly could not spare enough men to work that huge ship. It was possible, from his medical advice, that a considerable number of the lascars survived, however, and under resolute command, they might be able to sail her downwind to Ceylon. It was his duty to try to preserve the valuable ship and cargo for the Company, but not at the expense of crippling his squadron in the process.

"Signals: 'Prepare to get under way, course north, a point west.'" There was barely enough light left to read the flags. "And now, to *Comet*: 'Send Keese on board with kit.'" It would be a while before Comet could ferry him across, and Merewether went down to the sick bay.

Buttram was hovering over a cot on which young Kinney lay. There was no visible sign of respiration, and Buttram pulled the sheet up over the waxen face and shaven pate.

"He's gone. A massive internal hemorrhage." Merewether barely knew the lad, but he had appeared alert and likeable. *Rapid* had pumped two raking broadsides, and *Comet* one, through that French cruiser without wounding a man, while the two hits the privateer managed had killed a Royal Navy warrant officer and wounded five seamen.

"Call the sailmaker, and I'll try to have the service at two bells in the forenoon watch. And what's wrong with that fellow?" There was a seaman, head bandaged, lying on another cot.

"Oh, Stokes got a nasty knock and cut on the head. I'm keeping him here tonight in case he has concussion."

66

"Very well. I've ordered Keese on board. When he comes, bring him to the cabin." Merewether went on deck and aft through the gloom, hoping *Comet*'s boat would soon arrive. At the break of the poop, he encountered Wolfe, still wearing his sword and cocked hat.

"Merewether, I must see you immediately!"

Merewether led the way below to the cabin, and Wolfe entered, propelling a man dressed in the semblance of a uniform ahead of him. The man was ashen, trembling visibly, and held his left wrist in his right hand. The left hand was wrapped in a bloody rag. Merewether took off his hat and seated himself at the desk.

"Yes, Captain?"

Wolfe's face was wreathed in smiles. "That was a beautiful maneuver, Commodore, you even deceived me! The feint, and then wearing back immediately to cross his stern again—ah, beautiful! Nelson could not have improved upon it." Merewether felt a glow of satisfaction at this unexpected praise.

"Thank you, Captain. I found myself in a fortunate position."

"Where you deliberately placed yourself," continued Wolfe. "I certainly shall see that Admiral Pellew receives a full account of this action!" He paused portentously. "And I've pulled off a bit of a coup myself this afternoon! This is the captain of the brig. Luckily, I have a fair command of French, and with a little persuasion"—Wolfe smiled triumphantly—"he gave me their operational plan." He paused again and leaned forward. "Sir, he parted company with two schooners only this morning. Since the Indiaman was his prize alone, they refused to help him try to save it, but are heading for a rendezvous off Ko Phuket with a third ship a week from today."

"Excellent, Captain, and what is wrong with this man? I thought there were no casualties in the Frenchman."

Wolfe laughed shortly. "As I said, I had to persuade him to talk. He only has two fingers damaged, though he was a bit stubborn at the outset. A Spanish trick I learned when I was serving at Gibraltar."

Merewether kept his face impassive. This officer had used torture to extract information from a prisoner in violation of the conventions of war. There was no question, the intelligence was valuable, but the means by which Wolfe had obtained it was barbarous.

"Thank you, Captain. I shall act upon this information as soon as that Indiaman is secured." He stood up in dismissal. "And send this man to the sick bay."

Wolfe's mouth came open, face crimson. He sputtered a moment, then blurted, "I'm damned! Vital and urgent intelligence, and you delay to secure a stinking John Company packet!"

"That's enough, Captain," said Merewether sharply. "And by the way, your aide, Midshipman Kinney, died a few minutes ago from a wound received in the action this afternoon."

"Oh, Kinney; died did he? Well, not much loss there. He was a dirty fellow without ability or future." The flush faded from Wolfe's face. "Well, God rest his soul!" he added almost inaudibly, and turned away for a moment, then turned back to face Merewether, a tear glistening on his cheek. "I'll put this remarkable failure to act on this information in my report. . . ."

"As you will," broke in Merewether. "You are excused." Wolfe went out, followed by the Frenchman, still holding his wrist, passing Buttram and Keese in the passage.

Merewether sat down wearily again at the desk. Much as he would prefer to go charging off in pursuit of the privateers, he must first try to preserve the Company's investment in the Indiaman. He called the messenger and sent him with instructions to the watch officer to order execution of the previous order and get the squadron under way. He left the boats in the water, towing alongside from a boom, to be used in the impending operation.

When the two surgeons entered, Merewether came bluntly to the point with Keese. "I had intended to give you an acting warrant as surgeon in the Marine, Doctor. Now, it seems we have come up with your ship, and you are her senior officer present."

"Yes, sir, but only a surgeon."

"Precisely what we require at the moment, Doctor. If I can give you a man qualified to sail her, and one able to navigate, assuming there are some healthy lascars left, are you willing to help take her to Ceylon?"

Keese's blue eyes snapped. "In a moment, sir! And I'll have

her disinfected and clean too. There should be enough drugs and disinfectants left in the apothecary locker, I doubt if anyone has meddled with more than the medicinal brandy."

"Very well, hold yourself in readiness. We should come up with your ship in another hour. I had intended to do no more than get a line on her tonight to hold her off the beach, but in light of certain information I have received, I must move immediately. Now, Buttram, there's a French officer waiting in your sick bay with an injured hand, and on your way out, ask the watch to pass the word for Eldridge and Webster to lay aft to the cabin."

As Merewether waited the few moments before the knock came, he thought sourly that Wolfe continued to be a problem, though he had produced the intelligence so desperately needed. He recalled Buttram's concept of two personalities inhabiting the same body. Well, tonight the suppressed one had leaped out again and quite unpleasantly. Possibly he could endure the man through the rest of this commission, but he was afraid something might snap. When the knock came, he invited Eldridge in, asking Webster to wait.

"Sit down, Eldridge," he told the boatswain's mate. "You read and write, I know, but how much more education did you have?"

"Not much," Eldridge confessed, uncomfortable at being seated in the cabin. "I don't cypher very well, sir."

"All right. That Indiaman up ahead has been infected by fever —typhoid, typhus, the doctors are not sure at this point. We are reasonably sure the French prize crew is dead or disabled, but that a number of the lascars probably survive. Given enough hands, can you get her under sail and take her to Columbo?"

"Get her under sail, I can, and steer any course that's set, but I can't navigate, sir."

"Very well, you're truthful. Are you afraid of the fever, Eldridge?"

"Not much, sir, I guess. I had a case of it when I was a boy."

"I had in mind," said Merewether slowly, "issuing an acting warrant, master's mate or boatswain, take your choice, to you to sail the Indiaman to Ceylon. I'll provide you with a navigator.

Are you game?" He watched Eldridge's face as determination succeeded surprise. "And if you'll take some instruction in navigation along the way, I'll recommend the permanent appointment to Bombay Castle."

"Yes, sir," said Eldridge. "And if you don't mind, I would as lief be a master's mate."

"Very well, Mister Eldridge," said Merewether rising to shake the young man's hand. He went over to a locker under the transom and pulled out a well-worn book. "Mister Burcham, lately a midshipman in this ship, left this behind. It details every step and calculation in the navigational process, and with some practical instruction, it should teach you enough to pass an examination for master's mate." Eldridge took the volume almost reverently. "Now get your gear and bedding together, draw pistols, powder and shot from the gunner, and I'll give you this to help you along in case of trouble." He pulled one of the four blunderbusses from the rack beside the door and handed it to Eldridge. "A gun like this made me a captain in the Marine, and it may bring luck to you. I was a topman and a boatswain's mate, too. Now understand this, provisions and water will come from this ship; do not eat or drink anything you find in the other. Obey the doctor's orders as to matters of health and the disposition of the ship once you reach Ceylon, but you are captain of the *Duchy of Lancaster*." He watched Eldridge stride out of the door, book and blunderbuss in either hand, and hoped that he had not just imposed a sentence of death upon him.

Webster came in, a bony man approaching middle age, who would have been handsome except for the ravages of disease and dissipation in his face. Merewether had discovered his education last year and customarily drafted him to assist in making fair copies of orders and reports in his classical handwriting.

"Sit down, Webster. What rating do you hold at the moment?"

"Ordinary seaman, sir."

"Let's see, you were rated quartermaster off the Cape of Good Hope and disrated for drunkenness at Calcutta."

"Yes, sir."

"Rated again, and disrated at Macao. Rated once more, and

disrated at Bombay. Drink each time. You are an excellent quartermaster."

A tinge of red appeared in the sallow cheeks as Webster met his gaze squarely. "Yes, sir, drink and women, they've been my ruination. I threw away an inheritance in London, went bankrupt as an underwriter at Lloyd's, and escaped to sea ahead of my creditors. I was gently born and had a good education, but I can't let women or spirits alone. No hope for me this late date."

Merewether looked down at his desk. He had known the man was educated and possessed ability, but on each appearance at the mast, Webster had interposed no defense and accepted his punishment. "Very well, Webster, I do not intend to reform you; I think and you think it is hopeless. I do want to borrow your considerable talents for a time, if you will consent." Webster looked at him impassively, the touch of color still in his face. "This Indiaman up ahead has been stricken with disease, evidently killing all the white men aboard her. Doctor Keese, her surgeon, and Eldridge have agreed to board her, and if there are enough lascars surviving, to try to take her to Ceylon. They need a man acquainted with the theory to navigate her. What do you say?"

Webster looked aside for a moment. "And why not?" he said at last. "I can navigate, and it's as good a berth as any for me. I'll do it, but I make you no promises once we arrive at Columbo!"

"Good, Webster, we understand one another, and I am rating you quartermaster again. Now, if you will, please give all the instruction you can to Eldridge in the theory and practice of navigation during the voyage." Merewether pulled down another of the blunderbusses from the rack, and handed it to Webster. "I gave Eldridge the mate of this. It often serves to preserve good order and discipline at sea. And good luck, Webster!" The man took the weapon and went out, while Merewether sat for a moment, wondering at the vagaries of fate. There was no guarantee of success or happiness in this world, even with a gentle birth and a classical education, he concluded.

CHAPTER SIX

The weather was making up, wind freshening, no stars visible, and an occasional whitecap appearing among the swells. The darkness to the east foretold the approaching squall, and stinging drops of rain splattered down as the launch pulled away for the *Duchy of Lancaster*. Merewether sat in the stern, bareheaded, in shirt and trousers, preferring to be wet with rain rather than sweat under a boat cloak. Doctor Keese, Eldridge and Webster had their baggage beside them, and three large parcels, wrapped in oilskins, containing rations and a water breaker each, were stowed forward. The coxswain steered for a dim light which must be on the Indiaman. She appeared to be lying quartering into the wind and sea as the boat pulled around the bow and into her lee, then circled to come along the port side at the gangway.

"And Eldridge," said Merewether suddenly, as the thought struck him. "Be sure to get rid of that hawser she was being towed by—be like an anchor underfoot otherwise."

Eldridge had a lighted lantern in hand and was anxiously looking up the high side of the ship.

"No ladder," he said, and picked up the grapnel. He hurled it up into darkness, heard it strike wood, jerked the line taut, and tested its hold. The ship was both pitching and rolling in the swell, and the bow hook and stern hook were fending off, as the oarsmen held the launch close. Eldridge gauged the pitch and roll, leaped to take as high a hold as he could, and went up the line as the Indiaman rolled to port, disappearing from sight like a fakir performing the rope trick. A moment later he shouted down. "Tie the lantern on the line!"

It seemed an interminable time before there was another shout from above, and a Jacob's ladder cascaded down.

"Up you go," Merewether told Webster, and the quarter-master scrambled up. There was a flaw in the wind for a moment, and a nauseating stench came into the boat.

"Good God!" said Keese. "Those French corpses must still be aft. I'll have to get them overboard somehow."

"All right, Doctor, can you make it? Let me know as soon as you can if there are enough able-bodied men to work the ship." What he would do if there were no lascars able to work Merewether refused to consider at this point.

Keese took hold of the ladder, swung himself up, was slammed once against the side as the ship rolled to starboard, and went out of sight. The boat crew had its hands full, holding close, and fending off, as the rain came down with increasing force. It must have been a quarter of an hour before the voice of Keese came down out of the darkness.

"Boat ahoy! There seem to be thirty-nine lascars healthy, including their leading seaman. Eldridge thinks he can manage, and now, we're ready for our gear and provisions."

A hook at the end of a line came down, and one by one the items were hauled up to the deck. Lanterns were now hanging in the shrouds casting a yellow glow on the wet side of the Indiaman. A head appeared over the bulwark.

"Are you ready, Eldridge?" shouted Merewether.

After a hesitation, there came the reply, "Yes, sir, I think so."

"Well, good luck!" Merewether turned to the coxswain, "Shove off, return to the ship."

The launch was a quarter of a mile away, pulling hard against the wind and seas, when the faint sound of a shot came from downwind. Merewether whirled to look back at the Indiaman, lanterns now mere pinpoints to mark her position. There was nothing he could do, he justified himself. It was sink or swim for Eldridge and his party; he could not risk the chance of bringing infection into *Rapid*.

The launch pulled on toward the ship.

Eldridge came back from the locker under the break of the poop with three more lighted lanterns and set them on deck while he looked for the Jacob's ladder. The stench coming from the open companionways leading aft was almost unbearable. He found the ladder, rolled and lashed against the bulwark, and cut it loose, then slipped the eye splices over the cleats at the gangway.

"Heads up!" he shouted, and kicked the roll over the side. A moment later, Webster appeared on deck, and after an interval, the head of Doctor Keese materialized at the top of the ladder, and he and Webster pulled him over the side. The doctor's knuckles were skinned, and he was rubbing his knees.

"I'll look for the charts and navigating instruments," said Webster, picking up a lantern and heading aft.

"Come on forward," said Keese. "There are a few hands speak some English, but Sharma is their leading seaman, if he's still alive."

At the forecastle entry, Keese paused. There was a lantern hanging inside, smoked and guttering, and a stench came out, not of death and corruption, but of sickness and feces.

"Sharma!" shouted Keese. He paused to listen, then, "Sharma, on deck!" There was a rustle of movement below, and a gray-bearded Indian appeared at the foot of the ladder.

"Sah!" the man said in astonishment. "You have returned!"

"Sharma, how many able-bodied men have you?"

The Indian thought a moment, counting on his fingers, then replied, "Thirty-eight, sah, and me, and eleven more still sick. All the Frenchmen are dead."

"Very well, Sharma, now get them on deck. We have to get the ship under way."

The man went back out of sight, and Eldridge led the way back to the gangway.

"Can you handle her with that many men?" asked Keese.

"Yes, sir, I think so, if I can make those buggers understand me."

"Well, Sharma will relay the orders in their lingo, and they appeared to know their business on the way to China. I'll tell the Commodore to send up our gear."

Once the baggage and provisions were on deck, there appeared to be no further necessity for the boat to stand by. Eldridge put his head over the side as he heard Merewether shout the question. He hesitated a moment, feeling suddenly lonely and abandoned, full of doubts of his ability to control this huge ship with

74

skeleton crew that spoke so little English, or to take her a thousand-odd miles across the Bay of Bengal. He wondered if he might sicken and die like those men aft, to become a liquid mass of corruption in a derelict doomed to drift until it wrecked against some god-forsaken coast. He had been confident enough a few hours ago, elated at his promotion, temporary though it might prove to be, and accepting the envious congratulations of the other petty officers. They had wondered that he had chosen to be a master's mate when the rank of boatswain was the pinnacle of ambition of nearly every rating in the lower deck. But Eldridge had made that choice deliberately. He had long since observed that a qualified boatswain was far too valuable a warrant officer ever to be promoted to commissioned rank. That scarfaced captain down in the boat had risen from the lower deck by way of topman and a boatswain's mate, to be a commodore now, it was said, and what one man had done, another might.

The memory of that misty morning five years ago when he left the stone cottage in Northumberland crossed Eldridge's mind. After his father died, the eldest son came back to assume the lease on the croft. He had told Eldridge bluntly that what with his wife, mother, and two younger sisters still at home, as well as his own three toddlers, there was no room for a well-grown sixteen-year-old lad. So Eldridge had walked to the Tyneside and found a bare subsistence digging and clearing ditches for the Corporation of Newcastle, and later became a navvy on the docks. The chance to sign on as a landsman in a coastwise brig was irresistible, but she had paid off after the voyage at Liverpool. Two years of swinging a pick and plying a shovel had broadened Eldridge's shoulders and developed his muscles, and with the advantage of being able to splice and tie the correct knot, he had found a berth in the slaver *Rapid* as an ordinary seaman on her last voyage to the Congo and West Indies.

This past year had been astonishing. Drafted into a service he had never heard of, the Bombay Marine, Eldridge had been carried from London around the world to India and China, and he had progressed from ordinary seaman to topman, then to boatswain's mate, and now to acting master's mate. Ambition flooded up again. He had fought by the side of Captain Merewether, and

75

Merewether had been fair to him. By God, he would justify Merewether, take this towering ship to Ceylon, and learn enough in the process not only to be a master's mate, but reach commissioned rank!

Eldridge shouted down his answer to Merewether's inquiry, "Yes, sir, I think so!"

He heard ". . . good luck!" almost drowned out in a splatter of rain, then saw the launch fend off and pull away into darkness. As he turned from the side, Eldridge heard the twitter of conversation in a foreign tongue, and looked forward to see movement flowing from the forecastle to gather in the shadowy waist. Sharma and Doctor Keese stood together at the base of the mainmast, a lantern casting dim yellow light on the scene. The rain came down harder, with gusts of wind out of the northeast. Webster came forward, water trickling from his chin.

"She answers her helm all right, sir," he told Eldridge. "Compass seems true, though I'm not sure about the table of corrections. The chronometers were run down, but I've wound and reset them to agree with the watch I brought from *Rapid*. There are charts in the roundhouse, though I can't find one for the approaches to Columbo. I'm ready to get under way, but that smell aft is more than I can bear."

"And me," said Eldridge, unwrapping the oilskin, and taking out the blunderbuss and pair of pistols he had had the gunner load and prime for him. There were scraps of oilskin tied over the locks of the guns to protect the priming from the rain. He thrust the pistols into his waistband, and went forward, laying the blunderbuss beside the mast outside the pool of light.

"Are all the hands on deck?" he asked Keese.

"Yes, sah," interposed Sharma. "I've told them what you plan, sah."

"All right, Sharma, but first I want those bodies aft out and over the side. I want all bedding, clothing, baggage, slop buckets, and everything movable after them! Tell all hands to go aft and turn to."

The lascar looked at him sidewise, his eyes gleaming in the lantern light. "Sah . . ." he commenced.

"Tell them!"

76

The leader turned to the assembly and began to speak, looking anxiously over his shoulder twice at Eldridge. There were several shrill cries, apparently of protest, from the group, and Sharma spread his hands, then gestured with his thumb toward Eldridge. The men moved restively, and a little hum of conversation arose.

Eldridge lost patience. "Turn to!" he grated, and Sharma took a step back in alarm.

"Sah, they are afraid, and some—their religion does not permit . . ."

Just then a man with glittering eyes and a stylized beard stepped forward and began to speak with vigorous gestures. He turned to the hands and shouted, pointing forward. A half dozen men turned and started toward the forecastle entry. The others looked undecided.

"Sah, this man is telling them not to obey, not to risk sickness or defile their hands with the rotting corpses of Christians!"

God damn, thought Eldridge in a cold fury, faced with outright mutiny before he had even taken command! He could not tolerate the stench, or the risk of infection for himself, Keese or Webster; the after quarters must be cleared at any cost. He stepped back, picked up the blunderbuss, stripping the oilskin cover from the lock, and pulling the hammer back to full cock. The bearded man was still shouting and gesturing toward the forecastle, as more lascars were now heading toward it.

"You!" roared Eldridge, stepping back into the lighted area. The bearded man whirled, and Eldridge fired the blunderbuss at point-blank range into his chest. He turned toward the crew, swinging the bell muzzle from side to side, smelling the acrid powder smoke as it blew by him. He was conscious of a movement to his right, and there stood Webster, the mate of his blunderbuss menacing the assembly.

"Tell them to turn to!"

Sharma spoke briefly. The men hesitated only a moment, before filing aft, looking with alarm at the grim faces of Webster and Eldridge, and the short, ugly weapons in their hands.

In an hour, the cabins aft were emptied. There had been five French corpses taken out on mattresses, wrapped in bedding, and dumped over the side. There had been no time for a commit-

77

tal service, even if he had known the words, Eldridge reflected. Everything portable followed the bodies, and then Keese sent a dozen pails of a shrewd-smelling liquid in to be splashed across the deck in each room and passage before they were swabbed out.

It took another hour to get topsails, spanker and a foresail set, then with Webster at the wheel, Sharma positioned to pass the word to the hands at the braces, Eldridge gave his first command.

"Starboard your helm." With the ship's head almost east, the wind was on her port bow.

"Starboard it is, sir." The sternway on the ship pulled the stern slowly about to port, as the rudder bit, then the foresail and main topsail filled with tremendous reports, the sternway checked, and the ship payed off as the scanty crew heaved at the braces to trim the yards as she came around.

"Shift your helm."

"Port it is, sir."

"Midships. Meet her," said Eldridge, as the vessel gained headway. He stepped over to look at the compass in the lighted binnacle.

"Your course is . . ."

". . . south-southeast, sir," interposed Webster.

". . . south-southeast," continued Eldridge. "Look lively!" he shouted to Sharma. "Trim her more—that's it!" On the port tack, under topsails, spanker, and one headsail, the *Duchy of Lancaster* staggered sluggishly across the heavy swells, raindrops bouncing on her decks, as Eldridge, swaying automatically with the movement of the ship, watched the compass, and then the trim of the sails. He was not weary: the exhilaration persisted; he was the captain, and he would take this great ship to Ceylon, come what may!

As he watched the straining sails and felt the movement of the ship, a thought struck him. Thunderation, the cable! He ran forward without explanation to Webster, found the boatswain's locker and an ax, and groped his way to the forward bitts. The cable went out through the fairleads, rigid as an iron bar. It must be dragging a hundred feet below the keel, impeding the ship's progress almost as much as would an anchor. It took three sharp blows with the ax before the severed end vanished over the bow. As he made his way aft, Eldridge felt that the ship was free at last, no longer staggering, but fairly dancing over the swells. He decided to catch a catnap in the lee of the roundhouse. After an hour, he relieved Webster at the wheel.

Daybreak was late and gray, rain still falling, but Great Nicobar Island was now on the starboard quarter. Webster came out of the roundhouse and touched his forehead.

"I recommend you change course to due west, Captain. It may give us a landfall well north on Ceylon, but it will be easy enough to coast around to Columbo, and I can't trust these chronometers since I set them. They're already two minutes out with the watch I brought to set them by."

"Very well, take the wheel." He went to the break of the poop to find Sharma and the watch on deck sheltering from the rain. "Hands to the braces, Sharma." The ship wore around to the west and settled on her new course. Sharma produced two lascars who could steer a course, and one relieved the helm. Eldridge found the parcel of food and the water breaker still on deck by the gangway. He took a drink of water in a tin cup from the cask and a dollop of lime juice from the jug, blunting his hunger with biscuit, cheese and raisins. From time to time, he looked up to see how the sails drew, and then to starboard toward that island. It was now broad on the starboard beam, and a recollection struck him.

"And now, Webster, suppose you commence teaching me how to navigate a ship."

"Aye aye, sir. You might just take a bearing on Great Nicobar, sir, and if she bears due north, as I think she does now, write in the log"—Webster paused to extract the big silver watch from his pocket—"'Seven hours, ten minutes ante meridiem, local time: Took departure, southern tip of Great Nicobar Island bearing due north, distant four miles, course west, making good five knots.'"

Eldridge headed for the roundhouse. It was a small step, but in the right direction.

CHAPTER SEVEN

Merewether took another reading from the boat compass. The Indiaman was going to leeward much faster than *Comet* or *Rapid*, and the distance had widened appreciably. He wondered again at the shot he had heard and hoped that Eldridge had survived to get some sail set. The squall had struck, gusts of wind picking up spume from the wave crests, and hurling the salt taste, mixed with rain, into his face. A dark shape with pinpricks of light loomed ahead, and he thought of the orders he must give tonight for the next phase of the operation.

"Steer for *Comet*," he told the coxswain. MacRae had not been informed of the fresh intelligence Wolfe had supplied this afternoon, and a brief council of war would be helpful.

A quarter hour later, MacRae said flatly, "I don't put much stock in information given to escape torture." He turned to the chart spread on his desk. "And why Ko Phuket as a rendezvous, unless it just happens to be the point that's dead in the eye of the wind? It's either a long reach north away from the shipping lanes, or a longer, harder reach south through the Strait before we could hope to be able to run down to it. . . . I just don't believe it. Diamond Point on Sumatra right opposite Penang would be more logical, if those Frenchmen actually plan a rendezvous, which I doubt." It was nearly the longest speech Merewether had ever heard the little Scots officer deliver.

MacRae remained standing, leaning over his desk, hands flat on either margin of the chart, the eye with the cast in it focusing almost straight as his gaze bored into Merewether's. It was the officer in tactical command's sole responsibility to evaluate the intelligence Wolfe had produced, and if he were wrong, the consequences would likewise be his alone. Still, there was no profit in a cruiser making a long reach north, away from the shipping lanes, merely to conclude a rendezvous. The date, a week hence, was persuasive. It would roughly mark the midpoint of a normal privateering venture, based upon the information supplied by

Ross in the Cocos Islands two months ago. Then again, those Frenchmen rarely acted in concert, as witness the fact that they had refused assistance to *Majeure* in salvaging the Indiaman, if her captain could be believed at all.

"What you say is logical, MacRae." Merewether shifted in the chair, uncrossing his legs, breaking the spell of MacRae's gaze; and he sat back down behind the desk. "But in addition to the torture, the man had some motive, resentment, if nothing more, to betray his consorts; he had already lost his own ship and prize, and misery loves company." He thought a moment. "And if three cruisers did show up at the rendezvous, there would be a good chance that we might be taken, and the captain rescued—"

—"Which would be little enough comfort for a man who has lost his own ship, and a prize that would have made him wealthy for life. I tell you, Captain, the thing does not ring true!"

Merewether had never before heard such conviction in MacRae's voice, and he wondered for a moment if the man might possess the fabled Celtic gift of second sight.

By nature, Merewether disliked compromise. While it might be easier, there was no overwhelming reason to make his reach to the north through untraveled waters, when he could possibly make enough easting by running back down the Strait past Penang, and he would again be in the "small end of the horn."

"Very well, MacRae, you are most convincing. I'll send Dillon on north with the prize, and we will go back southeast through the Strait. But I do intend to look in on Ko Phuket before the week is out."

On deck, he found the squall had passed, wind and rain abating, and he entered the launch again to pull over to *Majeure*. He gave Dillon, a tall, broad, calm man, his orders, spoke briefly to Whitfield, made sure the prize was in capable hands before parting company, and came back on board *Rapid*. He was so weary he thought he would drop, but he remained on deck until he was sure the prize was moving, then signaled *Comet* to get under way.

Doctor Buttram intercepted Merewether on his way below. "Sir, I need to talk again with you."

"Certainly." Merewether pulled off his soaked clothing, rubbed himself dry, and shrugged into the silk gown he had brought back from Canton last fall. The tea Sangh had prepared was hot and comforting.

"I told you this afternoon I'd discuss the matter of Kinney's death, or rather some events preceding it, further with you."

"Yes," Merewether said, "and I must mark the place in the prayer book for the service in the morning."

"You saw his head," continued Buttram inexorably. "Shaved to the bare skin."

"Yes, but only in passing, an hour or so before he was wounded."

"It was done yesterday morning by that servant of Wolfe's, but at his direction. . . ."

"Why, in Heaven's name?"

"It seems," said Buttram slowly, "that Captain Wolfe was convinced the boy was infested with lice or some other kind of vermin. I examined him three times in the past week and found nothing, though I did give him an ointment, just in case. This morning, as I understand the matter, Wolfe called the boy to his room and had Dyer shave the hair off his head. Kinney was terribly upset, though he went about his duties as usual."

Merewether recalled Wolfe's reaction to the news of Kinney's death this afternoon. "How did he happen to be on the main deck, anyway?"

"He was assigned there to observe the time it took for powder charges to come up from the magazine to the guns. I have his notes. They were still clutched in his hand when he was carried into the cockpit." Buttram handed Merewether a foolscap sheet.

"I'm damned." Merewether looked at the cryptic figures. "Only two broadsides; I'm afraid we didn't give him much to work with."

"It's beside the point," Buttram continued. "Legitimate enough information, I dare say, if one is inspecting the state of readiness of a warship. The point I am making is: Wolfe is insane!"

"I believe you tended toward that opinion in our last discussion."

"Yes, but now I am ready to certify him!" said Buttram in a high, strained tone.

Merewether sat silent a moment, then said deliberately, "Doctor, Wolfe would make a fool of you. He is entirely normal in his appearance and could make a convincing and logical explanation of any of the actions you relied on. A flat assertion that he saw lice in Kinney's hair would outweigh your negative statement. True, he was drunk once, but no harm resulted. His attack on the Malays was merely an impetuous act of valor. We have no evidence as to the matters of the woman and the cat. Now, what else have you?"

"Great balls of fire!" exploded Buttram, leaping to his feet, face livid. "You've become a sea lawyer!"

"I'm not, and sit down, Doctor. I am only stating how the matter would appear to a disinterested person. Wolfe is in this ship under orders as an observer for the Royal Navy. I can require him to conform to reasonable rules of conduct, which I did in the matter of the wine, but, legally, he is not under my command, and I conceive my authority is limited to an order to leave the ship." A thought struck him, and Merewether asked, "What was wrong with that French captain?"

"That is another thing. The man had the joints of two fingers crushed in such a manner as to damage the nerves and cause intense agony. I've read about the device, a trick brought to Spain by the Moors and then refined by the Inquisition. The pain was insupportable, gangrene a certainty because of the destruction of circulation, so I had to amputate both fingers; luckily, it was the left hand." Buttram shook his head.

Merewether told himself in disgust that he shared the guilt of Wolfe's barbarity, had condoned the matter after the fact, and intended to act ultimately upon the intelligence produced by the torture, though it violated the conventions of war. He dissembled, and a subdued Buttram took his leave, as Merewether retired to roll and toss halfway through the midwatch, dreading the coming morning and the burial service for Kinney.

It was slow going, the wind had drawn almost east after the unsettled weather, becoming light and variable in the process. It took two days to cover the distance from Great Nicobar to a position where a blue smudge on the horizon indicated a landfall on Diamond Point. Merewether wished a dozen times that he had disregarded MacRae and made the easier reach north, but he had developed an almost superstitious belief that he would find the French at the point MacRae had mentioned. Wolfe had appeared on deck in full uniform just before the committal services for Kinney yesterday morning, looked at the compass, and then at Merewether.

"A reach north would have been easier, Commodore," he had said. "You may be cutting this damn fine."

"Five days yet," Merewether replied. "And I cover the narrow seas again, as well."

"True," said Wolfe, more pleasantly. "And it is a matter upon which reasonable minds may differ." He had paused and looked down at the waist where the hands were beginning to gather in response to the word the boatswain's mates were shouting down the companionways. "And Commodore, would you mind if I read the service for poor Kinney? It would be a comfort to be able to say as much in the letter I shall write to his mother and father."

"Why, not at all, Captain," said a startled Merewether. "I should have made the suggestion myself."

Wolfe made a surprisingly professional affair of the service, his voice sounding out as he read the prayers with sonorous grace over the bare heads of the crew. *Comet* was hove to on the starboard beam, her hands ranged along the side, flag at half-mast. The plank tilted, and the canvas-shrouded body slid from under the red ensign into the sea.

"Hats on." Larkin looked to Merewether for permission to dismiss.

"Just a moment." Merewether during his last commission had made a custom of announcing promotions after a burial at sea; two boatswain's mates had been temporarily promoted and transferred, and the boatswain had recommended that Lyle, coxswain for the launch, and Briggs, foretopman, be given temporary ratings. "By virtue of the authority vested in me by the Articles for the Government of the Bombay Marine, I hereby rate Lyle and

Briggs to be boatswain's mates for the time being. You may dismiss the hands, Mister Larkin."

Wolfe had been standing by, prayer book still in hand. "You read an impressive service, Captain," Merewether told him.

"The words are in the Book of Common Prayer," said Wolfe, looking a little embarrassed, "but I read them with a full heart. And I have another headache; I must get a potion from Buttram." The man was a perfect enigma, Merewether thought, as he watched him go below.

Now, there was that distant cloud on the horizon that Dobbs insisted must be Diamond Point, the sun already up and hot, and the wind shifting again almost northeast. It was inspection day for *Rapid*, and Merewether followed Larkin, Tompkins, and the gunner along the weather decks, examining standing and running rigging, the boats, catted anchors, the pumps, and main capstan, before looking at the polished brass of the guns.

"You might consider using chafing gear when you replace those lines, Mister Tompkins. That main-topsail brace seems to cut like a saw."

The boatswain made a note.

"Otherwise a very good topside inspection."

The party filed below, to be met by Doctor Buttram, the purser and the carpenter. The two shot holes had been sawed square, plugged, caulked and painted. The galley was clean, kettles and pots gleaming, knives and cleavers hung neatly in their places. The party progressed on into the sick bay and then the cockpit, both scrubbed spotless. The cooper joined the group, and they went down to the hold to inspect water casks and the victual storerooms, sweat beginning to drip from Merewether's chin here in the bowels of the ship.

"Sir!" At the top of the ladder, a head appeared, and Merewether recognized Hamlyn's voice.

"All right?"

"Sir, sails bearing about northeast. Mister MacCamy thinks two ships are chasing a third."

Merewether pondered the situation. *Rapid's* course was already southeast, as close-hauled as she would lie, and Diamond

Point was almost dead ahead. There was no reason to alter course at this time with so little information.

"Very well. Tell Mister MacCamy to hold on, and signal the sighting to *Comet*, if she hasn't already seen them herself." He went on behind the doctor, cooper and purser to thump casks, make sure they were full and properly secured with enough dunnage to hold them against any roll or pitch the ship might make. Impatience surged up; he chafed to be on deck, but compelled himself to follow through the routine for another half hour until he could terminate the inspections as fully completed.

"Very good. I am pleased with our state of readiness," he told the group as it finally came back to the main deck. "A few repairs and corrections are yet to be made, but on the whole, very good." He forced himself to climb the ladder deliberately.

On deck, nothing seemed to have changed. The ship was still close-hauled on the port tack, heading southeast, Diamond Point still an indistinct blur ahead. He could see nothing from the deck of the sails reported, but Mister MacCamy came rolling over in his round-shouldered gait to report the targets were apparently headed southeast also. Merewether looked at the signal log, saw *Comet*'s acknowledgment of the message, and invited Larkin and Buttram below for tea. He saw Wolfe emerge on deck, and on impulse, extended the invitation to him. The burial service yesterday had exposed a facet of the man he had not suspected.

Half an hour later, he could restrain himself no longer and took the glass to the maintop. He found the targets, but could make no more of them than had already been reported. There did appear to be three, all presenting their sterns to him, their masts almost in line, so that he could not even determine whether they were ships or schooners. One appeared much smaller, but whether it was smaller, or merely more distant, he could not tell from this angle. They appeared to be comfortably weathering Diamond Point, and he came back down to go in the cubbyhole with Dobbs and make sure his own course would do the same.

"Damnation," he grumbled to Dobbs, as they emerged. "Except we need the easting, this may be another water haul. I don't think we've gained an inch, and if we did come up with them, they'd probably be country ships at that."

86

"Well, sir, I doubt it. They appear to be sailing right smartly."

The morning wore on, the breeze slackening, the sun an intolerably bright brass disk in a cloudless sky. Merewether had found a bit of shade cast by the mizzen topsail against the starboard rail and remained there, his shirt sticking to his back. Sangh brought up a bite of lunch and cold tea laced with lime juice. The last cast of the log had indicated less than four knots, and the targets were not yet in sight from the deck, though Diamond Point was now distinctly outlined off the starboard bow. Larkin relieved MacCamy for the afternoon watch and came over to discuss the situation. Merewether was a bit short with him, and then despised himself. Larkin found his own spot of shade.

This had been a frustrating operation, now over a month old, with one privateer and an infected Indiaman to show for it. Somehow, he had thought he would sweep clear the Bay of Bengal and capture or destroy the enemy in short order. He had understood the immensity of the area in which the cruisers could operate, but his plan to seek them in the shipping lanes, the narrow seas, and the small end of the horn had appeared sound, and in fact he yet could perceive no defect in it. Possibly, those sails up ahead were French, but the odds were against it. Depression settled upon Merewether as it had before his first visit to Penang. He was even now risking his career in the face of Wolfe's positive intelligence, coming back southeast at the illogical insistence of MacRae, when he should have gone north. "Cutting it damn fine!" Wolfe had said yesterday morning.

Merewether wondered if he would ever rest easily as a commander, and wished for a moment that he were still a first lieutenant, responsible for no more than the efficient internal workings and discipline of a single ship, while a lofty captain made the decisions. He had spent two reasonably happy years in that estate before he was catapulted into command of a ship. And now, he found himself charged with a mission beyond his abilities, he told himself, and with the Royal Navy peering over his shoulder to observe and document his downfall. He was in a blue funk, doubting and pitying himself. He shrugged his shoulders, as though to dislodge the demon perched upon his back, and tried to think of a more cheerful subject.

He had sent Eldridge and Doctor Keese, along with that ruined gentleman Webster, to risk death in the *Duchy of Lancaster* in an attempt to take the pest ship a thousand-odd miles to safety for the benefit of the Company. He remembered Eldridge, young and keen, though uneducated, and his cynical appeal to the man's ambition with a temporary appointment to warrant rank. His conscience did not trouble him so much as to Keese and Webster—they knew their chances. But he had sent the party to carry out a mission he would have shrunk from himself. Cold steel and gunfire he could understand and face; pestilence, deliberately courted, was another matter. He wondered again at the shot he had heard as the boat pulled away from the Indiaman, and hoped Eldridge survived.

Hell's bells, this train of thought was no better than the last! He tried to think of Lady Caroline, but her image blurred in his mind, somehow overlaid with that of the other widow, Kate Hartley, at Penang. She had connived with Livie Raffles to use him, agreeable as the matter had been, but he still felt a touch of resentment at the assurance with which those two females had manipulated him.

"Deck there! Two ships hauled their wind." The hail from the masthead brought him back to the present with a jerk.

"What course?" shouted Merewether, diverted from his bitter thoughts.

There was a pause, then, "Looks about north-northwest sir." There was another appreciable interval, then, "Sail ho! Broad on the port bow."

Merewether could stand the suspense no longer. There was too much activity on the horizon. He snatched up the glass and went into the rigging to see for himself. At the main trucks, he braced himself and sought the targets. There was no doubt now; they both were large schooners, almost the mates of *Comet*. They were now on the starboard tack, headed almost north-northwest. Beyond them, he could see a sail, still headed southeast, some kind of a small country trader, scuttling to safety.

He shifted the glass and picked up the fourth sail, well to the east of the schooners. She was ship-rigged, and the cut of her sails was unmistakable; she must be the Royal Navy sloop *Argus* he had seen refitting at Penang, with Captain Ackroyd about to make contact with potential prizes. She was in a favorable position, holding the weather gauge on the schooners, while *Rapid* and *Comet* were far to leeward of the course they were now making good. Even as he watched, the sloop's shape altered slightly, and she headed to intercept the privateers.

It was a fluid situation and Merewether struggled to come to a decision. There was a bare chance that if *Comet* went about now, she might, with her superior windward qualities, just intercept the schooners. And unless the sloop was close enough by then, she might very well be overwhelmed by superior force. On the other hand, the Frenchmen could wear about at any time and go back southeast without hindrance. The sloop would be much more valuable to windward and astern of the enemy, while *Rapid* and *Comet* attempted the interception, but there was no way to order her there, even if a Royal Navy captain would obey a signal from the Bombay Marine.

His action might be misinterpreted, but it was essential to prevent the doubling back of the cruisers when they saw their escape northwestwardly cut off. Someone must plug that avenue of escape.

"Signals!" he shouted down. Hamlyn raised his face far below, slate in hand. "To *Comet*: 'Engage the enemy.'" He saw Dobbs looking up expectantly, the hands already poised at the braces in anticipation of the command to go about. "Execute," he told Hamlyn, coming to the deck, and to Dobbs, "Steady as you go."

Comet came to the wind, and went about alertly on the starboard tack. Merewether knew MacRae, with his passion for navigation, would set the best possible course for the interception. He consoled himself with the fact that *Comet* carried ten eighteen-pounders and had added two long nine pivot guns last month at Calcutta. *Rapid* plunged on southeastwardly, as close-hauled as she would lie, Diamond Point still almost dead ahead.

All the vessels were now visible from the deck, the schooners hull up, but dead to windward. *Comet* was well ahead of them, but still to leeward, slanting toward a point of intersection of their course to the northwest. The sloop was to windward of the targets, also aiming toward a theoretical point of interception, while *Rapid* thrashed on southeastwardly, striving to reach a position where she might shut off the open avenue of escape in that direction. It was mid-afternoon, and the pitch was literally bubbling in the seams of the deck under the pitiless glare of the sun.

Wolfe was on deck in his shirt, a wetted blue kerchief tied about his head, but he made no comment on the situation. There came a flaw in the breeze, and Dobbs ordered the helm over to starboard, gaining a few yards to windward by the maneuver. Merewether took another bearing on the schooners. He was not yet in a position where he could go about and join in the chase; it was still possible for the schooners to pass to windward of him if they decided to go about. Nothing to do but hold on, fighting for every yard to windward gained. He came back to his bit of shade and thankfully drank the cool cup of water that Sangh offered him.

"Well, Captain . . ." he had commenced to Wolfe, when the shout from the masthead interrupted. He looked aft and saw the schooners turning together, their profiles visible for a moment, then narrowing again as they came almost bows on. The movement had been beautifully timed. A few minutes more, and both the sloop and *Comet* would have been in position to cut them off. Now they had nothing more than a stern chase, and Merewether feared he could not get far enough to windward in time to interfere with their escape. Still, there was a chance he might be able to make contact with them, what with the flaws in the wind that Dobbs was alertly taking advantage of to gain every inch to windward.

Merewether took the time to examine the schooners carefully through his glass. They were beautiful examples of the Yankee shipbuilder's art—built fast enough to catch almost any other vessel, or run away from frigates or sloops, and yet carry sufficient armament to make them most formidable to a ship as lightly armed as *Rapid*. That young republic, though officially neutral, could not resist the opportunity to give the old British lion's tail a twist, even though it were by proxy.

Merewether took the glass away from his eye. "Send the hands to quarters, Mister Dobbs." The sound of the drum and shrill of whistles erupted, precipitating a flurry of disciplined confusion. Nearly every man had been on deck sight-seeing in anticipation of the order.

"All stations manned and ready," Dobbs soon reported.

"God damn!" said Wolfe. "Any fool could have foreseen that. All *Argus* had to do was hold the weather gauge on their quarter, not try to intercept, and we would have had them!"

Merewether was startled at the outburst, but for once he could agree with Wolfe without reservation. He went back to the binnacle and confirmed the bearing. There was yet a bare chance he could throw *Rapid* across the enemy's course and cripple or interfere with them enough to give time for *Comet* and *Argus* to come up.

Larkin commanded the starboard battery and customarily remained forward at the pivot gun, thus making the widest possible separation of first lieutenant and captain. It was a sensible precaution, minimizing the possibility of the loss of both in a single broadside. Merewether went forward, greeting the gun captains in the starboard battery by name as he passed, to join Larkin on the forecastle. He looked at Diamond Point, still almost dead ahead, and then back at the French, holding on as close-hauled as they would lie, hoping to pass to windward of *Rapid*. He took time to look at the sight mounted on the long nine-pounder pivot gun, with its measured scales for elevation and deflection, the invention of his old first lieutenant, MacLellan, and hoped the bill for a hundred pounds he had drawn on Bombay Castle last year in payment had been honored.

"Larkin, last year MacLellan overloaded the after gun, a charge and a half, as I remember it. Do you think you could risk the same?"

Larkin's pale blue eyes sparkled. "Of course, sir, the gun may jump her track, but I don't believe it will burst. I'll try it!" He turned to Totten, the gunner's mate, "See if we have cartridges

91

made up with half loads for saluting, and bring up a dozen for each gun in copper buckets with lids."

Totten and his striker headed below for the magazine, while Merewether strolled aft, speaking to the port gun crews as he passed.

At the binnacle, he took another bearing on the schooners. By God, they had drawn a quarter of a point to starboard from dead astern! He was to windward at last, however small the advantage might be. Unless there was an appreciable shift in the wind, the French could not now weather Diamond Point without first coming to grips with *Rapid*. MacRae was almost three miles dead astern of the cruisers, every sail set, while the slower sloop was farther behind, and well to the east. There came another minute flaw in the breeze, and Dobbs snapped out his order to the helm. A few more yards gained to windward!

"Mister MacCamy, I'd be obliged if you would exchange stations with Mister Larkin for a bit." MacCamy silently touched his hat and rolled forward.

Larkin and Totten critically examined the shot in the rack, finally selecting a half dozen of the roundest, with no visible imperfections. The powder charge, plus a half cartridge, went down the bore, followed by a wad, the ball, and another wad.

"Don't prime it yet," Larkin cautioned the gunner's mate, looking astern. The nearest of the schooners must be a mile and a half away, and gaining on *Rapid*. He checked the bearing of Diamond Point again; he could still weather it, but it would be an extremely close matter for the Frenchman.

Buttram and Davis, dripping with sweat, came on deck from the cockpit to observe the situation, then hurried back to their station when the word was passed for both batteries to load and run out their guns. Wolfe had belted on his sword, pistol butts now protruding from his waistband. Sangh brought up his sword and the pair of double-barreled pistols, and Merewether told him to lay them beside the skylight. Too soon to burden himself with their weight, he told himself. It was already an hour into the first dogwatch, and the sun was setting on the starboard quarter, outlining the sails of the privateers. There might be a land breeze after sunset to help edge them out, he thought, as impatience boiled up.

"If you don't mind, Captain," said Larkin, "I'll try a ranging shot now."

The quill was inserted in the touchhole, priming powder trickled from the horn, the lock was cocked, and Larkin set the sight at extreme elevation, and a quarter of the way to the left on the deflection scale. He squatted behind the gun, peering through the sights, adjusting the quoin, then directing the rotation of the platform to correct the train.

"Mark and lock. All clear!" The crew scattered to either side and turned their backs, as Larkin stepped off the platform, paused a moment as the stern rose gently on a swell, and twitched the lanyard.

The report was excessively unpleasant, the gun recoiled violently, and leaped six inches into the air as the tackles checked it. But it did not jump its track, Merewether was thankful to see, as he shifted his gaze to the cruiser. The splash appeared to be right under her bow. On her forecastle, he could see a group gathered about a gun, now trained out toward *Rapid*.

"A little left and a little short!" he called to Larkin. The crew was already swabbing out, and the new charge went down the bore. Larkin moved the sight a notch to the right on the deflection scale.

"Loaded, primed and cocked!" sang out Totten. There was a tiny adjustment made in the train, and the gun blasted out again.

Merewether caught the hit in the field of his glass, apparently right on the carriage of the bow chaser on the cruiser's forecastle. The gun was on its side, half a dozen men sprawled on the deck about it.

"Good shot! You disabled their bow chaser, but try to hit a little more aft, spars or rigging, if you can!"

Larkin made another minute adjustment of the sight, and the gun was heaved back to battery. Merewether thought of the contrast between the methodical MacLellan, with his "over, under, and halve the difference" system of laying a gun to find a target, and the intuitive corrections that Larkin applied.

The long nine fired again, and Merewether could see no sign of

93

the fall of shot. Either it was just over, or had hit the hull. He had started to take the glass from his eye, when he caught motion in his field of view. The square-rigged foretop hamper was bending down to leeward, as the gaff fell, collapsing the foresail. The jibs and forestaysail, cut loose at the top, blew over the bow to drag under foot. The shot must have hit right at the truss bands of the foretopmast, cutting halyards and forestays, and wreaking damage that would take hours, if not days, to repair.

"Well done, Mister Larkin!" shouted Merewether, and a cheer erupted from the hands, capering at their stations. The schooner fell behind, now almost dead in the water, as the second privateer pressed on leaving her crippled consort behind. Merewether wondered what her next maneuver would be, with Diamond Point now looming dead ahead. He was tempted to close the distance, but his windward position had been too hard won, and if he came closer, there was a possibility that the enemy with her handier rig might slide by him to escape.

Here the coast of Sumatra slanted back to the northwest from Diamond Point, before it again trended out to the northeast, to form a wide sound. Once a ship had penetrated to any great distance, it would be on a lee shore, with a long laborious beat to windward to escape it. The cruiser had the choice of making the turn back to the northwest and spinning out the chase a little longer, with a chance of escape in the dark, or of trying to force its way past *Rapid* to weather Diamond Point.

"Why don't you close on him?" demanded Wolfe. Merewether was too concerned with the situation to feel irritation, watching the other ship for the first telltale indication of her intentions. He saw her rudder kick over, hands tailing on to the braces controlling the square topsail, and had opened his mouth to give the order to his own helm when some instinct halted him.

The schooner's rudder came back midships, the topsails were trimmed back, and she plunged ahead on her original course. It had been a feint, designed to lure *Rapid* into a turn that would have lost just enough ground for the enemy to make his escape.

"There's your answer," he told Wolfe absently. The die was cast, the enemy intended to fight its way past *Rapid. Comet* was still almost three miles behind, and gaining slowly, but if that privateer could shoot away a spar and cripple *Rapid*, she had little chance of coming up in time. The sloop had abandoned the chase and was approaching the other cruiser, already hoisting out her boats to take possession of the prize.

The boatswain's mates were hanging up battle lanterns, dim enough in the light remaining, but necessary to light the stations as darkness fell. The two vessels were slanting toward a point of intersection not far ahead.

"You may fire when ready," he called forward to Larkin. It was still too far, even for the long nine, but the range was lessening.

The Frenchman held on. He could not afford to sag off any farther toward the land if he were to retain any chance of weathering the point. Merewether looked through the glass again. The schooner's decks were crowded with men. Evidently, she had not yet furnished any prize crews and carried her original complement. The forward pivot blasted out, making him jump, but he could not make out the fall of shot. The after gun fired, and he saw the hole appear in the schooner's mainsail, but no crippling damage. Larkin came down the starboard battery, conferring briefly with each gun captain. *Comet* was coming, but it was up to *Rapid* to stop the enemy at this juncture.

The starboard battery was trained around as far as it could point, the guns at maximum elevation. Merewether saw the orange glow of the privateer's broadside, and heard one shot howl overhead, but the splashes of the other balls were nearly a cable's length to starboard. Both pivot guns fired again, but he could see no effect. Less than half a mile now, he judged, and closing rapidly.

"Starboard battery, fire!" came the command from Larkin. The smoke went down in a solid cloud, obscuring the enemy. There was disciplined activity along the deck as the gun crews reloaded and hauled the pieces back to battery. Every gun captain was looking forward to Larkin, who stood holding his hand up, gazing at the enemy.

"Half elevation," he called, and quoins were knocked in. "Fire!" The broadside blasted out and the red-orange glare blinded Merewether momentarily. When the smoke blew clear, he saw the schooner still coming, her flying jib blowing free and gaps in her bulwarks, but undaunted. She fired her broadside again, and there was a crash right beside him as a ball came through the bulwark and shattered the skylight.

Rapid's third broadside exploded, and over the smoke, Merewether saw the spars of the schooner only a few hundred feet away. The enemy, he realized, was giving him the choice of being rammed, or of letting the schooner pass. That captain was no poltroon!

The battery was run out again. He had heard the word "grapeshot" passed down a moment ago, and the sound of the guns was deeper this time. Grape on top of a round shot at this range should be deadly, but the spars were still visible above the smoke, undamaged.

If both ships held on, they would come together a cable's length ahead, he calculated, or the Frenchman conceivably could turn astern of him at the last moment. He held on, watching intently for the first sign that would indicate the schooner's intention. The privateer fired again and there was a horrendous crash aloft. He saw the main-topmast sway halfway up its height, then hang for a moment, supported by its shrouds.

"Heads up!" he shouted forward, as the hands amidships scattered.

There was another rending crack, and the mast parted. The port shrouds held it momentarily against the pressure of the wind, then the whole upper works, half the topmast, with the royalmast and pole above it, came straight down, the splintered butt smashing through the pinrail and penetrating the deck beside the mainmast. There was a tangle of shrouds and canvas above, caught over the stump of the topmast that momentarily held the wreckage upright. Four marines assigned to the maintop had come down with it, and they came sliding and jumping out of the wreckage to reach the deck.

"Topmen!" shouted Merewether. "Get a turn around that mast!" If he could get lines secured about the wreckage and the stump of the topmast to hold it upright, he might yet be able to work the ship. He saw Lyle, boatswain's mate, and Briggs, topman, his most recent promotions, climbing into the tangled mess, even as he heard Larkin's command to the starboard battery. The gunners, ignoring the risk of being crushed by the precariously balanced mast, ran back to their guns, and the broadside flamed out grapeshot at point-blank range.

"Port your helm!" called Merewether, not taking time to observe the effect of the broadside. He looked up; the shattered mast still held upright, and the men were now throwing hitches into a length of cable that encircled the fallen topmast and the lower mast. Sails on the fore and mizzen masts were still drawing, and the ship was closing toward the Frenchman.

"Grapnels! Grapnels!" he shouted forward, and saw Mister Tompkins and three of his mates already poised to throw. Thank God for the drills and training this past year! *Rapid*'s bow was swinging to starboard, but the privateer was moving faster, her stern already opposite him at the break of the poop. Even as he watched, he saw her rudder go over to starboard, white foam visible under her counter in the last bit of light as she turned downwind. It was his last chance. He could never catch her. She would pull away a bit, and then turn back to weather Diamond Point!

"Throw! Throw!" he shouted in desperation. With the swing of the bow of *Rapid*, and the turn downwind of the schooner, the distance was less than a hundred feet, but it would widen in seconds as she settled before the wind. It was a long heave for an iron grapnel attached to a six-foot length of chain.

The four men swung the grapnels like slings, then released them almost simultaneously in high arcs. Two fell short by yards, one hit the stern quarter of the schooner, and bounced back into the sea. The fourth sailed right over the taffrail, and the seaman jerked the line to set the points in the rail, then took a double turn about the forward bitts. Merewether prayed that the workmanship of those Yankee shipbuilders had been honest, that that rail would hold, and that the hemp in that slender line was sound.

"Midships," he told the quartermaster, to take some of the strain off the line. It was almost black dark now, but by the forward battle lantern, he saw the men retrieving their grapnels, and throwing again. Two of them apparently made connection and were snubbed to the bitts. The schooner would not run away now!

Men with axes and lanterns appeared on the stern of the privateer, striking and prying at the imbedded grapnels and slashing at the chain lengths. Merewether opened his mouth to shout the order, then heard the musket volley follow Gunny's command. The men on the poop fell, and the three threads of hemp stretched tight as fiddle strings.

"The helmsman!" shouted Merewether. The marines in the foretop fired, and in a moment the schooner's rudder slammed to port under the pressure to leeward. The schooner, her rudder jammed hard over, came about, heading into the wind, as *Rapid*, of necessity, followed suit. It was as though he had hold of the tail of a tiger, he thought, just before the port battery of the privateer erupted in a ragged broadside as her guns bore for a moment before *Rapid* sagged away astern.

There were hits forward, leaving the foot of the flying jib flying loose with the forestay severed. There had been solid hits in the hull as well, Merewether realized, but there were more urgent matters to deal with. The schooner's backed topsails were giving her sternway, and she was coming down on *Rapid*'s bow. In a moment, the ships would come together, and the men he had seen on the privateer's deck would swarm over the side to board him. The forward pivot gun blasted out, its orange flame lighting the stern of the enemy. He could not see the effect of the shot in the darkness as the acrid powder smoke blew aft. No other gun would bear, but the marines were keeping up a steady fire with their muskets from the foretop and forecastle.

"Repel boarders!" Merewether shouted forward, and heard the cry echoed along the deck as the men seized cutlasses and pikes from the racks at the base of each mast. He tried to find his pistols and sword where he had laid them beside the shattered skylight, but could not put his hands upon them. He straightened up, looking out to port, but he could see no sign of *Comet* in the darkness. He groped again and touched the polished wood of one of the pistols, then abandoned the search for his sword to snatch a cutlass from the rack at the mizzenmast before running forward.

The poop of the schooner was almost against the starboard bow. There was a continuous banging of muskets and popping of pistols now from the decks of both ships, but no one could see much in the darkness to aim at. The ships came together with a grinding crash, and a cheer went up from the Frenchman, echoed a moment later from *Rapid*. Merewether gained the fore-castle where the marine detachment was drawn up in a double line with bayonets fixed.

There was a moment of hiatus, both ships suddenly silent as though time had been suspended, while enemy peered through darkness at adversary across a narrow gap. Then the ships came together again with a screech of wood rubbing against wood, and the spell was broken. A shout came from the privateer, and a mass of men rushed across her poop to pour into *Rapid*.

"Hit them !" Merewether roared.

The marines' volley knocked down the leaders, but the rest of the invaders met the party from the waist led by the boat-swain and MacCamy head on. Merewether found himself on the forecastle in the gap between the marines and the waisters, and slashed at a face in the dim light of the battle lanterns burning in the rigging, then drove his cutlass into the mass of bodies pressing forward. He felt it penetrate, but it was wrenched from his hand as the man fell. He found himself pinned momentarily against the forecastle railing, and while he pulled the pistol from his belt, he looked to the right to see Wolfe driving forward, his sword a flicker of light as he mercilessly cut his way into the boarding party. The man was an absolute marvel with the sword, he thought, as he got the pistol loose to fire one barrel after the other into the enemy.

Two men fell, making a little space, and the marines surged forward with bayonets. Merewether gave a wordless shout of en-couragement to the men and realized that he was unarmed, cut-lass lost, pistol empty. He saw the gleam of a cutlass lying loose on the deck and bent to snatch it up. Too late he saw the French-man driving the pike down at him and tried desperately to twist aside. Someone came between them, deflecting the pike with a sword, then deftly driving the blade through the man. He regained his feet, cutlass in hand, and realized that Wolfe had been his benefactor.

"Thank you, Wolfe!" he shouted, and charged back into the melee.

Wolfe continued his attack, using his sword with the detached finesse of the expert. A Frenchman sidled to the left out of Wolfe's sight and aimed a pistol at him. Merewether had only an instant to slash the cutlass backhanded and upward, feeling the edge bite into bone in the man's forearm, and saw the pistol fly into the air as it discharged.

"Much obliged, Captain!" Wolfe shouted over his shoulder as he pressed forward again.

The man had been unpleasant, was possibly even insane, as Buttram insisted; his judgment had been poor on occasion; he was cruel and ruthless; but his courage could not be questioned. He had owed his life to Wolfe, but now they were quits, the debt repaid. Merewether turned back to the fight and saw the sails close aboard to port.

Comet came grinding along the port bow, and a flood of men poured onto *Rapid*'s forecastle led by little MacRae with a pike longer than he was. The reinforcements swept the boarders from the deck, driving them back into the privateer, then joined with *Rapid*'s men to pursue them up the deck of the Frenchman. There were cries for quarter, and in a few minutes, the cruiser had struck her colors.

Merewether accepted the surrender from a tearful, dark young second lieutenant, with Gunny serving as interpreter. The schooner's captain was dead, killed by a musket ball as he stood by the helm, and the first lieutenant was down in the cockpit with a foot mangled by grapeshot.

"Well," said MacRae, looking about the deck in the yellow lantern light. "I don't like the smell of this at all."

"What do you mean?"

"That there are more men below than on deck. Of course, the marines are flushing them out, and the gunner and his mates have control of the magazine and armory, but I suggest a search be made from the bilges to the crosstrees for arms. I would expect an attempt to retake the ship."

Merewether paused a moment. He had acquired an almost superstitious respect for the perception MacRae possessed since his prediction of finding the cruisers off Diamond Point had so uncannily proved out.

"I intend to order Larkin into her as prize master and send Gunny with all the marines as a guard. We will make the search, of course. Do you have a junior officer you can spare to be second in command?"

"No, sir, I have only two watch-keeping officers on board, since Dillon took command of the first prize. But, if you'll consider him, I have a crackerjack quartermaster, MacFee's his name, served his apprenticeship in the herring fleet out of Mallaig, a distant cousin of mine, too."

"If you say so, I'll issue an acting warrant as master's mate to him."

"Better make it boatswain, Commodore."

"Very well. And now, if you will look after matters here for a bit, I'll send Larkin over to take command. I don't know how badly *Rapid* is damaged yet, but I'm afraid that main-topmast wreckage will fall any minute."

"One thing more," said MacRae slowly. "That sloop abandoned the chase and took the prize you crippled. Of course, it makes no difference, we were all in sight and share the prize money, but it was in a better position to come up with you than I was!"

"Quite right," replied Merewether, wondering how much weight it would carry with Pellew. "I intend to cover the matter in my report." He made his way wearily back to *Rapid* and came down into the waist, listening to the rhythmic thump of the pumps, to meet the carpenter coming forward.

"She's holed twice on the starboard bow, right at the waterline, sir. I've stopped the leaks for the time, but she took on a good bit of water first," the carpenter reported, wiping the sweat from his face. "No other damage to the hull, except where the deck is holed by the butt of the topmast. And your cabin is a mare's nest, Captain, glass and splinters all over!"

A party was aloft in the wreckage with lanterns, dismantling the rigging and sending down the yards. The sails had been cut loose, reducing the wind pressure against the wreckage, and several additional turns of cable now secured the royal mast upright against the mainmast. Merewether could not see the boatswain in the group, which seemed to be under the direction of Bowman, now the senior boatswain's mate, with Larkin standing by.

"Where's Mister Tompkins?" inquired Merewether.

"Wounded, sir," said Bowman, keeping his eyes fixed aloft. "Handsomely! Handsomely!" he shouted, as the royal yard revolved in the air, and then started down with a run at the end of a whip too lightly snubbed about a cleat. The hands managed to check it, at the expense of the skin of their palms, just before the iron-bound end struck the deck. Merewether was in the way here, distracting the men from their work. He moved away and called Larkin.

"I'm sending you into the schooner as prize master," he told the tall man. "MacFee from *Comet* is acting boatswain, and I'll give you Gunny and twenty marines. Take your crew from *Comet*, I can't spare the hands. Do you have any report of casualties yet?"

"Yes, sir. Three dead, fourteen wounded, including Tompkins, who has a pistol ball through his right arm." Merewether shook his head. The butcher's bill had been more expensive than he had bargained for, and *Rapid* was holed and crippled as well.

"Get your things together and relieve MacRae. As soon as the search of the prize is completed, I propose to pull the ships apart, then anchor until daylight."

"Aye aye, sir. The hands have not messed yet."

"Very well, you go on, and I'll see what we can do." He started for the ladder to the cockpit and met the purser emerging from the hatch, his shirt splattered with blood.

"The doctor is about finished, and I thought I would see what could be scraped up for the hands. The cooks are still busy helping with the wounded, sir," reported Davis. "Would you authorize an issue of rum, sir?"

Merewether hesitated. Lord knew the hands deserved the treat, but he looked back at the men hanging precariously in the rigging of the mainmast and decided that he would be doing them no favor to give them rum until the wreckage was cleared.

"Not now," he decided. "See if you can get enough biscuit and cheese in the hands of the mess cooks to satisfy them for the time being." He forced himself to make the descent to the cockpit, finding it still oppressively hot here below decks.

The scene was macabre, the operating table laid across chests, its white canvas cover now glistening with blood, and a nauseating odor of vomit permeating the stale air. To one side was a charcoal brazier, glowing with coals, the cauterizing irons thrust into them, handles protruding. A black-haired man lay on the table, head back, breathing stertorously through his open mouth, as Buttram took precise stitches to close the gaping slash that extended from his right shoulder diagonally down across his chest. Two other men were seated propped against the bulkhead, bloody rags tied about their heads. Buttram looked up quickly, then continued his work as the cook and his mate held the man still.

"Almost finished, Captain," said Buttram in his cheerful manner. "A few more stitches here and on those two heads over there, and I'll be through. I've used the laudanum freely, so there's not much trouble holding them steady."

"Who were killed?"

"Petty, sailmaker's mate; Evans, topman; and O'Brian, ordinary seaman. Barring infection, I don't account any other wounds to be mortal." He tied the last knot and covered the wound with a bandage over the man's shoulder and then around his chest. "Sangh was hit by flying glass from your skylight— fifteen stitches in his face and arms, and just missed his eye. He'll be in pain for a while, but he says he can still perform duty."

"Doctor, when you finish here, see if they need any help in the schooner." Merewether climbed back up the ladder to the deck, emerging with relief into the cooler night air.

The cabin had been cleaned up, but half the glass panes were missing from the skylight, and it was covered with a tarpaulin. Wolfe was seated on the transom, a dark bottle of Scots whisky beside him and a half-filled glass in his hand.

"Hope you don't mind, Commodore. I broke my parole. Since

103

you have my cellar padlocked, I prevailed on Sangh to get me a bottle from yours. With all that sun today, my head is throbbing. Have a dram?'' Merewether felt a sense of comradeship for the captain, quite different from his feelings even this afternoon.

"No, thanks, I have too much to do. I will have a bit of tea." On impulse, he continued, "And here is the key to your locker." Sangh came in, both forearms bandaged and court plaster obscuring his forehead and the left side of his face. "I'm sorry you're hurt, Sangh. Please rest, if you wish."

"That was quite an action, Commodore," Wolfe said. "It really was touch and go whether you would be able to intercept that cruiser, and the whole affair was so unnecessary. If *Argus* had only held the weather gauge when the French first turned north, cutting off their escape, you and *Comet* could have run them down much sooner. That boy, Dobbs, did a magnificent job of working this ship to windward enough to make the interception, too. I quite enjoyed the fight on deck, and, I must say, you have as well-trained a crew as that of any Royal Navy ship I have seen."

Merewether, surprised and grateful, wondered too, if the Scots whisky had inspired this flow of praise. "Your performance was above and beyond the call of duty also, Captain."

"One other thing," growled Wolfe. "The Admiralty gave Calder a Court of Inquiry last year for stopping to take prizes and not following up on his interception of Villeneuve, and he had bad weather to excuse him. I shall see that the action of *Argus* this afternoon is brought to the attention of authority!"

Merewether agreed with the statement, but said only, "I must be on deck."

Mister Tompkins was on the scene, his weathered face pale and drawn under the tan and his splinted right arm in a sling.

"I'm sorry, Tompkins, no need for you here."

"Nothing serious, Captain, the ball broke both bones when it passed through, and I am a little weak in the knees, but I want to see these masts down, so we can rig the mains'l, set some stays'ls above it, and work the ship halfway decent." The pole had been detached from the royal mast and lowered, and the hands were commencing the ticklish task of separating the royal mast from the shattered topmast.

Tompkins continued, "I oversaw the rerigging of this ship two years ago, before the Company bought her. New masts and spars, Norway pine from the steps up, with new ironware and cordage. This mainmast is seventy-seven feet, six inches; that topmast was forty-six feet, nine inches; the royal mast is twenty-three feet, six inches; and the pole they just got down is eighteen feet, six inches, making a sum of a hundred and sixty-six feet, three inches." He hesitated, then mopped his brow and said in a changed tone of voice, "I think I will go below, Captain. That dollop of brandy the doctor gave me a while ago has fuddled me!" He walked aft, a little unsteadily.

MacRae and Larkin appeared before him. "Captain," said MacRae, "no sense of us rubbing off any more paint alongside. We are both going to pull away and anchor. I get a sounding of fifteen fathoms, and we're on a lee shore."

"Very well, I will anchor too." The officers left, and in a few minutes, the prize cast off, going downwind a cable's length before she dropped and swung round to ride to the anchor. *Comet* boomed off and slid another cable's length astern before coming to anchor, while Merewether acted as his own boatswain and moored *Rapid*.

Hamlyn had the watch, the weather was clear, stars bright, and the moon just rising as he went below. The bottle was still on the transom, a quarter empty, and Wolfe was gone. He pulled himself together with an effort, looked with longing at the Scots whisky, then forced himself to sit at the desk, open the quartermaster's notebook, and commence the composition of his report. The action of the sloop this afternoon still rankled, but he compelled himself to be objective.

CHAPTER EIGHT

At daybreak, Merewether came back on deck. The royal mast was secured, all the ironwork had been removed from the shattered topmast, and it had been extracted like a bad tooth from the hole it had punched in the deck. A party was bending a sail on the main yard, and the lanyards in the deadeyes of the new shrouds were being tightened. The boatswain, looking much improved, came up with the sailmaker.

"Captain, with the mains'l and two stays'ls, we think the ship can work to wind'ard. Another hour should see us finished," said Tompkins, lowering his gaze. "It may be a mite different steering; the rig doesn't exactly balance, but I think she'll do. I hope we can find a new topmast at Penang."

"Thank you. Let me know when you are ready," said Merewether, glad that he had seen fit to mention Tompkins' services in his report.

The sloop and the first schooner were nowhere in sight. She must have been able to get the prize under way during the night and head for Penang. *Rapid* hoisted the signal to get under way, and the hands wound in the anchor. She did handle differently, he soon discovered, but adjustments were made, and with the helmsman carrying a little lee rudder, she would lie almost as close to the wind as before.

At mid-morning, in five hundred fathoms, he hoisted the signal to heave to and then the church flag. Wolfe was on deck, but he did not volunteer to read the committal services for the three casualties, and Merewether labored through them. The issue of a double ration of spirits was greeted with cheers, and the squadron resumed its voyage.

With the necessity of working to windward, it was mid-afternoon the next day before the three ships reached the anchorage off Penang. The pilot had reported that *Argus* and her prize had arrived just after daybreak, and Merewether could see them at anchor off the dockyard, the blue ensign flying above the tricolor.

"I think you may give the port watch liberty," Merewether told MacCamy. "And I am going ashore to Government House to make a report."

"Aye aye, sir." MacCamy went forward in his round-shouldered gait, whistling tunelessly to himself; and in a few minutes, the gig had hooked on to the gangway.

He caught Raffles coming out the door to enter his barouche. "Hello, Commodore, back again with booty, I see." Raffles shook Merewether's hand with vigor. "No use going in there; all the offices are closing early. Tonight's the Governor's Birthday Ball." Raffles paused, and made a wry face. "This is the damnedest place for social events I ever saw, but Livie loves it, though she pretends it's dull. Now I must pick her up and take her home. Do jump in; I insist you come along with us!"

"I hadn't planned . . ." commenced Merewether.

"No excuses, and I'll invite your officers and that fellow Wolfe, too!" He pulled a card from a pocket in his ornate waistcoat, reached into the barouche, and took out a writing board, complete with pen and bottle of ink. He scribbled a note on the back, called to a small brown man sitting on a bench, gave him rapid instructions in Malay, and the man loped off. "I sent him down to your boat with the invitation. Now, off we go."

The barouche moved off at a trot along the carriage road that wound up the hill west of the anchorage, and soon drew up at the door of a bungalow surrounded with flowers. Raffles jumped down and after a few minutes returned. Merewether bowed to Mrs. Raffles.

"Commodore, I'm delighted to see you again and to hear you've been so successful, too!"

"Thank you, Madame, and I'm happy to see you and Tom again. You've been so kind . . ."

"Not at all. You have been most entertaining and accommodating. And now, Tom, let's go home. I must prepare for the ball." Merewether wondered for a moment just what she meant, then decided it was merely small talk.

Raffles handed her into the barouche, and they rattled off a half mile, to pull in before the Raffles' residence. There was the same flow of conversation between this high-spirited pair as they rode along that Merewether had listened to during his first visit, as Raffles detailed the events of the day and Livie passed shrewd judgments on them.

He pricked up his ears when he heard Raffles say, "And just before noon, Captain Ackroyd of *Argus* came in with a petition for condemnation of the prizes, *Chasseur, Mercure,* and another taken off the Nicobar Islands, name unknown. . . ."

"But," she broke in, "the charter for the Court of Record has not yet arrived."

"Precisely," said Raffles. "We have a magistrate and coroner, but no court with power to adjudicate a prize. I told Ackroyd he would have to send his petition to the High Court of Judicature at Calcutta. He insisted on seeing Governor Dundas and demanded that he convene or sit himself as a Prize Court of Admiralty."

"Impossible !" declared Livie.

"So the Governor told him," said Raffles, turning to Merewether. "Wasn't that *Mercure* you brought in this afternoon?"

"Yes," said Merewether. "And the ship taken off the Nicobars was *Majeure,* on its way to Calcutta now, with my prize crew aboard."

"I understand that Captain Ackroyd is taking the position that he shares in all prizes taken by any forces in the Strait, or their approaches, under his commission."

"He was not in sight," said Merewether shortly, as the barouche stopped. There was no doubt, he thought, that *Argus* shared in the two prizes taken day before yesterday—she was in sight. But the claim to a share in *Majeure,* taken five hundred miles northwest of here, was preposterous.

Inside the cool dim sitting room he remembered, the Malay girl brought Straits Coolers after Livie had excused herself. Tom Raffles and Merewether sat companionably in silence for a bit, sipping the tart drink, while Merewether thought of the latest events. This had been an ill-starred operation from the outset, he told himself—from the distasteful scene when he returned on board to find Wolfe drunk, to the present, when he found himself about to be embroiled in controversy with Captain Ackroyd. True, he accounted his mission three-quarters complete, and it would be difficult to accuse him of failure. There might yet be a fourth privateer lurking out there, but three had been taken and the Indiaman recaptured. He wondered if Doctor Keese, Eldridge and Webster were still alive and in control of the *Duchy of Lancaster*. If they were, the ship should be approaching Ceylon by now. But this latest development was disquieting, and it was not the law of prizes, as he had understood it. He had heard that Admiral Calder had submitted a claim for a share in the Trafalgar prize money last year, though he was a thousand miles away from the action.

Merewether's train of thought was broken as Raffles cleared his throat and spoke. "Don't worry about the matter, Commodore. The case will have to go to Calcutta, and I am sure the Company's solicitors will see that the law is followed."

"There is little enough I can do about it," admitted Merewether, thankful to put the matter aside for the time. "Did I tell you, it's in these reports, we found the Indiaman and sent her on to Ceylon?"

"What? Oh, wonderful! Tell me the story." By the time it was told and a brief account given of the other events of the cruise, Livie had returned, wearing a plain gray dressing gown, and the girl came in to light the lamps.

"Since there will be supper at the ball, we will not dine formally, Commodore. There's a buffet laid in the dining room when you are ready, and if you would like to freshen up, take the last door to the left." In the lamplight, Mrs. Raffles looked ravishing, and Merewether caught a hint of scent in the air.

Merewether went to the room and found a pitcher of water, still hot, with soap and towels on the washstand. He took off his coat and stock, and rolled up the sleeves of his shirt. In the mirror, he saw the dark tan of his face and hands and the almost milk-white skin below and above them. The white of the scar across his cheek stood out, and he concluded from the fine-drawn appearance of his face that he had lost weight in these past weeks. He completed his ablutions, brushed his hair, and went back to the sitting room.

Livie was sipping Madeira. "Tom's changing," she said. "There are spirits and wine on the sideboard." Merewether poured a glass of London gin, cut a lemon, and rejoined the woman.

"Tom just told me you recovered the Indiaman. You know, her officers are still here, and it might be possible for them to make their way to Ceylon and take her home."

"Yes, but at this point, I can only hope she reaches Ceylon, with an acting master's mate, a doctor, and a drunken quartermaster to manage her." He felt uncomfortable in the absence of Raffles.

"You remember Kate Hartley, I am sure."

Merewether was suddenly wary.

"I wish I could have known you'd be here tonight. She accepted an invitation to go with the Sperrys, but"—Livie looked speculatively at Merewether—"perhaps she could come back with us."

Merewether made a noncommittal sound, and Mrs. Raffles continued, "You are not married, I think?" He shook his head. "Or betrothed?"

"No," he said, and added unaccountably, "not yet."

"Oh, there is someone you're interested in?"

Merewether began to sweat. This woman would have it out of him. "I have been seeing a young lady at Calcutta," he began, and wondered, if in fact, he did have an interest in Lady Caroline, or more importantly, if she were the least bit interested in him.

Livie looked away and said absently, "Of course, Kate is quite well off, no children, and her husband was general agent for the Company and had interests in three country traders, as well. She plans to return to England later this year, when his affairs out here are finally settled. And she was quite complimentary of you." Merewether recognized the matchmaker, realizing that Kate had confided her entire adventure to this woman, and one or the other of them had decided that she was now interested in a conventional relationship. He sought to withdraw and tiptoe around the pit he saw opening before him.

"A most gracious and attractive lady," he said carefully. "But, you know, I am under some obligation back at Calcutta." It was an outright lie, and the telling of it made him uncomfortable. He was relieved when Raffles came in, resplendent in civilian full dress, and the conversation shifted to less hazardous subjects.

They had another drink, then dined sparingly at the buffet. Raffles consulted his watch. "We should be away, dear." And to

Merewether, "In effect, I'm the majordomo for this affair, and I should be there early."

They were the first to arrive. Raffles immediately going off with a corpulent man in livery and Livie vanishing into the ladies' retiring room. Merewether wandered about for a few minutes in the empty expanse of floor, then went outside to catch the breeze coming in from the harbor, seeing the lights on his ships and hoping that all was well. He worried for a moment about the possibility of finding a satisfactory spar from which a new topmast could be fashioned and damned himself for not going to the dockyard this afternoon to look for one.

Half an hour later, MacRae and his third lieutenant, Cowan, came up, precisely at the appointed hour, and Merewether chatted with them until Dobbs, Buttram, Hamlyn and Wolfe arrived. Several carriages had drawn past the entrance, and shortly the sound of instruments being tuned came from the windows.

"May as well join the party," suggested Wolfe. He was in full dress, the new-gold lace marking his rank as a captain of less than three years' seniority flashing in the light from the doorway. He appeared to be in high spirits, and Merewether wondered if he had used the key to his cellar before leaving the ship. The group of officers went in, blinking in the bright light.

A functionary took the names, beginning his announcement, "Commodore Percival Merewether, Captain James Wolfe . . ." on through Midshipman Hamlyn. Before he was half finished, Raffles had popped out, and Merewether made the presentations.

"The Governor has not yet arrived, gentlemen. He wishes all of you to be presented to him in recognition of your recent services. In the meantime, there are punch bowls in those alcoves, and young ladies will soon be arriving for the dancing." The group drifted toward the punch, feeling self-conscious in the sparsely occupied room.

Mrs. Raffles intercepted them halfway across the room, and Raffles recited the names faultlessly. She managed to put MacRae on one arm, and Hamlyn on the other, leading them merrily to the punch bowl.

"Damned attractive woman," said Wolfe, *sotto voce*. "How do you manage to know one in every port, Merewether?"

"I am irresistibly handsome and possess a fatal charm." Merewether was entering into the spirit of high good humor.

Livie saw the officers served, then dimpled and curtsied as
with one accord they drank her health. She enjoined them to
wait and went into the retiring room to emerge with five young
ladies.

"The dancing will commence as soon as the Governor arrives
and his reception is over," she told them, and pirouetted in a
step or so with a flash of ankles. Even quiet little MacRae and
stolid Dobbs were soon chattering with the young ladies, and
Wolfe had instantly claimed a tall girl with dark hair and
sparkling blue eyes. They were interrupted by the announcement of the Governor's arrival, signaled by the playing of a
sprightly march by the musicians.

The reception was quickly in progress, Governor and Lady
Dundas, the Company Resident and his wife, Mister and Mrs.
Raffles, and several lesser dignitaries making up the receiving
line. The girls scattered to join their families for the formalities,
and Merewether herded his group together to take their place in
the line. The affair moved more rapidly than many such, and
Merewether soon found himself being presented by Raffles to the
Governor and his lady and, in turn, presenting his officers and
Wolfe.

"Yes, Commodore, I am delighted to make your acquaintance.
George Barlow wrote me to give you all assistance if you called
here. I should like to discuss the situation at greater length tomorrow, if you are at liberty."

"Certainly, Your Excellency," said Merewether, hoping for a
new topmast, and moved on.

Back at the end of the slowly moving line, he saw the flash of
gold lace and recognized Captain Ackroyd, accompanied by
three lieutenants and two midshipmen of the Royal Navy. He
went back to the punch bowl and took another cup, sipping
slowly while he watched the crowd from the entrance to the
alcove. The music struck up as the receiving line disintegrated,
and the alcove filled with thirsty guests. Merewether stepped out
of the way and put his empty cup on the tray. He felt it his duty

to find Mrs. Raffles and lead her in to the dance, since her husband was so caught up in the management of the affair. As he crossed the floor he saw Mrs. Hartley being led out to the dance by a man of middle years whom he recognized as the first officer of the *Duchy of Lancaster*. He bowed to her, and she responded with a distant nod. He found Livie, and they danced the first set.

"Oh, Commodore, I don't think Mrs. Hartley will be coming home with us tonight. She met this widowed officer of the Company's service yesterday, and she says he's most insistent on taking her home tonight." Livie paused, then continued, "He thinks his party may take passage for Ceylon next week in a country ship, and he has already mentioned marriage to her!"

"Quite all right," said Merewether with relief, and then illogically felt a twinge of jealousy. She had chosen him to satisfy her needs, but with marriage in sight he became an embarrassment to her.

The gaiety engendered by Mrs. Raffles carried on, fueled by the punch bowl, and each of the officers had his turn at treading a measure with her during the evening, as well as with the small number of daughters of Company functionaries present. The release from the strain of the past weeks at sea was something to be savored to the utmost. Merewether, close to midnight, escorted Mrs. Raffles to the entrance of the retiring room and strolled toward the alcove. Supper would be announced soon, but he was thirsty again after the dance. Just inside, he saw Ackroyd and one of his lieutenants.

"Here, you!" called Ackroyd, starting across the room. "You, Merewether, just a moment!" Merewether, startled, turned to face him as Ackroyd approached, followed at an interval by his lieutenant.

"Good evening, Captain," said Merewether pleasantly.

"Merewether, I resent the statements you have made reflecting upon my courage and performance of duty!"

Merewether tried to think of any statements he had made, other than the bald recitation of fact concerning the action off Diamond Point contained in his report.

"Don't deny it; I hate a liar!" shouted Ackroyd, red in the face and trembling. "I demand . . ."

Someone brushed by his shoulder, and Ackroyd shifted his gaze. Merewether glanced sidewise and found Wolfe beside him.

"I am the person who made the statements, Ackroyd! And I repeat the charges to your face: You abandoned the pursuit of a French cruiser to seize a prize already crippled by the Bombay Marine! Do you desire further specifications?"

"Now, gentlemen," cried Merewether, attempting to intervene. "Captain Ackroyd was addressing his remarks to me!" He had never been involved in an affair of honor, but this was the unmistakable prelude to one, and Wolfe had shifted the provocation to himself. Merewether felt that he was without fault in the matter, but if Ackroyd believed otherwise, he felt enough resentment for his recent actions to give him satisfaction. The scene was distasteful, and it had already drawn a large audience. Through a gap in the crowd, he saw Raffles hurrying across the floor toward the alcove, and the Governor hovering discreetly in the background.

Wolfe disregarded Merewether's protest. "Do you challenge me?" demanded Wolfe. Ackroyd had gone quite pale and hesitated a moment. "No? Then I name you a poltroon, and I challenge you!"

A shade of color returned to Ackroyd's face, and he said steadily enough, "My seconds will wait upon yours before noon tomorrow. Whom do you choose?"

"What about me?" demanded Merewether. "I thought you had addressed your complaints to me!"

"No offense, Commodore; I have found the guilty party," said Ackroyd. "And I shall give him satisfaction soon enough!" He looked back at Wolfe. "And who are your seconds?"

"Commodore Merewether and Doctor Buttram, both in *Rapid*."

Raffles pushed through the crowd, just in time to hear Wolfe's statement.

"Now, gentlemen," he commenced smoothly. "No need for an affair of honor. Indeed, the Governor disapproves of the practice. Can't this matter be composed? I feel sure there must be some misunderstanding. . . ."

"None whatever!" said Ackroyd. "I have been publicly insulted, humiliated and challenged. However, if Captain Wolfe desires to confess to these persons present that he lied, withdraw his remarks, and apologize, I may accept that as satisfaction."

Merewether looked at Wolfe. He was entirely composed—cold and deadly in manner. Except for Ackroyd's disavowal, he could well be a principal in the affair, and he wondered if he could have maintained the poise Wolfe displayed.

"No chance!" grated Wolfe. "And damn your impudence for intruding, as well!" he told Raffles.

"Very well," said Raffles cheerfully, taking no offense. "I shall inform the Governor of your decision." He walked rapidly back across the floor.

"My seconds will be Lieutenants Shropshire and Wyatt," said Ackroyd, then turned and strode away, followed by the two lieutenants. The bystanders broke into a buzz of comment and drifted away as Buttram came up.

"Did I hear correctly. You are to fight a duel, and I am to be a second?"

"Yes," said Wolfe, a little ruefully. "I'm afraid I've made a fool of myself. I wasn't thinking straight. A moment more, and he would have challenged me. I could cut his ears off with the sword, but since he knows my skills, pistols will make the matter more even, and he gets the choice of weapons." He rubbed the back of his head and closed his eyes a moment.

The die was cast, Wolfe and Ackroyd would fight a duel, and he would be Wolfe's second. Merewether had never issued a challenge, nor had he ever been challenged, though that certainly had been Ackroyd's intention tonight. He was illogically regretful for a moment that the diversion had occurred and that he was not a principal in the affair. He heard supper announced and went to find the Raffles pair.

The impending duel was the subject of a constant buzz of conversation at the Governor's table where Merewether found himself seated with Livie and Tom. Apparently, Livie was already fully informed of the facts, for she made no further comment. As soon as he decently could, he made his excuses and went back to the ship, passing close aboard *Mercure* and hailing the watch to make sure all was well in her. He had no trouble falling asleep. Just after eight bells in the morning, the messenger reported that the gig from *Argus* was approaching. At least, Ackroyd's seconds were prompt and he would not have to wait out the morning for them. He sent for Buttram, and they held a brief conference with Wolfe, just awakened, bleary-eyed and yawning, in his dressing gown.

"Any time, any weapons," he told them, his words slurred and indistinct. "I have a fine pair of pistols, but I'll use any you agree on, provided the gunner inspects and passes them." He reached over, pulled a drawer open in his chest, and produced a rosewood case. "Show them these, if pistols are Ackroyd's choice. At least, I have confidence in them."

"Very well," Merewether told him. "I think the seconds are coming on board now." He and Buttram went back to the cabin, where the skylight had been removed for repair, and in a few moments, Hamlyn escorted the two lieutenants in.

"Good morning," said Merewether rising. "Pray be seated, gentlemen." There followed a moment of silence, punctuated by the clearing of throats, while the officers looked about curiously.

"Your quarters suffered a bit, sir," offered the elder of the two, a tall, light-haired man named Shropshire, who had been with Ackroyd last night. The other officer, Wyatt was his name Merewether remembered, was slight and dark.

"Yes, the carpenter has removed the skylight. He hopes he can find glass enough to make twenty-one panes over in George Town. If not, we shall have to board it over, and I will miss the light."

"You seem to have been hulled twice, as well as losing your main-topmast," said Wyatt.

"Things were rather hot for a few minutes, but we are making repairs; and if I can find a suitable spar for the topmast, we should be able to return to sea shortly." He wondered when they would get around to the business in hand.

The two officers looked at one another. Evidently, they were as inexperienced at this game as Merewether and Buttram. Then Shropshire cleared his throat. "Sir, you know our mission, and Captain Ackroyd says there is no chance of composing this

116

quarrel except by a complete retraction and apology from Captain Wolfe. . . ."

"That is out of the question, of course."

"Of course, sir, but it is my duty to propose it." He hesitated. "There is a level bit of greensward just behind the dockyard, no residences close, and it has been used for this purpose in the past, I am told."

"Quite satisfactory, and your choice of weapons?"

"Pistols, sir, ten paces, and no second shots."

Merewether opened the case to display the gleaming blue steel and polished walnut of Wolfe's pair, complete with powder flask, perfectly cast balls, steel ramrod, and silver charge cup.

"How do these strike you?"

Roberts looked briefly at the pistols. "They appear quite adequate, but we'll want them inspected by our gunner."

"Fair enough, send him over. And now, the time?"

"It should be daylight by four bells in the morning watch. Shall we fix that time tomorrow morning?"

"Agreed," said Merewether. "Doctor, do you have anything to add?"

"No, sir." Shropshire and Wyatt rose and bowed.

"Good day, gentlemen," said Merewether, also rising to see them out the door.

"Well," said Buttram, "that was quick and pleasant enough. And now, I must see my patients. I have two incipient infections I'm trying to head off."

"And I am going to see the Governor and try to find a topmast." Merewether ordered the gig called away and went around to Wolfe's room.

Wolfe was shaving, now fully awake. "Pistols?" he guessed.

"Yes, at six o'clock tomorrow morning. One shot each at ten paces with your pistols."

"Confident, isn't he?" said Wolfe calmly. "He is a crack shot. You know, I served with Ackroyd three years ago in the Mediterranean when he was first, by two numbers in the Navy List, and I was second in *Aphrodite*, thirty-six. We had a dustup then, and I challenged him; but Captain Rogers would not hear of it. I had a chance to come out here as first in *Apollo*, and I took it. Then the bastard showed up here, as impossible as ever." He washed lather, flecked with blood, off his face, toweled it, and sat heavily back in the chair.

"I realize, Commodore, I haven't been the best passenger you could hope for this cruise. I've done some things I'm ashamed of, and I apologize for any grief I've brought you." The man was in dead earnest, Merewether saw, aware of the possibility of death within the next twenty-four hours. The second personality that Buttram had visualized in him was completely subordinated now, for how long Merewether could not guess. Wolfe continued speaking very slowly, "But you have been a gentleman, when you had the provocation not to be. And I must say, you have demonstrated, in two classic examples, the art of winning naval engagements by superior seamanship, gunnery, and plain good training, so that your officers and men do the right thing in the heat of battle without being told." Wolfe reached over to his desk and picked up a packet, folded and sealed. Merewether caught a glimpse of the superscription addressed to Pellew.

"I had written most of this report earlier, and then added the account of the engagement off Diamond Point night before last, while the facts were fresh in my mind. Last night, after my return aboard, I composed my critique of the operation and of your tactics." Wolfe handed over the packet. "There are copies for your Commodore and the Governor-General." He paused and rubbed his hand across his forehead, eyes closed, then continued, "And here is the letter for Kinney's parents."

Merewether felt embarrassment. It was almost as though he were listening to the deathbed words of the man. He took the packet. "Thank you, Wolfe," he said. "I shall place them in my strongbox for safekeeping until you call for them. And now the Governor has asked to see me, and I must try to find a new topmast."

Wolfe opened his eyes and said a little thickly, "Lord knows, I had little enough to drink last night, but my head is splitting. I think I shall rest awhile."

CHAPTER NINE

Raffles buttoned his waistcoat and slipped into his coat, then
adjusted his neckpiece and watch chain, and led the way in to
Governor Phillip Dundas. He was formal in his way, but by no
means in the manner of Sir George Barlow. He indicated chairs
for Merewether and Raffles, and looked undecided for a moment.
His color was bad, jaundiced, and his hands shook. Prince of
Wales Island had a climate that was not conducive to long life
among the European inhabitants of the large government establishment here at George Town in this young Presidency, and
health was a serious concern, in spite of the succession of balls,
routs and picnics, all duly reported in the *Prince of Wales
Gazette*.

"A sad thing, Commodore, that two young men seek to kill
one another, and both promising officers of the Navy," he began.

"Yes, Your Excellency. I was almost involved myself. Ackroyd thought I had made the statements that Wolfe acknowledged."

"A sad thing," said Dundas again. "I am informed there is no
chance of composing the matter."

"None whatever, as of an hour ago. They meet tomorrow
morning with pistols."

"I tried, Your Excellency," interposed Raffles.

"I know, and I am not going to interfere," said Dundas
tiredly. "Now, Commodore, I am acquainted with the terms of
your commission, and I know that three of the supposed four
French cruisers have been taken. Your ship is damaged and re-
quires a new topmast. We have a dockyard, and it was thought
when this Presidency was established that we would build or
repair many ships here. Unfortunately, there is no suitable timber for the purpose this side of Rangoon. When *Argus* required
new masts, we were four months finding and bringing them in."

Merewether's heart sank. The Governor was telling him that
there was no material here for essential repairs, impossible as

that appeared. He commenced, "But, sir, Your Excellency, I require only a spar of sufficient size. I can fit it, and I have all the ironware. . . ."

Dundas shook his head. "I have had MacDonald, the superintendent of the dockyard, in already this morning. Mister Raffles has told me of your requirements. He says he has teak planks and a few oak beams, but no timber of the variety and dimensions you require. . . . I sympathize with you, Commodore. Is it possible for you to continue under, I think the term is, jury rig?"

"Possible, sir, but the strain may spring the fore- and mizzenmasts, if long continued, and the ship is unbalanced as well. I would be derelict in my duty if I took her into action in this condition."

"Yes, I suspected something of the sort," said Dundas slowly. "I regret our lack. And now, the surgeon insists that I return home at this hour to rest. I have been unwell, Commodore, and I leave the matter in the hands of Mister Raffles, with authority to give you all assistance."

"I am sorry, Your Excellency, and I wish you a speedy recovery," said Merewether, rising and bowing. The hand of death was on the man, he surmised, and wondered if Raffles anticipated it, as he did that of the first secretary.

Back in his chamber, Raffles divested himself of his coat and unbuttoned the waistcoat. He pulled out his watch, attached to the chain with its jingling seals, and said, "Another hour, and I shall take you home to lunch with me."

"It is too much," demurred Merewether. Then a thought struck him. "But could we go to the dockyard meanwhile and let me see for myself?"

"Certainly." In a few moments, the barouche was at the door, and they rolled down to the harbor.

They passed a low, spreading building on the principal street of George Town. "Our best public house," said Raffles, with a wave. "A Londoner by the name of Moulton established it last year. He has the finest selection of wines and spirits in the Presidency, and roast beef every night. You should arrange to dine there before you depart."

"At the rate I am going, I may dine there every night for the next year," said Merewether bitterly.

Raffles laughed and said, "You take matters too seriously, Commodore. *Carpe diem*, live for the day, enjoy things while you may, you're a long time dead. Of course, I would not deliberately pick this Presidency as the place to spend it. Even the Admiralty, which insisted on making it the headquarters base for the eastern half of the fleet, now recognizes the mistake, so we have one twenty-two gun sloop here." They drew up at the dockyard.

MacDonald was a thick-set, bald man of about his own age, surly in manner, who spoke with the accent of the Highlands. "No, Commodore, I told the Governor not an hour ago, there's not a stick of pine, or anything else that would make a topmast, this side of Rangoon. The trees that grow here, or over on the mainland, are all too hard or too soft, too heavy or too light, for masts and spars. Four months, it were, to find the timber for two masts in *Argus* out there, and that bastard Ackroyd gigging me three times a day and then complaining to the Governor because my artisans take a siesta."

Merewether loked out the window of the office. It was situated in the corner of a fair-sized sail loft, with fly-specked schematic drawings of vessels tacked on the walls. Along the waterfront were moored a number of small craft, a pilot lugger, scows, barges, lighters and work boats. On the ways a hundred feet distant, was the keel, with stem, sternpost, and half a dozen rib frames erected and temporarily braced, of what promised to be a considerable vessel. The timbers had weathered almost gray, and weeds grew thick about them.

"That was commenced as an Indiaman two years ago," explained MacDonald. "Joseph Parker and Sons commissioned her, but what with the Frogs cruising about out there, we ran out of timber, and there she sets."

Anchored a little way offshore were the two barges Merewether had seen alongside *Argus* during his first call at Penang. Each carried a pair of shear legs, joined at the top and spreading like the letter A, braced and guyed, with tackles running through a block at the apex, and leading down to a windlass. One was not much more than thirty feet high, but the other must be fifty. Merewether estimated. These were the implements by which the damaged masts had been lifted out of *Argus* and the new ones stepped.

"Might I borrow your glass a moment?" asked Merewether, took the telescope, and stepped outside.

The two spars forming the longer of the shear legs were undoubtedly pine, probably salvaged from some wreck. While weathered, they appeared sound through the glass, no obvious cracks or checks, though one was studded with iron spikes to serve as a ladder, and he judged them to be at least fifty feet in length. In front of the building was a flagstaff with a signal yardarm and halyards. The flag bag was inside the sail loft, and it took only a moment to pull out the necessary bunting. Raffles came out, followed by MacDonald.

"What in the world, Commodore?"

"Signaling my ship," replied Merewether, then whispered, "Now you stand by me, Tom!" He bent on *Rapid*'s number and two-blocked it, then lowered and two-blocked it again half a dozen times to attract attention. He was rewarded finally when a bit of color blossomed on the mizzen halyards, acknowledging her readiness to receive the message.

"Boatswain and carpenter, come on shore." *Rapid* repeated the signal, then two-blocked, "Understood," and Merewether hauled down the hoist, signaling execution of the order. He detached the flags and restored them to their bag, then came back to the mystified Raffles and MacDonald.

"Oh, Mister MacDonald, I have to be in attendance on an affair of honor tomorrow morning. Could you show me the green used for this?"

They walked through the empty, echoing loft and emerged on an open lawn, sickled smooth. "The sun will be rising right behind that tree over there," said MacDonald with relish, "so generally they face off at right angles to the sun's bearing, so there'll be no advantage."

"How often do you have such affairs?" inquired Merewether.

"This will be the third in three years. Last one, Mister West, of the Company, wounded an ensign from the garrison for the attentions he paid to his wife. Then West died within the month of fever, and his widow married the ensign, though how much comfort he is to her I don't know, seeing as where he was wounded!" He laughed uproariously, and they went back to the office, with Raffles impatiently consulting his watch.

The launch was pulling for the jetty in front of the office as MacDonald said, "I am due for a siesta. Never dreamed of such a thing back in Clydebank, but it comes in handy out here in the heat of the day. Back at four."

"Go ahead," Merewether told him. "I must wait a moment to give orders to my boatswain." MacDonald put on a wide straw hat and departed toward George Town.

The launch hooked on to the jetty, and the boatswain swung nimbly ashore in spite of his broken arm, followed by the carpenter.

"Mister Tompkins, you see those shear legs out there on the barge? I think one of them might serve as a topmast. Will you and Mister Svenson take a look at it and, if sound, dismantle it and take it back to the ship."

"Aye aye, sir."

"Good God, Merewether!" exploded Raffles. "You can't commandeer the dockyard's equipment. Why, MacDonald . . ."

"The Governor said, 'Give me all assistance.' To be honest, Raffles, I interpret that to mean you stand between me and MacDonald when he finds his shear leg missing."

"Well . . ."

"And now, I accept your kind invitation and look forward to seeing your charming wife again."

By the time they reached the Raffles residence, the high-handed confiscation of a vital part from the Company's equipment had become a joke. Raffles hastened to tell Livie the gleeful story over Straits Coolers.

"But of course, my dear, once MacDonald sees what has happened and comes to me, he may be of a mind to call me out!" he concluded. Livie laughed again at the absurdity, and they went out to the verandah to dine.

"Commodore," said Raffles, settling back in his chair after lunch. "I think I shall emulate Mister MacDonald this afternoon. What with the ball and the late hour, I feel the necessity of a siesta." Merewether saw Livie look quickly at Tom, a sparkle of pleasure flashing across her face. Evidently, she anticipated more from the afternoon than a simple nap. For a moment, he envied Raffles and coveted Livie, then heard him continue, "Of course, you're welcome to stay for a siesta, too."

"No," he said, wondering for a moment how Kate Hartley might be employing the afternoon. "No, I should be on board when that spar arrives, closely followed by MacDonald. If you will have your man take me to the landing, I'll be most appreciative."

He came on board in the blinding heat of the day, seeing in passing that the shear legs off the dockyard had now assumed a lopsided aspect, and the launch was pulling toward the ship with the new topmast towing astern.

The sun was almost touching the tops of the hills to the southwest when MacDonald made his appearance. Mister MacCamy let him come on board without hindrance, where the first sight that met his eyes was his shear leg, now trimmed off at either end and wedged on saw horses along the port side. The carpenter and his mates were fitting the ironware to one end, while the carpenter from *Comet* was at work on the other end, a selection of chisels, saws and augers spread on deck around them. Two carpenter's mates were trimming and trueing the spar with drawknives and planes, while curls of shavings blew unheeded across the deck. Mister Tompkins stood by in a bit of shade, contentedly smoking his pipe, as he watched the topmast take shape.

"Here, now!" shouted MacDonald, whipping his straw hat off and throwing it to the deck. "I've found the thieves!" He was in a towering rage.

The boatswain looked around at him. "Have you lost something, sir?"

Merewether, at word from the messenger of the approach of the visitor, had come to stand on the ladder, just looking over the coaming of the after companion. At the response, MacDonald became inarticulate, bouncing up and down, and appearing on the verge of assaulting the boatswain, broken arm and all. Bowman, the leading boatswain's mate, lounged up beside Tompkins and stood there, hands on hips. He was a man over six feet tall, with a protruding jaw and broken teeth, who weighed an easy fifteen stone.

MacDonald calmed a little and began, "My shear legs . . ."

"Here you are, sir," said Davis, the purser, bustling up and handing over a folded paper. "Your bill of exchange drawn on Bombay, nine pounds, seven shillings, and thrippence, appraised value, one unfitted pine spar." MacDonald took the paper and unfolded it, his mouth working open and shut as he looked at it. Then he crumpled it savagely and threw it into the scuppers.

"I'll . . ." he commenced, and saw Bowman move toward him. He retreated across the deck, paused when he saw there was no pursuit, and shouted, "I'll see the Governor! You'll hear from this!" He went to the gangway, and as he started down the ladder, a seaman handed him his hat and pressed the crumpled bill of exchange into his hand. MacDonald looked at it, then thrust it into his pocket, clapped on the hat, and climbed down into his boat. From a hundred feet away, he turned once more to shout, "Damned Bombay Buccaneers!" and headed for the George Town boat landing. Raffles was in for an uncomfortable quarter hour, Merewether could predict.

The appropriation was justified, Merewether told himself. There might be some repercussions from Bombay, but taking a pine spar from another agency of the Company in time of need was certainly not a hanging or even a court-of-inquiry offense, particularly when liberal payment was offered. The barge saw only limited use, and for such a purpose, surely one of the local trees would provide an adequate leg. And at the rate the boat-swain and carpenter were going, assisted by the carpenter and his mates from *Comet*, the mainmast should be completely set up and rerigged by day after tomorrow. The thought of the morrow depressed him, and he thought of the inn that Raffles had pointed out in George Town this morning. A drink and a meal ashore in a public house would be a novelty after these weeks at sea. He called Sangh.

"Would you ask Captain Wolfe, Doctor Buttram, Mister Dobbs, and Mister Hamlyn if they will consent to be my guests at dinner ashore this evening, and tell the messenger to come down."

In a moment, the messenger knocked, as Merewether finished scribbling his invitation.

"Send this to Mister Larkin in *Mercure* and Captain MacRae in *Comet*. Private."

Larkin needed a run ashore, away from the strain of watching over a ship full of sullen, dangerous prisoners, undoubtedly plotting to retake the prize at the first opportunity. Dobbs, in his steady, quiet way, had proved himself during the past nine months since he had come aboard as a passed midshipman. Hamlyn was gaining confidence and knowledge, and promised to become a competent officer. Merewether recalled that it was more than a year ago, in London, just before *Rapid* sailed on that desperate mission to meet Abercrombie, that he had last invited his officers in a group for a celebration ashore; and only three of that group were here now. Then too, he wanted to cheer Wolfe up and take his mind off the affair of tomorrow morning.

"Sah, I cannot awaken the captain."

"What?"

"He breathes, but does not awaken."

Damnation! Had Wolfe drunk himself into insensibility on the eve of his duel? Merewether stepped around to Wolfe's room. There was no bottle or glass visible, and when he bent over him, he detected no odor of spirits.

"Call Doctor Buttram." The man was lying across the bed, still in the dressing gown he had worn when Merewether left him this morning, his eyes half open.

When Buttram arrived, he sent Sangh to get a spill and light the lamp, taking Wolfe's pulse while he waited in the twilight. The lamp lit up the room and showed Wolfe's half-open eyes. Buttram pushed back the lids and muttered something, then felt the forehead and explored areas of the knees and elbows. He stood back, one hand holding his chin and looked steadily at the chest of the recumbent figure, with its measured rise and fall.

"No reactions, pupils irregularly dilated, and in a deep coma, if ever I saw one," said Buttram, as though he were talking to himself. "And the slight clumsiness of the left hand and leg, speech a little slurred of late—I confess I thought he had been tippling again since you gave him back the key to his cellar—added to his erratic actions these past few weeks . . ." his voice trailed off.

"Well, what is the trouble?"

"Of course, it could be a stroke, but not likely at his age. My guess—no I cannot even guess at this point."

"What can you do for him?"

"Nothing that I know of, except a little blood-letting should not harm him, and could be beneficial." He instructed Sangh to bring him his medical kit. "I am no great believer in bleeding, as a rule, but sometimes it will relieve humours, or restore consciousness after a stroke." He hummed tunelessly as they waited. Sangh came back into the cabin, and Buttram took out the instruments, and a graduated vessel.

"Six ounces, should be enough," he said briskly, gripping Wolfe's arm just above the elbow, and causing the veins in his forearm to distend. A stroke of the knife, and the flood flowed smoothly into the cup, dark red, almost black, in this light. "That's enough." He closed the incision, and pressed a bit of lint, wet with brandy, over it. "No visible effect," he said after a bit. "But we shall wait and see."

"What do we do about tomorrow morning's affair?" asked Merewether, knowing the answer before he had completed the question.

"It's obvious; the man is incapable. We so inform Ackroyd, or more correctly, his seconds."

"Well, I have already invited you and a party ashore to dine at the public house, and I will not disappoint. You say there is nothing more you can do, so make him comfortable, and we will stop by *Argus* on the way to the landing."

Buttram and Sangh straightened Wolfe on the bed, pulling his limp arms and legs straight, and then laying a damp rag across his eyes to protect them from gnats or flies. "I can't give him water," said Buttram abstractedly. "I fear he would not swallow, and would strangle. He cannot live long in this condition but I'll have Dyer stand by."

It was a subdued group that left *Rapid*, picked up Larkin from

Mercure, and then MacRae from *Comet.* The word of Wolfe's mortal affliction had quickly spread.

"Pull for *Argus,*" Merewether told the coxswain. The absentee pennant was flying, but he needed information as to where Ackroyd might be found. They were hailed fifty yards off her gangway.

"*Rapid*!" shouted back the coxswain as they came alongside.

"Can you tell me where I might find Captain Ackroyd?" Merewether called up to the master's mate at the gangway.

"Sir, I think he and Lieutenants Shropshire and Wyatt are dining at the public house in George Town."

"Thank you. Give way," he told the coxswain. "The public landing." At least it was convenient to find Ackroyd and his seconds at their own destination.

Inside, the public house was a bit of old England transplanted to the tropics. True there were punkahs, never seen in Britain, waving slowly back and forth overhead, propelled by cords that led outside to Malay boys, to keep the air in motion; but one look at the host with his red John Bull face, and the roast of beef, already carved half its depth, suspended on a spit over a drip pan beside a bed of coals, carried Merewether right back to London. The place was half full of warrant officers of the Royal Navy and from *Comet* and *Rapid,* with a considerable contingent of army personnel from the garrison, led by a haughty sergeant major.

The host bustled forward. "Good evening, gentlemen, and you'll be Commodore Merewether?" The cockney accent was familiar and comforting, reviving memories of his boyhood.

"Yes, Mister Moulton, and could you accommodate the six of us for dinner?"

"Certainly, sir. Roast beef is the main dish, but I have puddings, relishes and kickshaws, too, and spirits, wine and ale."

"Excellent, I'm sure we will do them justice, and see what these gentlemen will have to drink."

"Right this way, gentlemen." Moulton led them to an alcove opening off the public room, furnished with a long table, chairs and sideboard. As they passed another such alcove, Merewether caught a flash of blue and gold. Ackroyd and his two lieutenants were in a group that comprised five women, and two men in

128

civilian dress. They were in high spirits, he gathered, as the last words of a song floated out. Ackroyd was conveniently located and appeared settled there for a bit. His party passed the entrance without notice or remark.

"Well, gentlemen, your preferences?" The innkeeper took their orders, and a Malay boy soon slipped in, balancing a tray of bottles and glasses to set the sideboard. Toasts were proposed and drunk, and Wolfe was forgotten for the time. The officers relaxed from the strain of the past weeks. Merewether kept an eye out, however, and when he saw empty dessert dishes carried by from the adjoining alcove, he caught Buttram's eye, and they went unobtrusively outside.

Wyatt was just coming out. "Could we see you and Mister Shropshire a moment?"

Wyatt nodded, and in a moment he and Shropshire emerged. Merewether looked about, other than the two private rooms, there was no privacy, but no one was paying any attention, and this was as good a place as any to give the news.

"Gentlemen, I fear there will be no meeting of our principals in the morning," said Merewether carefully. "Captain Wolfe is physically incapable, as Doctor Buttram will explain." Both officers looked startled and doubtful, as they looked to Buttram.

"Gentlemen, Captain Wolfe lapsed into a deep coma sometime earlier today. Recovery is most unlikely, death inevitable, in my opinion." He paused and looked at Merewether.

"Therefore, gentlemen, will you inform Captain Ackroyd of the circumstances, and we will wait a moment for your reply."

It was only a moment before they returned, accompanied by Ackroyd. "What is this all about, Merewether?" he demanded. He was a little loud, but perfectly steady on his feet. Several heads turned among the patrons in the public room.

Merewether felt irritation at the tone of voice, but replied civilly, "Why, I thought the doctor had made it perfectly plain. The man is unconscious and on his deathbed."

"In less than twenty-four hours? A likely story!"

"I beg your pardon, and how am I to interpret that remark?"

"I said, 'A likely story!'" said Ackroyd, in a loud, insulting voice, ringing across the suddenly quiet room. "And you can interpret it anyway you please!"

Merewether was aware that his own officers had come to the entrance of their alcove, the women and civilians staring from the other, and that every eye in the big room was on him. He realized with a perverse pleasure that the man was intent on making a scene and that it was impossible to withdraw with dignity. He had, in effect, been named a liar before fifty-odd witnesses and Wolfe branded a coward as well. Distasteful as the prospect was, he must accept the challenge or walk under a cloud the rest of his life. Anger and animosity toward this arrogant man, who had abandoned the chase to take a crippled prize from him three days ago, steeled him. He spoke from a full heart and was surprised by his own vehemence and stilted language.

"Why, then, I think you have called me a liar, and I demand a retraction and an apology for that and your false reflection upon the courage of a mortally ill man!" he said in a clear, ringing voice that carried across the room.

Ackroyd flushed beet red. "Why, you damned John Company pirate, I'd rather kill Wolfe for the sake of old scores, but you'll do as well!"

"Do you challenge me then?" Merewether demanded. "You fail to make yourself clear." The reckless perversity of spirit and deep anger that had possessed him from Ackroyd's first sneering statement carried him along. "Very well, I accept your challenge! And in view of Captain Wolfe's disability, I shall suggest to my seconds that we meet at the time and place appointed for his meeting with you, and with the same weapons."

Ackroyd appeared a little taken aback at the quick response. He looked to Shropshire, and then to Wyatt, and said in a lower tone, "My seconds remain the same."

"I request Doctor Buttram and Lieutenant Larkin to act for me." Merewether went back into the alcove, hoping that MacRae would not be hurt by his unhesitating choice of Larkin, hearing the excited buzz of conversation rise in the public room, and poured a drink. He was unaccountably exhilarated, and yet there was a tremor in his hands as he lifted the glass. Larkin and Buttram soon came back.

"It's settled, same time, place and weapons," said Buttram, shaking his head with a humorous expression of resignation. "All this time, all unknowing, we have nurtured a tiger in *Rapid*'s cabin, gentlemen!"

Merewether laughed with the rest, feeling the comforting influence of the gin spread through his body, engendering a sense of bravado. He might be dead tomorrow, but he was damned if he would let the prospect spoil his evening!

CHAPTER TEN

Merewether awoke when the morning watch was called. There was a minor throbbing in the back of his head—he had drunk one gin too many last night, he decided—but his hands were steady. It was still black outside, and through the remnants of the skylight he could see stars, promising a fair day. He rang for Sangh, had the lamp lit, and asked for tea and hot water. He began to shave himself. The brown face and neck contrasted with the white of his shoulders in the mirrored lamplight, and he discovered that the scar on his face had broken open again, the result of frequent shaving, sun and sweat the past few days. He skirted the raw area with the blade, leaving a little patch of stubble, so as not to irritate the wound further. He wondered if he would go to his grave with the patch of bristles still growing about the raw edge of the old scar. He forced himself to think about the new topmast, now fully equipped with its fittings, and then inevitably wondered if he would live to see it hoisted into place. Hell, he had been sanguine enough last night, light-heartedly brushing aside the possibility of death or injury; but matters appeared differently in the hours before dawn!

He washed off the lather and dressed, selecting a blue stock to match his coat. No use giving Ackroyd a better point of aim by wearing white. He wondered for a moment at his unhesitating choice of pistols when he had killed a man last summer with a sword in single combat. He knew in his heart, though, that it had been a fluke, and he had escaped with his life only by the merest luck. He thought fleetingly of Lady Caroline, far to the north, and wondered what cavaliers might be courting her in his absence. He could not keep his mind upon her, his thoughts veered right back to the lonely meeting an hour or so hence. He had known officers in the Marine in years past who had been involved in such affairs, but not so many of late. Commodore Waldron frowned on the practice, and he had often noted a personality change in them after a successful meeting. It was as though a man having once tasted blood, must drink it again and again, defying fate, until he met the inevitable opponent who was as reckless, quicker and more accurate than he.

He still was not sure of his motives in taking offense and reacting so quickly to Ackroyd's unconsidered comment. Part of it, true, was honest resentment of Ackroyd's conduct, carried forward from the day of the action, and another part was his suspicion that he had too willingly stepped aside and let Wolfe make the quarrel his own night before last. But possibly the most compelling factor to Merewether was the sneering slur upon the courage of Wolfe, even then lying mortally stricken. He had not liked the man, but Wolfe's courage could not be faulted, and the slander was inexcusable.

The thought of Wolfe reminded him, and he stepped around to his room. Dyer, his servant, snored in the chair; there was an acrid odor of urine in the air; and Wolfe lay as he had last night, chest slowly rising and falling. There was a rasp in his breathing that indicated dryness of throat and nasal passages, but Buttram had said that he could not give him water for fear of strangulation. He shook Dyer awake and directed him to bring fresh bedding; then he removed the rag, now bone dry, from Wolfe's eyes. They were dull and sunken, and he wet the rag in the pitcher and laid it back across them. As he left, he met Buttram coming down the passage.

"He's still alive, Doctor," Merewether told him, and wondered if he might be able to say the same for himself two hours from now.

Back in his cabin, Merewether drank another cup of tea, freshly brewed in his absence, and put on his coat. Time to embark, he decided, since the gig must call by *Mercure* for Larkin on its way to the dockyard.

Buttram came in and said, "The gig is at the gangway, Captain." Buttram was in undress uniform, and at the ladder was Davis, carrying the medical kit, and a landing-force packet of bandages, splints, tourniquets and lint compresses. These grim implements and accessories for the care of the wounded were disquieting, but Merewether followed Buttram into the boat without comment.

Larkin came aboard carrying Wolfe's pistol case wrapped in oilskin under his arm and a powder horn slung over his shoulder. He spoke briefly, and the gig pulled for the landing. To the east, the sky was lighter, and the stars had almost faded. By the time they came ashore, it was light enough to see their way around the sail loft, past the ropewalk, to the grassy plot. They were the first to arrive and stood silently in a cluster.

Merewether remembered with a shudder the mirth of Mac-Donald yesterday morning at his mention of the unfortunate wound to the ensign. There were always men, sadistic and expert enough, who would seek to punish an opponent by shooting to wound him in the genitals or in the kneecap, leaving him alive and crippled. Merewether had no opinion as to Ackroyd, but the possibility was there, and Wolfe had said he was a crack shot. He heard the sound of voices, and Ackroyd's party came around the building.

Larkin and Buttram, with Shropshire and Wyatt, went over to the center of the green, while Ackroyd and a beefy man in the uniform of an assistant surgeon of the Royal Navy stood, backs turned, staring out over the harbor. Merewether saw Shropshire pointing and gesturing and Larkin evidently objecting. Finally, the two laid a kerchief on the turf, and stepped off, together, ten paces, then laid down another. He noted absently that the markers lay almost east and west and remembered MacDonald's comment yesterday about the sun rising above that tree. Oh well, the thing would be over by the time the sun rose over those hills enough to matter. The four seconds came back.

"Gentlemen," said Larkin. "I am going to load these pistols.

If anyone has any objection to them, speak now, or forever hold his peace."

He uncased the first pistol, blew through the muzzle to make sure the touchhole was clear, then poured the silver measure full of powder, leveled it with his thumb, and dumped it down the barrel. Wad, ball, and wad followed, and he handed it to Wyatt to hold while he loaded the second. He pushed the frizzen forward, poured a pinch of powder in the pan, and snapped it back, following suit with the other pistol.

"Loaded, primed, and at half-cock," he announced. "Gentlemen, are you ready?"

Merewether came forward. The scene was unreal, and his skin crawled at the thought that in a moment or two, Ackroyd and he would be firing at one another in cold blood.

"Now, gentlemen," asked Shropshire formally. "Is there any chance of composing this quarrel?"

"None!" said Ackroyd and Merewether almost in unison.

"Very well, you will each take position at the markers, facing one another. The pistols will be held pointing down, uncocked. I will give the word to cock, and then Lieutenant Larkin will count, 'one hundred and one, one hundred and two, one hundred and three.' After the word 'three' you may fire at will. . . . Commodore, call this coin for the choice of positions." He spun a gold piece in the air, catching and covering it with his hand.

"King," said Merewether. It was exposed, showing the spade.

"I'll take that one," said Ackroyd, pointing to the eastward marker.

"Gentlemen, take your positions."

Merewether clumped over stiffly to the westward marker, facing Ackroyd, and Larkin put the pistol in his hand. "I wanted the thing north and south," Larkin whispered, "but I think it is not important."

Merewether could feel the sharp-cut checkered walnut of the grip filling his hand, and his thumb automatically sought the hammer. The sky over the tree at the edge of the green was bright red now, promising the momentary appearance of the sun. The seconds had withdrawn well out of the line of fire, leaving the two men facing one another.

"Cock your weapons!" Merewether drew back the hammer and felt the sear engage with a well-oiled click.

"Are you ready?"

He heard Larkin begin the count, "One hundred and one . . ." Ackroyd's figure was hazy, and he blinked his eyes to clear them. "One hundred and two . . ." The sky behind Ackroyd was much brighter now, and he tensed himself to swing the pistol up and aim it. "One hundred and three!"

A dazzling ray of sunlight burst through a gap in the leaves of the tree, blindingly, right in his eyes. Merewether snapped his head instinctively sidewise, to the left, eyelids almost closed to escape the brilliance. He felt the hot breath of the ball as it passed his right temple before he heard the sound of the shot and saw the smoke. Ackroyd had aimed at his head with the full and explicit intention of killing him and would have succeeded except for the involuntary movement of his head to escape the dazzle of the sun in his eyes!

The pistol was still at Merewether's side. He had only begun to raise it. Ackroyd stood in place, mouth open, looking incredulously from Merewether, down to the pistol in his hand, still smoking. For an instant, Merewether considered firing in the air—Ackroyd would almost certainly be punished when Wolfe's report was delivered to Pellew—but the thought of Wolfe, dying out there in *Rapid*, and the shot at his head hardened his heart. He brought the pistol up smoothly, head still tilted to the left, eyes narrowed to slits against the sun, seeing the gilt buttons on the blue coat through the sights. Ackroyd took an involuntary step back, then froze, his face a pale mask of horror.

The trigger pull was light and crisp. It let off before he expected it to, and the gun jumped in his hand, smoke jetting from the pan and muzzle. For a moment, Ackroyd was obscured by smoke and the sunlight still in Merewether's eyes. Then he saw his gun fall to the turf, and the man clutched his left arm above the elbow, blood blossoming red through his fingers. He had missed the heart shot for which he aimed, the muzzle diverted to the right by the unexpected lightness of the trigger pull, but evidently he had inflicted a substantial wound. He was suddenly and irrationally glad he had not killed Ackroyd, and a tremendous sense of relief flooded through him that the affair was over and he was alive.

The naval surgeon and Buttram were hurrying toward Ackroyd, and Larkin came over to Merewether, taking the pistol from his hand.

"God, Captain, I thought you were gone! That sun struck right in your eyes at the count of three. I had argued the point, but there were children back there on the hill who might otherwise have been in the line of fire, and we thought the affair would be over before sunrise."

"It saved my life," said Merewether in wonder. "I moved my head to escape the sun, and the ball just missed." He walked over to where he had left his hat; Larkin diverged to pick up the other pistol. Wyatt stood by as Larkin cased the pistols and secured the lid.

"We should wait a moment for Buttram," Merewether reminded him. The naval surgeon had cut off the sleeves of Ackroyd's coat and shirt, and Buttram was holding a tourniquet on the upper arm as the surgeon probed in the wound. In a few minutes, Buttram rejoined them.

"A painful wound, but not serious," he told them. "The humerus is broken, but the ball is out. He may have a stiff elbow, though." He picked up his medical kit and the landing-force packet.

Just as they came around to the front of the sail loft, they saw the barouche coming from George Town. Raffles was driving it himself at a gallop, and he reined the horses to a halt in a flurry of dust.

"Am I too late?"

"All over and done," volunteered Larkin. "The surgeon is patching up Ackroyd out back."

"Really? Splendid! You stand vindicated, Commodore!" Merewether wondered for a moment what Raffles' reaction might have been had the matter gone otherwise, then decided it did not matter. He liked the fellow in spite of his equivocations. "I should step around and say a word. You know, what with one thing and another, I did not return to my office yesterday, and only learned of Wolfe's illness and this affair an hour ago. I had hoped to arrive in time to mediate the matter. And now, if you gentlemen have no better plans, wait a moment, and then we shall breakfast at the public house." He trotted off around the loft.

Merewether felt a little faint—weak in the knees—as reaction set in. He would welcome breakfast, with a bit of brandy and a cup of tea first; but he could not help speculating, even at this moment, as to the cause that had detained Tom yesterday afternoon: Mrs. Raffles, unquestionably. And for a moment he again envied Raffles and coveted Livie.

The breakfast in the tavern was pleasant, and the brandy calmed his nerves. Raffles charmed Buttram and Larkin with his flow of wit and comment. Ready to depart, Raffles asked, "You have at least another several days before you are ready for sea, I suppose?"

"No, I don't think so. The boatswain expected to have the topmast in place this afternoon, and all the rigging set up by tomorrow. I would expect to sortie early the next day."

"Most regrettable. You will miss our Ides of March Rout just a fortnight off, everyone dressed as a character from *Julius Caesar*. Oh, it will be a gay occasion!" continued Raffles. "But there is a minor entertainment tomorrow night sponsored by the garrison, and I am commissioned by the commandant to invite the officers of the ships in port."

It was an hour into the forenoon watch when they came back on board. Buttram handed over the cased pistols to Totten for cleaning and went below to see Wolfe. Merewether stopped to look at the topmast, now with lines laid out to be hooked on.

"We're setting up the tackles to lift her into place now," volunteered Lyle, the junior boatswain's mate.

There were men in the fore and mizzen rigging spinning an intricate web of blocks and lines. Dobbs and Hamlyn, followed by MacCamy, approached him with inarticulate congratulations on his successful encounter. Merewether went below to find the carpenter's mates, freed from work on the mast, replacing his skylight, a box of glass panes set carefully to the side. He found the cabin untenable, however, and went back on deck. Hell, there was no place to rest, even the wardroom furniture was being polished! His restless mood persisted, and he decided to go back ashore and walk about, exploring the town and island. While he waited for the gig to be brought around, he saw one of the dockyard work boats being sculled toward the gangway. The workman only handed up a folded paper to the watch and sculled back toward the landing. He wondered if it were a writ, procured by MacDonald from the magistrate, as the messenger brought it over to him. After MacDonald's wrath yesterday afternoon, anything was possible. He broke the seal and read the message written in a large hand:

Honored Sir: I see you fight that Royal Navy swell a bit ago, and you done well, what with the sun in your eyes. I think you pay 2 pounds, 4 shillings more than used spar is worth, and I credit your B/E by this amt. C. MacDonald, Supt.

Chapter Eleven

There was a substantial bazaar in George Town, and Merewether was soon strolling through the crowds it attracted in this island of almost fifteen thousand persons of varied races. He saw wares from Siam, Burma, Java, India, and a few from China, displayed along the narrow way. Some of the hopeful merchants had regular stalls with racks and tables, while others squatted in the dust, their stock-in-trade heaped about them within arm's reach. It suddenly occurred to him that he owed the Raffles pair a gift for the hospitality they had extended, and he began to look with more purpose. He hesitated over a display of jade and filigreed gold, then decided such items were not appropriate. Toward the end of the way, he came to a decrepit bungalow almost overgrown with flowering vines. Half obscured over its verandah was a weathered sign, "Prize Agent." Beyond was open country, rising to the hills, with scattered dwellings. This place did not look as though it had much custom, here at the end of the marketplace.

A woman came out of a byway ahead, European by color, but grossly fat, with a skirt that exposed legs in white cotton, swollen like sausages.

"Ah, there ducks," she said, exposing blackened, broken teeth in a smile. " 'ow about it? Only ten shillings, and change yer luck!"

"No," said Merewether, stepping to the side for her to pass.

She pressed on toward him, exuding a powerful odor of gin and stale sweat, saying, "Now, don't yer be bashful, and if it's a bit short yer are, why five will do!"

Merewether turned to escape the woman and went up on the verandah of the "Prize Agent," leaving her muttering curses before she rolled on down through the bazaar.

"Ha!" said a disembodied voice. "Old Dolly's early today, must be out of gin." Merewether paused to let his eyes adjust to the shade after the blinding glare of the sun outside. There was an old man sitting in an armchair, propped against the wall at the end of the verandah. "You would not have passed her by ten years ago when she first came here. A raving beauty, she were, and I used to stop around to see her too, in those days; but gin and the syphilis and the climate has done her in. And what can I do for you, Captain?"

"Well . . ." he commenced. "I'm not sure; I was looking for something as a gift. . . ."

"Don't have much anymore," interposed the man. Merewether could now see that he wore a patch over his left eye and that close-cropped white whiskers covered his cheeks and chin. "Since the Company made this place a Presidency, there's no prize business any more. I come down here with Captain Francis Light from Ko Phuket in 'eighty-six and built this house. There was nothing here but jungle and a Malay village over there. Captain Light—he was commissioned in your Bombay Marine, too—called the headman of the village on board and tried to hire them to clear the land for this settlement. Work? Why those chiefs laughed at him, even when he showed them a sack of silver coin! 'More than one way to skin a cat,'

139

says Captain Light, and sends a party ashore to set up a flagstaff on the beach. 'Have to fire a salute to the flag, now,' he says. 'Seven guns.' Well, the gunner loads the nine-pounder battery, and Captain Light pours a hatful of coin down each muzzle. 'Now fire the salute,' he tells the gunner, and seven charges of silver pieces goes flying over into the bush." The old man chortled at the recollection. "They dove right over the side and swam ashore." He stopped to laugh again. "And in three weeks, them natives had skinned this place off to bare ground looking for the coins. Captain Light laid out his gridiron of streets for George Town, just like they are now, and the bag of dollars not half empty!

"I used to do a monstrous trade. I was second only to James Scott in the trade here; of course, they was mostly pirates, but their goods sold as well as any and came cheap. I made my pile, and now I mostly just sit here and watch to see what the fools in Government House will do next." The man spat over the railing of the verandah. "They call this a 'Presidency,' like it was Bombay or Madras!" He snorted in contempt. "We got a sick Governor, too, and that young dandy Raffles, with his fancy waistcoat and gold chain, smiling like a mule eating briars and going behind yer back ruling the place. Bah! And they say he married that woman in exchange for his appointment." He snorted again, and Merewether wondered if he had escaped the attentions of the prostitute only to fall into the clutches of this garrulous old man. "Well, I still got a few things to sell. Look about, Captain."

Merewether hesitated to enter the dim interior, then decided he had nothing better to do and went in. There was a mishmash of goods, furniture, china, bolts of silk, muskets, fowling pieces, pistols and swords of every description, even a spinning wheel in the corner, all jumbled together without pretense of order. At first glance, he saw nothing that remotely resembled a gift to a couple in appreciation of courtesy, hospitality and assistance and turned to leave.

"Don't see anything, eh, Captain?" said the old man, unexpectedly standing in the doorway. "And about what did you have in mind to spend?"

"Why," said Merewether, a little disconcerted, "I might go as much as five pounds. . . ."

"I have just the thing." The man stepped over to a corner of the room and moved several rolls of matting to expose a Chinese desk, lacquered black and inlaid with mother-of-pearl and graceful silver designs, almost the duplicate of one he had seen last year in the Company's hong outside Canton. "Had it a long time," grumbled the old man. "Dusty, but sound." He shouted in Malay, and two men came in to carry it to the verandah and wipe it clean. It was sound, and a beautiful piece, Merewether decided, and would make a useful addition to the Raffles' sitting room.

"I'll take it," he said, fishing for his money. "And can you find me a dray?"

"Ahem. I was going to knock a pound off the price for your shooting that high and mighty Ackroyd," said the old man. "But since you're going to give the desk to that fellow Raffles, I'll have to penalize you a pound. So that makes five pounds, net."

Merewether was startled—the man apparently could read minds—but he paid without comment. "And the dray . . ."

"My men will take it in the cart. Will you go along?"

They stopped by Government House, and he intercepted Raffles dashing down the hall. "I've a meeting of the Council, and then I must verify the books of account with the Resident. I am delighted with the gift, but take it on, Livie may even give you lunch."

At the bungalow, the two Malays set the desk on the verandah as Merewether knocked. The girl admitted him. It was a few minutes before Mrs. Raffles appeared, wearing a yellow silk dressing gown, her hair tucked under a white scarf.

"Why, Commodore, this is an unexpected pleasure! I slept late and just finished bathing. Tom was called out before daybreak, about that duel this morning. And who won it, Wolfe or Ackroyd?" Merewether became aware as she moved across the light of the shaded window that the yellow silk gown was all Livie wore.

"Wolfe, by proxy," he managed, feeling a wave of heat and shifting his gaze. "And what I came for was to give you and Tom a token of my appreciation for your hospitality. He told me to bring it on, since he is otherwise engaged. May I have it brought in?" He opened the door, and the two men carried in the desk. Merewether handed each a shilling, and they left.

"Why, it's beautiful, simply beautiful!" Livie was obviously pleased and came over to run her fingers across the inlays. "Thank you!" He caught a whiff of her scent as she turned, threw her arms about his neck, and kissed him hard upon the lips.

Passion flamed. He had coveted this woman, and envied Raffles, ever since he had met her. He kissed her back with ardor, feeling the firm body under the yellow silk press against him, and was suddenly aware that he could have Livie this instant if he only pressed his attentions. Merewether had no idea of her past before she married Tom, but she was older in years and experience than either Raffles or he. Then he knew that however compliant she might be, he could not face himself if he cuckolded that likable young man in his own home. He did not want such a matter between them. He disengaged and stepped back.

"That was quite the nicest 'thanks' I ever received," he told her lightly. "And now, I must be back on the ship. We raise that new topmast this afternoon, and I should be there." He courteously brushed aside her protests; he had survived temptation, and he did not dare expose himself further.

At the public house on the way to the landing, he had two gins and lemon, already a little remorseful that he had not pressed his advantage, then went on to the ship. The cabin was redolent of paint and putty, but the skylight was whole again, and the windsail was diverting a pleasant portion of the breeze inside. He slept the afternoon away, unmindful of the thumps, shouts and footfalls on deck as the topmast rose into place.

Wolfe died an hour into the midwatch the next morning. Buttram awoke him, and he went around to see the waxen, yellow face, already shrunken so that the bones stood out.

"He'll have to be buried ashore," Buttram reminded him. "And it should be by noon today in this climate. And now, Cap-

142

tain, I feel compelled to do a post mortem dissection to see if I can find the cause of his death. Will you give permission?"

"Certainly, if I have the authority." ·

"In the absence of a next of kin, and as the commander of the force to which he was attached, I feel certain you have the power."

"Very well, I'll enter the matter in the log. And Dyer, will you call the carpenter?"

When the carpenter came, Merewether told him, "No rest for the weary, Mister Svenson. Can you put together a coffin tonight?" The carpenter went off muttering to rouse his mates, and the sound of hammering and sawing lasted until after daybreak. MacCamy took a party armed with picks and shovels over to the fort to open the grave in the military cemetery to the north, while Merewether went back to George Town to find the vicar of the Church of England. He sent word to Raffles of the time and place of the services and then induced the Commandant of the garrison to furnish a caisson to transport the coffin from the landing to the place of sepulture. He had to obtain the Marine guard of honor from *Comet*; his own detachment was occupied with the prize.

The services were held just before noon, a surprising turnout appearing from the European community, the ladies sheltering under parasols. Twenty men each from *Rapid* and *Comet* marched in the procession, and there was even a contingent from *Argus* led by Lieutenant Wyatt and two midshipmen. He saw Livie and Tom in the group, as the vicar, a tall, raw-boned man in flapping vestments, read the service. Merewether, head bowed, wondered at the vagaries of fate that had brought Wolfe to lie for eternity here in this island in the tropics, halfway around the world from England. The crash of the volleys, muffled in this green amphitheater, made him jump, and he was glad to go with the officers from *Comet, Rapid*, and *Argus*, to the public house for a quick drink afterward.

He had just finished a gin and lemon when Buttram caught his eye.

"Let me see you a moment, Captain." They stepped around to the alcove where the party had dined three nights ago.

"Sir, I have, in effect, an apology to make to Wolfe. Fortunately, I listened to you last week, and did not take the drastic action of certifying him as insane." Buttram was dead in earnest, face shining with sweat in the midday heat. "And since he is gone, I can only make it to you, so that your report may be written to reflect the true state of affairs."

"Yes," said Merewether, wondering what the doctor was getting at.

"I was wrong, dead wrong, when I said the man was insane, Captain. I should have recognized the symptoms, since I have observed such a case twice before—the headaches, dizzy spells and clumsiness—instead of trying to be clever, and making a diagnosis from his actions by applying the theories of Mesmer and Pinel." Buttram wiped his brow, and turned to look out the window.

"I comfort myself, Captain," he continued slowly, "by the thought that even if I had made an accurate and early diagnosis, there is no cure for the malady."

"Have you confirmed the disorder?"

"Yes, I did the dissection this morning. First off, I opened the skull—I had to go no further. There it was, a horrible, crab-shaped growth, a tumor! It had displaced one lobe of the brain, and finally choked off the flow of blood, causing unconsciousness and coma!" Buttram turned back to Merewether. "Of course, he died quickly after that, no possibility of getting liquids into him, and in this climate!"

Merewether turned the matter over in his mind. He had attributed Wolfe's erratic behavior these past weeks to insanity, drink or some innate defect of character, but during the past few days, the man had exhibited still another personality change, and he had come almost to like him. He wondered for a moment what Wolfe might have been had he not suffered from that horrible disorder that had warped his mind, and changed his personality. He had certainly been more likable in the terminal stages, and may well have come full circle in the progress of the disease.

"No need to blame yourself, Doctor. You say yourself there is no treatment for the malady. There is nothing in my reports so far that reflects upon Wolfe, and there will not be. Thank you, and have another drink."

He had almost decided not to go to the entertainment at the garrison, knowing that Raffles and Livie would be there. His conscience was clear; he had stopped short. But he would never be at ease in their presence again. Still, Major Anderson, the Commandant, had made a special point of reiterating the invitation to the affair, and as a matter of courtesy and interservice relations, he had felt compelled to accept.

By the end of the first dogwatch, MacCamy and Tompkins came to the cabin. "Sir," said MacCamy. "The mainmast is complete, set up, yards crossed, sails bent on, and brailed up."

"We'll have to take up some on the shrouds and stays once we've been in a seaway a bit," chimed in the Boatswain. "The new cordage will stretch, of course."

"Of course," said Merewether. "You have been magnificent, both of you. And I intend to get under way north at daybreak." He looked at the splinted arm suspended in its sling. "Your wound is healing, Tompkins?"

"Yes, sir. Doctor says there's no sign of infection."

"Very well. Mister MacCamy, please pass the word to make all preparations for getting under way tomorrow morning."

Merewether sat back to consider the next phase of the operation. The French captain had insisted on the truth of his statement made to Wolfe as to the rendezvous off Ko Phuket, but the time he had given was long past. Still, two of the privateers had been found here in the Strait of Malacca, and interrogation of their officers had failed to reveal any such plan or any lead as to the possible whereabouts of the fourth cruiser. The likeliest area would be northward, along the shipping routes to Rangoon and Calcutta, what with *Argus* now back in commission, and patrolling the Strait area. All the officers of the prizes had been transferred to a prisoner-of-war camp maintained by the garrison, but it lacked facilities for the large crew of *Mercure*, and Larkin would have to take it in the prize to Calcutta. He could escort him part of the way, but it would be up to Larkin and Gunny to keep control of the French crew, and he did not envy them their assignment.

His thoughts jumped from the impending operation to Livie. The remarks of the retired prize agent intrigued him. He wondered if the rumor that Raffles had exchanged his marriage to her for the appointment as secretary here at Penang had any basis in fact. He was capable of such a bargain, but the young man appeared devoted to her, and Livie was a charmer. He regretted for a moment again that he had not pressed his advantage yesterday, and then immediately concluded that his instinct had been correct. He wondered a moment more about Kate Hartley, whether she had decided to marry Pickens, the first officer of the *Duchy of Lancaster*, accompany him to Ceylon, and thence back to England. Obviously, she did not care to be reminded of that casual liaison that Livie had procured now that a suitor with the intention of marriage had appeared.

He came full circle to Lady Caroline, the vision of her face and hair now distinct in his mind. On short acquaintance, she was a difficult person to understand. He speculated that she had plunged into her almost mystical preoccupation with poetry and literature, in an unconscious effort to forget her dead husband and absent child. Perhaps, if she was still about when he returned to Calcutta, he would try to jar her out of the mood. In the meantime, he was reading the plays of Shakespeare and a collection of the poetry of Walter Scott in Buttram's small library in an effort to discover for himself their fascination for her.

The party in the armory was much as he had anticipated, Merewether decided, after listening to an Irish sergeant sing saccharine ballads of home, mother and faithless love in a high tenor voice, followed by a young lady who gave a medley of romantic lyrics, most of them impossible to follow, while fiddles and flutes accompanied her. He sat in a group composed of Major Anderson and his wife, the Raffles, Mister Winningham and his wife, Kate Hartley and Mister Pickens, and several junior officers of the garrison.

The musical renditions came to an end, and the audience drifted to the other end of the armory where a buffet and punch bowls had been established, served by Malays under the direction of the same Irish vocalist who had just performed. One of the captains came up and touched his arm.

"Commodore, you'll not want any of that swill. Come with me." He led Merewether back to a small room, already full of officers, where two corporals were serving spirits neat. He took a glass of gin and a quarter of lemon and eased back out of the room, finding a place in the corner of the armory to sip his drink, standing there watching groups gather, mingle and melt into others. He would stay, he decided, only long enough to satisfy the requirements of courtesy.

He was sick of this island of Penang, he thought. It had brought death, unpleasantness, an affair of honor, and temptation to him, and he hoped that he would never call here again. He finished the gin and went over to place the empty glass on a tray. As he turned, he found Kate Hartley in his way, and bowed, looking past her for Mister Pickens.

"Ah, Commodore," she said in a low voice. "And are you enjoying the occasion?" He was startled at the warmth in her voice after the deliberate snub at the Governor's Ball.

"Why, yes, I suppose so," he replied. Kate drew him back into the corner, and he followed reluctantly.

"Now," she said. ". . . Mister Pickens has asked me to marry him, but I've not yet given him an answer. . . ." She looked up at him with luminous, expectant eyes.

Merewether was astounded. The woman was quite evidently inviting a proposal of marriage from him. Livie had sounded him out on the subject some days ago, and he thought he had diverted her with his lie. Then the matter had appeared to become academic with the intervention of Pickens. Yet, here was Kate, tremulous as a girl, telling him she was uncommitted, with the evident expectation that he would seek her hand. The woman was attractive, but since that heartbreak last Christmas when he found that Flora Dean had married Lord Laddie in his absence, he had entertained no thoughts of marriage. The matter was delicate. He had no desire to offend. But he had no desire to be caught up in marriage to a widow in George Town either. He elected to misunderstand her.

"I am delighted, Mrs. Hartley!" he said. "And I wish you all good fortune in your new life with Mister Pickens."

An expression of disappointment crossed Kate's face, followed by a flush of anger. "You . . ." she commenced, then paused. "You are obviously not a gentleman of perception and breeding!" she blurted illogically, then turned and marched away. Merewether escaped to the temporary sanctuary of the spirits bar and mopped his brow in relief as he considered for a moment the unfathomable nature of woman.

It was only a few minutes, his glass was barely half empty, when Pickens sought him out. With the commencement of the dancing, the little room had emptied of all save MacRae, nursing his glass of Scots whisky and making desultory conversation with one of the corporals, who spoke with the accent of Inverness, and two of the garrison officers.

"Merewether!" Pickens was a man taller and broader than he, with a blunt, weathered face, and obviously nervous.

"Yes?" said Merewether, a little sharply, nettled at the tone.

Pickens hesitated, unsure of himself, and then commenced lamely, "Kate, Mrs. Hartley, that is, is much upset by your boorish conduct toward her!" The accusation came out almost as though by rote. Evidently this officer was no more experienced in affairs of honor than Merewether had been a few days ago. Merewether felt indignation rise in him. He had certainly not been boorish toward the woman, though she might feel herself scorned, and he was sure he could take the measure of this Company Maritime Service officer, either with pistols or swords.

He opened his mouth to issue the challenge, but checked himself. A fortuitous, involuntary movement of his head yesterday morning had saved his life. The subsequent wounding of Ackroyd had given him a taste of blood and was making him a ruffler and a bully here, already anticipating the duel with this plain, honest, uneasy man. Hell! He was like the others—a successful encounter, and he was ready to take any offense to the field of honor. Kate Hartley certainly was not worth it to him, nor to her anxious champion standing here before him. He had no idea of what face she had put on the thing in making her complaint to Pickens, but it did not matter. He was suddenly sick of the entire affair and despised himself most of all for even considering fighting a duel on such flimsy grounds.

"Why, Mister Pickens, I had no idea that I had offended Mrs. Hartley in any particular. She informed me of the approaching event, matrimony with you, and I offered my felicitations to her, as I now extend my heartiest congratulations to you! If I was clumsy in expressing myself, I offer my abject apologies and beg her forgiveness." He bowed, as MacRae, the garrison officers, and the two corporals looked on in amazement. "And now, I must return to my ship, since we weigh anchor at dawn." He bowed again and went out to find Anderson, Raffles and Livie and to take his leave. Pickens did not follow him.

PART II
ILE DE FRANCE

CHAPTER TWELVE

The hounds were in full cry northwestwardly up the Bay of Bengal. *Rapid*, her gun crews standing easy, was positioned a mile and a half off the starboard quarter of the big French schooner, while *Comet* was to leeward just abaft her beam. With the wind steady out of the northeast, the two could instantly counter any move the Frenchman might make to escape, and she would soon run out of sea room against the Sundarbans Coast and the shifting sands off the Ganges Delta. With only an hour of the forenoon watch gone, the hounds were in no haste to close in for the kill; they could take this fox at their leisure.

"Set the flying jib," the Captain called to Lieutenant Dobbs. "Come a point to port," he told the quartermaster. He saw the maneuver accomplished and drifted toward the lee rail.

Rapid was desperately shorthanded after furnishing her share of the prize crews for three French privateers. Every idler in the ship was now distributed among the gun crews. The Captain's eye ran over them, stolid and competent at their stations, and reflected that most of them were well into the second year of their enlistments. Somehow, he would have to convince them to reenlist within the next few months, or else find and train a new crew.

Forward, he saw the round-shouldered figure of Mister Mac-Camy, the second lieutenant, beside the long nine-pounder pivot gun. Larkin, his first lieutenant, together with the entire Sepoy Marine detachment, had been sent into the last prize taken two weeks ago. That ship had been so crammed with men that it was essential she be under resolute command, even with the precaution of distributing her officers and leading seamen among the ships of his squadron. MacCamy had no flair for gunnery, but

Totten, the gunner's mate, would set the sights and lay the gun.

The schooner still showed no colors, but her identity was plain. The alteration of course and additional sail area had almost exactly balanced one another; *Rapid* was closing on her prey, but the relative bearing remained unchanged. In another quarter hour, he might try a ranging shot with the bow chaser. He hoped *Tiger*, the big top-heavy brig with her fourteen twenty-four-pounder carronades, was on station off the delta. An overwhelming show of force might persuade that French captain to surrender without a serious engagement.

Captain Percival Merewether of the Honourable East India Company's Bombay Marine braced himself against the bulwarks, his eye automatically measuring the steady gain on the privateer. It had been an interminable three months at sea, patrolling the eastern approaches to the Hooghly River in the Bay of Bengal, a period of unremitting vigilance and tedious boredom, with the additional weight of responsibility for the Bengal Squadron upon his shoulders. Even the courtesy title of "Commodore," given him as the officer in tactical command, had failed to cheer Merewether's spirits. Fortunately, he thought, this day might conclude the cruise; intelligence had reported only four commerce raiders from Mauritius, though in the past six months they had taken shipping of the value of more than three hundred thousand pounds, and three of them had been captured since the new year.

It was amazing, Merewether thought cynically, how a few thousand pounds, now safely invested in the Company, could change a man's outlook. Last year, a pauper, dependent upon his pay as a captain in the Marine, he had been eager for continued employment at sea; now, after a little luck in the way of prize money, he resented this confinement in a ship at sea. He was approaching middle age, he considered. He had turned twenty-nine last New Year's Day; he had neither wife nor family; and by his own cross-grained stupidity last year had lost to another man the woman he loved.

Inevitably, the thought brought to mind Lady Caroline Austen, niece by marriage of Sir George Barlow, the Acting Governor of India. She was a beautiful woman, with her red-

154

gold hair and stately carriage, younger than he by five years, but widowed since Trafalgar, and the mother of a five-year-old son in England. Sir George and Lady Barlow had almost transparently thrown her in his way, had made him her dinner partner at several of the entertainments during the holiday season while his squadron outfitted for this operation. Lady Barlow had confided that Caroline had been deeply grieved by the loss of her husband, that her family had sent her on this visit to give her a change of scene. Well, in that respect she was in no different category than the other hundreds of young ladies who came out each year to Calcutta, Bombay, or Madras for extended visits, in the hope of finding a husband or escaping an undesirable suitor in England.

Still, Lady Caroline was a different sort of woman, Merewether decided, different from most of the women he had known. She had no fund of small talk to bridge the intervals at dinner and appeared to have only the politest interest in the foibles and scandals of Calcutta society. The second time he had been paired with her at dinner, the man to her right had made some mention of a poet named Walter Scott. It was as though a spillway had opened; she poured forth a torrent of quotation and comment, leaving Merewether silent and forgotten beside her. The next day, he had found some of the works she had mentioned in the canteen at Fort William, and had undertaken to improve his education. It was difficult, he had no ear for poetry, but found Shakespeare a bit more palatable since he could follow the story line. Armed with this knowledge, he was able to lead her on and at least carry on a conversation. During the past three months, he had read more widely through the monotonous days between actions and had even exhausted the small library that Doctor Buttram owned, a souvenir of his days at Cambridge. Probably it was wasted time; he had no idea whether Lady Caroline considered him to be a suitor, or, for that matter, whether he desired to be so considered.

Merewether drifted toward the starboard side, checking the compass as he passed. Almost within range, he decided, measuring the distance with his eyes. He saw Dobbs's expectant gaze and turned aside ignoring him. Against the weather bulwark, his view of the quarry was obstructed, and he soon moved back to leeward.

The thought of Lady Caroline's widowhood was uncomfortable, as was the recollection of her unknown child in England with his grandparents. The title she bore was by courtesy of her late husband, he knew; she had none of her own. If she married him, she would automatically become plain Mrs. Merewether. This thought was even more uncomfortable; it served to resurrect demons he had painfully exorcised last year when he hoped to marry Flora Dean.

There was, he assured himself, no record in the Company, or the Marine, to prove his illegitimacy. His grandfather, the old groom on Lord Spencer's estate in Surrey, had simply signed the articles as guardian of an orphaned twelve-year-old boy, apprenticing him to the ship's husband of the Indiaman, *Dunvegan Castle*. Yet in marriage, there must be some inquiry as to his antecedents. If he had children, they might demand to know their pedigree, even if the wife was discreet enough not to press the point.

He thought of his mother, worn out by the struggle to rear her bastard son, dead at twenty-nine, and wished savagely for a moment that he might find and take revenge upon the man who had wronged her by fathering him. Hellfire! This was almost as absurd as some of the Greek tragedies he had read in translation last month. With an effort, he focused his attention on the privateer; she was within range.

"Sail ho!" came the hail from the masthead. "Two points on the starboard bow." There was a brief pause, then, "Looks like *Tiger*, sir."

"Signals," called Merewether. "To *Comet* and *Tiger*: 'Engage the enemy.'" He shouted forward to MacCamy, "You may fire when ready."

The trap had been sprung. *Tiger* was in a fortunate position to run down before the wind and intercept the Frenchman. With nowhere to go, it would be hopeless for the French captain to fight against these odds. The spiteful, ear-splitting report of the pivot gun cracked out. Merewether caught the splash in the field of his glass just to starboard of the schooner before the

156

powder smoke momentarily obscured his view. Even while the gun crew was sponging out, the Frenchman altered course and came up into the wind. She ran up colors, then hauled them down and hoisted a white flag.

While *Rapid* ran down to starboard, Merewether watched *Comet* round to and station herself a cable's length off the port quarter of the prize, ready for any trick that might be attempted. MacRae, in *Comet*, was an excellent officer, entirely deserving of the promotion he had gained last year at Bombay.

Rapid rounded to, and the port battery was run out, a grim deterrent to any treachery in the mind of the French captain.

"You may take a boarding party, but *Tiger* will furnish the prize crew," Merewether told the hovering Dobbs. *Tiger* had not contributed to a prize crew and still had her full complement of officers. He looked forward and found her almost hull up. "Flag to *Tiger*," he told the quartermaster. " 'Man the prize; Evans is master.' "

The boats from *Comet* and *Rapid* reached the schooner almost simultaneously, just as the prize unaccountably sagged off to leeward, seemingly out of control. Merewether snatched the glass from the rack. The rudder was jammed hard over to port; some diehard had cut the tiller ropes! He saw Dobbs lead a rush aft, lining the Frenchmen on the poop up against the rail, while another party disappeared below. It was only a matter of minutes until he saw the rudder move, midships, then to starboard, while seamen tailed on to sheets and the ship came back under control, hove to again. Evidently only the lines to the wheel had been cut, while the relieving tackles below remained intact. Still, there would be a delay while the boatswain's mates rove new lines to the helm.

Tiger came lumbering down and hove to, hoisting out her launch almost immediately and filling it with the prize crew. Morrison was a good officer in a clumsy, unhandy ship that had been designed to carry the maximum number of guns with the minimum of draft. He heard seven bells strike and decided it would be more than an hour before the schooner was ready to get under way.

"Private, official," Merewether called to the signal quartermaster. " 'Captains come on board.' " With time to waste, it might as well be improved with a brief social gathering over lunch. The sea was calm, and even a conscientious commander could leave his ship for this brief period. "Sangh," he called down the companionway. The little Hindu steward emerged. "Dinner for three, no, four," he said catching sight of Doctor Buttram emerging from his cockpit below. "And set out the spirits as well." He regretted he could not yet authorize the issue of a ration of grog to the crew; with the boarding party away, there would be endless confusion. Better to wait an hour for its return.

Little MacRae was first aboard, a smile creasing his saturnine face as the pipes twittered. Captain Morison, thin and intense, was close behind. In the cabin, Merewether proposed a quick toast, "To His Majesty, God Bless Him, and may this commission soon be ended." The amens echoed about the table; even Doctor Buttram had taken brandy instead of claret.

"Now, gentlemen," continued Merewether, "I am of the opinion that our immediate mission is complete. Sir George and Admiral Pellew had information of four privateers. Thanks to your efforts, they are now ours. Is there a contrary opinion?"

He paused, conscious of the fact that both these officers were older than he in years, if not in experience at sea. He was ready to listen to any recommendation—that actually was all they could offer—but it would have to be exceedingly persuasive to change his mind at this point. He realized again how tired he was, feeling the compelling necessity to escape the prison of command in this ship and of the squadron, if only for a fortnight. "I don't disagree, sir," spoke up MacRae. "I'm down to the last pannikin of lime juice, and I reduced the water ration by a third three days ago."

"Nor I," rumbled Morison in the startling bass voice coming from so spare a figure. "I have enough supplies yet. Took on some from a store ship off the Sandheads last month. But the men are restive. A run ashore would be most welcome, sir, clear the air."

"Agreed, gentlemen. As soon as the Frenchman is ready, we sail for the Hooghly and Calcutta. If the wind holds, we should be off the Sandheads by midnight. Now, another drink before we dine?" Only Buttram declined.

Sangh was clearing the table and the two captains were shuffling their feet in the restive fashion that indicated they would prefer to be dismissed when the messenger knocked.

"Come," invited Merewether.

"Sir, Mister Dobbs and the launch are alongside, and he says, please sir, can Doctor Buttram come on deck."

"Certainly," said Merewether, looking at Buttram. "You may be excused, Doctor. And gentlemen, delightful as this occasion has been, we must be about our duties. Give the gigs a hail," he told the messenger. "And call away the boatswain's mate and side boys."

On deck, waiting for MacRae's gig to hook on the ladder, Merewether was conscious of other activity at the port gangway. Buttram was standing by while a boatswain's mate rigged a whip through a block at the end of the boom. The pipes squealed. He shook MacRae's hand and saw him over the side. Curiosity compelled him to move across the deck as the seamen walked away with the line.

"Handsomely!" shouted the boatswain's mate. " 'Vast heaving; now lower away, handsomely, damn you!"

The object dangling in the cat's cradle at the end of the line was a litter, improvised from planks and canvas and steadied by hand lines at either end. It touched the deck with a barely perceptible thump bringing forth another stream of maledictions from the boatswain's mate.

Lying on the litter was a shadow of a man, every bone outlined under the blackened skin; only the eyes, unnaturally large in the hollow sockets of the skull, appeared to be alive. The eyes moved searchingly back and forth—apparently the man was too weak to move his head—seeking something. Buttram knelt beside him, felt his pulse, his forehead, pulled his lower lip down to expose the gum, then prodded two fingers gently against the abdomen just below the breastbone. The wince was barely noticeable, but then the roving eyes caught sight of Merewether standing behind Buttram.

"Sah!" the croak startled Merewether as though it had come

from a corpse. "I am Lowjee, Havildar in the Third Company, First Bombay Marine Battalion. I have escaped from Mauritius!"

Merewether had heard of no Marine prisoners on Mauritius, but the identity of this man and his bona fides would be simple to confirm once Gunny, Commander of *Rapid*'s Marine force, was back on board. "Very well, Lowjee. You are safe in the Bombay Marine cruiser, *Rapid*. Now, Doctor, see what you can do for the Havildar." The staring eyes rested their gaze a moment on Merewether's scarred face, then closed wearily as Buttram directed the removal of the litter to his sick bay forward.

"Mister Dobbs, may I see you in my cabin once we are under way?" Merewether began. Then he told MacCamy to make sail.

He could see the gigs being hoisted in on *Tiger* and *Comet*, and the preparatory flag was now two-blocked at the masthead of the prize. He remained on deck until the squadron was under way with the Frenchman carefully shepherded along between the ships.

Dobbs knocked and entered half an hour later. "Yes, sir?"

"Have a chair, Mister Dobbs. Tell me what you know about that apparition you brought aboard."

Dobbs settled his thick frame back into the chair, and his pale eyes sought the lamp swinging overhead. He was not the most articulate man aboard, thought Merewether, but he had proved to be a dependable, if unimaginative, officer since he came aboard nine months ago.

"Sir, we made a search of the Frenchie, as always. There was a lazaret aft below a bosun's locker. The hatch was padlocked. Naturally, I broke it open, and found the man inside. I thought he was dead, but then he moved and cried out. The French steward could speak a little English; he said the man was a prisoner, had escaped from Mauritius and stowed away. When he began to starve, he came out and was caught. The captain put him back there, a gill of water and a biscuit a day, to teach the Marine dog a lesson."

It was the quite the longest speech Merewether had ever heard from Dobbs. And yet, there was a story. Buttram would do his best to save the man's life in the meantime.

"Thank you, Dobbs. May I say that I have been most pleased with your performance of duty this cruise and shall say so in my report to Bombay Castle." Dobbs's blunt face was red as he rose, stammered his thanks, and escaped.

Two hours later, Buttram knocked and entered. "Never saw a man in worse condition from scurvy and plain starvation, and still alive," he said cheerfully. "He's a challenge to all the medical science old Doctor Gray tried to teach me. He can't retain water, lime juice, spirits; it all comes right up. So, I've had some sugar teats made. . . ."

"Sugar teats?" demanded Merewether, remembering the soggy rags he had seen protruding from the mouths of grubby infants.

"Well, on the same order, sir. A rag wrapped about a bit of sponge and soaked in sugared lime juice. It keeps the mouth moist, and some liquid is bound to drip into him. If I can get enough into him to strengthen him, he has a chance of life."

"Very well, Doctor. We should be in Calcutta by day after tomorrow night."

The young man's face lighted up. "I hope I may have leave, sir. Jennifer . . ."

"Certainly. Of course, your son might be at the landing to greet you."

"I hope not. I want a full-term child, and I should be with Jennifer when her time comes."

Merewether resisted with difficulty repeating the hoary naval chestnut that the father had to be present when the keel was laid, but not for the launching.

Once Buttram had left, Merewether found himself reading the reports left with him by MacRae and Morison, comparing them with the reports he had completed for each phase of the operation. He must have his own over-all report in hand for the Commodore and Governor-General upon arrival at Calcutta, and with the necessity of being on deck for the ascent of the Hooghly River, it was not too soon to commence. Dusk had fallen and the pilot boat was in sight when he completed the chore.

CHAPTER THIRTEEN

Merewether's estimated time of arrival was in error. It was almost noon the third day when the flotilla came in sight of the anchorage off the dockyard at Calcutta. At the point where *Rapid* had been accustomed to anchor, there was a towering frigate moored bow and stern. Merewether recognized her before he could make out the pennant flying at her masthead: *Pitt*, thirty-six, built and launched two years ago at Bombay by the Parsee shipbuilder, Jamsetjee, and now flagship of Commodore Sir John Waldron, Commandant of the Marine.

"Deck there. Signals!" came the hail from the foretop.

Hamlyn, midshipman of the watch, sprang up the starboard ratlines and focused his glass. Merewether reflected that three months at sea under the demanding eye of Larkin and the heavy-handed tutelage of Dobbs had erased some of young Hamlyn's sulky reluctance to do a day's work at sea.

"No salutes," Hamlyn translated. "Captains come on board."

It was typical of Waldron, Merewether thought, a practical man, certainly entitled to the honor, to avoid the waste of powder and disturbance of the native population. He was happy that he would be able to report that Mister Hamlyn, son of the Commodore's dearest friend, was shaping up and might become a competent warrant officer. He had opened his mouth to give the order, when he heard Hamlyn's command to the signal quartermaster to repeat the signal to the squadron. The boy was learning.

Rapid came to anchor and carried out a stern anchor. Only then did Merewether order the gig over. He remained on deck to see the other ships moored, the prize safely between *Comet* and *Tiger*, the Bombay Marine ensign flying proudly over the tricolor. Sangh had his full-dress uniform laid out. He came on deck five minutes later, buckling on his sword, and descended to the gig as the pipe wailed.

Waldron, in company with Commodore Land, Master Attendant at Calcutta, and Tollett, his flag captain, received the three officers in his cabin. Broad-shouldered and balding, he was not distinguished in appearance, but his abilities were unquestioned.

"Welcome, gentlemen. I see the Bengal Squadron has completed its mission. Now, where do I employ you?"

Merewether was stricken. He glanced at MacRae and Morison, standing impassively by his side. No comfort there. "Sir, I think we must refit, perhaps careen, clean our bottoms. . . ."

Waldron laughed. "Tollett, take those reports from Merewether. Be seated, gentlemen. This occasion calls for a round of toasts, and I want an informal report before I have to read those documents."

The affair was soon over. In an hour, the toasts had been drunk, details of the capture of four French privateers extracted from Merewether, MacRae and Morison, and a light luncheon consumed. Waldron dismissed the group with a cheery, "I shall see you gentlemen tonight."

On deck Commodore Land explained, "Sir Thomas Jeffrey is entertaining, a dinner for the Honourable Alfred Robert Percy, one of his old friends in the Foreign Office. Since your ships were reported from downstream, I am directed to invite you gentlemen to the affair. It begins at ten." The Commodore's barge hooked on at the gangway, and he went over the side as the pipes squealed.

The dockyard work boat was pulling away as Merewether's gig came alongside *Rapid*. Hamlyn handed him a sealed letter. Forward, the purser and his mates were hauling the mailbags from the gangway to the shade of an awning, to be opened and sorted. Merewether continued below, cast off hat, sword and stock, and seated himself at the desk.

The superscription was in the handwriting of Lady Caroline, he realized, as he broke the seal and unfolded the sheet.

"*Dear Percival*." Well, that was a twist. Lady Caroline had been quite formal in her addresses to him, usually "Commodore" or "My dear sir." It was, however, no more than a note of invitation to foregather at the Governor-General's palace an hour before the dinner, since he was to be her escort for the evening. Merewether sat a moment looking at the brief note, trying to

163

read some other, deeper meaning into it, then laughed at himself. He shouted for the messenger to summon the officers and warrant officers. Liberty would be granted in an hour, but he wanted the task of refitting *Rapid* to commence tomorrow morning.

Doctor Buttram had gone ashore with the mail boat, he soon discovered.

Lady Caroline received Merewether in her sitting room, extending her hand with apparent warmth. There was time for only the barest murmur of amenities before Sir George and Lady Barlow entered.

"Ah, Commodore, we are delighted at your safe return, and most successful, too." Servants came in with wines and spirits; the party was joined by MacIntosh and Locksley, secretaries to the Governor-General, the Captain of the Guard, and three anonymous young ladies. Amidst the chatter, Merewether did his best to be attentive and responsive to Lady Caroline. Her eyes were darker in this light than he remembered, but the red-gold hair glittered in the candlelight, and her complexion was unblemished. Truly a beautiful woman, widow or no, he decided, wondering again if the "Percival" of the note meant she considered him a serious suitor. He was by no means sure of his own feelings and desires, he thought, finishing off the glass of dry sack.

Sir George appeared to be more reserved tonight than Merewether had ever seen him at such an affair as this. Ordinarily, he would dominate the occasion, but now he sat in a corner, content to sip his wine without joining in the conversation. He kept his eye on the clock, however, and at a quarter of the hour, decisively led the party out to the carriages, to arrive at the entrance to Sir Thomas's residence on the stroke of ten.

Merewether, with Lady Caroline on his arm, took station in accordance with the whispered directions of Locksley. He was conscious of a blur of color, the sounds of violin and flute in the distance becoming audible as the buzz of conversation ceased with the entrance of Sir George. He soon found himself making

164

his bow to Sir Thomas and Lady Jeffrey, and in turn, being presented to the guest of honor.

The Honourable Alfred Robert Percy was an alert man in his middle forties, with regular, unremarkable features that just missed being handsome. "Ah, yes, Commodore," he said briskly. "Thomas here was telling me of your voyage to China last year; most interesting. I should like to talk to you at some point. I was out there almost twenty-five years ago and slipped into Canton myself."

"Indeed, sir? I don't imagine it has changed very much. But then, I saw very little of the city."

"It will be interesting to compare notes, however, and now I see Thomas is ready to dine," Percy said in dismissal.

There was dancing later, and Lady Caroline did not lack for partners. In her stately, but graceful way, she appeared to possess boundless energy. Sweating under his full-dress coat from his exertions, Merewether finally sought out the cloakroom he remembered and found it empty. Unbuttoning the coat, he opened it wide to catch the breeze at the window. He heard the door close behind him.

"Well, Commodore, will you share a bit of that breeze?" said Percy, unbuttoning his coat. "I'd forgotten how hot Calcutta can be in the spring."

"Certainly, sir," replied Merewether moving aside.

"It was in eighty-three that I made a voyage out to China as supercargo in my cousin's ship, *Carlton Castle*. I had some notion of a career in the Company, being a younger son, but when I got back to England I found a place in the Foreign Office, and I've been in that line ever since." He glanced sideways at Merewether. The breeze was serving its purpose: the shirt no longer stuck to his ribs.

"I was ashore in the Company factory outside Canton when I became acquainted with a young Chinese who spoke very passable English, not pidgin. He was being educated as a scholar and was serving as something of an apprentice to the Co-hong at the time. I invited him out to the ship to examine our sextants, charts and chronometer. In turn, he invited me to his home. He dressed me in a robe, stained my face and hands, put a wig and cap on me, and I went along." Percy laughed deprecatingly. "Don't know what would have happened had I been caught."

"I was tried by a Court of Inquiry at Bombay Castle last year for the same thing," said Merewether.

"Yes, I know, but you accomplished your mission and then came clear. . . . I spent three days ashore, pretending to be a deaf-mute, attended two banquets, and saw most of the city. I found that Chinese family most hospitable." Percy looked again at Merewether with a slight smile. "My host even provided a companion for my bed."

Well, thought Merewether, customs did not change much in twenty-five years in China. "I was treated to very much the same courtesies, sir," he managed.

"I thought as much," said Percy with a chuckle. "We must discuss the specifics of Canton at greater length, and now, I must go back to Thomas and George. A guest of honor should at least be visible. By the way, Commodore, what part of England are you from?"

"London, sir, born and bred there until I went to sea."

"Oh, but you don't have the accent of Bow Bells. This is only the second time I've encountered the name Merewether. Not a very common one."

Merewether turned and looked at Percy as he buttoned his coat. The man had a faraway expression on his face, staring out into the darkness.

"It's been thirty years, yes, thirty years this month, for I celebrated my sixteenth birthday there, got a beautiful fowling piece as a gift, still use it when I get back home. I spent the spring holidays with my cousins, the Spencers, in Surrey. I was mad about horses, still am for that matter. There was a groom in charge of their stables named Merewether, a quite knowledgeable horseman. I must have worried him half to death with questions, what kind of tack was best, whether the Eclipse or Matchem lines were better stayers — my family bred from Eclipse. I did learn a great deal from him, and he had a pretty little daughter, just my age. Ah, we had a wonderful time, my cousins and I, that spring!"

Merewether felt a hand of ice seize his heart. He stared at

this man for a moment, seeing the bright blue eyes, the hair, once brown, now graying, the regular features, not scarred or powder burned. He did not trust himself to speak, but turned away, held the door open for Percy to precede him into the corridor, and escaped to search out Lady Caroline.

It was three in the morning when Merewether brought Lady Caroline back through the gates, past the sleepy guard, to be admitted to the entrance hall by the Indian doorman. His hopes of a goodnight kiss were dashed as he saw the door to the left leading into the library open, light streaming from it, and the shadow of Sir George looming in the doorway.

"Goodnight, my dear Lady Caroline," Merewether murmured, bowing over her hand. "It was a delightful evening." He straightened up as she passed through the curtained entrance at the end of the hall, conscious of the presence of the Governor-General.

"Come in a moment, Merewether," said Barlow.

In the library, a cigar smoldered on a plate, and a silver coffee service rested on the long table.

"Coffee?"

Merewether poured a cup and took the chair indicated.

"Hell of an hour to be about," growled Sir George. "But I couldn't sleep anyway. Different for you young sprouts, dance all night, and none the worse for the next day." He picked up the cigar, looked at it critically, and stubbed it out on the plate. "I'll not deny it, I was upset by the news. I thought Burghley would hold his ground, but he switched, went over to Minto lock, stock and barrel. He'll regret throwing mud in the eye of Wellesley someday, but too late for me."

Merewether felt blank. He did not understand what had happened and drank a bit of the coffee as he saw that no reply was necessary.

"It happened last July, news only reached me in January, but it will probably be a good while before the appointment is publicly confirmed, and even longer before the new Governor-General reaches Calcutta," continued Barlow. "Of course, once the news gets about, my authority is crippled. Everyone will be looking forward to the new man and paying little enough attention to the Acting Governor. Only bright spot in the affair, my people managed to get a commitment to commission me Governor of Madras. I'll at least be able to relieve that popinjay, Bentinck, there."

Light dawned on Merewether. Sir George had been denied the permanent appointment as Governor-General of India! He felt a curious regret; the man was cold, hard, merciless in many respects, certainly not a likable sort, but during the past year he had acquired a great deal of respect for Barlow and his abilities. The man was honest and courageous, doing his best to govern India in the interests of King and Company. He finished the coffee.

"I guess I've come a long way, at that," said Barlow slowly. "My father was a silk mercer in London. He did manage to give me a decent education, and I've made the most of it. But Percy told me tonight that counted heavily against me, swung Burghley over in fact; they concluded they wanted a blue-blooded baron to follow Cornwallis and Wellesley." He shook his head. "I always thought the man and his abilities counted, not his pedigree. At least I told myself that." He shook his head again.

Merewether realized that commiseration at this point would be presumptuous and decided to change the subject.

"Sir—Your Excellency—this man Percy I met tonight, who is he?"

"Another politician mainly, holds an appointment in the Foreign Office with the rank of under secretary. He has served in Italy, Sweden, Portugal and Spain, so Thomas tells me. His mission out here is ambiguous to me. He came through the Mediterranean and overland to the Red Sea, only ten weeks from London. I suspect he represents the Minto interests and is here principally to look over my shoulder for the time."

"I mean his family," said Merewether trying to appear offhand.

"Oh," said Sir George looking at him sharply. "He's a younger son of Lord Percy of Bennington, if that's what you want to know. The family is a collateral offshoot of the Percys of Northumberland. The title was granted by Charles the Second for services during the Restoration, not an ancient one as such things go, though his family is very old in England. His mother was a Spencer, and his brother holds the title now, with male issue, so Percy is not in the line of succession.

"Hotspur's family!" Merewether thought, then said, "He was quite courteous to me tonight. He told me he had been in Canton some years ago under very much the same conditions as I was and wanted to talk further about China. I was curious."

Sir George stifled a yawn. "Well, Merewether, I shouldn't keep you any longer. I feel as though I might sleep now. This conversation is entirely private, you understand."

Sir George stood up in dismissal, and Merewether found his way back to his tonga and thence to the ship. Two bells of the morning watch struck as he came alongside. No more than time for a nap before he must be up and about, he thought wearily, hanging his clothing on a chair and stretching out on the bed.

He had barely dozed off when he came wide awake with a start. He turned over, sought sleep again, and found it quite impossible. The evening had created tensions that made sleep hopeless at this point. He felt as though he were on the verge of some great discovery, if he were only able to think the matter through. Gray light was visible through the skylight as he heaved himself off the bed and sat at his desk staring into the gloom.

The coincidences were devilishly convincing. He remembered his drab, gentle mother, toiling in the kitchen at Bellflower House on Belgrave Street until she died quietly in a consumptive coma. He had been twelve and she twenty-nine at the time. Her father, an old groom with a close-trimmed white beard, had come up to London to take the coffin and Merewether back to Lord Spencer's estate in Surrey. The burial service in a country churchyard had been read hastily by a rural curate, with only his grandfather and two other men, who Merewether understood were his uncles, and their wives present. The next day, his grandfather had brusquely taken him back to London and signed the articles that made him a ship's boy in the Indiaman, *Dunvegan Castle*.

Merewether rubbed his smarting eyes with his knuckles. The

reminiscence last night by Percy of his visit to Surrey was exactly thirty years ago this month, and he was then sixteen, as was the "pretty little daughter" of the groom, Merewether. He had turned twenty-nine last New Year's, and suddenly Merewether was convinced: he had seen and conversed with his father.

This conclusion caused no exaltation in Merewether's soul. He approached and examined it warily; there were enough other alternatives in what might have occurred in the affairs of a sixteen-year-old girl thirty years ago in the springtime to make the matter by no means certain. But, the physical resemblance was there—eyes, hair, features, even the manner in which Percy carried himself. And the name "Percival," just such a variant of Percy as a romantic young girl might bestow upon her bastard son in memory of the cavalier who had seduced and deserted her—it was God damned circumstantial, he told himself in the gray daylight, as four bells sounded.

Sangh came in with a tray of breakfast. It was then, without conscious logic, that Merewether decided he would declare himself as a serious suitor for the hand of Lady Caroline.

CHAPTER FOURTEEN

Larkin, the prize crew and the Marine detachment from the third prize came on board just before noon. They were sweat-soaked and dirty, a week's growth of beard on their faces.

"God, Captain," Larkin told him, refusing the chair lest he soil it, "It was like guarding the door to a lion's den. Sixty men to control two hundred!"

"It was all we could spare," Merewether told him sharply. "That was why I sent Gunny with you."

"Of course, Captain, but the Frenchies had two enterprising able seamen—we couldn't identify them till this morning—and they made four serious tries at retaking the ship, the last at five bells in the midwatch this morning. We've been at anchor off Fort William for a week while they built more prison quarters ashore. That major," Larkin snorted at the memory, "said he couldn't spare even two files of soldiers to give us a little relief."

"Any casualties?" inquired Merewether.

"Five men, including two marines, wounded; none serious. The marines killed eight Frenchmen and wounded seven more this morning with a volley, after they broke open a hatch forward and managed to get quite a party on deck, armed with axes and capstan bars. We were standing watch and watch, and Gunny was on deck"—Larkin mopped his brow—"Fort William took the prisoners, and Commodore Land sent a shipkeeping party. They'll be busy awhile, the Frenchmen made a holy mess of everything below."

"Very well, take a rest. I have given orders to MacCamy and Dobbs for maintenance and replacement, but there will be no supplies before tomorrow."

Larkin mopped his brow again, pale blue eyes above the stubble of beard glancing wearily from Merewether out the port to the dockyard and back. "Thank you, Captain."

Merewether concluded that a tour of duty that could affect the steel-and-rawhide Larkin in this fashion must have been exceptional. If time permitted before another operation, Larkin should have a holiday. He turned to the stack of requisitions as the purser came in with more.

Late in the afternoon, Merewether called away the gig. He felt again as though he should explode unless he escaped the confines of *Rapid*. A drink and dinner at the club, probably with his old friend MacLellan, would help to clear the air.

At the arsenal, he could see no sign of MacLellan until a European artificer pointed far down to the other end of the building. The clang of hammers on anvils, the whit-whet of two-man rip saws cutting through teak, and the buzz and shriek of metal on grindstones combined in a deafening cacophony as Merewether threaded his way through men and machinery.

MacLellan, his first lieutenant of a year ago in *Rapid*, and now in command of the arsenal, was standing behind a Chinese artisan. The man was pushing a handle on a pumplike mechanism back and forth. The device was inserted through a hole in the side of a heavy box. MacLellan's lips were counting silently with each stroke of the handle. Just as Merewether came up, MacLellan touched the shoulder of the Chinese.

"Two thousand!" he shouted over the noise. "Enough!" MacLellan stepped around to the back of the box, reached in and unscrewed something. He emerged with a metal flask which he shifted rapidly from hand to hand as though it was hot. He laid the flask beside three others on a bench, and only then saw Merewether.

"Ah, Captain," he shouted. "Welcome, and come outside!"

In the shade outside the building, the din subsided to a gentle mutter. MacLellan mopped the sweat from his big red face and took the hand Merewether extended. This big Scots officer possessed one of the most inventive and ingenious minds Merewether had ever encountered. Indeed, Merewether still was using the accurate adjustable sights that MacLellan had designed on the long nine-pounder pivot guns that served not only as bow and stern chasers, but as broadside guns as well for *Rapid*. Those sights had earned him some thousands of pounds of prize money last year—though, of course, MacLellan had shared in it, too.

"You know, Captain, that first prize you sent in, *Majeure*...."

"Yes, the brig."

"I inspected her ordnance, of course, and found two cases of muskets in her armory, never been opened. There was German lettering outside, must have been some loot Boney took in Austria and put up for sale to the privateers. I was curious to see the quality of Austrian arms and opened one." MacLellan paused, lips pursed portentously. Merewether wondered what he was getting at.

"Captain, they weren't muskets at all; they are air rifles!"

"What, air rifles? I never heard ..."

"Rifles, sir, in which the ball is propelled by air," MacLellan continued. "Those flasks I have just filled form the butt stock of the gun and hold enough pressure to fire at least twenty shots at very near the velocity of a musket ball, with little noise, no flash and no smoke."

"Oh," said Merewether, "I see." He made an effort to show interest in this phenomenon which was obviously of such importance to his friend, MacLellan.

"I had heard of them, of course. Old Benziger, the German clockmaker in London, saw a test of them in Vienna twenty years or so ago. They were invented by a Swiss named Bartolome Girandoni and actually used by Austria against the Turks. These must have been stored away in some arsenal and then captured by Boney. I have twenty-four of them, each with two extra air flasks and a pump. I don't believe they've ever been used," Mac-Lellan said with satisfaction. "You are just in time to witness a test of one."

The shade was pleasant, there was even a bit of breeze off the river to evaporate the sweat, and it was much too early to visit the club. Merewether accepted the invitation.

MacLellan came back carrying what appeared to be a conventional musket, except that its butt stock was one of the metal flasks. He snapped his knuckles against it and it rang like a bell.

"There were some ordnance instructions printed in German in the case. My master mechanic is from Hanover and could read them. They said, two thousand strokes of the pump for full capacity. I have no idea of the pressure, and so we filled them in the box in case the flask should explode." MacLellan's Scottish burr had thickened with excitement.

He took a pouch out of his pocket and poured gleaming, smooth-cast lead musket balls into his hand. "Even have the molds, fifty-one caliber," he said. "It holds twenty balls, but I shall fire only ten." He dropped the balls into a metal tube located at the right side of the breech, pointed the barrel up, moved a crossbolt back and forth, and then pulled back the hammer with an audible click.

Merewether became aware of a buzz of conversation and looked around. A dozen European artificers and twice that many Indians had ranged themselves along the wall of the arsenal building. The same little Chinese artisan who had sailed with him to the Andaman Islands, and later to Bombay last year, came trotting toward MacLellan. He saw that a plank, tall as a man, a foot wide, and an inch thick had been erected across the yard some fifty paces distant.

MacLellan put the piece to his shoulder, sighted, and pressed the trigger. There was a light, high-pitched "whap" that did not disturb persons walking along the river path a few yards away—quite different from the forthright flash, roar and cloud of smoke of a musket. Merewether could see the hole in the center of the board, a foot from the top, daylight showing through. MacLellan raised the gun, manipulated the lock mechanism, and fired again. A second hole appeared beside the first, and he continued to fire until the tube holding the balls was empty. Less than half a minute had elapsed from the first shot. It was miraculous! The plank was cleanly pierced by each ball in a pattern about six inches in diameter.

"Not very good shooting," grumbled MacLellan. "But then, I can improve these sights. The velocity and striking force compares very favorably with the service musket, I think."

He took the air rifle back inside the arsenal building as the artisans gathered about to examine the target. The bell at the dockyard gatehouse tolled the end of the working day as Merewether waited for MacLellan to get his hat and coat.

Merewether and a board of officers from the dockyard concluded that *Rapid*'s bottom was not so foul as to require careening. The fresh water of the Hooghly would improve it even more by killing off the barnacles. Standing and running rigging were renewed, and with the assistance of a legion of Indians, the sailmaker was cutting a complete new suit of canvas in the sail loft ashore.

Commodore Sir James Waldron remained at Calcutta, lazily, he said, awaiting the southwest monsoon before he continued east on his tour of inspection.

Larkin was granted his leave and improved it by hunting tigers up the river in Bengal, bringing back four magnificent skins as proof of his marksmanship with the long Kentucky rifle.

Doctor Buttram had come racing up the ladder this morning, his face one radiant smile, with the breathless report, "A daughter, sir, prettiest girl you ever saw!"

"And Lady Jennifer?"

"Fine, sir, fine! We've named her Catherine Anne after her grandmothers."

"Well, congratulations, Doctor. We must drink to the young lady and her father, if you'll be my guest at lunch," said Merewether, wondering what it must be like to be a father. "And now, whatever happened to that Havildar that came aboard from the Frenchman?"

"Oh, he's improving. The sugar teats worked fine. He retains solids now and can sit up, though he is still quite weak. With the repairs on deck finished, I'll move him up under an awning, sir."

"Good. Is he strong enough for an interview yet?"

"I think so, Captain," said Buttram slowly. "I don't want to tire him, and then he has lost most of his teeth—just fell out from the scurvy."

"Tomorrow will be soon enough," Merewether told him in dismissal. "I want Gunny present, and he is over at Fort William today."

Below in the pleasant draft from the windsails, Merewether considered how almost two weeks of freedom to leave the ship at will had improved his perspective. The last few days at sea had been torment, but after a few hours ashore now, he found himself as anxious to get back aboard as he had been to escape its confines. It was one of the penalties of command, he decided, the compelling, continuous necessity to assure himself that all was well with the ship.

He thought of the orders issued by Commodore Waldron last week. MacRae, in *Comet*, would sortie south tomorrow to find the Royal Navy squadron east of Ceylon, deliver dispatches, and then show the flag of the Marine up the Coromandel Coast, at Pondichéry, Madras and Ganjam. There were still Company packets and country ships holed up along the coast in fear of the French. Morison, in *Tiger*, would sail east in company with *Pitt* to the Strait, and then return along the westbound shipping lanes to Calcutta. Only *Rapid* was still without orders, but the Bengal Squadron had been effectively disbanded. Merewether felt no regret at the loss of his courtesy title of "Commodore," but the lack of orders for *Rapid* was ominous. Pray God, it would not be the furnace of the Persian Gulf!

Merewether's thoughts shifted abruptly to Lady Caroline. He

would see her tonight for the seventh time in thirteen days. He felt a thrill of anticipation; her kisses night before last had been passionate. He had tried to tell himself that she was a woman of experience, a widow, not a trembling maid. But it made no difference; the resolve he had made two weeks ago at dawn solidified. Tonight, risking rebuff and ridicule, he intended to ask Caroline for her hand in marriage.

Merewether was still stunned. It must be halfway through the midwatch, he computed, but he would not strike a light to see the time. He had been back on board at least two hours. The proposal, once hesitatingly ventured, had been almost instantly accepted.

Sir George and Lady Barlow had offered their felicitations and congratulations, with bumpers of sparkling wine to toast the happy couple. Sir George had called him aside later to explain that Lady Caroline had no dowry or fortune of her own; her living was for life or widowhood, and the corpus was entailed upon her son. This was a minor relief to Merewether; Calcutta and Marine gossip would have no peg upon which to hang.

Lady Barlow told him that, by agreement with her sister, she stood *in locus parenti* to Lady Caroline and planned to announce the betrothal a week hence at a reception and dinner.

"That Minto may arrive at any time now," she said, curling her bitter mouth. "I hope to have the wedding reception here. No need for a long engagement, neither of you are children."

The one other thing Merewether remembered of that hectic two hours of festivity and plans was the expression on Caroline's face. Under the crown of red-gold hair, the trembling lower lip and luminous eyes fairly shouted her love to him across the room. Her stately reserve had vanished, and she was plainly and simply a woman in love. He hoped he could reciprocate enough. He promised himself he would justify her love and felt an unaccustomed tenderness well up in his breast. Suddenly, he wondered what that man, Percy—his father?—would think of this marriage.

CHAPTER FIFTEEN

Buttram had the Havildar on deck in a litter, screened from the sun and occasional showers, but open to the variable breezes that forecast the southwest monsoon. His arms and legs still appeared to be no more than sticks covered by skin, but the eyes, which had appeared so disproportionately large in his face two weeks ago, seemed to have shrunk. Jemadar Gunny, of the Marine detachment in *Rapid,* stood by impassively.

"Remember, Captain, the man has lost most of his teeth, he is still quite weak, and he may not be able to speak distinctly," said Buttram.

"Very well, Doctor. Now, you, tell me your name, rank and organization."

The reply was indistinct, a whistling note overlaying the words, but intelligible.

"Sah, I am Lowjee, Havildar in the Third Company, First Bombay Marine Battalion. I have escaped from Mauritius!"

Almost the same words he had uttered when first brought aboard *Rapid,* Merewether remembered.

"Tell me how you came to be on Mauritius," Merewether urged.

"Sah, my platoon was in *Camel,* transport, with two companies of Sepoys last August, bound for Mangalore from Bombay. It was said we were to reinforce the garrison there after the mutiny at Vellore." The indistinct voice failed, and the man closed his eyes. Buttram leaned forward, gaze intent upon him, then the man opened his eyes and continued. "A French ship captured us, sah, and we were taken to Mauritius." He closed his eyes again, and Buttram motioned to the Indian boy-of-all-work he had brought on board last week to spell his assistants while they were on leave.

The boy picked up a cup of lime juice and held it to the man's lips. He swallowed twice and lay back, licking his lips, the shrunken, toothless gums exposed. After a moment, the man continued.

177

"The Frenchmen offered us our freedom if we would enlist in their militia. Many of the soldiers did. Not a single marine enlisted, though they starved and beat us and set us to breaking stones for roads!" The man's eyes flashed, and he raised his head to look proudly at Merewether.

"How many of your men were alive when you escaped?"

"Thirty-one, sah. Nine had died."

"And where are they confined, Lowjee?"

"Three miles north of Port Louis, sah, in a stockade near Tombeau Bay. When I escaped, I thought to stow away in the American ship bound for Madras. Alas, it had left, and the French privateer was in its berth."

"And when was this?"

"Three months ago, sah."

"Very well, Lowjee," said Merewether. "I am glad you are gaining strength. I shall report your story to Commodore Waldron."

"Thank you, sah." The Havildar lay back and closed his eyes. Merewether nodded to Gunny and went aft.

"Sah," said the Jemadar a quarter of an hour later, the gray in his hair and beard quite visible now under the skylight. "I have seen this man at Bombay Castle. Two of my men have served under him, and another is from the same village. He is no spy and tells the truth."

"Thank you, Gunny. I am of the same opinion." The erect, military figure about-faced and marched out.

Merewether leaned back in his chair and gave the matter consideration. The rescue of a man who claimed to be a noncommissioned officer of the Bombay Marine Battalion had, of course, been included in the report he had submitted to Commodore Waldron, with the footnote that his physical condition precluded questioning. Now, it appeared some thirty other marines were imprisoned by the French but remained loyal to the service under the severest treatment. He had not heard of the loss of *Camel,* but Sir John would know of it. The matter must be reported, he decided, as he found paper in the desk, lifted the lid of the inkwell, and took the pen from the shot bowl. A half hour later he dropped the packet into the pouch to be delivered to the flagship by the guard-mail boat in the usual routine.

"No, by God!" exploded Commodore Waldron. "I will not delay until the Royal Navy and the powers that be decide to take Mauritius!"

Tollett, the flag captain, showed his dismay. "But, sir . . ."

"No buts, Tollett. If I were not already committed to the east, I should go myself. The Bombay Marine takes care of its own. Those marines are suffering for their loyalty to the Crown and Company, and I say we rescue them!"

Tollett subsided in his chair with an injured expression. Merewether, sitting beside him with Commodore Land to his right, thought Tollett's presentation had been entirely logical. Only thirty-one Sepoy marines involved, at last account three months ago, and the island was sure to be taken within the next year.

"There's a break in the reefs along the west coast giving entrance to Tombeau Bay, and the camp appears to be on its south shore," continued Waldron. "A ship can edge in close after nightfall and land a party of marines. Much simpler than a cutting-out expedition. Such a prison camp will not be well defended from outside, and knowing the Creole militia, I'm sure the ones on duty will not be too alert. Should be an absolute surprise!" Sir John's eyes were flashing, his hand whacking the desk to emphasize his points. "Only a matter of two hours or so for you, Merewether, once you reach the island."

Merewether was not surprised. He had anticipated something of the sort ever since Midshipman Hamlyn had delivered the message an hour ago to report on board *Pitt*. He wondered how he could explain to Caroline and Lady Barlow that an important figure on the betrothal party next week would be absent. It was not too early, he consoled himself, for Caroline to learn the realities of the fortunes of war in the Bombay Marine.

Waldron was continuing. "Naturally, you'll keep this Havildar on board; he may even be strong enough to guide the landing force by the time you reach Mauritius."

A voyage of six thousand miles, Merewether thought, for thirty-one men, less those who might have died under punishment or from disease in the past three months. Still, this was a matter of high principle—one man or a thousand, it made no difference. As the Commodore had said, the Marine took care of its own, European or Indian, and demanded in return the very loyalty that had brought these marines to their present straits.

Commodore Land spoke up. "I think we can get the balance of your supplies and water aboard today and tomorrow. I think you may get under way by day after tomorrow. Soon enough, sir?" he asked Waldron.

"Oh, yes," replied the Commodore. "It's going to be unsettled for a week or so anyway, what with the southwest monsoon setting in. I'll have your orders delivered by noon," he told Merewether in dismissal.

Caroline was merely stricken; Lady Barlow was furious, but she received no encouragement for her complaints from Sir George. He told her flatly that this was a private matter within the Marine, and of no concern to Government or Company. The betrothal party would be held, and the announcement made in the absence of one of the principals. It was even a minor relief to Merewether to escape the glittering crush, the knowing eyes, the simpering or falsely hearty congratulations that he had witnessed at a similar affair before Doctor Buttram's wedding last year. In any event, he should be back before the tentative date for the wedding the third week in June.

Merewether came into Commodore Land's headquarters in the dockyard the next afternoon to pick up the Admiralty chart of Mauritius, last corrected in 1803. There should have been little change in four years, but the information was still sketchy, he found, as he looked at the reefs indicated along the west coast, north of Port Louis, and the gap that permitted entrance to Tombeau Bay. It was uncertain, from the few soundings indicated, if he could anchor off that coast close enough in to permit a quick trip with the boat. It might be more satisfactory to rig the drogue and supplement its drag with the second launch towing *Rapid* into the wind. As Waldron said, it should be for not much more than two hours, provided he could edge in close enough.

"Bad luck," said the voice of MacLellan behind him. Merewether had imparted his happy secret and had asked MacLellan to stand up with him at the ceremony. "But ye should be back in plenty of time"—he paused and winked—"for the great event."

"I'm only concerned about Caroline's feelings for my desertion of her this week," Merewether said anxiously. "It's a bobtailed announcement party if the groom isn't present."

"Never fear," replied MacLellan. "Ye'll never be missed. All eyes will be on the joyous bride-to-be. The groom is of no more account on such an occasion than a teat on a boar hog." He laughed, and then sobered. "Captain, you'll be my guest at the club tonight? I've a bit of a suggestion to make."

"I shall be delighted, though I have a later engagement with Caroline."

After an afternoon of interviews with the officers and warrant officers as to the state of readiness of *Rapid,* the glass of gin was delicious, and the common room in the club was dim and cool. MacLellan lowered the glass of Scots whisky, smacked his lips, and set it down.

"Good, Captain, good! And now my suggestion. You know the air rifles I showed you? Well, this morning I presented a petition to the Prize Court for valuation before condemnation— I made the appraisal myself—and obtained a decree awarding the rifles to the Marine at five pounds each, complete. What it means is, the Marine has bought the rifles in advance of the condemnation and sale of the prize because of urgent need for them."

"What urgent need?" inquired Merewether.

"Why your landing force, certainly. One musket shot would bring down the whole garrison of Port Louis on your party, and cold steel might not reach far enough." MacLellan sipped his drink and continued. "I had Gunny and the Marine detachment over this afternoon, gave them full instructions on the weapons, and let each man fire five shots. With the two spare air flasks, they'll have sixty shots a man before they need to recharge the air."

"Well, I'm damned." Merewether was nettled. It had not occurred to him to demand the use of the almost noiseless weapons for his mission.

*

181

Lady Caroline was both warm and sad that last evening. Her reserve had apparently melted for good at his proposal two nights ago, and she accepted his attentions with fervor. Merewether suspected that he might have had her, wedding or no, but that was not the way he wanted this marriage to commence. He still felt no all-consuming passion for her, not at all the madness for Flora Dean that had possessed him last fall on the voyage back from Bombay. Rather he had a gentler emotion, one of tenderness, a desire to protect and cherish this splendid woman. He sensed her loneliness, that she had lost a husband and was separated from her child — he still felt a pang of jealousy at the thought of either — and that she was in love with him, scarred face or no. He had made a discovery: When a woman truly loves a man, it is difficult for him not to respond.

They parted at two in the morning. "Take care, my dear, my love," Caroline whispered.

"I shall, Caroline. I shall count the hours." He kissed her again and resolutely strode out to the tonga.

CHAPTER SIXTEEN

Close-hauled against the southwest monsoon, *Rapid* made a long reach, steering as near south as she could, to pick up the southeast trades near ten degrees south latitude, then ran down almost to twenty-five degrees south, before she went about to make the approach to the west coast of Mauritius. Almost four weeks, commencing with squalls and rain, and then fine weather. The heat was not oppressive at sea. Lieutenant Dobbs was developing into as competent a navigator as MacRae, and Midshipman Hamlyn was able to stand a complete watch under the cold blue eye of Larkin without prompting. Merewether relaxed and enjoyed the cruise, spending long night watches on deck, sometimes dozing in the canvas chair rigged at the weather bulwark or carrying on a desultory conversation with Larkin, or MacCamy, or Dobbs, or Doctor Buttram, or even Mister Hamlyn. He thought a great deal about Caroline and watched the calendar anxiously. The voyage back with the southeast trades and then the southwest monsoon would be much quicker than this roundabout, slow trip south, he calculated. Finally, the noon sights put *Rapid* squarely on the latitude of Mauritius; longitude was more uncertain, but Merewether was sure he was west of the island. He changed course to east-northeast a half east and called Briggs, boatswain's mate, aft.

"Do you know a man on this ship with better eyesight than you?" he demanded.

Briggs scratched his head a moment. "No, sir," he replied.

"All right, take the glass. Now I want you right at the hounds of the mainmast. The island has tall mountains, and they say a cloud hangs over the peak of the tallest at all times. It could be" —Merewether hesitated—"anywhere from dead ahead to the starboard quarter. Sing out the moment you sight it."

Briggs took the glass, and went, agile as a monkey, up the ratlines. It was five bells in the afternoon watch when the hail came, "Land ho! One point on the starboard bow."

Merewether held on course. It was extremely unlikely that anyone should be on one of the peaks barely visible from the masthead and even unlikelier that *Rapid*'s royals could be identified at that distance. When the peak bore due east, Merewether hoved to. With this fair breeze, it would be a matter of less than four hours to run in.

An hour later the Marine detachment formed up on deck for inspection. By the side of Gunny as he passed down the rigid ranks was Havildar Lowjee, still thin and toothless, but in health again after five weeks at sea. He would go ashore with the landing force to guide it to the prison camp. Twenty men carried the air rifles, with two extra air flasks, a pump and bullet pouch each at their belts. The other ten men of the party carried an assortment of pikes, axes and crowbars, with coils of line slung over their shoulders.

"Very well, Gunny," Merewether told him. "See that they are fed. I shall get under way at sunset."

Dobbs and Hamlyn were in charge of the boat. Muffled oars

were a nuisance, Merewether decided, and of no value approaching a shore upon which surf broke. He called the officers into his cabin just before sunset.

"Gentlemen, you know your mission. I shall accompany the landing force, but it is entirely under the command of Gunny in the execution of the attack. The camp is less than half a mile inland. Two hours should be sufficient to make the rescue. After three hours, the launch will return to the ship regardless of whether the party or I have returned, and you will get *Rapid* under way."

Half an hour later, Sangh came in to clear away the dishes, while Merewether struggled to pull on the landing-force boots he had not worn since that nightmare at Vellor last summer. He stood up, twisting each foot to settle it firmly on the sole, and found Sangh bowing before him.

"Sahib, since you do not carry your sword ashore, do honor to this humble one and carry this jambiya." He presented the traditional Indian knife, green agate handle, brass hilt, sheathed in a wooden scabbard covered with purple velvet. Merewether drew the knife, looked at the watered-steel, slightly curved blade, doubled-edged half its ten-inch length, and sheathed it.

"You warrant, of course, that it will bring me luck?"

"No, Sahib. Only that without it, I fear misfortune." The large liquid eyes of the little Hindu steward bore an expression of real concern.

Merewether laughed. "Thank you, Sangh. I shall carry it with gratitude." He slid the dagger inside his waistband, the hilt just above the belt buckle, and went on deck.

By two bells of the first watch, the island was close ahead. The moon had risen but was yet invisible behind the hills. The leadsman in the chains monotonously repeated, "No bottom with this line." To the south, the point with its fort guarding the harbor of Port Louis was identifiable by its lights. The shore was steep, and there were reefs both to the north and the south. Merewether decided he was close enough, came into the wind, and launched the drogue; shortly, the sea anchor took a strain.

The two launches went over the side in succession, one to receive the marines at the port gangway, the other to take a line from the bow of *Rapid* and commence pulling steadily into the wind to hold her in position.

Merewether climbed down into the boat a little awkwardly with the air rifle slung over his shoulder and its accouterments at his belt. The swell was only moderate and the launch made good progress, even against the land breeze out of the mouth of the little harbor—a breeze that carried to his nostrils the acrid odor of the hot metal of the dark lanterns stowed under the thwarts, along with the smell of vegetation on the island. The lanterns would be necessary to rouse out and move the prisoners. He cautiously cracked a lantern to read the heading on the boat compass.

"Come starboard a point," he told the coxswain in a low, conspiratorial tone, and then laughed at himself for the bit of melodrama.

The moonglow revealed breakers to port and starboard, and the calm gap between that led into Tombeau Bay. Merewether steered through the entrance, and then, at the whispered directions of Lowjee, changed course boldly to starboard. The beach loomed ahead, as a seaman in the bow of the launch tested the depth of water with a sounding rod. The boat was close to the beach when the rod found bottom, and a moment later, the keel grated on gravel. Half a dozen men went over the side to tail on to the painter and draw the launch securely onto the shingle. Gunny led his force over the bow, dry-shod, and formed up along the beach.

A moment later a party of four departed south to establish a block point and pickets on the road that ran a few hundred yards inland. The balance of the force moved southeast, angling away from the bay, led confidently by Lowjee and Gunny. Merewether followed close behind them, pushing through tough, knee-high scrub. They stumbled over an occasional rock but moved in relative silence. In a few minutes, they crossed a gravel road, then paralleled a deep gully to the edge of a modest slope. The moon was just becoming visible, and two hundred yards ahead, Merewether could see the stockade, a lantern burning at the north gate. On stilts, at each corner, was a canopied platform, open on all sides, that must hold a guard. A house with light streaming from its doorway stood beside the gate, and a man sat in a chair tilted against the wall, a musket leaning carelessly beside him.

Gunny drew the detachment together, sent two men toward each of the back corners of the stockade, then after a calculated interval, led his main party through the shadows to complete a flanking movement toward the gate. Merewether held his point of vantage on the rise beside the gully. This was marines' work, and he could only admire the precision of the operation.

The first "whap" made him jump, then it was followed by three more in quick succession, then three more again from near the gate. The man in the chair stood up, clutching his chest, and then fell on his face. A group of marines burst through the lighted door of the guardhouse; another party swung the gates apart and disappeared into the stockade. There had been no outcry and not a musket shot fired. Merewether relaxed and congratulated himself.

A quarter hour passed, only an occasional flash of light from an incautious dark lantern marking the activity within the stockade. Finally, Merewether saw the group come out. He tried to count, lost his tally at twenty-three, and then saw the marine detachment form up and start toward him, escorting another group. It was almost over. The operation was a success.

It was only the click of two stones together, but it was close behind him. There was no time to unsling the air rifle. Merewether snatched the jambiya from its scabbard as he whirled, and drove it upward in the knife-fighter's stroke he had learned in his days in the lower deck, designed to penetrate soft flesh below the armored rib cage. He felt the knife strike home, hoped the man was not a stray marine. Then the shattering blow exploded in his brain.

Larkin pressed against the port bulwark, his gaze sweeping continuously across the mouth of the bay. With the moon up, breakers were plainly visible, as the launch should have been by now. MacCamy and the quartermaster took another bearing on the light at Port Louis. There had been no measurable drift, what with the resistance of the sea anchor and the influence of the pulling boat. Two hours and forty minutes! The landing force must have run into trouble, though shots should have been heard

186

even out here. Larkin recalled his explicit orders and made a decision.

"Call in the launch," he told MacCamy. "We're not making enough leeway to matter." He regretted the gratuitous explanation.

MacCamy turned to go forward in his round-shouldered, rolling gait. Larkin watched him go, thinking that the man had no more enterprise or spirit than an ox and wondered what had brought him to sea in the first instance. Larkin thought again of his orders. No doubt it was better to lose a marine detachment and boat crew than a ship like *Rapid*, her men and armament. He agreed with the logic of the order, but it was hard to go off when a little more time might resolve the matter. The second launch came alongside, the hands a little noisy in their relief at having an end of the monotonous task.

"Leave the crew in the boat for the time being," he called to MacCamy on a sudden impulse, not certain himself of his intentions. He poked his head into the cubbyhole. Ten minutes left of the allotted three hours. He waited a moment for his eyes to readjust to darkness and picked up the night glass. Coming out of the shadow of the island through the entrance of the bay was the launch.

Relief flooded through Larkin. "Mister MacCamy," he called. "Heave in on the drogue. They're in sight! You may hoist in the boat."

He relaxed against the bulwark as the boat made its way like a beetle across the swells. He did not mind, he thought, the responsibility of command, but he was glad that Merewether had it at this point. The voyage back should be accomplished in half the time it had taken to sail down to this God-forsaken island in the Indian Ocean, but as a free soul, Larkin felt he would be trapped were he burdened with the lonely responsibilities thrust upon a commander at sea. Better by far to be a first lieutenant and sleep well.

He thought for a moment of Merewether. The man was a good captain, courageous, intelligent and enterprising, possessed of an indomitable sense of fair play, not nearly as hard and merciless as his scarred face made him appear. He seemed to bear lightly the weight of duties imposed upon him and to accomplish them without apparent effort, but Larkin had seen his soul completely naked on that occasion off the Andaman Islands when he would have exchanged his career for the lives of two helpless women. It was uncomfortable to realize that Merewether would never have left the marine detachment and boat crew behind, whatever his orders. By now he would have been ashore with another party to learn the trouble, Larkin told himself with a little contempt. But a first lieutenant acquired the habit of obeying orders unquestioningly, or he did not last for long in the Bombay Marine.

The thought brought on a bit of wonder to Larkin that he found himself in such a service, halfway around the world from the farm on the south bank of the Ohio River in Kentucky where he had been reared. He wondered for a moment if his sisters were still alive or had long since starved to death, considering the two worthless men they had married. He felt a little nostalgia for the cold winter mornings of his boyhood, the smell of wood smoke and the swirling mist above the river, as he went out to pull down fodder for the cattle and the old mare, who had produced, his father boasted, sixteen mule colts in her time. For a moment, he considered resigning his commission in the Marine and going back to Kentucky. It was a state now, since 1795, and might yet hold a future for a man of his experience.

The boat came alongside, the marines disembarked in their orderly fashion, followed by a band of ragged men, and the boatswain supervised the hoisting in. Dobbs and Gunny appeared abruptly before him.

"Sir," commenced Dobbs. "We've lost the Captain!"

"What?" said Larkin.

"Sah," broke in Gunny. "The mission was a complete success. We killed or overpowered the guards and rescued our Marines. Twenty-four men survived. When we moved against the stockade, we left the Captain on a little rise overlooking the prison camp. Upon our return, he was nowhere to be found. I made a complete search, sah, even using our dark lanterns."

"That's right," said Dobbs. "I just couldn't believe it. Gunny and I went back with a party and the lanterns, even shouted a bit, and scoured the area."

"We are a quarter hour late now," Larkin said slowly. "If we are to be out of sight by dawn, we must be under way. Do either of you think there's a chance if we took a party back ashore?"

Dobbs hesitated, obviously wanting to continue the search.

"No, sah," said Gunny decisively. "We might find him by daylight, but we certainly would be discovered, and the ship might be lost. I assure, sah, the search was thorough."

The messenger panted up. "Sir, Mister MacCamy says the drogue's in sight."

"Tell him to hoist it in and get the ship under way. Course, due north."

The decision was made. In five minutes, the ship was on the starboard tack, headed north. It was four bells in the midwatch as Larkin went below and entered Merewether's cabin.

The council of war was brief. Dobbs and Gunny were obviously distressed; MacCamy had no suggestions; and Buttram, as surgeon, could only concur with the decision of the executive officers. After their departure, Larkin continued to sit in Merewether's chair at his desk. He reached into his pocket and pulled out the keys, each neatly tagged, left with him four hours ago, to the strongroom and box, the magazine, and the lockers under the transom. Whether he willed it or not, Larkin thought sourly, he was in command and might as well enjoy its perquisites.

"Sangh," he called, and when the little Hindu appeared, told him, "Coffee, please, a bit of toast and preserves." He realized as the small man turned to go that the face under the headcloth was crumpled and wet with tears. Hell!

Finished, he looked at the brass bed. He decided not. He would have to use the cabin for his executive duties; the records were here, and it was the only adequate space in which to hold a conference with his officers. But he would retain his own room and sleep in it. He could only conclude that some straggler had surprised and killed or captured Merewether. There was no other explanation for his disappearance.

Larkin thought of the betrothal, already announced, and the wedding to that beautiful young widow scheduled not much more than a month away. Bad luck! Not only for Merewether, but for her, widowed once and now deprived of her intended before she was even bedded. Once the dust had settled, he might call around himself.

Larkin put the thought aside as unworthy. It had touched a sore point, however, as it brought to mind Jane Wisdom, one of the twin daughters of the Comptroller of the Company he had met at Bombay last fall. He had felt an attraction for her during their evening together at the ball and had called upon her half a dozen times before *Rapid* departed for Calcutta. He had declared himself, asked her to wait for him, and had thought from her actions that she reciprocated. The long, artless letter he wrote and dispatched from Calcutta at Christmas had contained an explicit proposal of marriage. The reply he received last March was a brief note announcing her impending marriage and a falsely courteous wish that they might remain friends. Hell!

Larkin found himself on deck again as the midwatch ended. The light at Port Louis was no longer visible, and he thought he could detect a faint glow on the horizon to starboard that forecast dawn. Hamlyn had the watch, a little anxious at the new responsibility, but the ship was on course, all sails trimmed and drawing, and homeward bound.

It was difficult to go to sleep for the brief period before reveille. Command, he reassured himself, was no stranger to him. He had commanded prizes full of sullen, fierce men, scheming to retake the ship at the earliest opportunity, without a qualm. Still, in the days that followed, he found it difficult to delegate many important duties to his subordinates. During the night, he came on deck at least twice each watch to check course and the trim of sails. He hung over the shoulder of the harassed Dobbs as he worked out the noon sights. Small defects in the ship and derelictions of duty that had passed without remark by him as first lieutenant became major concerns.

The confrontation came five days later. Larkin was prowling forward when he came upon five men who had been set to picking oakum as penance for minor sins of omission or commission by the Master at Arms. Four were new men, shipped at Calcutta only last month, and the fifth was a recruit enlisted at Bombay Castle last fall. All five had dropped their work and were lying back idly while strands of hemp blew across the deck.

"Here now," said Larkin, in the manner he thought Merewether would have used on such an occasion. "Best get on with that."

Two of the men jumped guiltily and picked up their lengths of hawser. The other three simply stared at him without expression.

"You heard me?" inquired Larkin a little sharply. The three men did not alter expression or make a move to resume their work. They were, he realized, testing him.

The nearest man, heavyset, with bristling side-whiskers, turned his head and spat on the deck beside him. Something snapped in Larkin. With a single movement, he caught the man by the neckband of his shirt, jerked him erect, heels six inches off the deck, and slapped, then backhanded him on either cheek. He thrust the man from him and realized someone was beside him moving into the group, flailing a rope end and kicking vigorously.

"Enough!" he told Bowman, the leading boatswain's mate.

In this ship, Larkin remembered, no man had been flogged since Merewether took command. These men were new, he realized; they had thought to test the new captain, even at the expense of their backs. He remembered Merewether's comment in the South Atlantic last year after the memorable wrestling match that settled bad blood between two seamen.

"The cat is not a good teacher, Larkin," Merewether had said. "When you reach the point you feel you are compelled to use it, the man is usually past redemption."

Perhaps so, but he was yet quivering with rage. He forced himself to appear calm.

"Sir, shall I bring them to the mast?" Bowman inquired.

Larkin saw a trickle of blood at the corner of the mouth of the man he had slapped. His eyes met Larkin's, not defiant now, but with an expression almost of admiration. The others stood a little hangdog, but in the attitude of respect. No useful purpose would be served, Larkin decided, by further action in the matter. He understood them, and they understood him.

"No," he said flatly. "Put them back to work."

The air was cleared; Larkin settled into the command of *Rapid* as she picked up the southwest monsoon again and plunged northeastwardly toward the equator. Eleven days later, the Royal

Navy sloop on picket duty off the southeast point of Ceylon intercepted her and delivered the second counterpart of orders from the Commandant of the Marine to proceed to a rendezvous at the eastern approach to the Strait of Malacca.

CHAPTER SEVENTEEN

Merewether became aware of an agony in his head. He managed to open one eye and found himself in a green-lighted tomb. Close above his face was an overhang of raw earth, while to his left was an almost impenetrable screen of rank vegetation. A crushing weight was on his feet and ankles. He raised his head and saw the curly black hair, above staring brown eyes of a dark man dressed in the remains of some sort of uniform. The man was dead, the hilt of the jambiya protruding from his belly just below the breastbone. Merewether opened the other eye as he pulled his feet from beneath the body. His vision was blurred and double, the movement sent additional paroxysms through his head, and he closed his eyes as pain shifted to his feet while circulation was restored.

It was obviously after dawn, no sunlight yet with the hills rising to the east. *Rapid* should have been long since under way north. Merewether rolled on his left side and pushed at the springy bushes. He managed to wriggle himself against them, forcing the stems over until he was out from under the overhang and staring at the sky, cloudless, but not yet blue at dawn. He was at the bottom of the deep gully he had waited beside last night to observe the Marine operation.

Merewether sat up, bringing on a wave of nausea that almost overpowered him. He closed both eyes and held his head. There was an egg-sized lump on the top left side, painful beyond his experience. He felt about it, decided there was no obvious fracture, and then managed to get on his feet, supporting himself against the steep side of the gully. A gleam of metal revealed the air rifle under the cut-bank; he snaked it out and hung it over his shoulder by the sling as he sought with one open eye a way out of this pit. As an afterthought, he managed to withdraw the jambiya, wipe it clean and sheathe it.

A hundred feet up, the gully widened until he reached a point where he was able to climb out. He headed toward the sea, feeling exposed and defenseless, but compelled to make sure that *Rapid* was gone. The gravel road he had crossed last night appeared through a break in the undergrowth, and he was sure he could see from it the harbor entrance and the sea beyond. He plunged into the road, heard an exclamation of surprise, and unslung the air rifle to cover the two men standing to his left.

They were an odd pair, he could see that with his one open eye. One, a dark young man was barefoot, clad only in a pair of white canvas trousers; the other, a bent old man, white-haired, with watery blue eyes, was dressed in white breeches, half boots, and a blue coat that hung to his knees, an old-fashioned cocked hat perched on his head.

"Hold!" croaked Merewether and looked out to sea. He could just observe the mouth of the harbor, but the sea beyond was plainly visible. No sail was in sight, north or west. Larkin had obeyed his orders! He turned back to the pair standing in the road.

The old man spoke in a voice like a rusty hinge. "Captain, I am an Englishman!"

Merewether tried to assimilate this remarkable statement into his aching brain. The man might pass for white, but he had a touch of the tarbrush too.

"I am Jamie Plantain, Captain. My father," he continued proudly in the hoarse old voice, "was Captain James Plantain, the great pirate and King of Madagascar!"

The sun had risen by now above the hills to the east, its heat touching Merewether's head. He felt giddy, opened both eyes, saw the double image of the men, and sat down in the gravel with a thump. He was conscious of being assisted in a stumbling way along the road, up a path through a vegetable garden, and into a substantial stone cottage set against the hill. When things became a little clearer, he was in a chair in a bare room floored with black stone slabs, and a woman, strongly resembling the young man but a little older, was holding a cup of tea that reeked of rum under his nose. He managed to take a sip of the steaming brew, then took the cup from the woman and drank it down. He felt the heat of tea and spirits expand through his body, but salmon, blue and pink clouds still floated across his vision, with every now and then a patch of gray mist that blotted out the scene. Merewether dimly realized that he must be suffering what Buttram would call a concussion and that he was helpless for the time either to plan a course of action or to carry one into execution.

The young man lounging in the doorway spoke rapidly in the Creole patois to the old man seated in a cushioned chair across the room. "The day relief guard just passed along the road," the rusty old voice said. "When they find what your men did at the stockade, they'll be along to see if we know anything. Best put ye out of sight, Captain."

Merewether felt no energy, no desire to rise or escape. He found a firm hand under each arm, hoisting him out of the chair and toward the back of the cottage. They emerged into a narrow patio, roofed with an arbor on which grapevines grew, the young man and woman propelling him toward a rock wall against the hill rising steeply behind the house. At the wall was a rounded parapet of stone, apparently a well or cistern. The young man removed a wooden cover and pointed down. There were iron rungs set into the stone inside.

"Down," said the woman urgently. "Four steps, then to your right."

At the bottom, Merewether could see the sky and his head reflected in water. He was uncertain of himself as he swung over the edge, but the instinct of an old topman came to his rescue. His feet and hands found the rungs; he lowered himself, feeling with his feet from one to the other, then found an opening beside him. He stepped into it, seeing dim light ahead, and emerged into a low room, apparently a cellar under the cottage itself. Light came in from a series of narrow slits in the walls against the overhead on either side. The floor was roughly covered with flat stone slabs, and against the opposite wall was a large chest. Beside the further wall was a low cot. He stumbled thankfully toward it and lay down, oblivious of the cloud of dust he stirred from the blanket.

*

Merewether awoke to find himself in total darkness. He was uncertain of his whereabouts, the air was still and musty, but there was a pleasant medicinal odor in it. He put his hand to his brow and found a bandage swathing his head, holding a moist poultice. He had time only to realize that he was marooned on the Ile de France before his lethargy took him off again into sleep.

When he awoke, light was coming through the slits, and he found the woman offering him a cup of water. He sat up, drank thirstily, and at her gesture, got to his feet. His vision was no longer blurred and double, but he had to pause a moment while he assured himself that he was steady. He went through the passage to the well, swung onto the rungs, and climbed out on the patio. It was, he guessed, early morning. He must have slept the clock around, and while still feeling weak and washed out, his strength was returning; he was ravenous.

"Ah, Captain, ye look a sight better this morning than yesterday," the old man—what was his name—said. "When Eleanora told me ye was asleep, we left ye lay, with a bit of medicine for your head."

"Yes, sir. I'm sorry, but I don't remember your name."

"Plantain, Captain, Jamie Plantain. My father was Captain James Plantain, the great pirate and King of Madagascar. My mother was Eleanora Brown, granddaughter of King Dick of Messaleague, but her father was an Englishman, too. And now, Captain, a bit of tea and breakfast and ye'll feel better."

Merewether watched the woman through the doorway to the kitchen as she moved about the brazier, pouring boiling water from the kettle into a silver teapot. As she leaned over, the thin cotton dress outlined her figure, and he realized that she was a beauty. She turned and caught his gaze, bold brown eyes, set in the oval, pale-gold face under curling mahogany hair, meeting his, then turning deliberately away as she loaded a tray. He felt a flush of heat in his face, despite his weakened condition.

The hot tea, boiled eggs and brown bread were soon consumed. Over a second cup, Merewether asked, "Are you in danger with me here?"

"Oh, no. The Frogs know ye came to rescue those Bombay Marine soldiers, and they don't suspect anyone was left behind."

He continued in the creaking old voice. "The militia came by yesterday to ask if we heard anything the night before. Of course we hadn't, and this is the only house in half a mile. It was plain enough, they said, what had happened. The track of your party from the shore and the marks where your boat was beached were still clear. Oh, they'll not be looking for ye, but then this is a small place, and a stranger will be noticed. Best stay out of sight."

Merewether's mind was beginning to function again. He was still weak, his head unhealed, not in condition to move about much; so it would be just as well to remain here for the time. The thought of remaining hidden until the Royal Navy, and the powers that be, decided to take Mauritius next year or the year after was intolerable to Merewether, however. Even the vision of the woman sitting across the room with eyes downcast could not affect his intention to escape.

There must be neutral ships, American, certainly, possibly Portuguese or Norwegian, calling at Port Louis from time to time, he told himself. There was the possibility that he might buy passage from a friendly captain, or at worse, stow away as the Havildar had done. It certainly was best to follow the advice of the old man to lie low for the present, he concluded, settling back more comfortably in his chair. He was at the mercy of this unusual group, but he felt no apprehension; he had accepted at face value the old man's statement, "I am an Englishman."

"And now, Mr. Plantain, how did you know me to be a captain in the Bombay Marine?"

"Oh, Captain, many's the time in the old days I've seen your officers in Port Louis, and then when my mother was alive, I sailed as supercargo on ships carrying her sugar to Goa and even Bombay. After that I was a harbor pilot for a score of years. The uniform has changed some, but not that much. And by the by, Captain, what might your name be?"

"Merewether, sir, Percival Merewether."

"Oh, and I've told ye mine. These are Pierre and Eleanora Lefèbre—I had only the one daughter, and she married a Creole —my grandchildren."

Merewether was reaching back in his memory for the name "Plantain." It seemed to be associated somehow with England

196

and Taylor, the pirates of the Malabar and African coasts of almost a century ago, and there was some story, still current, of the Englishman who had built a castle at Ranter's Bay to make himself King of Madagascar.

"Your father sailed with England and Taylor," Merewether ventured.

"No, Captain. England and Taylor sailed with my father. They danced to the tune he called," said the old man proudly. "My father fought a war with King Dick to win my mother, Eleanora Brown, and then celebrated the marriage with England and Taylor as guests at the ball."

"But this must have been a long time ago."

"I am eighty-one, Captain. My father became weary of being a king and decided to join the forces of Angria on the Malabar Coast—they were pirates after his own heart—and he left Madagascar, taking my mother and one servant"—Plantain spat on the floor—"Nelly, a hot-bellied bitch. My mother found herself with child—me—and that Nelly persuaded my father to leave her off here." He spat again. "Of course, he provided well for my mother, the chest ye saw in the dungeon was full of louis d'or, and many's a cyclone day as a child I counted and stowed the gold pieces back into the chest."

"Five men, I'll not call them husbands, for she'd always expected my father back, my mother had. She bought this land when it was cheap, and slaves to clear and plant it with cane. The gold lasted a long time, and she sold her sugar every year. Ah, she were a rich woman and sent me to the academy in Port Louis to learn to read and cypher. When I was eighteen, I went to Bombay and tried to find my father, but no one knew of him by then."

The old voice quavered a little. "The last man she had was a Frenchman. He stole all her gold, a little at a time, and then took ship for France. All I have now is this house and a few worn-out acres left. My mother only died ten years ago at ninety. Ah, Captain, she were a marvel! Scripture by the yard, and knew all the prayers and catechism by heart, too. Her father were Edward Brown, an Englishman and a schoolmaster, shipwrecked on Madagascar; ah, he learned her well."

It was a fascinating story, Merewether decided. The old man was three-quarters English, one quarter black by his own account, but in spite of the injury to his mother by his father, he was proud to call himself an Englishman. Merewether relaxed further; this man was safe.

The morning wore pleasantly away as Merewether sat listening to the account of days long gone by on this lonely ocean island, the ships and men, wars and trade that had washed across it during the past three quarters of a century that the old man could remember. He came back to the present, conscious of his bandaged, poulticed head, the grime of the dungeon on his hands and face, and the crawling itch of stale sweat on his body.

"I wonder, Mister Plaintain, if I might get a bucket of water and clean up a bit." He was sitting in shirt, trousers and boots. Somewhere, since the night before last, his jacket, belt, hat and air rifle had disappeared.

"Better than that, Captain. There's a small pool behind the house at the end of the patio, screened by a hedge. The water runs from a spring in the hillside, cold, but ye may bathe to heart's content."

Merewether soon found the pool, a rock-lined oval, ten feet across, closely surrounded by thick thorn bushes clipped into a head-high hedge. The woman had just stepped out of it onto the flagstones, her wet, golden body glistening as she folded a bright cloth about her head. Her eyes caught his; she flashed a smile, picked up the robe that hung on the hedge, and brushed by Merewether into the house.

By the next day, Pierre had reported that no foreign ships were in Port Louis; only a French privateer brig was at anchor, apparently out of commission and refitting. The French naval squadron was absent. That day a party of ragged men, escorted by militia, had passed along the road toward the stockade. Most of them appeared to be Europeans, bearded and stumbling along as though half starved. Pierre reported that night that they were the remnants of the crew of *Polaris,* a Bombay Marine survey ship, taken two years ago in the Maldive Islands. Merewether pricked up his ears. He had counted twenty-nine Europeans and six lascars in the party. Possibly there were some officers who survived, and he must make contact with them to ascertain their temper.

"Where will these men work?" he inquired. He was beginning to understand the limping English that Pierre spoke.

"Some break rock up the side of the hill. Others take it down in hand barrows. The rest spread it on the road."

"How closely guarded are the men in the quarry?"

"One man, usually. There is no place to run away. The guards are there only to make them work."

"And if they have a call of nature?"

"Sor, they hold up two fingers, and the guard gives them permission to go into the bushes. They dig a latrine in one place for this."

Better sanitation than the Company's European troops usually practiced in the field, Merewether thought. He tried to remember how the road ran past the prison camp, but his memory of the sketchy map drawn by the Havildar was foggy.

"Is there a place from which I can see these men at work?"

"Ye might go around the side of the hill, Captain, before daylight, and look right down on them from safe cover," old Jamie broke in, his faded blue eyes sparkling. "I know just the place— on the hill where I played in a little cave as a boy. It can't be found unless ye know where to look."

Merewether was turning the entire matter over in his mind. It would serve no useful purpose, he decided, to contact the prisoners at this point. He had no means of escape available, and the chances of betrayal were too great. It might be valuable, however, to know the terrain and the routine the prisoners and their guards followed.

"I would like to see them," he told Plantain.

CHAPTER EIGHTEEN

It was cool and still dark, the breeze coming down from the hills with enough force to make him shiver. He wore a pair of duck trousers, a rough cotton shirt and a round straw hat. The stars were beginning to fade as Pierre led Merewether along a faint path up the side of the hill behind the cottage to a crest, then northward nearly half a mile. There he went down a slope, passing between large boulders, then turned abruptly to the right. Screened a narrow foot behind a boulder was the entrance to a little grotto, showing blacker in the dim gray light. Merewether squeezed through the narrow entrance and stepped on a rock floor, hearing the trickle of water in the recesses behind him. He looked out over the boulder concealing the entrance and in the increasing light could see the slope down to the road, Tombeau Bay and the sea beyond.

"Take care, Captain, and I'll be back after dark," said Pierre, then vanished into the gloom up the slope.

Merewether sat down on the cold stone and wondered if what he might observe this day would be worth the risk and discomfort. A half hour later, he heard a distinct whistle and shouts, several times repeated. Reveille, he concluded, at the prison camp. It was still not light enough to see any distance, and he leaned back against the rough wall and dozed. When he awoke, it was broad daylight and the party of prisoners was just coming into view along the road.

It was a long day. The trickle of water a dozen feet back in the cave filled a basin lined with smooth black pebbles, and the overflow appeared to drain out through a crack in the floor. The quarry was two hundred yards down the hillside to his right. Ten men swung sledgehammers in deliberate arcs, breaking the stone. A dozen others, two to a barrow, loaded and transported the stone to the road. They appeared to be filling a sort of swale where others spread and tamped the rock.

At intervals, a man would hold up his hands, two fingers extended, catch the eye of the guard, and at a nod, drop his tools and go into a clump of bushes to the left. He had the terrain fixed in his mind, the prison camp to the left, the quarry and road here at the head of Tombeau Bay, and the river to his right out of sight, but emptying into the harbor. In half an hour's time, he had satisfied himself and concluded that the balance of the day would be wasted.

When the sun was near overhead, a whistle sounded. The

prisoners dropped their tools and sought the shade of a tree, breaking into groups, each about a pot that appeared to contain beans or peas. The five guards withdrew to the shade of another clump of trees, and two of the Indian prisoners appeared, each carrying two baskets. Bottles were passed around, evidently wine, as the two men who carried muskets leaned them against trees and the others unfastened their belts and laid aside their pistols and braided leather whips. After half an hour, one guard heaved himself to his feet, blew a whistle, and the prisoners plodded back to work. The guard took up his musket and posted himself in the shade near the entrance to the quarry where he could observe the entire operation. The four others remained lying in the shade, evidently taking a siesta. It was a loose and casual procedure.

At sunset, the prisoners were assembled and marched back out of sight to the camp. Then, at dusk, Pierre arrived to lead Merewether to the crest of the hill and back down to the cottage.

"A long day ye had, Captain," Jamie greeted him, "and did ye learn a bit?"

"Enough," said Merewether. "I'd not care to be a prisoner of the French."

The old man had a cup cradled in his hands, and Merewether could catch a whiff of the aroma of spirits. "Rum, Captain. Will ye join me?"

The fiery liquor expanded through Merewether's body and brought an immediate sense of well-being that sent him early to sleep.

Two days passed without incident; Merewether began to feel the galling effects of boredom. He improved the time by picking the brains of old Jamie and Pierre as to the geography of the island. The peaks rising steeply back of Port Louis were named Pieter Both and Le Pouce, he knew from his charts, with the lesser ones of Virgin's Peak, Cantin's Peak and L'Echelle Rock to the northward.

"I climbed Pieter Both when I was a lad," said old Jamie proudly. "Never was done again until a Frenchman named Claude Peuthe did in 1790. I told him how I got up to the final knob: I shot an arrow attached to a cord over the summit and pulled a line over by it. He did the same."

"Tell me about Port Louis," Merewether urged. "The Citadel, I know is on a hill in the town, but what other defenses does the harbor have?"

"There is a battery in a fort on Tonnelier Island on this side of the harbor entrance. It is separated from the town by a marsh called Mer Rouge. This battery is not manned except in time of danger, because the marsh causes the malaria. The battery on the south shore is manned, they keep a good watch there, and the barracks are on the hill behind it. Ah, but the malaria! It drives all but the poorest into the hills to escape it. Even the Governor's mansion is five miles from Port Louis."

"Five miles? In what direction?"

"Why, right south, I guess. Le Reduit, they call the mansion, a beautiful place, and with the high road right into town. The Governor only comes to town twice a week in his carriage, the lazy Frog."

The next morning, Plantain and Pierre left to walk into Port Louis to buy staples not produced by the garden that Pierre tended in front of the house. Merewether emptied his purse of sixty-odd silver rupees—they passed current in Port Louis, Jamie said—and pressed them on the old man as payment for his lodging. He sat in the front room with a view out the door along the road, hearing an occasional clatter or snatch of a song from the back of the house as the woman went about her household duties. The homely sounds brought back memories of the great kitchen at Bellflower House in London where he was reared as a backstairs child. He thought briefly of his mother, and then of Caroline, almost forgotten during these past few days. It was only a little more than a month until the wedding, an engagement he was most unlikely to fulfill on time.

Eleanora came in, a broom in hand, and began to sweep the black flagstones. He watched the smooth, graceful rhythm of her movements. He saw that her face was averted, the dark, luminous eyes intent upon her task. A haze of dust arose, dancing in the shaft of sunlight from the window. She turned toward him, starting to say that he should go out to the patio to escape the annoyance. The memory of her emerging from the pool flooded over him, obliterating the thought of Caroline. He caught her about the waist and kissed her, felt her respond. Then she led him to her little room, stepping out of her dress as they came through the door.

The click of a heel on stone at the back of the cottage alerted Merewether; Eleanora lay quiescent and relaxed beside him. He slid off the cot, pulled on shirt and trousers, and emerged barefoot into the kitchen, then backed through the doorway into the front room, picking up the jambiya from the table as he went. There were scuffing sounds, then a figure appeared in the back doorway, hesitated a moment, and slipped through into the kitchen. He was a thin man, obviously European, with a mustache and side-whiskers worn in the colonial French style. He was dressed in the uniform of an artilleryman in the French regulars and appeared to be unarmed. He looked about, evidently adjusting his vision to the dim interior.

"Here, now! Who are you and what do you want?" Merewether blurted out.

The man jumped, eyes wide, mouth open, hands extended, as Merewether advanced, knife in hand. "Inglis!" he shouted, snatched a pot from the table and hurled it with a crash against the wall to the right of Merewether, spun about and ran out the door.

By the time he could get to the patio, the man was almost to the road, running diagonally across the garden. No chance to catch him, even if he wanted to, Merewether decided sourly, and came back inside. Eleanora, her dress clutched in a bunch against her bosom stood wide-eyed in the kitchen.

"It was Jules!" she cried. "Back again. Gran'ther and Pierre told him never to come again!"

"What? Who is Jules?"

"My husband, the worthless one! He left me last year and took up with a Creole slut at Quatre Bornes. She peppered him, and then he wanted to come back to me. *Ptah*," she spat, "but Pierre and Gran'ther drove him off! He must have seen them at Port Louis and hoped to surprise me alone."

"And now he's gone to give the alarm," said Merewether.

"I'm sorry; I've brought trouble to you and Mister Plantain."
Almost as an afterthought, Eleanora pulled the cotton frock over
her head, and the golden body disappeared. She slid her feet into
sandals, tied the headcloth, and started for the door.

"I must find Pierre and Gran'ther," she told him. "No place in
this house is safe now, not even the dungeon. You must hide
somewhere else."

"My gun and uniform?" asked Merewether, with some confused thought that so dressed he could not be charged with
being a spy. This, however, solved nothing so far as Eleanora,
Pierre and old Jamie were concerned. In fact it would make the
case against them stronger: treason; harboring and giving comfort to the enemy in time of war.

She ran to an alcove, pulled aside the curtain, and pointed to
the undress uniform he had worn ashore, bloodstains and grime
washed out, and smoothly ironed. The belt with its accouterments hung on a peg and the air rifle was in a corner. Footsteps
sounded at the front, and Jamie came in followed by Pierre with
a basket in either hand. Eleanora launched into a torrent of
speech in the patois, while Pierre and Jamie stood listening,
their faces blank. He could only understand the names "Jules"
several times repeated.

Without a change of expression, Jamie turned to Merewether.
"Well, Captain, now ye have played hell!"

"Yes, sir," said Merewether. "I'll get out and away. The man
saw no one else here; you and Pierre were in Port Louis, as you
can prove, and Eleanora was in her room. You can tell them I
was a mere interloper, an English thief in your house." He
thought of another point. "You drove Jules away. He has cause
to hate you, and it is only his word against three." He paused
and tried to think how MacLellan would handle such a legal
point. "He probably was absent from his post without leave,
and you may impeach his motives. Anyway, I'll go."

Jamie took off the old blue coat and hung it with the cocked
hat on a peg. He sat in his chair, motioned to Eleanora, and she
brought in two cups of rum. Merewether stared at the cup of
aromatic spirits, then at the calm old man.

"No tearing hurry, Captain." He sipped from the cup. "An

204

hour to town and then around the bay to find someone with authority in the garrison. Another two hours to form up a party and march it out here. And it being in the heat of the day, I doubt it will be that soon. Time enough to make some plans."

"Yes, sir." Merewether's impulse had been to bolt out into the undergrowth on the hills rising to the east: little enough chance of survival that way if there were a determined search. He sat down and tasted the rum.

"Yes, Captain, I think ye're near right. I have complained to the gendarme of this district, asked him to warn Jules away, and told him why: he's peppered. He'll have a bit of explaining to do himself, why he was here. Oh, they'll make a search, no doubt, but there will be no proof once we hide ye."

"Where?"

The old man took a swallow of the rum, set the cup down, and coughed gently. "Ah, there's a dozen places, but only one in reach now. Even Eleanor and Pierre don't know of it. At the bottom of the well, a stream flows through, and beside it there's a sort of pocket in the rock. Cold and damp, but out of sight and safe until we can move ye on."

Merewether began to chafe. It was almost an hour since Jules had run across the garden, but Jamie insisted on taking the noon meal. "Might be a time till ye eat again, Captain," he told him cheerfully.

Finally, they came out on the patio. The cover was removed from the well, and a sturdy hemp line, with a large iron grapnel eye-spliced into one end, was lowered, the hooks firmly gripping the parapet. "Ye'll take this line with ye, Captain. In case they take us away, ye can throw the grapnel up and over the edge of one of the iron handholds, climb right out."

That was a relief; he would not be trapped helpless at the bottom of the pit. He went over the side, down the irons, took hold of the line, tested its anchorage, and let himself down. Just before his feet touched the water, he saw the dark opening beside him and swung in. A moment later, his uniform, gun and belt came down on a cord, together with a small basket with bread, cheese, a cup and a flask of rum.

"Heads up!" the rusty old voice echoed, and the grapnel

plunged into the water. He hauled it in, neatly coiling the line. He was in an almost round recess, a volcanic bubble in the basalt, four feet in diameter. A thump echoed down the shaft, and light was blotted out as the lid went on the well. Merewether settled down, listening to the gurgle of the water close beside him. In five minutes he was asleep.

He was awakened by the reflection of light on the surface of the water. Voices came echoing down the shaft, and then he heard leather scrape on the iron rungs at the top. Merewether restrained himself from poking his head out. He could see no reflection in the water from this angle, but it lightened up as he heard the man step into the entrance to the cyclone cellar above. A moment later, he heard him call up in French, and the sound of leather on iron again. A babble of voices came down the shaft for a moment, then died away. The well cover had not been replaced.

It must have been two hours, the light was diminished as the sun put the shadow of the cottage across the parapet, before Merewether heard Eleanora call down.

"They've gone, but Gran'ther says wait a bit."

He settled back as darkness engulfed the well. The bread, cheese and rum were untouched, still held as a reserve against contingency. He was wide awake, and his conscience began to torment him. Merewether told himself that he was not as yet under any formal vows to Caroline, not married to her, but the moralities of the matter were implicit. He had been unfaithful, however he might justify the matter. He squirmed against the cold stone and looked out and up to see stars framed in the small circle of sky. He was a weak, susceptible man, without morals or principles, unworthy of a woman such as Caroline, he decided with contempt. But, uncomfortably, he knew that given the opportunity, he would seek Eleanora out again.

Half an hour later, a whistle echoed down the shaft, and he heard the voice of Pierre.

"Tie on your baggage, Captain."

Merewether reached out blindly and found the dangling cord. The uniform, basket, gun and belt were hoisted away. Another whistle, and he tied the cord to the grapnel. It was a simple matter to go up the line, hand over hand. He emerged on the patio, seeing the dim features of Jamie and Pierre before him.

Pierre led the way, up the path they had followed two days ago, but then right and along the side of the hill, then up again, as Merewether followed blindly. They reached a crest, turned right again, passed along level ground, then went down a slope through thick trees. Ahead, he heard the sound of a brook, and shortly they waded through water, ankle deep, rushing over a gravel bottom. Fifty yards beyond, Jamie took the lead. The moon was just becoming visible, and in the dim light, Merewether could make out a low bluff against the hillside, trees growing closely against it. Jamie squeezed between the trunks and the rock, and disappeared. Pierre pushed him forward, he stumbled, and found himself in a hole.

"Here," said Jamie. "Lower your head, bend over."

Merewether bent over and shuffled toward the voice. He felt his back scrape, bent still lower, and went into Stygian darkness. He heard the rasp and pop of flint on steel, and in a moment a coal of fire gleamed, then a candle was lighted.

"Hideout of the old Maroons, Captain, slaves that escaped from the Dutch before the French came. It should be safe enough for a while."

Merewether looked about in the flickering light. It was a musty little room, barely high enough to stand in, dug out of the face of the hill, the front wall made of stones roughly laid up, with a low entrance at the side. It appeared to be reasonably dry and well ventilated.

"There's always a bolt hole out the back, Captain," Jamie told him, pointing to the back corner on the left. A low tunnel entrance was visible near the overhead. "That leads a dozen feet into the side of a ravine. Ye can get out without being seen from the front. The Maroons still hid out from the French in places like this when I was a boy."

Pierre was laying down blankets and a basket of provisions against the back wall. The gun was against the wall, and the uniform and belt were hung up.

"Now, ye best lay low a day or so, see how the wind blows,

Captain. Pierre will come back tomorrow night. Ye've food and drink enough till then. There's peepholes in the front wall but ye'll have to find them by daylight. And now we'll be off —oh, I almost forgot—a schooner privateer came in this morning to Port Louis with a prize, but all she carried was coir and coconut oil. That American prize agent laughed at the privateersmen!"

"Thank you, sir." The old man and Pierre ducked out through the entrance into darkness. Merewether sat on the blankets, ate a bit of cheese and bread, drank water from the jug and blew out the candle. An hour later he awoke, clutching the jambiya, hearing the scuff of leather on rock in the passage entrance. The whisper reassured him. It was broad daylight when Eleanora departed.

CHAPTER NINETEEN

The morning sunlight became visible through chinks in the wall. Merewether could see past the trees and vines that grew against the front of the dugout into a grove below. He ate and considered slipping out to wash in the little stream, then decided not. The day wore on, past noon, the light in the dugout growing dimmer as the sun moved westward. Merewether wondered at his patience, his willingness to remain hidden in this burrow, but then he had few alternatives, and, he told himself cynically, Eleanora might come again tonight.

A little after noon, he heard sounds on the slope below. He applied an eye to the peephole and saw a squad of soldiers deploying across the hillside. Another was filing to the left, and in the center, a young lieutenant stood with a spyglass to his eye, pointing directly toward Merewether. Beside him was the jaundiced artilleryman Jules. He had been betrayed!

Merewether did not hesitate. Into the basket went uniform, belt and blankets, with the gun laid across its edges. He pushed it ahead of him into the bolt hole as he crawled along on hands and knees. A dozen feet, and he saw green-tinged light ahead.

He found the entrance, peered through the bushes that screened it, heard the tramp of feet coming a hundred feet down the ravine, and realized he was caught like a rat in a trap. He pushed through the entrance, saw that the ravine bent to the right below him and that the soldiers were not yet in sight. He scrambled down into the ravine, up the other side, and behind a clump of bushes. As quietly as possible, he climbed to the top of the hill, screened by the trees from below. Panting, he paused at the crest, saw a crevice under a shelf of rock, and pushed the basket in out of sight, retaining only the jambiya in his belt. He headed south at a trot toward L'Echelle Rock rising two miles ahead.

In an hour, Merewether had reached the bench from which the peak rose steeply. He found a place between two boulders with a sharp drop below, and sat down, drenched with sweat. From here, he could see most of Port Louis, the bay and the two forts. A large schooner was at anchor well inside the harbor, a smaller vessel anchored astern. On the south side near the shore, a sizable brig was moored, her yards and topmasts struck. Other than lighters and small craft, these appeared to be the only ships present.

He rested a few minutes, then pulled himself erect and headed southeast around the base of the peak, down the slope, to skirt what must be Cantin's Peak and Virgin's Peak, toward Pieter Both towering beyond. He stayed on the overgrown benches above the occasional houses and cultivated fields he could see stretching eastward. He found a little stream, where he drank and washed his face and hands. By night, he might slip down to one of the garden plots and find some vegetables, but he could not risk it now. Ahead, he saw a track tending toward Port Louis and hid as several carts piled high with cut cane came lumbering along behind bullocks. It was late afternoon before Merewether rounded the southeastern approaches to Pieter Both and found a highway barring his progress. He paralleled the road westwardly around the base of La Pouce, and at sunset took shelter in a clump of trees where a trickle of water squeezed out into a pool. From here he could see the road and gates opening on a drive to what appeared to be a substantial, well-kept estate.

Hungry and tired, Merewether settled back and tried to evaluate his situation. Until now, he had been intent upon putting as much distance between himself and the detachment of soldiers as possible. Probably there was a general alarm out over the island by now, and distance was no safeguard. He wondered whether Eleanora or Pierre had betrayed his hiding place. Old Jamie he did not doubt, and he really could not believe the others had. Well, it made no difference now; he might play out this string for a while, but eventually he must be taken. He became conscious of his sweat-soaked clothing, now drying stiffly as the sun set. No use to wash them out in the pool, he would do it in the morning when a few minutes of sun would dry the garments.

In late afternoon, he saw a barouche with a tasseled canopy come along the road, drawn by two handsome gray horses. It held a man lounging at ease in the back seat, as the team turned into the drive and the gates swung open. Two men in the uniform of regular French infantry closed the gates behind the carriage as it disappeared through the shrubbery. Merewether decided that he had just witnessed the arrival of the Governor, and that the mansion at the end of the driveway must be Le Reduit. Certainly, it was unlikely that a private citizen would have military guards at his gate. And yet, it was a slight force for a governor's mansion, even one constructed as a refuge from the malaria, in the hills away from the capital. He wondered if some larger force lurked in the background. Surely by now the Governor must know there was an Englishman at large on the island; and then he realized that one man reported by a jealous husband would scarcely be worthy of note by any-one of higher rank than a district gendarme. He found a place under thick bushes and slept uneasily.

It must be midnight, Merewether decided; the moon was up, and he could hear music in the distance. He pulled himself into the open where he could see lights across the road, flam-beaux burning at the gates, other lights beyond twinkling through the leaves. The gates were propped open. No one was in sight. He was hungry and desperate, with little to lose. He moved on an impulse down the slope, scuttled across the road a hundred yards east of the gates, and climbed a stone wall. Beyond a belt of shrubbery, he came to an open lawn in which flower beds were spaced. The house was ringed with another screen of trees and shrubbery. He drew a deep breath and walked boldly across the moonlit lawn and into the shadow of the trees by the side of the house, passing a broad verandah where he could hear voices. He had no plan except to see what forage he might find for himself.

The windows spilled out light and the sound of music through mosquito netting. They were too high to see in, and he passed rapidly by, close to the fountain of the house, around toward the kitchen. Here the windows were at eye level, and he crept beside a bush where he could catch a glimpse inside. Maids were passing back and forth, carrying laden trays; apparently supper was just being served. No chance there, and Merewether turned to move back the way he had come, emerging from the shelter of the bush.

A calloused hand seized his neck, and his right arm was jerked excruciatingly far up behind his back in a hammerlock.

"Now just stand quiet," said a voice in his ear, "and I'll break no bones."

There was nothing else for Merewether to do; the jambiya was out of reach of his left hand in his belt. The pressure on his neck was intense. Only then did Merewether realize that the man had spoken in English.

"Sir, I am an officer of the Bombay Marine." The grip relaxed almost imperceptibly.

"Let's see what you look like."

Merewether was pushed into the light from the kitchen window, the hand left his neck, but took his left arm, twisting it behind his back to make a double hammerlock. He saw a bearded face thrust into his, in the light of the window peering at him, and smelled the aroma of wine.

"Well, I'm damned! I'd never forget a face with a scar like that. I met you last year, Captain, at Calcutta. I'm Andrews, master of the brig *Liberty* out of Philadelphia, but I don't recall your name."

"Merewether."

"Oh, yes. You took me to your Governor, and then captured that God damned Frog privateer, I heard. Well, what in hell's name are you doing here?"

"I might ask the same," said Merewether. He moved a little, and Andrews released the hammerlock.

"I only came out of the party to pump ship. I'm a prize agent buying cargoes the Frogs bring in, but there haven't been any lately. Coir and coconut oil! No market for that in the States. I sent the *Liberty* back with a full lading three months ago, but it looks as though I'll have nothing for her next voyage."

Merewether was anxious. This conversation was in normal tones, in English, but no one in the house seemed to have noticed.

"Well, Captain Andrews, I am delighted to meet you again . . ."

"Wait a minute, Captain. You look a mite peaked. Now just stay here, this ain't one of the sit-down suppers. I'll be back." The bearded figure marched off toward the front.

Merewether was of two minds, cut and run, or wait. Hunger overcame his fears, however, and he remained crouched in the shadows against the side of the house. It was more than half an hour before he heard footsteps, and Andrews appeared in the moonlight and handed over a napkin-wrapped parcel. Never had there been a more delicious combination, Merewether decided, as he rode in Andrews's light wagon rattling down the long grade into Port Louis, where they stopped before a bleak building facing the waterfront, and Andrews unlocked the door.

"There's a room above, ladder just inside the door. I must stable the horse." Merewether found the ladder, climbed up onto a sort of mezzanine above the main floor, and collapsed on the rough boards.

Merewether awoke to find a young, sandy-haired man shaking his shoulder. "Captain Andrews says come on down."

Merewether rubbed his eyes and stretched, every bone and

muscle aching, then rolled over and went down the ladder. He found himself in a dim storehouse, half filled with bales, boxes and barrels. He followed the man to a door in a corner that opened into a room furnished with bed, table, desk and a large iron strongbox bolted to the floor.

"Good morning," offered Andrews. "And have a bite. There's coffee and lime juice, too, and a bucket of water behind that door to wash in," continued Andrews. "And these are Harris and Starr, my clerks, Captain Merewether of the Bombay Marine."

He saw a black-browed man turning from a pan on a charcoal brazier and nodded to him and the sandy-haired man. He was dished out a steaming portion of porridge and poured a cup of coffee. The breakfast was delicious.

Andrews lit a spill of paper at the brazier and then lighted a cherry-bowled pipe. "And now, Captain, what do I do with you? I'd had a bit of that Dago wine the Governor served last night and wasn't thinking too straight, I'll admit. Of course, the States are neutral, no great love for either France or old England, but I've a job to do here, and I'm accountable to my principals to make a profit." He puffed a cloud of blue smoke toward the ceiling and looked perplexed. Behind the black beard was a square, resolute face with shrewd hazel eyes.

"I'll leave tonight, Captain," Merewether ventured. "I do not want to endanger you. I'm most grateful for your hospitality."

"Well, you were courteous to me at Calcutta, and I don't forget a favor. Now, I've people to see. I'll lend you a razor and soap, and you can stay out of sight above. Maybe by night, I can think of something."

It was delightful to scrub himself clean with a bucket of hot water and shave the bristle from his cheeks. He used the last of the water to rinse out the canvas trousers and blue shirt, leaving them to dry in the sunlight and air from an open window overlooking the harbor.

He was in little better circumstances than he had been in the hills, Mereweather considered. The bold movement from the Governor's mansion last night had succeeded because anyone who might have noticed Andrews's departure had simply assumed that the man with him was one of his servants, brought along to attend the rig. Here, there must be people coming and going; the warehouse of an American prize agent must attract custom. The neutral nations' willingness to trade in the captured goods of Company and English ships had sustained Mauritius and made fortunes these past four years.

Merewether remembered the report of old Jamie and looked out the window. A cable's length off, the brig he had seen from the mountain was moored bow and stern to buoys. There were half a dozen men visible on her deck, most of them busy with brushes and pots of paint. A carpenter was using an adze, his upward stroke almost coinciding at this distance with the chuff of the blow on the timber he was shaping. She was pierced for six guns a broadside, but the newly painted buff ports were closed. Clearly, she was out of commission.

A half cable's length astern of her was the schooner that had brought the prize in, what, two days ago? The snow was almost hidden beyond her. He could make out a languid petty officer lounging at the schooner's gangway, no other men visible on deck. A crew of ten practiced seamen could get a fore-and-aft rigged vessel like that under way, given the chance. The batteries at the narrow entrance to the harbor were the problem. He felt the clothing, found it still damp, moved it into the rectangle of sunlight, and dozed off.

It was midmorning by the time he awoke. He heard sounds below, voices, hoofbeats, and the thump of boxes or barrels on the floor. The clothing was dry, and he pulled it on, then forced his sore feet into the stiff landing-force boots. The sounds below ceased, and the young man, Harris, he remembered, came up the ladder.

"A short day's work," he said cheerfully. "The Frogs haven't had much to sell the past three months. The report is out now, they've lost their best four privateers off Bengal, taken by the Bombay Marine."

"Yes," said Merewether. "I heard as much myself."

"What we have here won't half fill the *Liberty*, and with Jefferson threatening an embargo, we may as well go home."

He looked at Merewether, a fresh-faced, intelligent young man, barely twenty, at a guess, not handsome, but with the strong structure of jaw and nose forecasting the man of affairs. The bland, expressionless blue eyes gave him an air of wisdom beyond his years. "Captain Andrews says you are a captain in the Bombay Marine. My father commanded a sloop of war in the old Continental Navy during the Revolution," he continued proudly. "Captured an Indiaman off Land's End in seventy-eight."

"Indeed?"

"Lost her, though, when two frigates showed up. Lucky, he always said, to get away himself."

"Fortunes of war," said Merewether.

"I could have had a warrant as midshipman myself, five years ago, from Commodore Edward Preble in *Constitution*. He'd been a midshipman in my father's sloop, but Mother thought I should go to Harvard College a bit longer and then learn the trade. My father's dead now, but we still own shares in ships trading from Philadelphia and Boston to the West Indies. This is our first venture out here; we own seven tenths of *Liberty*."

"Oh. Do you speak French?"

"Yes, a bit. It's not real French most of the people speak, but I've learned to get along."

Merewether's mind had been active during this brief conversation. Andrews was a sensible man, not one to risk ship or man needlessly for a marooned officer of the Bombay Marine. This young man evidently held a controlling interest in the trading venture here, though he nominally was only a clerk to Captain Andrews. And obviously he was a man of spirit. His conscience pained him briefly as Merewether set out to seduce Harris into a venture to escape from Mauritius.

"That schooner out there, where's her crew?"

"Most of them are ashore now. The men usually keep an establishment, a woman and a place to stay ashore while they're here; no more than an anchor watch aboard now. Usually, they would rest, refit and revictual for a month before they go out again, but with no more to show for the last voyage than that

215

snow they'll have to go back and beat up for more. I hear it will leave in the next four or five days," said Harris.

"A determined party should be able to take that schooner and sail her right out," said Merewether, watching Harris closely for the effect.

"Well, yes, take her, but sail out? No, I think not. The batteries on the southeast point are manned and ready, a battalion of regular artillerymen with thirty-two pounders, and the channel's not much more than a cable's length wide. Every ship has to have clearance from the Captain of the Port, departure in daylight only, a pilot aboard, and hoist the day's recognition signal," replied Harris. "But I see what you're driving at, Captain—"

Merewether felt a little nettled. The young man was clever. He had instantly punctured the vague plan that had formed in his mind a few minutes ago: liberate the Bombay Marine prisoners, overwhelm a skeleton crew, and sail the privateer out.

"If there were a bit of a diversion, something to attract attention elsewhere, there might be a chance. Oh, Captain Andrews has let it be known one of our men from Souillac is visiting here a few days, in case you're noticed." Harris turned to go down the ladder, saying, "Time for lunch; short day, but I'm getting used to these tropical ways, take a siesta myself now, not here but up on the hill. Beautiful girl."

Merewether idled the afternoon away. He watched a water hoy go alongside the schooner in late afternoon and pump her cargo in. A half dozen men handled the operation on deck. An hour later, a launch pulled out carrying eight men to the ship and returned with another eight; change of watch for the shipkeepers, he concluded. A few minutes later, a skiff paddled by two women, deep bronze in color, made its way to the ship and tied on to a boom forward of the gangway. Within an hour, seven women had boarded her. Merewether wondered for a moment who the lone celibate was on board. He became certain he could take the schooner with a dozen armed men, but young Harris had unerringly put his finger on the sore spot in the scheme.

Just before sunset, a lighter pulled by four sweeps appeared from beyond the schooner. It was loaded with six barrels and many bales of coir, apparently part of the cargo of the snow, unloaded out of the range of his vision. He watched as the barge laboriously made its way to his left and finally tied up at a jetty a few hundred yards westward, toward the harbour entrance. The men lashed a tarpaulin over the cargo and departed.

Merewether came down to find Harris and Starr in the captain's quarters, sharing a bottle of brandy. Andrews was absent.

"I clean forgot you were aboard, Captain," apologized Harris, pouring a liberal portion in a cup. "Confusion to Boney!"

The supper that followed was plain, but there was fresh beef with potatoes and carrots in the stew, and a French pastry for dessert.

"Captain Andrews went up to Pamplemousses for the night; a sugar planter thinks he can sell us a cargo of sugar. Small chance, there's no profit in carrying it halfway around the world when we can buy at the same price in Cuba or Hispaniola. He'll have a nice entertainment tonight though, a *sega*, an old African dance put on by the blacks. The drumbeat and rhythm are enough to make you want to get in it yourself!" Harris's eyes sparkled at the thought. "I'll have to get out at dawn to pick him up in the wagon. There's an auction at ten in the morning and a chance to pick up a few things worth taking back to Philadelphia."

Harris opened a box, extracted a long, thin West Indian cigar, offered it to Merewether, who declined, and then lighted it with a spill. "I'll have one more dollop of this brandy, Spanish, it is, and doesn't have the soapy French taste. It came from the master's cellar in the Indiaman *Royal George*, taken south of here last year. Then I'll retire. By the way, Captain, since you're more or less accounted for, would you like to ride along?"

"I would be delighted," Merewether told him. "The last time

I came that way, I was traveling through the bushes and in a hurry." Harris and Starr soon retired, and Merewether followed, to lie sleepless on the pallet he had made on the balcony overlooking the harbor.

It must be two hours after midnight, he thought. The three-quarter moon was above Pieter Both, plainly outlining the harbor. The three ships present each showed an anchor light. There was an aura of silence over the town and harbor, with only the occasional bark of a dog saluting the waning moon, when Merewether moved quietly to sit by the window again.

"Diversion," Harris had said. An uprising in the south? A fire in the town? A forged dispatch to the commandant of the garrison? The Governor kidnapped or assassinated? A powder magazine exploded? Merewether shook his head. None of these heroic expedients would empty the batteries commanding the entrance to the harbor, and a single salvo from the thirty-two pounders would cripple or sink any vessel attempting the narrow passage. Then too, he was putting the matter backward, he decided. First, he must have a force upon which he could depend to take the schooner. The snow was hopeless; it would be snapped up within a dozen miles of the harbor by that tall privateer. But now an inkling of a resolution of the problem crept into his mind; coir and coconut oil in the lighter now moored against the jetty a hundred yards to the east; the land breeze that he felt ruffling his hair through the window now.

There might be a chance he could provide a diversion.

Chapter Twenty

It was pleasant to ride along the gravel road in the dawn, listening to the cheerful conversation of Harris as he pointed out the geographical features of the landscape and commented on the economy of the island. Pamplemousses was a hamlet some four miles east of the head of Tombeau Bay. Half an hour later, Merewether recognized the stone cottage of Jamie Plantain against the hill as they rolled by. There was no one visible about it. A quarter of a mile further, they passed within earshot of the prisoner-of-war camp just in time to hear the whistles and shouts signaling reveille. A little farther on was the swale the prisoners were filling with broken stone. The wagon slowed, as Harris let the horse pick his way across the rough surface. There had been little progress made since the day he had watched the operation from the hillside.

Merewether touched Harris's arm. "Let me out here. I'll be back tonight," he told Harris, seeing the startled expression. He swung down and walked hurriedly up into the copse surrounding the latrine. One of the basaltic boulders dotting the hillside afforded shelter, and he tucked himself behind it, screened by bushes.

During the next hour, Merewether had ample time to reconsider his hasty decision. Still, he told himself, unless he could make contact with these prisoners, he had no chance of escape from this island within the foreseeable future. Finally, he heard the tramp of feet, then the clang of shovels, the squeak and rumble of hand barrows, and finally the thud of sledgehammers on stone. The day had begun for the prisoners.

It was more than an hour before anyone approached the latrine. The man was middle-aged, gray-bearded, and stooped, his hands gnarled by a lifetime before the mast. Merewether did not move, he wanted someone quicker of wit than this seaman appeared to be. The man dumped dirt in the pit from a broken shovel and went back. From his hiding place, he could see only occasional movement of the prisoners and guards. Two other ordinary seamen came and went, as the sun climbed in the sky. The buzz of flies in a cloud over the pit was soporific, he was almost dozing when he heard footsteps again.

The thin, scholarly face behind the scraggling beard he had seen before at Bombay Castle, he was sure, and then a name came without conscious thought to his lips.

"Wilkerson!" he said in a conversational tone of voice, moving from the shelter of the boulder. "I'm Merewether. Do you remember?"

The man stood in arrested motion, the end of his unfastened

belt in his hand, staring at him. "Well, I'm damned!" he said. "And what happened to your face?"

"No time for that," said Merewether. "If I can manage a way to escape, are you with me?"

"Certainly."

"And your men?"

"They'll come."

Merewether decided to take the risk. "Tell the officers and petty officers you can trust to stand by. When we move, it must be instantly." Hope flamed in the dull eyes as Wilkerson buckled his belt and turned to go, his mission here forgotten.

"I'll be back," said Merewether, and slid again into concealment. It was an eternity before the prisoners formed up and marched away at sunset.

Merewether pulled himself erect, and went stiffly up the hill. He found the path and moved in the dusk to the point above Jamie Plantain's cottage. In the afterglow he could see no sign of surveillance of the place, but he waited until the light faded and the glow of a lamp appeared in the back doorway of the cottage. His entrance caused consternation, old Jamie snatching up a huge pistol.

"Friend! Merewether!" he said urgently. He saw no sign of Eleanora or Pierre, but Jamie had a cup of rum at his elbow. "I should go on to Port Louis now."

"Just a moment, Captain," rasped Jamie. "What have ye done with her?" The faded blue eyes were fairly sparkling with rage in the lamplight, and the pistol was still pointed at him.

Merewether was speechless. Evidently the woman, Eleanora, was missing, and Plantain had concluded that she had gone with him. He opened his mouth to make the denial, but guilt was a dead weight on his conscience.

"I know Eleanora's a full-blooded woman, and she's been starved of a man these three months past," continued Jamie, finally laying the pistol on the floor beside his chair. "I suspected ye could not resist her and that she went to ye that night in the Maroon dugout, but she has not returned."

There was no reason to deny the fact at this point, Merewether

220

decided. The old man could possibly be a jealous grandfather, but then Eleanora was not a child, she was a mature woman. He realized suddenly that it was not the seduction which had outraged Jamie, but Eleanora's desertion of him. The possessiveness of the aged, and their tendency to cling to those who served them, often overrode other considerations. He decided to make a clean breast of the matter.

"Sir, it's true Eleanora came to me in the dugout, but she left at dawn three days ago. That afternoon two squads of soldiers appeared, and I barely squeezed out the bolt hole ahead of them. After that I slept in the woods." He was about to add that an American trader had taken him in, but a sudden caution curbed his tongue.

"Yes, Pierre found the dugout wrecked, and we thought ye had been taken, but he learned the soldiers came back to Port Louis without ye. Pierre's been there yesterday and today trying to find Eleanora. It must be that *cochon,* Jules, has caught her." The old man settled back in his chair wearily and lifted the cup to his lips. "Pour a portion of rum, if ye wish, Captain. We've no one to cook here now, naught but bread and cheese to eat."

Merewether relaxed. The crisis was past. The seduction of his granddaughter did not weigh heavily on Jamie's mind; it was her absence from his service that concerned him. As he lifted the cup for the first cautious sip of the fiery spirits, Merewether wondered if he would ever drink another civilized London gin and lemon.

There really was no reason to stay, but the night was young, Port Louis less than an hour's walk away, and the moon would not be up until well after midnight. Merewether found the remnant of a loaf in the pantry, cheese and some dried plums. He served Jamie and ate a bit himself. The conversation was desultory, then ceased as Jamie lay back and snored. He had almost decided to take his leave, when he heard footsteps. He slid into the kitchen and then heard Pierre's voice speaking rapidly in French. He eased back through the door and nodded to Pierre, who gave him only a quick glance, then continued his report to Jamie. When he finished, there was a dead silence as Jamie sat in his chair, head bowed.

"Captain!" he said, "Pierre learned Jules has lodged Eleanora in the house of Madame Torres. Some of the privateersmen keep their women there, but Jules has only the pay of a private soldier, and it must be more than he can afford. I suspect . . ." The old, creaking voice trailed off. "I want her back!" he said suddenly, raising his head.

"Yes, sir," said Merewether. "But if she's his wife . . ."

"No matter. She was my granddaughter first!"

This was ridiculous, the old man in a tantrum, able to think only of his own comfort. And Merewether had other concerns; he had in effect made a promise this morning to Wilkerson and his men. He was no closer to a solution of the problem than he had been last night.

"All right," he said. "You want Eleanora back, and I wish to go to India. I need a man able to get that snow under way with six men and take her out of the harbor. But first, I must recover my gun and uniform." He tried to tell them where he had left them under the ledge.

Old Jamie broke in. "I told ye I was a harbor pilot. Moving the snow is easy, except for the guns in the fort. Never worry about your plunder. I'll find it."

"And never worry about the guns in the fort." Merewether paused, conscious that he was moving faster than he had planned, then plunged recklessly ahead. "I'll take the day guards at siesta tomorrow, march the prisoners back to the stockade at sunset, and then wait for the night relief." It was only another step. "We take them to Port Louis, capture the schooner, then the snow, and sail them out. . . ." He stopped, thunderstruck at the stupidity of his oversight. "I need a boat, Mr. Plantain," he finished weakly.

"Never mind that," said old Jamie. "There's a ferry scow moored this side of the bay, near the north batteries. I know the way across the outer reef around Mer Rouge; ye may get your breeches wet, but ye need not swim."

Merewether realized that this was a simple plan, simply expressed. Its defect was that it led only into a dead end, trapped in the harbor by a battery of thirty-two pounders. Old Jamie came bluntly to the point. "And now, where's Eleanora?"

"She'll be back before morning," Merewether said.

The walk into Port Louis was pleasant in the cool of the evening in this season that passed for autumn in these latitudes, and the land breeze was beginning to come down from the hills. He went by a watchman at the edge of Port Louis, saluting him without breaking his stride. There was a glimmer of light in the upper window of the warehouse, and at Merewether's call, Harris came down to unbolt the door.

"I'd decided you'd been shot," he said cheerfully. "Captain Andrews fair took the hide off me for letting you out of my sight, but then he picked up some bargains at the auction and put it back on again."

They climbed onto the balcony where a lantern cast a yellow glow on an opened book. Starr was absent.

"Horace," said Harris self-consciously. "The Odes. *Carpe diem* intrigues my romantic nature, but I can't help dreading the cold, gray dawn of the morning after. It must be my puritan grandmother's blood showing through."

"Yes," said Merewether, realizing that he had no conception of what Harris meant. "Now," he continued, "I have made contact with the prisoners. They are game for the attempt."

"Oh, and you have found a way past the batteries?"

"Possibly. Are you familiar with the arbitary signals used by the French?" He saw the puzzled expression on Harris's face, and explained, "I'm interested in only one, the flag hoist for, 'I am pursuing the enemy,' or its equivalent."

"Not exactly," replied Harris. "They don't furnish us with their signal book. We've always relied on a simple dip of the flag in *Liberty* as an answer to any Frog flag hoist. Seems to work very well."

Merewether felt exasperation well up in his throat and started to turn away from this clever young man.

"I'm sorry, Captain," said Harris, touching his arm. "I didn't mean to be facetious, but I just don't know." He paused, then said, "Captain Andrews may know."

"Very well," said Merewether in resignation. "Perhaps you'll know more about the house of Madame Torres."

"Quite a bit," said Harris. "I spend my siestas there quite often. A very respectable woman, Madame Torres. All reckonings for lodging are paid in advance."

"And have you noticed a woman, just came there in the past two days, quite a striking Creole? Her name is Eleanora." He paused, conscious that he did not know her last name.

"Oh, yes, she must be the one who came in with an artilleryman from the garrison. A little bruised about the eyes, but she'll heal."

"I've promised to return her to her family," said Merewether. "Tonight, if possible."

"As a star boarder," said Harris, "paid in advance, I have certain privileges, such as a key to the back door of the establishment. I was going to nip up there myself after a bit. . . . If the soldier's not there, I'll have Hermione bring the girl out to you —that is, if she wants to come."

Harris was silent a moment, a little half smile on his face, but the blue eyes bored into Merewether's.

"And now, Captain," he said. "I'm a damned fool, but I guess I come by it honestly. My father slipped by a frigate and cut out a prize in The Downs one foggy night thirty years ago, the foundation of our fortunes. It had Lord Howe's paymaster and his chests on board. I can't go with you to India, much as I'd like to—family obligations, you know—but I don't mind giving you such assistance as I can, so long as I don't get involved with the Frogs. I'm not interested in heroic gestures; I want solid facts. If you can convince me, I'll see what I can do for you."

Merewether sat quietly for a moment. He had set out to seduce this young man into giving assistance for the escape, and here was the explicit offer; he need only present a logical plan, one that would appeal to the calculating intellect he recognized behind the nonchalant exterior. Misgivings beset him; this American was a neutral, and if the venture failed or Harris's part were suspected, the French government might inflict harsh reprisals, even some trumped-up charge of espionage or sedition. Still, he justified himself, Harris and Andrews were already tarred with guilt for giving him refuge, and a few more acts in violation of neutrality could hardly make the matter worse. He must have someone who knew the town, the military and official procedures, with access to more information than old Jamie and Pierre could ever hope to learn, and with freedom to come and go. He accepted the challenge.

"I am honored, Mr. Harris," he said. "And if you'll come along with me to India, I'll see you entertained by the Governor-General as though you were a visiting Raj."

"No," said Harris. "State your plan."

Merewether paused a moment to collect his thoughts, then commenced, "Diversion, you said . . ."

An hour later, Harris went up the hill to the house of Madame Torres.

Eleanora was shaking uncontrollably, hysteria suppressed, but close to overwhelming her. Merewether put his arm about her and moved along the byway Harris had recommended to avoid the watch. They walked in silence until the cottage was in sight, a light visible; apparently Jamie and Pierre were still awake.

"I'm sorry," Merewether told her as they halted at the edge of the garden. "I've brought you trouble."

She laid her head on his shoulder and wept, as he patted her back awkwardly. It was uncomfortable, this mature woman reduced to a whimpering child, and yet the pressure of her body against his awoke passion even here. His caresses became less comforting and more explicit, as she gradually ceased her tears. Merewether would have pursued the matter to a conclusion, when he found himself pushed away.

"No!" Eleanora said in a violent whisper. "Jules forced me, and I'll not have you take the pox back to your bride!"

The vision of Caroline leaped into his mind, as Merewether's arms dropped. How could this woman have known? He was sure he had said nothing to give her even an inkling of his betrothal, but his guilt must have shown through, and somehow, she had guessed. In foolhardy confusion, he reached for Eleanora again, found her moving away, and let her lead him through the garden to the cottage.

For the first time since Merewether had known him, Jamie appeared to be a little tipsy, his speech slurred, his eyes wandering.

This was the third cup in the past hour of incomprehensible creole gabble. It must have been close to midnight when Eleanora, still sobbing, retreated to her room.

"Now, Captain, there's your plunder hanging in the closet. A little rust on the musket, but unharmed, I judge. I'd draw the charge and reload before trusting it to fire after lying out in the dew."

"Thank you, sir, and now if Pierre can put it in the cave above the quarry, I'll be there by dawn. I intend to move tomorrow night." Merewether paused for a moment, trying to sort the confused plan in his mind into some sort of order, consecutive in time and coordinated as to movements. "I think I must wait until midnight to capture the schooner, but I should move my men earlier if I can."

"Well, Captain, I suggest ye bring your men around the coast road, and I'll meet ye when it turns back, south of Tombeau Bay, just about the place I first saw ye the other morning. I'd say an hour before midnight would be about right," said old Jamie with a yawn.

"Agreed," said Merewether, thankful for the decision, as he still sought to establish the chronology of the operation. The waning moon was just becoming visible as he came out into the garden. He covered the distance to Port Louis in less than an hour, passing through the byway without sighting the watch. To his surprise, a light was visible in the window of the warehouse. He tried the door, found it unbolted, and went up the ladder.

"Damn!" said Harris. "I thought you'd never come back."

Merewether was surprised at the heat in Harris's voice. "I thought you were at Madame Torres's," he said.

"And so I should be," exploded Harris. "Damn it, what I've been waiting to tell you since a quarter of an hour after you left is, there's a Boston barque anchored at Souillac. Captain Andrews just got the word tonight. It's taking on fresh water and sailing for Calcutta tomorrow—no, this afternoon."

Merewether came stockstill as the news sunk in. Harris and Andrews would not have mentioned the matter unless they were sure he could obtain passage in the neutral vessel. He felt exultation well up, sure that he could exchange the twenty pounds in notes in his pocket, plus a draft on the Company, for a passage to Calcutta, not working his way for once across the weary ocean leagues, as he had everywhere he went since he was twelve years old. The prospect was irresistible. He would abandon the harebrained scheme to take the privateer schooner and sail her past the batteries with a crew of liberated Bombay Marine prisoners. That was suddenly a puerile and desperate venture, doomed to failure. He was free, free to go and escape, and if the barque had any sailing qualities at all, he could still be back for that wedding day with Caroline. His mind glossed over his unfaithfulness in the jubilation of the moment. Even afoot, he could cover the thirty miles to Souillac in six or seven hours and be on board well in time.

"I can't do it, Harris," Merewether found himself saying, not believing his own ears. "I promised those men a run for their money, and I can't leave them in the lurch." The vision of Wilkerson's haggard face, hope flaming in his eyes, could not be denied and the prisoners left for rescue next year. He even wondered for a moment if the putative blood of Percy running in his veins had anything to do with his decision. Nonsense! he decided.

Harris looked at him, the bland blue eyes in the fresh, young face suddenly sparkling in the lantern light. "I think you're a bit of a fool, Captain. This is the Ile de France, not King Arthur's Court, and we've found you a sure way out." He hesitated a moment, his eyes still disconcertingly meeting Merewether's. "But, by God, if you've given your word, Captain, stand by it!"

Merewether felt relief flood up. Harris had called him a fool, but he understood his obligation. He and the prisoners might die in the attempt, but his conscience would not bear the burden of a desertion of his comrades for the balance of his life.

"Thank you. And now, I've little enough time if we move tonight, seeing it's not long before dawn and I have a way to go. Are you still with me?"

There was a momentary flicker of doubt across Harris's face, reasonable enough under the circumstances, after a man had refused sure escape.

"Certainly. And by the by, the signal you want is red, white swallowtail, blue. Logical enough when you think of it, the Imperial colors."

Merewether repeated the sequence to fix the flag hoist in his mind, then extended his hand. "I'm grateful, Mr. Harris. Perhaps you'll come to Calcutta sometime when I can properly express my thanks."

Merewether pulled the jambiya from under the pallet, secured it in his belt, and swung down the ladder. Outside, he encountered a drizzle of rain, the first he had felt on the island, though it was just at the end of the cyclone season. He set off at a fast pace around the harbor, then up the hill, conscious that dawn was breaking in the east, finally to take shelter in the cave above the quarry. He was soaked, and wondered for a moment if the French would work the prisoners on a day such as this promised to be. In the growing light, he found the bundle of his possessions, and stripped off the wet clothing to put on undress uniform. Seated against the rock wall, an exhausted Merewether went to sleep.

It was mid-morning, he judged, when he awoke. Merewether drank from the pool at the back of the cavern, splashed water on his head and face, and surveyed the situation. The prisoners were at work, the rain had stopped, and the sun burst forth intermittently from behind scudding clouds. An hour and a half later, the whistle blew, and the guards trooped up to their grove, as the lascars appeared with their hampers. The men clustered in their patch of shade about the pots that held their food. The routine was identical to that he had observed, what, four, five days ago? He could see the wine bottles passed out as the guards settled back in comfort.

Half an hour later, the whistle blew, one man with a musket moved indolently out to his post, and the prisoners straggled back to their duties, as the other guards settled in for their siesta. Merewether looked at the air rifle standing against the wall of the cave, then decided against assassination. By now, the guards must be asleep, except for the one man standing with his back to him. He buckled on the belt with the extra air flask and bullet pouch, took a deep breath and slid out the entrance. He walked slowly down the slope toward the grove, carrying the air rifle at the ready, conscious that some of the prisoners had seen him.

Wilkerson was loading rock into a barrow in the quarry a dozen feet from the guard. Merewether reached the grove, found the snoring figures sprawled before him, and turned his head just in time to see Wilkerson strike the guard in the back of the head with a broken piece of stone. Another man caught the musket before it struck the ground. Merewether pointed the rifle at the guards as they started up. Suddenly there were a dozen men beside him in the grove, the stacked muskets and pistols were seized, and sledgehammers raised threateningly.

"Hold on!" cried Merewther. "Don't kill them!" One squat, bullet-headed seaman seemed intent on doing just that, but Merewether barred his way and pushed him back with the rifle. He had the fleeting impression that the man's fury had been transferred to him, but just then Wilkerson intervened.

"Hold!" he shouted in turn. "Silence!"

The melee subsided, with the guards huddled together cringing away from the menacing circle. There must be many old scores here that wanted settling, Merewether concluded, conscious of the eyes now fixed upon his face. Most of them were hard and unfriendly, showing little respect for the uniform of the Bombay Marine.

"Now, men," he commenced, "Lieutenant Wilkerson will tell you, I'm Captain Merewether of the Marine, come to take you away from here." He paused, conscious that this was not entirely the truth of the matter, but it was close enough to be convincing. He went on, "But I need your help. We march to Port Louis tonight to take ship and escape to India. In the meantime you must still act as prisoners."

There was a momentary silence, then an angry mutter of voices. Apparently these men had thought that they would march straight off to a Company ship and an issue of grog. Even a few more hours of servitude seemed to be more than they could bear. Merewether slung the air rifle over his shoulder, butt down, and waited for quiet.

"Wait," said Wilkerson. "The Captain is in command."

Merewether stood impassively, the realization quickly sinking in that he was faced with mutiny. These men, long imprisoned and mistreated, were in no mood to carry out an operation under a strange officer or to submit to ordinary discipline. Even with willing men, the plan was slim enough, and the odds against success astronomical. He wondered for a moment if he could disengage himself here, and with the three or four hours left, reach Souillac in time to board the Boston barque. He raised his hand and tried to speak again, then stopped when it became apparent that no one would listen as the tumult drowned him out. The men had reached a frenzy of angry hysteria, and Merewether wondered what Wilkerson might have told them to raise their hopes so high, only to be dashed by his own simple statement of the plan of action.

He heard a voice shout, "Hang 'em all, I say, and take it to the hills!"

Wilkerson, face pale under the beard and sunburn, tried again. "Silence!" he shouted.

"Ah, shut your bloody mouth!" screamed a voice.

Merewether became aware of movement to his right. The squat man he had shoved out of the way with the rifle a moment ago, almost completely bald, with old scars of the cat crisscrossed over his bare back, was moving towards him. The man's face was crimson. With his feet wide-spaced, knees bent, head hunched forward, hands dangling, he was hopping stiffly back and forth, shrieking obscenities.

The noise subsided as the others watched the fury build up in the man. Merewether stood quietly, the rifle still slung over his right shoulder, grasping it by the barrel just above the lock, the toe of the stock swinging level with his knees. He had seen men of this type a time or so before, had witnessed them generate the berserk madness within themselves that compelled a senseless, murderous attack. This man was following the pattern. It would be only a matter of seconds before he launched his assault.

He would break his hands on that round bullet head, already laced with blue scars from old wounds, with little chance of stopping him, Merewether realized, and there was no time to unsling the rifle. He saw the frenzy reach its climax, and gauging the distance, took a half step forward, swinging the rifle butt upward, the sling of his shoulders serving as a pivot. The toe of the stock smashed against the lower jaw, two teeth popped out of the man's mouth, followed by a gush of blood. The steel air flask rang like a bell, as the berserker fell on his face.

There was a dead silence.

"Now," said Merewether in a conversational tone, "lay this man over there in the shade with someone to look after him and give him a bit of water when he wakes up." He turned to Wilkerson. "Who's your senior petty officer?"

"Case, gunner's mate, sir."

"Give him a steady man, a musket and pistols, to keep these Frenchmen." He saw the fallen guard in the quarry trying to rise. "And bring that man over here. Tear up a napkin and bind up his head."

Merewether turned back to the crew, now standing quietly before him. He decided that discipline prevailed, the men would accept orders, and he sent them back to breaking stone and spreading it in the swale. At sunset, the force marched off, their captives bunched in the center, guarded by prisoners wearing the jackets and caps of the militiamen. Even the berserker, his jaw supported by a napkin tied over the top of his head, was somewhat cheerful.

CHAPTER TWENTY-ONE

It proved to be a simple matter to ambush the night relief party as it came to the stockade, but twelve prisoners, held by only thirty men in his crew presented problems. Merewether finally decided to lock them, bound back to back, in the little guardhouse at the gate of the stockade, hoping that they could not free themselves before daylight.

After the men had been fed, he commenced the urgent briefing and rehearsing of the party in the roles they were to play in the operation. Wilkerson was the only surviving commissioned officer since the malaria last winter, and he soon found that he did not have the petty officers to fill the rough watch, quarter and station bill he drew up. On Wilkerson's recommendations, he rated seamen to petty officers, and promised Case, the gunner's mate, an acting warrant if all went well. There were oarsmen to be told off for the ferry scow, topmen, boatswain's mates and quartermasters to be assigned specific missions, and all to be impressed with the necessity to use cold steel, no firearms to be discharged except at a last resort. With this accomplished, Merewether was astounded to find that it still lacked two hours until midnight.

The night was overcast, a hint of rain again in the air. Merewether came out of the stockade with Wilkerson and decided he would walk the short distance to Jamie's cottage to make sure the old man was ready.

"I will meet you and the men on the road at midnight," he said. "Make sure the guards are secured before you move."

Merewether moved up the slope by the ditch where he had found himself nearly a fortnight ago. There were no lights visible in the cottage, and he found the door closed. His light knock was instantly answered by Pierre, who shoved the barrel of a pistol into his belly.

"Merewether!" he gasped, and the young man stood aside. There was only a flickering candle in one corner of the room and heavy shutters were bolted across the windows.

"Ye're early, Captain," said Jamie from the darkness in the corner. "But just as well. That damned Jules has been about again and upset Eleanora terrible. Right in the house, he came, and I missed him with the pistol!" Merewether's eyes adjusted to the light, and he saw the old man in his chair, wearing the long blue coat, white trousers, boots and cocked hat, that he now realized was his pilot's dress. He was thankful to see that Jamie did not have a cup of rum at hand.

"I have the prisoners ready to move, sir," Merewether told him. "We took the guards at noon."

"Very good," said Jamie. "I've had a bit of the colic since this afternoon. I'll just take no rum until I feel better."

Merewether was suddenly aware of the frailty of this man upon whom he depended to show the way around Mer Rouge and find the ferry scow.

"Naught to worry about," Jamie repeated. "I'll be ready, but I calculate ye're early here."

"Yes. I came by to make sure you were ready." He paused, and then continued boldly, "And to say goodbye to Eleanora."

Eleanora was subdued, her eyes swollen and downcast. Merewether bowed and made a stilted speech of thanks and farewell, and she withdrew, responding with only an unintelligible murmur. A sense of urgency possessed Merewether, though it lacked almost an hour of the appointed time.

"Sir, I think we should go. If Jules was about earlier . . ."

"We can move out along the coast. May take longer in this weather." There was no rain yet, but the smell of it was in the air. He stood up and reached behind the chair, then buckled on a cutlass in a well-oiled leather sheath, mounted with brass.

" 'Twas my father's, Captain James Plantain. He left it and told my mother if she had a son to make sure he was learned to use it. I'll leave the pistol here with Pierre, though I'm not thinking Jules will be back tonight. And now, Captain, we be off."

In a few minutes time, they were at the point of rendezvous. "I'll go down and get the men, while you wait here," Merewether told him.

At the stockade, he found Wilkerson, made a quick inspection of the guards, tied back to back in the gatehouse, slung the air rifle over his shoulder, and went back toward the road where Jamie waited.

A dozen yards from the road, he heard a shout and the pound of running feet on the gravel surface. Merewether jumped forward, unslinging the rifle and burst into the roadway. There was a clang of metal on metal, and he could just make out the flash of blades in the darkness between two shadowy figures. Metal rang again, but he could not distinguish friend from foe. There was another shout as one blade rose high in the air, then a scream of agony.

Wilkerson came stumbling up, a lantern shielded with a square of canvas in hand. In its light, Jules, the jaundiced artilleryman, writhed on the gravel, coughing out a continuous bright red hemorrhage. Old Jamie stood back, on guard, breathing heavily, the old cutless with its gleaming blade still pointing at Jules.

"Passed clean through him!" crowed Jamie. "Never cut when ye may thrust!" Beside the man lay a long cane knife, heavy and razor-edged. The coughing declined into a rattle, and movement ceased.

"Put him out of sight in the bushes," Merewether told Wilkerson.

Five minutes later, the party moved off, around the shore of Tombeau Bay, and down the coast toward Port Louis Harbor. Jamie led the way, a bit tottery, but without hesitation through the darkness. A fine mist began to fall and the shore breeze came down strongly from the hills. Merewether shivered as he became wet to the skin. It seemed an interminable time before Jamie called them to a halt on a gravel beach.

"Less than a mile, Captain, but we must wade and walk across the outer reef of Mer Rouge." The old man was wheezing, and Merewether decided to rest a few minutes. "Must be this rain has give me the rheumatics again in my arm," he continued, sitting down.

"We are ahead of ourselves at that," Merewether told him. "Plenty of time yet."

After a quarter of an hour, Jamie led them single file, wading through waist-deep water, then across rough coral, as he picked a way down the exposed reef. There was no surf with the wind blowing offshore, but it took an hour to reach the island where the unmanned batteries crouched under canvas covers in their redoubts. Jamie found the ferry scow at its moorings, half full of water, its sweeps laid carelessly along the little jetty. Wilkerson put six men to work bailing her out with two wooden scoops and the militiamen's caps.

Across the bay, Merewether could see the three anchor lights —from left to right, the brig, the schooner and the snow. Above them, a few lights showed in Port Louis and on the batteries directly opposite him. He rested the men half an hour, then ordered the embarkation. Jamie was still wheezing, his arms folded across his chest, but he took his place in the stern as Merewether shipped the rudder.

"Give way." The scow moved sluggishly out, steering first two points to port of the schooner, then adjusting to counter the shore breeze, which appeared to be still freshening. He had two men to each sweep, but progress was slow. Twelve men, all armed, and Wilkerson were crouched in the bow. At his whispered command, the oarsmen eased their stroke, and Merewether brought the scow about to port as the starboard sweeps came in. She slid softly along the port side of the schooner where a tall man could reach a handhold in her scuppers. The man pulled himself up by main force, wiggled over the bulwarks into the waist, and dropped the jacob's ladder rolled up beside the port gangway.

Merewether was the fourteenth man on board. The lone man on deck was already a captive, a horny hand over his mouth, arms twisted up behind his back.

"There are seven other men and women," whispered Merewether to Wilkerson.

It was ludicrous. The naked women were pushed into the lazaret aft, their clothing bundled in behind them, and the padlock snapped shut in the hasp. The steadiest man in the crew was placed on guard outside. These women-starved prisoners could not be afforded a chance to think about the matter, lest the whole venture founded on these lush Creole charms.

Merewether was in command of the ship. He sent the men to quarters, to find in darkness the halyards, sheets and braces that must be manned, the flag bag, the magazine, the pyrotechnics locker. Then he realized his mistake. He and Wilkerson intercepted the group coming out of the commissary pantry, and marched them with their burden of bottles aft to the cabin, there to deposit the spirits under lock and key. He thought wryly of his concern to make sure the women were secure, while ignoring the greater danger of the rum. It was a commentary on his character, he decided.

The crew for the scow went quietly back into her, old Jamie still sitting stiffly in the stern. They pulled away for the short distance to the snow. The two men aboard her offered no resistance. Both were asleep in their bunks.

Merewether faced Plantain on the poop of the snow. She

steered with a tiller, a small, crowded vessel, only a tiny cabin for her master and his mate, and a fetid forecastle for the dozen lascars who had composed her crew. She was a poor example of the country ships trading along the Malabar coast, south to Ceylon, and he shared the contempt of the agents at Port Louis for such a sorry prize. But she might serve his purpose.

"And now, Captain Plantain," he commenced slowly. "There's really no good reason for you to go further. Let me take you back ashore, and you may go home, no one the wiser for this night." He could see the old man, still hunched over, his arms wrapped about his chest, in the darkness.

Jamie straightened up. "Nay, Captain, I told ye I was an Englishman! My father was a brave man, though misguided, and I'll never equal him, but I'll see ye off this island this day. 'Tis not as though I had a lifetime yet to live. I'm old, a burden, and no use to myself. I'll take this stinking bucket out as ye say!"

Jamie was adamant, and Merewether was relieved. He needed every man he could muster to get the schooner under way, and he could hardly spare Wilkerson to command this little vessel. Then too, Plantain with his pilot's experience should be able to take her out along the northern limit of the harbor entrance. He told himself that he had made the offer, been refused, and did not intend to argue the point.

"Very well, Captain," he said briskly. "Half an hour before dawn, I'll show a light three times. That is your signal to cut the anchor cable and set sail. With this breeze, you should be well out of cannon shot by daylight."

"I understand, Captain," said Jamie, taking his hand. "And good luck to ye!"

"And to you, Captain Plantain. You are an Englishman after King George's own heart!"

He left the snow and pulled back to the schooner, his conscience still sore at his exploitation of Jamie's simple pride in his English ancestry. It might yet be possible, if all went well, to restore him to his home undetected. The misting rain drove into his face as the ferry rounded to alongside the schooner. The wind chilled his body through the soaked uniform during the brief ascent of the ladder.

There was one more task to be accomplished, he thought wearily, as he sat with Wilkerson in the cabin. "Ask Case to come in." The bulkhead clock showed nearly a quarter after three, two hours until daylight, and possibly more than that in this weather.

The acting gunner came in, a stocky, taciturn man who spoke in the broad accent of Devon.

"Yes, zur?" he inquired.

"You have inspected the magazines and pyrotechnic locker, Mister Case?"

"Yes, zur. All's secure, zur."

"I'll want rockets ready for launching, Mister Case," continued Merewether, emphasizing the "Mister" of the warrant rank. "But protected from the weather. And I'll want the stern chaser cleared away, made ready for loading and firing. You'd best have a slow match lighted. The lock may misfire in this weather."

"Aye aye, zur." The man was ready to go, as he halted him with another question.

"You are handy with flint and steel, I take it?"

"Yes, zur."

"Then leave your mate to lay out the rockets and clear away the gun. Bring two axes, two buckets and your tinderbox back here." The man stood for a moment staring. "You may go," Merewether prompted.

When he returned, axes and buckets in hand, tinderbox tucked into his waistband, Merewether told him, "Have a seat, Mister Case. We have a few minutes to wait." The man sat down stiffly in the unaccustomed surroundings of the cabin, and the presence of this strange captain, with his scarred, resolute face, who had so casually smashed the jaw of the berserker this afternoon.

"I need you to light a fire for me at the harborside," continued Merewether conversationally. "And the axes to break open some casks. It might be as well if you tied a kerchief around your head like this." He folded the square of cloth about his own head as he had seen Eleanora do, and knotted it. Case clumsily followed suit.

"Now, if you'll roll up your trousers and tie a bit of canvas about your waist for a skirt, you might very well be mistaken for a woman in the dark." After an incredulous pause, Case followed Merewether's example, then rubbed soot from the lantern glass on his face and hands.

"We'll take one of the wherrys at the starboard gangway."

Case grumbled but picked up his burden and followed Merewether on deck.

It was a bare quarter mile to the harborside. Pulling without haste, the wherry covered the distance in a few minutes. Wet and cold again, Merewether steered for the spot in the gloom he estimated to be the mooring of the lighter loaded with coir and coconut oil. It was barely fifty feet away when he made out its bulk alongside the rickety jetty. He altered course to port and pulled beside the pilings almost under the blunt bow.

"Take a turn," he whispered, and Case made the painter fast. "Wait a moment." Merewether scrambled up the scantlings, conscious of the clumsy encumbrance of the canvas skirt.

On the jetty, he paused to look about. There was a cobbled roadway leading from the jetty toward another broader street, and a dark warehouse beyond it. The sound of scuffing footsteps came from the street, Merewether froze for a moment, then sidled slowly to his right, head averted. He saw in the corner of his eye a figure carrying a bull's-eye lantern, then felt its yellow light wash over him as he turned away. A voice called out a French phrase, then laughed. Merewether made a disdainful gesture and minced with short steps along the jetty. Laughter came again, and the figure scuffed off past the warehouse. Praise God, the watch had thought him just another half-drunken Creole wench returning from an assignation! He waited an eternity, then called Case up from the wherry.

The jambiya cut the lines lashing the tarpaulin down over the cargo. Folded back, Merewether could feel the tops of barrels, and then he found a space between the casks and the bales of coir wide enough for him to stand in. The motion of the barge caused a continuous turgid movement of water in the bilges under the floorboards. He came back out, pulled the tarpaulin farther aft, exposing the bales of coir, pulled one down and cut it open.

"Give me an axe," he whispered to Case.

He swung and the blade glanced off the staves, almost striking

238

his leg. Hell! No sense in using brute force. He tapped the top hoop, then inserted the blade under it and pried. It came loose, and another stroke of the axe split the head of the barrel.

"Push it over," he told Case.

The gush of sweetish-smelling oil wet his feet before he could pull himself up. He pulled down more bales, cut their bindings, and heaped the coir in the bottom of the lighter, then opened another barrel and poured the oil over the mass, to drip into the bilges.

"Now, bear a hand with the buckets!" he told Case, and the two of them began to dip buckets full of water from the bay to wet down a whole tier of the bales. After a few moments, it felt as though his arms would come out of the sockets, but the bales must be soaked. Finally, hearing the harsh breathing of Case beside him, he decided the bales were wet enough. They rested for a moment, then piled the wet bales to form a chamber about the pile of loose, oil-soaked coir, and roofed it over with others.

"Now, strike a light!"

Case bent down in the shelter of the bow, and began striking steel on flint. A spark glowed in the tinder, and the gunner blew it alive.

"Light the coir." A tiny flame grew in the dry mass, and Merewether pulled the tarpaulin forward to shelter it. The flame waxed bright, as Merewether pushed it into the pile of oil-soaked coir, walled in with the water-soaked bales, and saw the fire flare up.

"Out!" He boosted Case up and scrambled after him. He pulled the tarpaulin forward almost to its original position, folding back only a corner to provide air, and watched the progress of the blaze. Still too much air, he decided and closed the corner, lashing it down to cut off the draft. Going aft, he cut lashings and folded back a corner. Some air was still getting to the fire forward, and a draft was now established. Smoke came boiling out of the opening at the stern and was carried by the land breeze almost horizontally above the water and out toward the harbor entrance.

"Back to the ship!" Merewether told Case.

All the way back, he kept swiveling his head aft, hoping the wet bales would contain the fire long enough for it to generate the smoke he needed for Jamie and the snow to slip out the harbor entrance behind its screen. Once it burned through the soaked bales and the tarpaulin, there would be no more smoke; the whole cargo would go up in bright flame.

On board the schooner, he ran aft. He could no longer see the lights on the battery. The smoke must have blotted them out.

Wilkerson brought the dark lantern to him on the stern. He flicked the shutter open three times, then repeated the signal twice more. He picked up the glass, found the dim loom of the snow in the field, and saw her alter shape as her bow fell off to starboard. She slid silently into the gloom before the wind.

Merewether managed to contain himself during the next half hour. The lights on the battery remained obscured, he could no longer make out the shape of the snow along the north shore of the harbor entrance, the lighter did not burst into flames, and no shots were fired. He sent Wilkerson forward to make sure the men were at their stations. For himself, he stood at the starboard rail, hands gripping the rough wood, the forgotten kerchief still tied about his head, tense and rigid as he awaited dawn and the ultimate test of his scheme.

Gray daylight came so gradually that Merewether was staring at the smoking barge a quarter mile away before he realized the fact. Even as he looked, a shaft of flame shot up, red and orange against the shore, and the lighter was ablaze from bow to stern. He stared at the phenomenon a moment longer, thankful that the tier of water-soaked bales had withstood the spread of the fire for so long a time.

The last of the smoke was drifting before the wind past the fort, lifting now to expose the emplacements. He searched the sea beyond the harbor entrance, at first seeing nothing, then caught an intimation of dull white sails. The glass showed the snow clearly in the growing light, a good three miles from the fort, sailing steadily northwestward, safe now from even thirty-two pounders.

"Load and run out!" Case and his crew rammed home

cartridge, wad, shot and wad again, and ran out the stern chaser.

"Fire!"

The bellow of the twelve-pounder reverberated around the harbor, an echo coming back from the Citadel on the hill to starboard. The smoke obscured the fall of shot, but that was of no concern to Merewether.

"Launch rockets!" Case extracted three rockets from their tin case, set them in their rack, and blew on the slow match. They rose, one after another, to burst vivid red against the low, gray clouds.

Merewether paused a moment to peer through the glass at the fort. A figure in white trousers and blue coat had appeared on top the redoubt, a spyglass in his eye, facing out to sea. The fort had the alarm, and the escaping vessel in sight! From across the water, he heard the thin, urgent summons of a bugle, as two more men joined the officer on the redoubt.

"Launch three more rockets," he told Case. Let there be no doubt, the schooner had discovered the escape, and was calling the attention of all concerned to it.

"Hoist the colors." The quartermaster hauled on the halyards, and the tricolor soared up, snapping in the breeze. The group of officers on the fort were looking back toward the schooner, attracted by the second series of rockets, and now the flag.

"Stand by to cut the anchor cable," Merewether shouted forward to Wilkerson. The quartermaster had the flags hooked on to the signal hoist, ready now, red, white swallowtail, blue, waiting for the order. The wheel was manned, hands standing by to hoist the sails. The boom at the starboard gangway was taken in, its cluster of wherrys cast adrift. Merewether opened his mouth to give the command, already thinking ahead to his order for the helm, when he heard the shout. It appeared to come from the water to starboard, as a man cried almost simultaneously.

"Man overboard!"

Merewether hurried to the rail, and there was Harris, hair plastered like a cap to his skull, treading water.

"Put over the ladder." In a moment a naked Harris was on deck.

"Don't hoist that signal, Captain!" he shouted, seeing the hoist already bent on. "The signal's changed."

"What?" began Merewether.

"Blue, white swallowtail, red, since midnight!" chattered Harris, shivering in the fresh breeze. "New Admiral's orders. And now, for the love of God give me something to wear, I'm freezing!"

Merewether guided the young man to the companionway, had the quartermaster reverse the signal, and tried to pick up where he had been when Harris shouted from the water. He did not for an instant doubt his bona fides.

"Cut the cable!" he shouted forward. "Two-block," he told the quartermaster. "Starboard helm," he ordered the wheel.

The signal hoist leaped up the mast as the ship gathered sternway, the bow swinging to starboard. He tailed on to the line to add his weight to the scanty crew and was conscious of Harris bearing a hand beside him, wearing a pair of flapping canvas trousers, as the huge, fore-and-aft mainsail rose in jerks.

"Midships! Meet her," he told the helmsman. "Sheet home!" he shouted to Wilkerson. "Belay," he ordered the after guard. "Mind the trim."

The schooner still had sternway on, but the bow was three quarters of the way around to pointing due west. The jib filled with a sharp report, and Wilkerson eased off on the sheet, trimming the sail to the wind. Sternway was checked as the mainsail filled, driving the ship ahead.

"Starboard helm," said Merewether to stop the swing. "Ease her. Midships."

The schooner was under way, heading out through the center of the harbor entrance. Merewether stepped back beside the wheel and took stock of his situation, conscious of the sweat drying on his body. Already a white wake boiled from under the counter, and Wilkerson was setting the flying jib. The tricolor and the flag hoist were blown out stiffly, plainly visible in broad daylight now.

The ship was coming opposite the redoubts on the point to

242

port now. He could see the ugly snouts of the huge guns through the embrasures, but he could not tell whether they were loaded. The group of officers on the earthworks had increased to five, then soldiers poured up behind them from the redoubt, and Merewether was sure that the guns would not fire. One, then all of the officers snatched off their hats and waved them as the schooner passed, the wind snoring through her rigging, almost drowning out the faint sound of cheering. From the fort, she must appear the very picture of vengeance in pursuit, he realized.

"Dip the ensign," Merewether told the signal quartermaster and turned to salute the group ashore. Already it would be difficult to hit this swift schooner. He steered to overhaul the snow, lumbering along three miles ahead.

Chapter Twenty-two

"And now, Mister Harris," he said to the young man, dried and clad in seaman's trousers and jacket from the scanty slop chest, no longer shivering, "You've played hell. I can't send you back to Port Louis with the prisoners on the snow. What now?"

Harris laughed shortly. "I guess not, Captain. And Hermione may miss me for a fortnight too, though she's already had her allowance and her rent is paid. But I've always wanted to visit India, and you've gained a passenger."

"You know," he continued. "That admiral who relieved Linois out here last year decided the British were reading his signals, so he concocted new ones, just published yesterday, effective at midnight. Captain Andrews happened to hear talk of the change and mentioned it casually last night. Took me awhile to find out the change—simple, just reversed them all!"

"I doubt that those officers in the fort took the time to verify the signals in the book," said Merewether. "The diversion spoke for itself. Though," he added, suddenly conscious of his debt to this man, "I'm most obliged to you, Mister Harris."

243

The schooner ran down to leeward of the snow and hove to. The small crew had already hoisted out a wherry, but they seemed to have difficulty in getting one man over the side and into the boat. There must have been some spirits left in her, Merewether thought sourly. Luckily they were not all drunk by now. The wherry finally pulled away for the schooner, as he fumed at the delay.

As the wherry came alongside, he saw a slight figure stretched in her bottom. Merewether realized that it was Jamie Plantain. "Need some help with the Cap'n, here," called one of the men. "He's in a swound, sir."

Jamie was soon lifted to the deck, where he lay ashen-faced. Respiration was barely perceptible.

"Brandy," Merewether told Wilkerson. He tried to get a little into the old man's mouth, but it had no effect; and in a few minutes, he realized that Captain Jamie Plantain was dead.

"A stroke," said Harris casually, and Wilkerson nodded in concurrence. In this remnant of a crew, there was no surgeon's assistant, not even a loblolly boy with a smattering of medicine. Merewether remembered Jamie's discomfort of the night before, the apparent pain in his arm, but the old man had doggedly carried through his mission and had even fought off the murderous attack by Jules.

"Just sort of sighed and slid down beside the wheel, he did," volunteered the leading seaman of the snow's party. "The Cap'n had just give the word to heave to."

"I'd like to put him ashore for burial," Merewether told Harris and Wilkerson.

"Better not, Captain," said Harris instantly. "The French squadron was in sight from Souillac yesterday, and it may show up anytime. I'd hate to see you lose this ship now that you have it!"

Merewether considered the matter. He was again responsible for more than his own safety, and these men deserved no needless risks after their ordeal on Mauritius. It was all very well, as a matter of sentiment, to see old Jamie laid to rest on the island, but then he remembered his simple pride in being an Englishman. And English seafarers from time immemorial had

244

been buried at sea. Such would be fitting and proper for Captain Jamie Plantain, he decided, rather than resting on that lonely ocean island where he had been born by the whim of fate and a hot-bellied bitch, who led his father on to ruin. He made his decision as the French prisoners and the seven Creole belles, now dressed, but gray with seasickness, were led out to be ferried over to the snow. Harris composed a note in French to Pierre and Eleanora, informing them of the death of their grandfather, which he entrusted to one of the women for delivery.

The schooner got under way and Merewether cracked on sail, taking advantage of this fresh breeze, chuckling at what those officers on the battery at Port Louis might be saying by now, seeing him sail on northwardly, while the snow commenced its weary beat back against the wind to Port Louis. At noon, the summit of Pieter Both was out of sight, and he hove to. There was only a Popish prayer book in the ship, and he called upon his memory to extemporize the committal of Captain Jamie Plantain to the deep in accordance with the rites of the Church of England. The crew was delighted by the issue of French brandy after the service, and Merewether took a dram himself, in company with Harris and Wilkerson, as a toast to the memory of a brave and able man.

"No, Harris," said Merewether patiently, for the fourth time in three days. "I really do not believe I have a bent for trade. Keeping books of account or computing profit on merchandise is beyond my experience." He thought with distaste that he should not be brusque under the circumstances. He had no idea of how Commodores Waldron and Land, not to mention Sir George Barlow, might view the affair of a senior officer of the Marine inept enough to be knocked on the head and marooned on Mauritius for nearly a fortnight. He could not yet afford to foreclose the opportunity in American shipping and trade that Harris was offering him.

"But, Captain," persisted Harris, "we'd give you one of our new full-rigged ships coming off the ways at Boston next year. We hope to try a voyage to China on our own account, and you've been there."

"Yes, but not in trade," replied Merewether, thinking of the cynical members of the co-hong he had seen last year in Canton being punished for their corrupt dealings with members of the Select Committee. "The Company and the co-hong would unite to deny you the right to trade."

Harris chuckled. "I've never yet seen a man who cannot be bought, if the price is right!"

"I'll keep the matter in mind and discuss it further when we reach Calcutta," said Merewether to keep this door open.

Harris strolled away from the canvas chair by the weather rail in which Merewether reclined. It was halfway through the first watch, already dark with brilliant stars in a cloudless sky. The schooner, under all the canvas she would carry, was surging north-eastward under the steady pressure of the southeast trade wind. In the next few days, she should run out of the trades and pick up the southwest monsoon to blow her across the equator and toward Ceylon. Merewether hoped the chronometer rate that Harris had translated from the French was accurate, and that the course he had set two days ago would bring the ship to the Bay of Bengal.

Aside from himself, there was only Wilkerson to serve as a watchkeeping officer among the rescued Bombay Marine men. And Wilkerson was primarily a surveyor and cartographer, not a seaman, having been engaged during most of his service in the Marine in charting the narrow seas through which the Company's ships must pass to reach their ports. It was astounding, with all the vast Indian and Pacific Ocean areas, how shipping must funnel through relatively tiny gateways, such as the Strait of Malacca, to gain its destination. The Company should, he thought, build a port to command that strait, and deny trespassers entry on its domain.

Harris had insisted that he could take a watch, that he had sailed as mate on two voyages to the West Indies. Merewether issued him an appointment as acting second lieutenant in the Marine, but waived any oath of allegiance to Crown or Company from this American. So far he had displayed judgment and ability under way, but then, the weather had been fine. Merewether and Wilkerson had taken the middle and morning watches, and Merewether remained on deck through the first watch to make sure, unobtrusively, that Harris had the ship in hand. He heard Harris come aft again, pass behind the helm to check the heading, and then lean against the taffrail twenty feet away. This young man would do, he decided, as he squirmed deeper into the chair.

The gloom that had hung like a pall over him since the sullen splash of Captain Jamie Plantain's body into the sea three days ago descended again. What had seemed at its outset, and even up to its virtual accomplishment, a rather simple operation for the skilled Marine detachment under Gunny, had left him helpless on Mauritius. True, he had managed to escape, but in the process he had been unfaithful to Caroline, had caused the death of a brave old man, and had compromised young Harris with the French.

He shifted in the chair, automatically looking up at the close-hauled fore-and-aft sails. This was his first experience with a schooner, but he found it exhilarating, the instant response to her helm, her ability to sail even closer to the wind than *Rapid* would, the relatively small crew that still could manage her. This thought brought to mind the berserker, now stretched on a litter under an awning forward, his jaw immobilized in court plaster, fed through the gap in his front teeth, drifting from delirium to rationality and back as his fever rose and fell. He wished he had not struck so hard with the butt of the rifle, and yet his whole escape had hinged upon that moment. He hoped the poor devil would survive.

His thoughts turned back to Caroline. It was a bitter draft to swallow, but he could only conclude that he did not love her sufficiently to marry. He had not forsaken all others, but at the first opportunity had bedded another woman. He tried to tell himself that Eleanora had led him on, that even old Jamie had recognized her temper and excused him. It would not wash, he decided; it was plain that he was unworthy of a woman such as Caroline, and he must confess at the earliest opportunity, freeing her to make a proper match.

The gloomy train of thought was interrupted as Harris materialized beside him.

"All's well, Captain, and you've time for a nap before the midwatch."

"No need," Merewether said, a little shortly.

"Well, sir, if you're going to stay here, may I ask a bit of advice?" The tone of voice was diffident, not the assured, almost patronizing manner of speech that Harris usually affected.

"Why, certainly," replied Merewether, a little startled.

"I've spoken rather freely of that girl, Hermione, I kept at Madame Torres's at Port Louis. And, of course, Andrews is a Philadelphia man, not one to pass judgment on another's morals, so he never said a thing to me." Harris paused, leaning back against the weather bulwark to scan the sails. Satisfied, he continued in a small voice, "But you get to thinking out here in the night under all those stars, and I'm a Boston man, born, baptized and brought up in the Old North Church. I knew I was wrong, but I went ahead, a long way from home, and Hermione is a beauty."

"Well, come to the point," said Merewether, already beginning to guess the rest of the story, Nothing like being homeward bound to awake the pangs of conscience, he thought, conscious of his own case.

"It's just that there's another girl back in Boston that I've spoken for, and she's agreed to wait for me. I don't know how I'll face her now."

Merewether did not laugh, nor did he admit to this young man the bitter thoughts concerning his own course of conduct. He sat up in the chair and cleared his throat judicially.

"This girl, Hermione, means nothing to you?"

"Oh, not really, I guess. After all, I was her third protector, but I am — was — fond of her."

"And the girl in Boston, how do you feel about her now?"

"That is what troubles me," said Harris almost in a whisper. "It's been nearly a year, and it's hard for me to remember now how Grace looked. She'll be eighteen before I see her again, too." Harris paused, then burst out, "What I mean is, if I can forget her so easily, take up with another woman, is it fair for her to wait, expecting me to come back and marry her?"

Merewether had already concluded that he had forfeited every claim to Caroline, but the case presented by Harris appeared by no means so clear-cut. He was a long way from home, in the vigor of his youth. It was only to be expected that he might succumb to temptation. But, should such a lapse be fatal to a marriage, where the liaison was only casual and not true love? He thought of Eleanor, beautiful and passionate, but he felt only compassion, not love by any means, for her now. He thought of Caroline, who had displayed the love she felt for him, and concluded again that when one is loved, it is difficult not to reciprocate. His mind formulated the answer to Harris's question, and he realized he had also solved his own dilemma.

"Why, Harris, I think I would go on back to Grace, see how she feels toward you, and how you feel toward her. She may very well have repented of her promise to you, for that matter," he said with a short laugh. "In any event, make no confessions. What's done is done. She may say that she forgives you, but the memory will canker in her soul, and she will chide you with it in the years to come. It may not be strict morality, but it is the practical solution."

In a few minutes Harris drifted across the deck to look in the binnacle, as the boatswain's mate sent his messenger to rouse out the watch below. Merewether went aft to the officers' head before he assumed the watch. His spirits were somewhat revived, though he had no firm intention of following his own advice.

Seven days sailing, the last five almost before the southwest monsoon, brought the schooner across the equator. It was the middle of June; occasional squalls marred the perfect weather; but she logged a steady ten knots. Rations were short, and Merewether reduced the issue of bread and salt pork by a third; but there was ample fresh water, and the supply of spirits, a harsh, brown apple brandy that Harris called calvados, was sufficient for a daily issue. At dawn, the tenth day out of Port Louis, Merewether made his landfall on Ceylon. He realized he was west of his destination and changed course to enter the Bay of Bengal. Late that afternoon, the Royal Navy picket sloop intercepted the schooner.

The Marine ensign, pieced together out of bunting ripped from the tricolors in the flag bag, was hoisted over the French flag. Merewether did not have the recognition signal for June, and he hove to, waiting patiently as the sloop ran down, her crew at quarters, guns run out. The boat carrying the boarding party came alongside, and a lieutenant came through the gangway as Merewether stepped forward.

"Ah, Captain Merewether," said the officer. "Southfield, sir. I met you last year off Madras when you took that Frenchie that had us prisoners. And how did you come by this one?"

Merewether soon discovered that *Rapid* had passed this way thirteen days ago and had been diverted to the Strait. She had left the rescued Marine detachment in the store ship for further transportation, either to Calcutta or Bombay. Pellew and his squadron had followed a day later as a rumor of a new Governor-General of the Dutch Indies, sent out by Bonaparte, galvanized the forces of the Royal Navy and the Bombay Marine to attempt an interception. He embarked Havildar Lowjee and his detachment of marines, and four days later was off the Sandheads, the pilot cutter in sight.

The schooner was inside the mouth of the Hooghly before Merewether remembered that he had no stream anchor, having left it on the bottom of Port Louis harbor. There were two kedges that together might just serve to hold the ship against a moderate bore in the river, but nothing heavy enough to secure it against the constant pressure of the current. Fifteen miles below the dockyard, he put Wilkerson ashore to ride ahead and alert Commodore Land to his necessity.

In late afternoon, he came in sight of the dockyard and saw a barge anchored in the stream, Wilkerson and a party waiting in it, to secure his cable until it could be spliced to the anchor cable leading up into the barge. It was tricky work, bringing the big schooner up against the current, close enough to get a heaving line across to the barge, and holding her there by wind and rudder, main strength and awkwardness, and the pulling longboat, while the heavy cable was snaked across to be made fast to the bitts.

For an hour, Merewether had perched on the bobstay under

the bowsprit, relaying his orders to helm and sails through Harris and Lowjee. He saw the cable take the strain, waited a moment to be sure, then climbed back on deck, sweat-soaked and weary. He leaned over to shout down a last admonition to the dockyard boatswain and his mates in the barge as they began the tedious long-splice to unite the bitter end of the cable from the schooner to that of the anchor upstream. As he turned, he caught a glimpse of color on the quarterdeck, the flash of red-gold hair in sunlight, and realized that Caroline, Sir George and Lady Barlow, and Commodore Land were on board.

Merewether paused in the shelter of the roundhouse to take stock of the situation and steel himself for the confrontation, uncertain yet of his decision. This voyage was not one of which he was proud, though he had managed to survive and bring back a prize. The advice he had so glibly given Harris last week was only a piece of sophistry, an unworthy foundation upon which to make a marriage. He must at the earliest opportunity confess his guilt and give Caroline her freedom. He mopped his streaming face, squared his shoulders, and marched aft, admiring the brave display the ensign of the Bombay Marine made above the French tricolor.

Harris was in the midst of the group, carrying on an animated conversation with Sir George, while the others stood by. He broke off as Merewether came up behind them.

"And here's the Captain now!"

The party spun about like marionettes. Merewether, conscious of his bedraggled appearance, had commenced his formal bow when Caroline put her arms about his neck, her tearful face radiant, oblivious of the grinning hands on deck. Over her shoulder, Merewether saw Harris close one china-blue eye in a conspiratorial wink.

PART III

THE PERSIAN ROAD

Chapter Twenty-three

Merewether awoke a little after dawn, conscious of soft buttocks pressed against his hip. After a month of marriage, there yet was novelty in awaking to find Caroline in his bed. He looked at the back of the tousled red-gold head and the curve of cheek, feeling a wave of tenderness for this woman who was now his wife. In private, all reserve had vanished, and he found her ardent beyond his dreams. He moved gently away, sliding from under the thin sheet to lift the mosquito netting and emerge in the dim light filtering through the blinds over the windows. There was enough of the dawn chill still in the air to make him shiver pleasurably as he stood naked, looking out into Colonel Harding's garden.

Here, at the end of July, every Englishman who was able had escaped the blistering heat of Calcutta to seek a cooler retreat in the hills. The colonel, now retired, and a member of the Council, had offered the use of his town house to Merewether and his bride until such time as he could make an intelligent choice of a place of residence. That time might never come, he thought, what with his ship still somewhere east of Malacca. It had been a fortuitous interlude, however, more free time than he had ever had, enabling him to give his bride his undivided attention.

He heard a door close at the back of the house, and then the twittering voices of the maid and man servant as they drew water from the cistern to fill the tub in the bath house. Colonel Harding suffered from the prickly heat and had built the facility at the rear of his house to enable him to soak in a medicated bath. Merewether had seized upon the unheard-of luxury of immersing his whole body in the tepid water daily. The thought recalled events of two months ago on Mauritius, and he wondered briefly whether Eleanora still bathed in the rock-lined pool beside the cottage. He put the thought resolutely from his mind.

"Percival!" said a sleepy voice. "It is very early."

He turned, seeing Caroline dimly through the netting sitting up in the bed, her splendid breasts frankly displayed. He felt a surge of heat at the vision; better not, he decided, there was no lock on the door, and he could not accustom himself to the casual manner in which these Indian servants came and went.

"Yes, my dear. Time enough for another hour's nap before breakfast." She wrinkled her nose at him and lay back down, as he pulled on the cotton robe, stepped into sandals, and went out to the bath house.

The man poured a kettle of boiling water into the tub, just enough to take the chill off, and went out. Merewether hung the robe on a peg and entered the tub. There was a cake of soap on the rim, but a little of that went a long way in this soft rain-water. He leaned back.

It was only a month ago that the wedding had been celebrated in St. John's Church, the culmination of three days of frantic preparation. The Chinese tailor near the dockyard gate had managed to put together a dress uniform, but the sword and cocked hat were borrowed. MacLellan and Harris had been pillars of strength during the ordeal. Merewether had not realized the tension that had built up within him until the day after the ceremony, when a great lassitude descended. He had no regrets. Gaining Caroline had made the ritualistic flummery, the false gaiety and the shrill pretensions at the reception seem worthwhile now.

Harris was up in Bengal still, due back at the end of the week, seizing the opportunity to hunt tigers. MacLellan had armed him with a brace of German rifles, heavy and slow to load, a far cry from Larkin's graceful Kentucky rifles, but accurate and powerful. He hoped there would be no misfires in the presence of a Bengal tiger. At that thought, Merewether cringed a bit, recalling his return of the air rifle to MacLellan.

"I relied on it, Mac, but never had to fire it."

MacLellan had taken the weapon, examined critically the pockmarks of rust that marred its finish, and then exploded, "Hellfire, Captain! There's no air in this container! It must have emptied an hour after it was filled."

Merewether remembered his confident capture of the guards at the quarry on Mauritius and shuddered. Ignorance was bliss; if he had had any inkling that the rifle was worthless, he could never have acted with the assurance necessary to cow that party of Frenchmen long enough for the prisoners to seize their arms. He relaxed and slid down into the water to his chin.

The nagging worry as to what effect his fiasco on Mauritius might have on his career in the Bombay Marine came again to mind. He tried to put the matter aside, but without success. Early morning had ever been a time for worry, when his failures, procrastinations, and shortcomings were crystal clear. By noon, they had been glossed over, postponed again, or pushed out of sight. *Rapid* was still far to the east, scouting the approaches and fortifications on Java in anticipation of the invasion next year. Only yesterday, dispatches a month old from the Java Sea reported that Captain Tollett had been ordered into her by Commodore Waldron as master. Larkin, however well qualified, was far too junior in the Marine to hold command of a major ship of war, and Tollett had been anxious for another sea command before his almost inevitable promotion to Commodore.

It was difficult for Merewether to reconcile himself to unemployment, though he remained a captain on the active list and lost only the extra pay for command of a fourteen-gun sloop. Yet Merewether deeply regretted the loss of his ship and the officers and men who had served with him for the past year and a half. The thought brought to mind Sangh, the sad little Hindu steward. Tollett would treat the man with consideration, but the jambiya that had saved his life was carefully wrapped and stowed in Caroline's trunk for safekeeping until it could be returned to its owner.

Another memory crossed his mind. Three days after the wedding, Merewether had awakened to find Caroline sobbing quietly in the night. When he sought to comfort her, he found that her grief was for the son in England, to be six this month.

"I've deserted James," she wept, "and he is still such a very small boy."

Merewether was disconcerted. The child heretofore had been an abstraction, only an uncomfortable token of the man who had possessed Caroline before him, not flesh and blood. He undertook to comfort her, to reconcile her grief with the impossibility of the distance to England.

"Of course, next year," he blurted out, "I'll complete ten years of commissioned service in the Marine and be entitled to three years leave with pay."

"Oh, Percival!" she had cried. "And we'll go back to England!"

It had been an unguarded statement. The matter was problematical, dependent upon many factors, the requirements of the Service, the situation, and whether he could find the passage money. The prospect had restored her happiness, however, and Merewether resolved to hold his tongue in the future.

His thoughts turned to his own schedule for the day. A fortnight after the wedding, Commodore Land had strongly suggested that Merewether keep duty hours at the dockyard— "Earn his pound and pint," in Land's words—and an adjacent office had been provided for him. He found himself buried under an avalanche of paper, requisitions, reports, adjustments of pay, all of which he must read and initial for Land's approval, or note disapproval and his reasons. He had never dreamed that this amount of correspondence was generated by the Marine here in Calcutta, and he was already chafing to be back in simpler surroundings at sea.

Today, he was to sit as senior officer on a board convened to examine several officers and temporary warrant officers who aspired to promotion, commissioned rank, or permanent appointment in the Marine. Three on the list he knew: Whitfield had been his leading boatswain's mate in *Rapid* for more than a year before he was appointed acting boatswain and second in command of the prize *Majeure* last February; Eldridge, acting master's mate, had taken the plague ship *Duchy of Lancaster* a thousand miles across the Bay of Bengal to Columbo, Ceylon, last winter with a skeleton crew of mutinous lascars; the third was MacFee from *Comet,* appointed acting boatswain in the prize *Mercure,* and he had the enthusiastic recommendations of MacRae and Larkin appended to his dossier. There would have to be the gravest of objections from the other officers on the board, Merewether told himself, to prevent favorable reports to Bombay Castle as to these three.

He climbed out of the tub, dried himself, and went back into the house. Caroline was asleep again, and he moved quietly as he dressed. He was all she had now. Sir George had been relieved by Lord Minto and had departed two weeks ago for his new post as Governor of Madras in a frigate supplied by the Royal Navy. As she had feared, the wedding reception had indeed been the last formal affair presided over by Lady Barlow in the Palace.

"I shall join you for breakfast," said Caroline unexpectedly, and he turned to see her slide from under the netting. She splashed briefly in the basin, and her white body disappeared into a yellow robe, her brighter head emerging at the top.

On the verandah, screened from the rising sun, a table was set. Caroline jingled the bell, and the servant came out carrying a tray, from which he unloaded two pots of tea, a jar of marmalade, and a plate of toast.

"I hope you will send the barouche back promptly," said Caroline. She rose and went over to a side table, picked up a slender volume, and returned to her chair. As she crossed the lighter square of the outside doorway, her figure was briefly outlined through the yellow silk, and Merewether was reminded of that morning—four months ago?—when he had resisted temptation in Penang. He wondered for a moment how Livie and Tom Raffles were progressing toward that fortune they had set their hearts on and wondered even more at the infatuation he had felt for that charming woman of the world. Certainly, she could not compare in beauty with his own dear Caroline, but he felt a cross-grained regret that he had not pressed his luck with Livie. "I have to discuss the imagery in *The Tempest* this morning," continued Caroline. "And the meeting of the Circle is over at Madge Foster's."

"I'll send it straight back," promised Merewether. The barouche and matched pair came with the house, to be exercised and maintained while the owner was absent. He finished his tea, pushed back the chair, kissed Caroline, and went in to pick up the cocked hat and sword.

He went out, entered the barouche, and the driver snapped his whip over the team. Presiding over the Examining Board required full dress and sidearms to maintain the solemnity of the occasion. There were two volunteers and three midshipmen, candidates for commissions as second lieutenants; three second lieutenants with more than five years service in the Marine aspiring to be first lieutenants; and six anxious petty officers seeking warrant rank. Some might be disappointed, but Merewether had made up his mind that Whitfield, Eldridge and MacFee would be be passed and recommended to Bombay Castle, come what may.

He alighted at the dockyard gate and instructed the driver to go back and await Lady Caroline. The chief clerk had already deposited a stack of requisitions on his desk, and he toiled through them, disapproving two out of forty-nine, then leafed through the incoming official mail. A name leaped out at him, Captain Richard Ackroyd, Royal Navy. Commodore—how long since he had held that temporary glory?—Percival Merewether of the Honorable Company's Service, was requested and required to be in attendance on a Court of Inquiry to be convened on board HMS *Terror* the 10th prox., then and there to give evidence concerning a certain action off Diamond Point, Malacca Strait. . . .

Hell, he had almost forgotten his resentment of Ackroyd's conduct last spring. He wondered suddenly if the man had a stiff elbow, as Buttram had predicted, from the wound he had inflicted in the duel, after he had taken up Captain Wolfe's quarrel. And then he wondered what Wolfe might have written in his report to the Admiral before he died. He could, in effect, be on trial himself. Merewether laid the notice aside, to be discussed with Commodore Land, as the clerk came in to remind him of the convening of his board.

There were four officers on the board, all senior first lieutenants, led by "Rhumb Line" Smith, now over seventy, a veteran of more than fifty years of service in the Marine and head of its

Bureau of Surveys and Cartography, temporarily in Calcutta to observe for himself the new channels cut by the Hooghly and the silting of the anchorage. Merewether remembered his own appearance before a selection board at Bombay Castle when he sought his commission in the Marine nine years ago.

"Mister, define a rhumb line," Smith had barked, and Merewether's mind had gone blank. He had stood before the glowering group of officers sitting behind the big table for what seemed an eternity, his mouth opening and closing, as he strove to recall the definition, if in fact, he had ever learned it.

"Why . . . Why . . ." he stammered, "why, it's the course . . . the ship's track . . . I mean, a line that intersects all meridians at the same angle. . . ."

"Close enough," Smith conceded, and Merewether had escaped, to find himself on the list posted later in the day as passed and recommended for a commission. It was only then that he had learned Smith was famous in the service for the question which accounted for his nickname.

Well, he had managed to get a note to Eldridge, come back from Ceylon in *Comet* two days ago, telling him to memorize the definition. It might be an unfair advantage, but that young man deserved a warrant after taking the *Duchy of Lancaster* safely to Columbo. He regretted the reported death of Webster, that failed gentleman, of the complications of fever and drink last month, and prayed repose for his tortured soul.

Merewether called the board to order at ten, with Smith on his right, and MacLellan to the left, Blair and Chastain, Land's staff officers, at either end of the table.

"Send in the first officer," Merewether told the junior clerk. His dossier identified him as Lawson, second lieutenant for the past six years and a midshipman two years before that, now serving in the armed transport *Antelope*.

The morning wore away, brief interviews with the three commissioned candidates and short discussions afterward. Their records were clean, and they had the recommendations of their commanding officers. They were passed as qualified for promotion, subject to vacancies occurring in the first lieutenant's List. One midshipman and one volunteer were failed; the board agreed that they did not yet possess the poise and experience for com-missioned service. Another six months at sea, and they might again apply.

Eldridge was the second aspirant to warrant rank to be inter-viewed. It was the first time Merewether had seen him since that night in the driving rainstorm off Great Nicobar, when he left him on the drifting pest ship, with the stinking corpses of the French prize crew still below decks. He was clean shaven and neatly dressed, but there was a tremor in his voice as he identified himself.

"Now, Mister Eldridge, you have held an acting appointment as master's mate for a little more than four months. Will you tell this board what duty you performed during this time?"

"Yes, sir," said Eldridge. "Sirs, I was appointed to be master of the *Duchy of Lancaster*, an Indiaman, found adrift off the Nico-bars, with her surgeon, Doctor Kees, and Webster, quarter-master, take her to Ceylon. We had thirty-eight healthy lascars on board . . ."

"I thought there were thirty-nine," interrupted Merewether.

"Yes, sir, but one of them refused to obey my order to move the dead Frenchmen out of the after quarters and told the others not to. I couldn't stand for mutiny, and I killed him with a blun-derbuss."

"Ah!" Merewether thought, that explained the shot he had heard as the launch pulled away that night. Evidently, the action had sufficed to quell the mutiny. "Go on, Mister Eldridge."

"Yes, sir. Well, sirs, we were under topsails, didn't have enough men to set and manage the courses, and it took nineteen days to raise Columbo."

"Who navigated the ship?" demanded Smith.

"Sir, Webster did the first nine days, but by then I'd learned to do a day's work in navigation, and I did the rest of the way. We never could get the chronometers to run right after they had run down, and we used Webster's watch."

"What did you do with that blunderbuss after you fired it," asked MacLellan.

"Cleaned and oiled it, sir, and reloaded too. It's in my seabag now, wrapped in oilskin, and the load drawn."

Merewether looked from Chastain, to Blair, to Smith, then hastily asked, "Mister Eldridge, can you define a rhumb line?"

"Yes, sir. A rhumb line is a line on the earth's surface which intersects all meridians at the same angle. Any two points may be connected by such a line."

Merewether stole a glance at Rhumb Line Smith and ducked away from his livid glare. "Very well, Mister Eldridge, you are dismissed." The young man about-faced and marched out.

"Well, I'm damned, Merewether!" complained Smith. "If I recollect rightly, you almost failed your own examination at Bombay Castle on that very question I was about to ask. It looks like a bit of hanky-panky to me!"

The vote for a permanent warrant was unanimous.

There was no satisfactory examination for boatswain, the qualifications being entirely empirical; a man proved himself at sea in every phase of seamanship, and the ability to make his men perform every duty assigned them, and if he had the unqualified endorsement of the commanding officer under whom he had served, the examining board was usually constrained to grant the warrant. Whitfield and MacFee were passed, their warrants signed immediately by Commodore Land, and they departed for new duties.

The board concluded its session at one o'clock. "Gentlemen," Merewether told the members, "I hope you will be my guests at the Calcutta Club, while I make my peace with Mister Smith."

Chapter Twenty-four

The Court of Inquiry convened on board HMS *Terror* at two bells in the forenoon watch a week later. Merewether came on board to the twitter of pipes, carrying his portfolio stuffed with copies of his operation order to the Bengal Squadron, his reports, and even the commodore's commission, now expired. He had read through them again this morning to refresh his recollection, though Land had told him that copies already had been furnished the admiral convening the court. These affairs were usually unpleasant and chancy for all concerned, an after-the-fact review of actions taken and decisions made in the heat of battle. Courts of Inquiry in the Royal Navy were designed to develop facts, rather than determine guilt or innocence and inflict punishment, though many a career had wrecked upon their findings.

A lieutenant led Merewether aft to the day cabin, and he took a chair in a row along the starboard bulkhead, "For interested parties and witnesses," the lieutenant told him. He looked about, seeing the long table set up athwartships, with five chairs behind it, and a chair at either end, already occupied by a yeoman-clerk and a stout, red-faced captain, evidently the recorder. After a few minutes, Ackroyd and Shropshire came in. Merewether inclined his head, but did not speak, and they took chairs at the other end of the row. He wondered at the fact he had actually tried to kill this little man last March. A few minutes more, and the master-at-arms came in, calling for all present to rise, and five captains filed in, to take their places behind the table.

The recorder immediately read the orders convening the court, "to inquire into all the facts and circumstances of a certain action off Diamond Point, Sumatra, the twenty-fifth of February, ultimo." He then administered the oath to the members of the court.

"The first item of evidence, gentlemen, will be the report of Captain Richard Ackroyd, commanding His Majesty's Ship *Argus*," said the presiding officer. "You may read it, Barton."

Merewether listened to the stereotyped phraseology, the recitation of command and orders, the successions of "in obedience thereto," and "thereupon proceeded," finally arriving at the concluding paragraph:

"Seeing that the French cruiser was in the process of repairing the damage to her foresails and foretopmast, I conceived it to be my duty to take possession of the prize, and thereby prevent her escape, or giving succor to her consort. . . ."

There was no comment from any member of the court, and the senior officer told the clerk, "You may read the report of Commodore Percival Merewether of the Honourable Company's

Naval Service." He listened as the voice droned out the words he had written in his wrecked cabin that sweltering night—it seemed years ago—while the hands dismantled the shattered main-topmast on deck. The language now sounded as stilted in its form as Ackroyd's:

"Conceiving that the enemy had a clear avenue of escape to the southeast, I undertook to place *Rapid* in their way. . . .

"Having suffered the loss of the main-topmast, with the enemy passing clear of *Rapid* to escape, Boatswain Samuel Tompkins and his mates grappled *Mercure*. . . .

"The enemy thereupon boarded in force over the forecastle, whereupon our forces offered resistance, most gallantly led by Lieutenants Larkin and MacCamy, Boatswain Tompkins, Jemadar Gunny, and divers other persons. Captain James Wolfe, Royal Navy, made a most determined and effective attack. . . .

"Whereupon, HEICS *Comet*, Captain Alex MacRae commanding, came along the port bow, the boarders were repelled, and the French cruiser *Mercure* secured as a prize of war. . . ."

At the conclusion of the report, there was no comment by any member of the court, and the clerk began reading the report of Captain James Wolfe, made while serving as an observer for the Royal Navy in the flagship of the Bengal Squadron:

". . . and holding the weather gauge, HMS *Argus* was then in position to deny the enemy's escape to the southeast while the Bombay cruisers made the interception to the northwest. . . .

"HEICS *Rapid,* under superior handling by Lieutenant Dobbs, managed to work to windward, and cut off the escape. . . .

"By outstanding gunnery under the direction of Lieutenant Larkin, *Rapid* scored two major hits upon the French cruiser *Chasseur,* the first dismounting her bow chaser, the second bringing down her foretopmast, topsails and foresails, leaving her unmanageable and incapable of escape. . . .

"By the most resolute handling, after the loss of all sail on the mainmast, her boatswain and his mates were enabled to grapple *Mercure,* bringing her to bay after the Marine detachment killed her helmsman and captain by musket fire. . . .

"At this point, HMS *Argus* did not proceed to give aid and assistance to *Rapid,* then in the process of repelling boarders and crippled by gunfire, but turned aside to take possession of the prize. . . ."

"There is an earlier report concerning an action off the Nicobar Islands between the Bombay squadron and the French cruiser *Majeure* that is not deemed relevant to the present inquiry," said the presiding officer. "However, there is a third document, entitled 'Critique of Operations of the Bengal Squadron of the Honourable Company's Naval Service, Commodore Percival Merewether, Commanding, January—March, 1807,' which may contain relevant evidence. Read it, Barton."

Merewether leaned forward, intent upon what Wolfe had written in those last hours of his life. The clerk droned through the formalities, and the references to the two reports, then read:

"I therefore reach the following conclusions:

First: The Bombay ships and forces observed during this period were in a superior state of readiness for action, as demonstrated in the two engagements observed.

Second: The state of training of commissioned and petty officers is excellent, and they respond with the correct action in the heat of battle without direct orders.

Third: The tactics employed by the commander of the squadron were classic examples of the maximum exploitation of the advantage of the weather gauge, positioning the ships so as to afford maximum opportunity for the batteries.

Fourth: The gunnery was superior, due to the use of adjustable sights of an ingenious design.

Fifth: The spirt of the entire crew was high throughout the operation, they working long hours in time of need without complaint.

Sixth: The ships and forces of the Bengal Squadron are entirely qualified to participate in any joint operations with the Royal Navy."

"Very well," said the presiding officer. "That concludes the documentary evidence in this inquiry. Now, Commodore Merewether, do you have additional facts not contained in these writings to present to this court?"

Merewether stepped forward and bowed to the court.

"No, sirs," he said.

"Does any member of this court desire to put a question to the Commodore?" There was no response, and the Captain continued, "Thank you for your attendance, Commodore." Merewether resumed his seat.

"And now, Captain Ackroyd, do you have additional facts to bring before this court, not contained in these writings?"

"Yes, sirs," said Ackroyd, coming forward, his mouth twisted in a bitter smile. "I object to the conclusions drawn by Captain Wolfe . . ."

"You are out of order, Captain. If you have additional facts, you may state them."

"Well, I was under challenge to fight a duel with Wolfe at the time he wrote that last report and critique at Penang. I did fight a duel with Merewether there. I submit these facts as evidence of prejudice, sirs."

"Very well, the evidence will be noted by the clerk. And now, does any member of this court desire to put a question to the Captain?"

"Yes," said the captain on the left, a swarthy man with a sardonic expression. "Why did you not hold the weather gauge, cutting off escape to the southeast, and let the Bombay ships make the interception?"

"Sir, I had no reason to expect they would take such action."

"Then, why did you abandon the pursuit of the French cruiser to take a crippled prize?" demanded a small captain at the other end in the accent of Devon.

"Why, the Frenchies were making rapid progress clearing the wreckage, and I feared its escape," answered Ackroyd, beginning to sweat.

"Very well," said the presiding officer. "I think the matter has been fully presented here. The court will retire to consider its judgment. Written findings and recommendations will be prepared and served upon the interested parties in due course. I declare this Court of Inquiry adjourned."

"How did it go?" inquired Land, as Merewether returned to the dockyard.

"Why, very favorably, I think," Merewether replied. "I think the members had the situation well in mind. I suspect Ackroyd will get at least a letter of reprimand and admonition." He detailed the questions asked by the two members.

"Humph," said Land, turning back to his desk. "Whitewash is thicker than water."

Three days later, the Royal Navy guard-mail cutter dropped off its pouch at the landing, and in due course, Merewether received a sealed packet. Omitting the formalities, the document said:

"We therefore respectfully find:

First: Captain Richard Ackroyd acted in a prudent and responsible manner in immediately taking up the pursuit of two French cruisers off Diamond Point, Sumatra, since he could not know what action, if any, the Bombay ships might take.

Second: The taking by boarding of the French cruiser *Chasseur* was justified, in view of the progress of repairs then being accomplished in her, to prevent her escape or succour of her consort, then heavily engaged with two Bombay ships.

Third: The reports and critique of the late Captain James Wolfe, Royal Navy, indicate prejudice, in view of the fact that he was under obligation to fight a duel with Captain Ackroyd at the time they were written. We therefore accord them little weight."

"Well, I'm damned!" exploded Merewether and went in to show the findings to Land.

"No more than I expected," said Land calmly. "At least they didn't recommend a court martial for you. White . . ."

"I know," broke in Merewether bitterly. "Whitewash is thicker than water!"

CHAPTER TWENTY-FIVE

Caroline had informed him this morning for the second time since their marriage that he was not an incipient father. Merewether did not mind, though he told himself it was not for lack of exposure to the peril this past month and a half. He came through the dockyard gate, tossing a careless return of the sentry's salute, and entered his office. Land had gone on some mission of his own yesterday and would not be back until Monday. The older man was enjoying his increased freedom, what with having a captain as an assistant for the time. The morning was still cool enough to be enjoyable; his cup of tea was brought in by the Indian boy of all work; and he attacked the pile of documents requiring attention with vigor.

Half an hour later, the chief clerk came in with a folded note. "Just brought by messenger, sir."

"Here," said Merewether. "I've finished with these." He pushed the basket of papers across the desk. "And send in another cup of tea."

His thoughts turned to his own problems. In less than a month, Colonel Harding would return from the hills, and he must find quarters for himself and Caroline. Accommodations appeared to be in short supply, and with most of his acquaintances gone, it was hard to obtain any information. Even Jennifer Buttram, absorbed in the day-to-day care of her infant daughter, was of no assistance. He might be reduced to taking lodgings next month, which could well be the most practical solution in view of his own unsettled affairs. Harris had come back from Bengal with three huge tiger skins and a font of harrowing adventures. The Boston barque that had called at Souillac last spring had been reported at Madras and was expected momentarily at Calcutta. Meanwhile, he was the guest of the Merewethers and had accumulated a monstrous stock of Indian, Burmese and Persian goods, all on credit, to be paid for on arrival of the barque.

Merewether picked up the note. The device indented in the seal was unfamiliar. He broke it open and read:

My dear Commodore Merewether:

You departed so soon after our meeting last spring that I did not have the opportunity to continue our discussion as I promised. Will you be my guest at the Calcutta Club today at one o'clock?

Resptfy,
A. R. Percy

Alfred Robert Percy? His father? He had scarcely thought of the man since last spring. He dashed off a note of acceptance, and when the boy came in with the tea, sent him to deliver it. The morning wore away in the succession of minor crises and decisions that tend to plague an officer in temporary command, as subordinates test his mettle.

Percy was punctual, extending his hand with a cordial smile. "Delighted to see you again, Commodore, and I'm told congratulations are in order, that you have taken a bride!"

"Yes, sir, thank you, but I'm no longer Commodore, my commission has expired, and I'm really more comfortable as Captain."

"Well, let us go in and have a drink, Captain."

They were soon served, Madeira for Percy and gin for Merewether. "Here's damnation to Boney!" offered Percy, and they drank.

"I've been up in the hills since the middle of June, only came back yesterday, and the heat here makes a difference." The man was tanned and fit-looking. "I was introduced to a game they call 'pulu,' quite popular among the cavalrymen up there. You try to knock a ball through a wicket with a mallet while riding a horse! I'd never played before and found it fascinating. . . ." The talk veered to Canton, the defenses and forces in Mauritius, the operations of the Bengal Squadron last winter, and then the mercantile future of Penang. Merewether found himself being led into various discussions, his opinions solicited, and then being adroitly prodded into an exposition of the purposes and functions of the Marine. After half an hour, he had gained a definite impression that he was being judged and weighed in the balance, his mind probed, explored and examined, and that Percy possessed a far shrewder, more perceptive mind than he had heretofore displayed.

Merewether declined a second brandy after the dessert, uncomfortably aware that it was past three o'clock, the dockyard was unsupervised, and the club almost empty. Percy seemed to pay no attention to the time, continuing to speak in the smooth, cultured voice, his eyes alternately hooded in the bland, conventional face, then startling in the intensity of a glance.

"I hear you met that Alley, the one who called himself Tipu Sultan, last year at Vellore."

"Yes, sir, he had been a schoolmate of my midshipman in England." Merewether did not elaborate. He had told no one of Tipu's astounding offer, back-handed though it was, that he might be Admiral of the Fleet in Imperial India, and the only witness had died a day or so later at the hands of Tipu.

"What impression did you form of him?" persisted Percy.

"Why, the man was a great leader. He inspired his followers. He was fearless, intelligent and absolutely ruthless—a natural king! Except for his death and the interception of the arms and munitions from the French, I think the whole south of India would be aflame by now."

"Indeed? Well, I think as much myself, and I never saw the gentleman. And now, I've kept you from your duties quite too long. We must repeat this delightful occasion!"

Merewether mentioned the luncheon with Percy to Caroline and Harris that evening before dinner.

"Percy? Oh yes, Uncle George had him to dinner with Sir Thomas last spring. He was most suspicious of his motives, and we were cautioned to make no comments on political matters in his presence."

"He is a man of considerable learning and ability," said Merewether. "I am still not sure what he wanted with me, since he is a Foreign Office man. Sir George told me he was descendant of the Percys of Northumberland."

"Hotspur's Percys?" asked Harris brightly. "He didn't look much like a great warrior when I met him up in Bengal last week, all covered with sweat and mud from that silly game they play there, 'pulu.' He tried to pump me as to the chances of Mister Jefferson's embargo being declared. I agree, though, he is a smart one!"

The conversation veered into other fields, as Merewether wondered absently again if the man could be his father.

Three days later, another note came to the dockyard, and this time Merewether recognized the crest of Sir Thomas Jeffrey.

My dear Merewether:
Could you lunch with me today, one o'clock, my house, and ask Land to let you off the rest of the day.

Yr obdt svt,
Jeffrey

Merewether took the note in to Land. "Hell's bells, these diplomats think the Marine runs itself! Oh well, go on. Sir Thomas is better than most."

"And the tonga?"

"Yes, I'll walk to my whist game, probably get a stroke. Little you young whippersnappers respect an older man!" Land's black eyes snapped, and he actually looked angry for a moment. Then he smiled. "I'm not actually that old," he said, "only be forty-eight tomorrow."

"Many happy returns, and thank you, sir."

Merewether rode in the tonga to the big town house, then sent the driver back to the dockyard. Damned if he would be responsible for a man's suffering a stroke on the eve of his forty-eighth birthday! He wondered at the return of Sir Thomas from the cooler hills to the heat of August in Calcutta. The Indian servant admitted him to the foyer, took his hat, and led him through the quiet house to a cool verandah, enclosed with cotton netting, overlooking a garden, two punkahs swaying rhythmically overhead. Sir Thomas and Percy rose as he entered.

It was an hour and a half of inconsequential talk, a light, delicious meal, and sweet, heavy wine for dessert before these two diplomats came to the point.

"I know you've been Barlow's man this past year, and you're married to his wife's niece, but Thomas here vouches for you, says you serve your master with unswerving loyalty," said Percy unexpectedly. "I had made my own judgment, and it is in accord." His face wore a bland expression, the bright blue eyes less piercing, less hard than they had been during that meeting last week.

"I serve the Crown," said Merewether, nettled at being termed "Barlow's man," and reminded of being related to him by marriage, "the Company and the Marine, as I have these past seventeen years . . ."

"No offense, Captain, it was merely a figure of speech. You have served all of them, Crown, Company, Marine and Barlow well," interposed Sir Thomas. "Rob is merely stating a premise; the decision has already been made, providing you see fit to accept."

"I don't . . ."

"Let me lay down a situation, Captain," said Percy easily. "You are experienced in evaluating matters and drafting operational orders to deal with them." He slid a bit lower in the wicker chair and sipped the tawny wine in his glass.

"Boney has courted Fath Ali Shah ever since he came to the throne of Persia ten years ago. He has one motive: Free passage through Persia to India. Of course, 'Boy' Malcolm made two treaties for us back in 1801, the first commercial, the second directed mostly against Afghanistan, though the French are mentioned in it. Then Russia annexed Georgia from Persia. We could give Persia no help, Russia was our ally at the time, so where does a country like Persia turn?"

"France," said Merewether.

"Of course," said Percy. "Her ambassadors met with Boney's at a castle called 'Finkenstein' last fall, just before I left London. I have learned that they reached agreement, a guaranty of territorial integrity at least, in exchange for free passage to India." He sipped the last of the wine. "And some arms, French officers to train the troops in the continental fashion, some Persian officers to be educated in France, oh, anything but money—Boney doesn't believe in paying that!

"Now, to confound the situation, the Czar is a great admirer of Bonaparte. His people and Boney's have been talking. We haven't been as prompt in paying some of our obligations as we should. We feel certain they will agree, may already have. If so, that leaves the Shah with a treaty that France will not honor. What is our move?"

"Inform Persia and persuade her to break the treaty with Bonaparte. Offer her arms, assistance and money as well," replied Merewether.

"Exactly what Wellesley and Gibby Elliott advised," said Percy. "Sir Harford Jones is on his way out here from London, commissioned to serve as ambassador to Teheran, and Gibby has already called 'Boy' Malcolm back in for the same mission."

"Gibby Elliott?" inquired Merewether.

"Oh, you probably know him as the Earl of Minto," said Sir Thomas. "George always just called him 'Minto,' the new Governor-General."

During the short silence that followed, Merewether wondered why he was being informed of this international diplomatic snarl between a self-crowned Emperor, a ShahnShah, and the Czar of all the Russias. Certainly not for his advice; eminent government figures had already agreed on the action to be taken.

"Now, Merewether," said Percy. "You're wondering why Thomas and I called you over here, and why we've bored you with this account of the political and diplomatic situation in a remote and backward kingdom. Well, I shall tell you a bit more. Thomas here insists I be entirely frank, but I must demand a pledge of absolute secrecy." Percy leaned forward, his eyes boring into Merewether's.

"I promise, sir," said Merewether uncomfortably, looking to Sir Thomas for confirmation.

"Very well," said Percy, sitting back. "Now, George Barlow thought I came out here to look over his shoulder for Minto, but he was wrong. I came because we in British Intelligence saw a pattern developing: The wavering of Czar Alexander, with the failure of England to pay the subsidy of six million pounds, and his fascination with Napoleon; the death of young Tipu Sultan, the only man with resolution, intelligence and force enough to raise and lead a successful revolt in India; the increased activities of the French engineers surveying a route through Persia; the defeat of Prussia and the Continental Blockade. If Alexander makes peace with Bonaparte—and one more defeat may very well have caused him to by now—there will be no more worlds for France to conquer in Europe. Bonaparte, with his peasant misconception of the 'wealth of the Indies' and his unemployed armies available, will be tempted to make his next move through Persia to India, in our opinion." He leaned forward to sip from a tumbler of water.

"I might say, Merewether," broke in Sir Thomas, "Rob here manned the French desk in Downing Street four years and is now the secretary in charge of British Intelligence."

"French desk?"

"You are not expected to know of such pursuits," said Percy. "British Intelligence is a secret agency under the Foreign Office. By common consent among the politicians, we are left undisturbed in any change of government. Our function is to gather and evaluate pertinent information from every part of the world, then make such deductions and reach such conclusions as appear justified. We then disseminate the information to the agencies concerned. Our agents may be such diverse persons as ship's officers, merchants, missionaries, priests, travelers, traitors to foreign states, even spies. We listen to anyone and the information goes into the hopper, though what comes out may be ground exceedingly fine. It usually adds up to a recognizable picture, and that is what we think we have here. We try to make it worth the while of our agents, and a little money does amazing things!" he added cynically. "For instance an account of your visit to Canton came from our man there just before I left London . . ."

"Dawson!" said Merewether.

"What? Well, I'm damned, the man's name *is* Dawson, a former Company officer and schoolmaster!"

"I saw him there, and I had served with him for the Company," said Merewether. "It was only a guess."

"Very well, Merewether, you are clever," said Percy taking another sip from the tumbler. "Now, let us get down to specifics. Harford Jones and 'Boy' Malcolm are both old acquaintances of the Shah and excellent diplomats. Given an even chance, either of them may be able to persuade Fath Ali to see the matter our way and act accordingly. What I am concerned with is the even chance." He looked at Sir Thomas. "You knew Pahlavi, I believe?"

"Yes, he was ambassador at Lisbon during the peace."

"What did you think of him?"

"I thought he was an excellent gentleman, educated in England and France, enlightened, perceptive, and with a sense of humor."

"Exactly. I have known him a bit longer, since I was in Magdalene College a term with him and took him home with me for the holidays that spring. When he came back to London four years ago, we renewed acquaintance; I had him down to Northumberland, wined and dined him, and ended up by recruiting him as our man in place at the Court of the Shah."

"I would never have guessed," said Sir Thomas with evident admiration. "Though I had wondered at the detail of some of the information that comes across my desk from the Governor-General. An outstanding accomplishment."

"He holds the equivalent post of Foreign Secretary now," said Percy with an air of pride. "He is our only minor nobility, but the Shah has taken his youngest sister as a wife, and Pahlavi has been preferred accordingly."

Merewether sat wondering at this discussion of a traitor in high office that passed between the two diplomats and speculated at the number of similar agents that might be sitting in Whitehall, or Downing Street, or even King George's Court, passing on each bit of information to Paris, to be ground small and finally distilled into a conclusion.

He became aware that Percy was addressing him.

"I was not aware until a week ago when I read the secret files in the Governor-General's Office and came across your report of last August on Vellore, that you were the man who actually killed Tipu Sultan in single combat. I had previously only assumed it was a force under your command. I was impressed with your analysis of the situation and your prompt and effective action to prevent the revolt that was surely coming. Also, I learned, you took Abercrombie, the pirate, brought his body back in a cask of spirits, and last winter, wounded a Royal Navy officer in a duel at Penang. Now, I want you to accompany me to Teheran as my aide on a mission intended to give our accredited envoys that even chance I mentioned."

Merewether sat still. He had gathered from the preliminary discussion that some such mission was in the offing, but he was not prepared for this blunt proposal. A sudden suspicion struck him.

"Am I to understand that I am to be employed as an assassin?"

Percy and Sir Thomas looked at him in amazement, and then Percy snapped, "Why certainly not! What gave you that idea?"

"I suppose it was your emphasis on the fact that I killed Tipu and Abercrombie, and wounded Ackroyd. I also killed a soldier on Mauritius three months ago, and broke a man's jaw so badly that he is only now returning to duty in the Marine," said Merewether.

"Not at all," said Percy firmly. "It was just that those matters stuck in my mind. I want a man with courage and resolution, initiative and unquestioned loyalty. And," he laughed, "if I require a murder, a man with some experience!"

"I confess I might have emphasized some of the more bloody aspects of your career," interposed Sir Thomas, "but it was only intended to show your abilities! Now, Minto has already consented to lend you to the Foreign Office, and the Superintendent of the Marine has been instructed accordingly." He continued in a kindlier tone, "I know it is hard lines on a man not yet married two months, but it is no worse than if you were down around Java with your ship."

Merewether was still suspicious, but he decided to put the best face on the matter he could. After all, the idyll of the past six weeks had to end sometime, but now he was faced with the immediate necessity of finding quarters for Caroline.

"When do you plan to depart, sir?" he inquired. "And by what means?"

"A week hence, if all is in order. Gibby Elliott has agreed to put one of your Marine ships at our disposal. *Comet*, I believe, is the name."

"Excellent," said Merewether. "Her captain was my first lieutenant last year."

"Now, a word more, Merewether. Do not speak of this matter to your wife or friends. The orders to *Comet* are only to Bombay, where other orders to Bushire will be given. Our mission in Persia is one of trade, under the Treaty of 1801. We shall want another session or so with you before we leave, and I suggest that you equip yourself as a cavalry officer, for there are no wheels in Persia. And now, thank you for your patience and willingness to help." Percy rose and shook his hand ceremoniously, as Merewether looked at him at this close range and wondered yet again if this hard, conniving man could be his father.

CHAPTER TWENTY-SIX

He had informed Caroline that he was expecting orders that would take him away from Calcutta for a time, and she appeared philosophical at this first parting. He told her only that it was a routine cruise to Bombay and the Arabian Sea, as an aide to Percy. But, he found her clinging to him in the night in spite of the heat, inciting him to excesses in concupiscence of which he had not dreamed he or she were capable. He wondered briefly on one such occasion if she were deliberately seeking pregnancy out of fear that he would not return, and then laughed at himself for the melodrama.

Lodgings were found, not elaborate, but adequate, and a quarter's rent paid for Caroline. He had to arrange for her to draw an allotment of his pay, and he placed another sum on deposit with the Company, subject to her order. He consulted a young solicitor for the Company, and made a will, leaving his estate to Caroline and her heirs without reserve. For himself, he had to have civilian clothing tailored, buy other clothing suitable to travel on horseback, and have thigh-high riding boots made. He had been on a horse possibly a dozen times in his life, in the courtyard at Bellflower House as a child, and once or twice since he had served in the Marine. He suffered some anxieties as to his ability to travel several hundred miles by such means. He had long since replaced the razors and other personal items that were still on *Rapid,* but what he missed in outfitting for this mission were the two double-barreled pistols he had carried since he took them from Abercrombie last year. He spoke to MacLellan and was able to borrow a pair of pistols, not double-barreled, but adequate. Percy had stated that swords would not be worn, so he did not replace his own. He attended an auction of effects of a deceased cavalry officer at Fort William and was able to buy a pair of brass-bound campaign chests, with drawers locked by broad leather straps, designed to fit on the back of a pack horse.

The night before departure, he had Land, MacLellan, Mac-Rae and Harris to dinner, with Percy as the guest of honor. The diplomat had previously met all of them with the exception of MacLellan, and he quickly won him over with his knowledge of fowling pieces and a discussion of the proper amount of lead to hold when shooting pheasants. There was a series of toasts proposed, first by Land, then by Percy, and last by Harris, due to take passage in the Boston barque tomorrow. Merewether felt subdued in the midst of the gaiety, even after two gins, when they went in to dinner. He had, he told himself, no enthusiasm for this assignment to Persia and was yet a little suspicious of Percy's motives in asking for his services.

Caroline looked more beautiful than ever tonight, her hair gleaming in the candlelight; and Merewether felt depression well up at the thought that this would be his last night with her for some uncertain period. He managed to address himself to his duties as host.

"Yes," he heard Percy say, apparently in answer to a question from Harris. "I was over there in ninety-four, and met your Washington. He was some sort of a distant kinsman to my mother . . ."

The evening wore on, this last night in the house of Colonel Harding, the old friends, the new friends, the banter and serious discussions between the guests, a savoury, and then brandy, and finally, their departure. He came back from the portico to find Caroline in tears.

"Why, what . . ." he commenced. She came over and put her

arms about him, her head resting on his shoulder, while she sobbed. "What did I do?" he demanded.

"Nothing. It's just that you're leaving me, and that Mister Percy . . ."

"What?"

She sobbed again, lifted her face, and he kissed her hard, his hands sliding down to caress her hips. "It's just that every time I looked at him tonight, I saw you, fifteen years older, and I am not sure that I liked what I saw," she said breaking away. "I don't want you to become as cold and hard as that man!"

Merewether was bemused. Someone else had noticed the resemblance between Percy and himself, and apparently objected to it. He had already concluded that the man was cold and hard, but those qualities were necessary in his line, and England needed such men. He speculated for a moment if he might become like Percy, possibly some of his subordinates already saw him in such a light, and then he wondered if the red blood of Merewether might have tempered the blue blood of Percy.

"Nonsense," he told her gently. "The man is a diplomat, and we require such men. I am nothing like him."

"Oh, but you are, you look enough like him to be his son or younger brother," Caroline cried. "And I do not want you to develop into that, become polished smooth as a diamond, and as hard, another Uncle George or Percy, 'seeking the bubble reputation even in the cannon's mouth.' " She put her head down on his shoulder and sobbed again. He recognized the quotation and congratulated himself on the reading he had done through the long night watches at sea last winter.

"Aha," he said lightly. "You prefer me as 'the justice' . . ."

"Not at all!" she snapped, lifting her head. "I prefer you as you are, 'the lover, sighing like furnace.' "

"Agreed!" he shouted, and gathered Caroline up in his arms, kicking and protesting, to carry her bodily to their bed.

"Was there enough sighing for your taste?" he inquired some time later, lying back relaxed in the big bed, their clothing scattered across the floor in the lamplight.

"For the moment," she replied. "But I shall probably provoke you again before you leave, sir!"

CHAPTER TWENTY-SEVEN

The journey down the Hooghly was a trial to Merewether. For the first time in his life, he was a passenger, charged with no duty to perform in managing the ship. On the quarterdeck, he caught himself half a dozen times about to give an order or admonition to the helm. He saw MacRae's sly smile and deliberately moved as far from the wheel and temptation as he could. Percy was on deck, shirt open at the throat, wearing loose cotton trousers, and a broad straw hat to shield him from the sun.

"Well, Merewether, I am happy to be under way. Once we clear this fetid delta and get into the clean sea breeze, I shall feel better. I always thrive on a voyage."

"Yes, sir, and are your quarters satisfactory?" Dillon had been dispossessed, and all the other officers moved down two spaces, and doubled up, to provide private rooms for Percy and Merewether. He sympathized with their dislocation, but he had often enough in the past suffered the same fate.

"Why, adequate, I think. Of course, I did not expect to live in a palace aboard a man-o'-war."

The next day, they dropped the pilot off the Sandheads, and took departure on the long reach southwardly to the equator which would enable them to go about and sail back up the west coast of India to Bombay. That afternoon, Percy handed Merewether a slender volume.

"You might read this memoir by a man who spent a number of years in Persia and was there at the time of the establishment of the Qajar Dynasty in 1779. Its founder was an eunuch by the name of Agha Muhammad Khan, and his opponent was Lutf Ali. He captured Ali at a place called Kerman and had him put to death by torture. Then, as punishment for the inhabitants of Kerman for allowing the man to take refuge there, he put out the eyes of twenty thousand of them!" Percy laughed. "You see, we are not dealing with gentle people. Of course, Fath Ali Shah is by no means as bloodthirsty as his uncle, but even under his regime, life is cheap in Persia!"

"I shall read it with interest," Merewether told him.

He had heard of the atrocity of Kerman years ago during his first commissioned service in the Marine, and he had been ashore in Persia, but never more than a few miles inland. He read the memoir, and two other books that Percy produced, as *Comet* crawled down the latitudes across the equator, there to go about and steer northwestwardly for Bombay.

Percy called ceremoniously on the Governor of Bombay, and then on the Superintendent of the Marine, presenting his credentials from the Foreign Office and the letters from the Governor-General to them, directing issuance of additional orders to Mac-Rae for the voyage to Bushire.

"You require that *Comet* await your return at Bushire?" asked Commodore Morris, acting for the absent Waldron as Commandant of the Marine.

"Yes," replied Percy. "I regret taking the ship out of service for the time, but it may be essential that we have immediate means of transportation upon our return from Teheran." Merewether pricked up his ears. It sounded almost as though Percy anticipated an escape to sea, though Bushire had a substantial Company establishment based there, and numerous small Marine vessels patrolling against the Arab pirates in the Persian Gulf.

They were only a day and night at Bombay before departing on the long, slow passage, west northwest, across the Arabian Sea to the Gulf of Oman, contending with contrary winds and suffocating periods of dead calm. Merewether had his instincts under control now and managed to suppress the impulse to give orders in MacRae's ship. But his ear was still attuned to every creak and thump on deck, and he woke automatically when the watch was relieved in the night. The ship worked around through the Strait of Ormuz, coming finally into the Persian Gulf, to catch a fair breeze for Bushire.

Percy had unbent as the voyage progressed, sitting late at table at the meals he and Merewether took with MacRae in the cabin, discussing the future of the Company, India and England, and the difficulties inherent in governing territories halfway around the world.

"No," he said on one such occasion in the Gulf. "I think the Company has nearly run its course, certainly as the governing power of a subcontinent. Of course, Government is taking a much stronger part in affairs now; the India Board has strengthened its hand, compared to the Courts of Proprietors and Directors, as witness Minto's appointment in preference to Barlow. Gibby Elliott was President of the India Board, you know." He looked through a port into the distance. "And there is no logical reason why a nation of at least a hundred million persons should be governed by a private company. The Company has managed to survive these two hundred years mainly by playing one native ruler off against another, keeping India fragmented, and employing mercenaries and bribes to hold its pet rulers in place." Percy looked back at Merewether and MacRae. "Why, if all the people of India could agree to piss at one time, they would sluice our few thousand British residents right into the sea!"

Even MacRae roared with laughter at the improbable event.

The Resident at Bushire, a man named Legg, was a precise person and uncertain of his liabilities in dealing with the Foreign Office, particularly in money matters.

"Why, it is right there," said Percy, stabbing his finger at the paragraph directing the Resident to procure horses and pack animals, drivers, equipage, rations and an armed guard of ten men for the use of Percy. "When the mission is complete, I draw a draft on London, payable at par in Bombay to the Company. You don't think I would haul a bag of gold specie around this heathen country, do you?"

"That is all very well, Mister Percy. I do not doubt you," said Legg, stealing another anxious glance at the Governor-General's letter. "But if something happens, the draft is protested, I have to pay it out of my pocket. I would feel a great deal more secure if you will draw the draft now."

Percy looked coldly at Legg, then unexpectedly said, "I'll draw a draft for half the outlay now, payable one month hence, and a draft for the other half when I return, and I think I am being generous." The man was still unhappy, but he acquiesced and commenced the arrangements.

"These are Shirazee Arabians, the finest horses in the world," said the wiry, bow-legged little Irishman, Keef, by name, as he led them out. Percy looked at each one critically, summarily discarded two, and finally settled on six animals, medium-sized Arabians that appeared fit and in good flesh.

"We rotate the animals, so they don't tire so easily and there's less chance of galling," explained Percy. "I'm aiming at fifty miles a day of twelve hours, though there are stretches when we won't make that much. I estimate at least twelve days to Teheran. And don't forget, Merewether, these horses are trained to be mounted from the right!"

Merewether looked at the restive horses with apprehension, though he dissembled. He shared the average Londoner's love of the beasts, but at a distance, not riding on the back of one going up a mountain gorge along a primitive track.

"Sor," said Keef. "I'll try to have this caravan ready to move by noon tomorrow. The road to Shiraz is good, and you may make a few miles before dark."

"Very well," Percy told him. "Make sure the tack is sound and that there's material for repairs."

They went back to *Comet* and had a drink before dinner.

"It is going to be a damned hard trip, Merewether, my bones ache at the thought of it. I suppose you are packed and ready to move?"

"Yes, sir."

"I have a pair of dragoon pistols in saddle holsters, and I hope you have some arms. The country, they tell me, is fairly pacified, but there are always a few nomadic brigands about. Of course, our escort should be enough to make most keep their distance, and I shall insist on a night guard, whether we are in a caravansary or not."

"Of course, sir." Merewether listened to Percy's extended comments, while his mind wandered back to Calcutta and Caroline. He had lived without a woman for most of his life, but now he wished desperately that he were back in Calcutta and just going home from the dockyard.

By dusk, the party had covered nearly thirty miles across the humid coastal plain. It halted for the night on the bank of a little river. There was a small establishment here with pens of laid-up rocks, presided over by a fiercely mustachioed old man. Keef dealt with him, then had the horses unpacked and led down to drink before they were fed. Merewether was so stiff and sore he had difficulty walking. The last fifteen miles had been sheer agony. He heard Keef speaking to Percy.

"Sor, I say pitch a tent here. Them shelters is crawling with bugs."

The tent went up, a ground cloth was spread, and the bedding unrolled. Merewether's two brass-bound cavalry chests were placed against one side of the tent, and Percy's against the other.

"Keef, is there any reason we can't bathe in that stream?" inquired Merewether.

"No sor. Just look out for leeches and potholes."

The cold water soothed the fiery skin of his rump, and Merewether came back to dine feeling refreshed.

The next day, they commenced the ascent of the plateau bordered by the Zagros Mountains, leaving the steaming plain and emerging finally into cooler territory. Percy and Keef, as well as every man in the train, were centaurs, but they condescended to give Merewether some instruction in the art of horsemanship. After a bit, he found himself achieving balance and was able to ride with the motion of the gait. After two more days, he became reasonably comfortable in the saddle. Up and away at dawn and moving steadily until dusk, they made their way through Shiraz, the old capital of Persia, toward Isfahan, through barren, almost deserted country. Only one incident marred the journey.

Merewether awoke in the chill before dawn at Percy's urgent whisper, "Get your pistols!"

He heard movement in the rock-fenced paddock fifty feet away, as he groped for his shoes, and then the pistols laid primed and ready on his chest. He emerged, bumped into Percy outside the tent, and they walked across the uneven turf toward the enclosure. Against the stars, Merewether made out the figure of a man on a horse at the entrance to the paddock, and behind him the clump and movement of other horses. Just then, another shape vaulted to the back of one of the animals, and there was a low whistle. It was obvious the horses were in the process of being stolen.

Merewether cocked both pistols, and at the clicks, the figure at the gate whirled with a shout, kicking his heels into the horse's ribs, with the evident intention of riding down Merewether and Percy. There was no time to do more than snap a shot at the figure, while leaping to the side. He heard Percy shoot, and the man fell off the horse. The second man, lying flat along the back of his mount, was heading off at an angle, a half dozen animals gathered together by a rope through their halters, trailing him out the gate. Merewether ran to intercept and saw the gleam of a blade pointing toward him. He checked his rush and fired the second pistol at the prone figure. The man cried out and rolled off the other side, as Merewether seized the halter. Keef and a half dozen of the drivers came running up, carrying the long-barreled guns they called "jinghals," just as a third figure on foot bolted from behind the paddock. A fusillade of shots from the jinghals failed to stop him, and he disappeared into the darkness.

"Well, one is dead, the other shot through the hip," said Percy in the lantern light. "And the third got clean away. Are there any horses missing, Keef?"

"No sor, and don't worry about this fellow here; Ali and his men will deal with him." The man was filthy, visibly crawling with lice, dressed in a sheepskin vest, and a felt skullcap. But he was young, no more than twenty. Blood had stained his legs, but the wound was not serious, and he was obviously begging as he addressed himself first to one and then another of the impassive Persian drivers about him.

The man on guard duty at the paddock had been found in a pool of blood, his throat gaping open like a second mouth. Two of the drivers seized the young man, raised and propelled him off into the darkness, as his voice rose in a shrill series of imploring lamentations. Ali followed, a strangler's cord dangling from his hand. The lamentations were shut off abruptly out in the darkness, and in a few minutes, Ali and his men returned. It was growing light in the east, and Percy ordered the party to break camp.

Teheran was a city built largely of sun-dried brick, with kiln-fired bricks reinforcing the corners of the buildings. In this semiarid climate, they appeared to endure well enough. The city was set nearly four thousand feet above sea level on the southern slope of the Elburz Mountains, and the climate was agreeable. They came to a brick-walled estate just inside the southern environs of the city and stopped before an entrance closed by massive iron-banded double gates. A guard lounged on a stool in a little kiosk at the side, a curved sword belted on. Keef hailed him in Persian, and the gates swung open, giving entrance to a courtyard with a substantial brick house in the background.

"The Company's factor here is an Armenian," explained Keef. "He keeps several apartments for visiting Company and Government people, and for the merchants he trades with, mostly rugs, you know. We will stay here."

A bandy-legged man, wearing an astrakhan cap above piercing black eyes, pockmarked cheeks, and a hooked nose, came out from the house and greeted Keef in excellent English.

"This is Avakian, meet Mister Percy and Mister Merewether. Seven languages, he understands, sors, so be careful what you say!"

"My house is your house, gentlemen." The man made a profound bow, motioning toward the doorway, "Enter." They were led to a spacious apartment of four rooms at the rear of the house, with narrow, barred windows looking out to a small garden. The baggage was soon brought in, and Percy turned to Avakian.

"Now, if we can have some hot water, we'll not require more for a while."

Merewether bathed, shaved, and dressed in the new civilian clothing he had never worn before. They had stood the journey remarkably well in the drawers of the cavalry chest, he decided. There was a knock, and Percy came in.

"Good, you've shifted. Now, Merewether, my next move is to contact Pahlavi, but discreetly, since I don't know the niceties of the internal political situation here, and I certainly do not desire to embarrass him, or compromise his position. What do you suggest?"

"Why, of course, a note . . ." He paused, and thought a moment. "This man, Avakian, do I understand he is to be trusted?"

"I suppose as much as you can trust any of these people out here. I'm told he has represented the Company's interests here for quite some time, and I understand he has provided the couriers for Pahlavi's messages from time to time."

"Well, then, I suggest you ask him how a note may be delivered, discreetly, I believe you said."

"Yes," said Percy slowly. "I don't like it. I prefer no writing, but it is probably the best way."

Avakian was reassuring. "I shall send my eldest son, he knows the way and the man, and he will deliver your message faithfully and unobtrusively."

The younger Avakian was a slender image of his father, but with a smooth olive complexion and an air of alert intelligence.

"You can find the man?" demanded Percy.

"Yes, sir."

"Can you remember the message?"

"Yes, sir. 'Magdalene sends greeting from the house of Avakian.'"

The young man departed, and Percy began to pace back and forth across the room. "I'd give my soul for a glass of Madeira, Merewether, but I shall deny myself until I get an answer. . . . Gad, I hope I get a prompt reply and a meeting with him! Perhaps then, I can form some opinion of which way the cat may jump." For the first time since he had known Percy, the man was showing signs of agitation and uncertainty, the assured, impassive mask had slipped just a bit to reveal human anxieties in the man behind it.

It was over an hour before the knock came, and young Avakian entered. Percy had resumed his usual manner, sitting negligently at ease in a brocaded chair, knees crossed.

"Sir, I delivered your message. Pahlavi says, 'Greet Magdalene at the house of Mossadegh, ten tonight.'"

"Where is that?"

"Only a little way west of here, sir. I shall guide you."

Percy looked at his watch. "Only five o'clock, Merewether. I think we can have that drink before we dine after all!" He turned to Avakian, pulling out his purse.

"No, sir," said the young man quickly. "I accept no rewards." He left, and Percy brought out a straw-wrapped bottle of Madeira.

"To Pahlavi, may his tribe increase!" Merewether touched his glass to Percy's and drank. He would have preferred gin, but the heady wine was pleasant enough.

Persia was not entirely a country without wheels, Merewether discovered, as they walked up a slight grade along a very fair lane paved with stone. Several high-wheeled carts and one wagon loaded with melons and produce passed them.

"Yes, sir, where there are streets or roads, they are used to carry goods, but there are a few places outside the city where the roads are passable," said Avakian in answer to Percy's comment. He pointed to a passing litter with enclosed top and sides pierced by curtained windows, swaying rhythmically to the gait of two mules between poles extending from the front and rear. "A 'takht-e-ravan,' as the Persians call it, used by the wealthy; but the poorer women and children ride in paniers slung on either side of a horse. The men, of course, usually ride."

"Quite interesting," said Percy as they turned into another street and went a hundred feet to stop before an undistinguished brick house.

"Here it is, sir," said Avakian. "Shall I knock?"

The door was opened almost instantly, and yellow lamplight flooded out. With the light behind him, Merewether gained the impression of an erect, medium-sized man in the doorway.

"Come in!" Percy stepped across the threshold, and Merewether followed into a large room, thickly carpeted, squinting his eyes against the light. The man closed the door and shot an immense iron bolt into its socket, then turned with arms outspread.

"Rob Percy!" he cried.

"Ricky!" Percy returned.

The two men embraced and then bussed one another in the continental fashion.

Merewether was now able to see that Pahlavi was a man of about Percy's age, with a slender, athletic figure of middle height. He was clean-shaven and possessed a resolute face, dominated by a prominent nose, high forehead, and curly black hair covering his head like a cap.

Percy turned. "My old friend and schoolmate, Reza Pahlavi, may I present Captain Percival Merewether of the Company's Naval Service."

"I am delighted," said Pahlavi, taking Merewether's hand. "Are you related, by chance? I notice a resemblance . . ."

"No sir," said Merewether quickly. "I am Mister Percy's aide."

Pahlavi gestured to a nest of comfortable chairs at one end of the room. Merewether sat silent, watching the interplay of expression and conversation between these two intelligent men.

"Ah, Ricky, and are you after the women as much as ever?" inquired Percy in a bantering tone. He glanced at Merewether with a smile. "A great lady's man, and I've always told him that even a Musselman's four wives would never be enough for him. How about it, Ricky?"

"True enough," Pahlavi replied easily. "The fires still burn, and that is the real reason for this little establishment I keep here at the edge of the city." He looked at Merewether, then back at Percy, and shrugged. "From time to time it is possible to acquire a European woman for a mistress—ah, variety is the spice of life, as you English say! Such attachments are usually brief, but delightful interludes while they endure. I have had one such here for the past three months"—he inclined his head toward the back of the house—"but she is so charming, so ardent, that I am not yet ready to send her away!"

Merewether marveled at the man's frank disclosure of the presence here of a mistress, in addition to four wives presumably at home. Oh well, standards out here were of a different gauge than in England, or even Calcutta, though he had often enough heard tales of women kept by prominent men in London. Pahlavi rang a bell, and a serving girl came in bearing a tray with glasses and a bottle of Spanish brandy, and they were soon served. Percy proposed a toast to the health and happiness of the host, then turned to Merewether.

"And now, Ricky and I have a brief personal . . ."

"I'll go outside."

"The other end of the room will be sufficient," Percy said quickly.

Merewether went to the opposite end of the room where another nest of chairs was placed. The rear wall was pierced with a high, barred window, the sill just below eye level, half covered with a curtain, and he absently glanced out. He realized that a wing of the house projected to the rear here, and the small, high window gave a view of a larger, lighted window ten or twelve feet diagonally across the ell.

A woman was seated before a large mirror, bright lamps hung on either side, her back to him, but her reflection was clearly visible in the glass. She wore an almost transparent silk gown that obscured, but did not entirely conceal, the image of her torso in the mirror. The face in the glass was hauntingly familiar, pale ivory skin, straight nose, high cheekbones, full lips, and bright eyes, their color uncertain in the lamplight. He knew he had seen this woman somewhere, but he could not place her. A moment later, she laid down the brush, dabbed at both cheeks with a pad, leaned close to the glass with her lips parted to expose the teeth, then stood up, and the small exquisite figure went out of Merewether's view.

He stood transfixed, then became conscious that he had paused with his glass of brandy halfway to his lips. He completed the motion, took a sip, and turned casually away to take a chair. The entire episode had consumed no more than a moment or so, but he realized that he must have caught a glimpse of Pahlavi's mistress.

"Merewether!" He came back to the present with a start. The two men had risen and were walking toward him. He still had half the brandy in his glass, and he drank it in a single gulp.

"Ricky and I have concluded our business for the moment. We will go back to our quarters," said Percy. "Good night, Ricky." The two men again embraced.

"Good night, sir," said Merewether, and Pahlavi shot back the bolt to let them out.

Avakian was waiting in the lane, and they went silently back to the big house. Alone in their compartment, Percy laughed. "Well, Ricky seems to have stayed hitched. I had to make sure, and I felt he would not want a witness against him. He admits there was a treaty made at Finkenstein Castle last spring with France whereby she will furnish arms and military instruction to the Persian army to enable it to regain Georgia from Russia in exchange for free passage to India. Exactly what I predicted! He insists he has no news of peace between France and Russia."

"If there is no peace, what can you do? I thought you intended to use the peace to induce the Shah to deny the French passage."

"True enough," said Percy. "It weakens my hand somewhat, but I have some other strings to my bow. . . . I confess I have some other misgivings, however. Pahlavi is so deep in this now that I do not believe he can withdraw, but there was an air about him tonight that disturbs me. To be sure, we were detaining him from his mistress, and that might account for it."

Merewether almost mentioned seeing the woman and instantly decided that an account of looking at an almost naked woman through a window would not reflect credit upon him. He held his tongue.

"What do we do next?" he persisted.

"I present my credentials to the Minister of Trade tomorrow, and we discuss the old Treaty of 1801. More salable Persian goods delivered to Bushire, and more British products brought in to exchange. It is no more than a smokescreen, but some small benefit may eventually come out of it." He yawned. "I am weary. Good night."

Merewether retired and tried to remember Caroline in the act of making love in the lamplight that last night in Calcutta. Somehow, the image would not come clear, and as he drifted off, he wondered again where he might have seen Pahlavi's lovely mistress before tonight.

CHAPTER TWENTY-EIGHT

The formal call on the Minister of Trade the next morning was an elaborate affair. His chambers were within the walls of the Palace of the Ark where the Peacock Throne stood, in a brick building with flowers and a fountain in front, the arms of Persia, a rampant lion over whose shoulders was a sunburst containing a human face, cut into a brass plate on the door. Percy and Merewether, dressed in their best and attended by the entire retinue of drivers and guards led by Keef and Ali, all scrubbed, dressed, shaved and trimmed to perfection, rode up on horseback. They were greeted by a chamberlain wearing a chain of office on which was suspended an enormous gold seal, likewise bearing the Persian arms. The formalities were conducted in French, and Merewether's role was limited to maintaining station to the right, and a half step behind Percy, since the left was the position of honor in Persia. Eventually, they were ushered into a large chamber and presented to the Minister, a tall man going to flesh, after which there were endless speeches in Persian and French. Percy was fluent in French, but the affair was like a mummer's show to Merewether. He subsided into his chair, managing to keep his eyes open, but his mind wandered some thousands of miles away to Calcutta.

Eventually, the audience ended, and the party moved to another chamber where a banquet was spread. As he came through the door, Merewether smelled mutton and wished he could turn and leave. He remembered when he was a child of six or seven, a large slice of prime roast mutton being placed on his plate by the benevolent old cook at Bellflower House, and his tearful rejection of it.

"Because the wool sticks in my teeth!" he had wailed, to his mother's embarrassment. In any event, he still did not care for mutton, and it was evidently the *pièce de résistance* today.

Percy was at the head of the table in the place of honor beside the minister, and Merewether found himself well toward the foot beside a stocky man in civilian dress with a large, perfectly round bald head.

"Captain Merewether, allow me to introduce myself," said the man with a smile. "I am Colonel Beziat, one of the Emperor's engineers. Since we are on neutral ground, we may as well be civil." Merewether bowed, and Beziat continued, "And this is Major DuFur, Captain, my associate." A younger man on the other side, small, dark and fox-faced, bowed and murmured in response.

"Perhaps, Captain, you care as little for mutton as I and would welcome a bit of beef instead?"

Merewether thought of the old saw, "Beware of Greeks bearing gifts," but could see no harm in sliding a slice of beef onto his plate when it was offered. The affair lasted until mid-afternoon, and Merewether found himself discussing many subjects with Beziat that had nothing to do with his mission here or with the war in general. As they parted, Beziat bowed. "I hope we will meet again, Captain," he said. "I have enjoyed our discussions, and there is no reason for us to be enemies here in Persia." Merewether made a polite response and rejoined Percy for the ride back to the house of Avakian.

"Who was the bald chap you were so thick with this afternoon?" inquired Percy when they reached their apartment.

"Colonel Beziat, one of the French engineers, sir."

"What!" exclaimed Percy. "And what did you talk about?"

"Well, a good many things. First, he doesn't like mutton and told me why, and then I told him why I don't either. After that, we got into a discussion of Shakespeare. The man knows Shakespeare, and even a good bit about Dryden, Burns and Coleridge."

"I'm damned!" said Percy. "Oh well, if you stick to poetry, no harm done." He looked searchingly at Merewether.

"The thing that puzzled me," said Merewether slowly, "was the fact he knew my name, and I have not been announced or presented at the audience."

"He probably knows a great deal more than that about you," said Percy. "He may call himself an engineer, but my guess is he's the chief French intelligence officer in Persia. I must trust you to be discreet."

Percy had audiences with the Minister of Trade for the next three days, while Merewether sat by in boredom. There was really no agreement to be made—the Treaty of 1801 already covered the matter—but eastern protocol demanded high-flown and protracted discussions. He saw Beziat each day as the audience terminated in the anteroom, and the man was cordial. Evidently, he was keeping a close watch on the proceedings. Each night, Percy went alone to confer with Pahlavi at his establishment, returning each time in a gloomy, frustrated mood.

"Damme, Merewether, there is something amiss with the man. One of the unwritten stipulations at Finkenstein was that the Shah would issue an actual invitation in writing to Bonaparte to come to Persia. You know, the Corsican is a great believer in legalities when it suits his purpose, and then we could not cry, 'invasion.'" Two months ago, Pahlavi reported that the Shah had repudiated this agreement outside the treaty on the advice of Pahlavi himself until such time as Bonaparte actually moved to help recover Georgia from Russia. Now he tells me that such a document is being drafted, and the Shah will sign it!"

"What difference does it make whether the Shah issues such an invitation?" inquired Merewether. "I would think the treaty speaks for itself."

"Afghanistan and Sind are no friends of England. The overt invitation and welcome to Bonaparte to enter Persia would be most persuasive for them to follow her lead, and it would influence all the native rulers in northwest India. We have counted on my friendship with Pahlavi to prevent delivery of such a document before Malcolm or Harford Jones could reach Teheran and intervene directly with the Shah. Then, if France and Russia make peace, the Shah might be persuaded to renounce the Treaty of Finkenstein."

There came a knock on the door, and Merewether answered. It was young Avakian. "The Company courier from Bushire just arrived," he said. "Two dispatches for Mister Percy." Merewether handed the two oilskin-wrapped packets to Percy, who laid them absently on the table.

"You see, Merewether," he continued, looking into the distance, "our course was charted in London early this year. The

Foreign Office, in consultation with the India Board, has ordered Minto to launch a three-pronged move to try to head off Bonaparte. Harford Jones is coming here from London, and Malcolm should already be on the way from Bombay. Elphinstone is going to Kabul to influence the King of Afghanistan to resist, and Metcalfe will attempt the same at Lahore. All of them will insist that Persia will not grant free passage to the French. I am here to make their representations true!"

Merewether tried to sort out the complicated affair in his mind as Percy picked up the dispatches and slit the covers with his knife.

"Praise the Lord!" shouted Percy in triumph. He waved the message at Merewether, and said, "The Russians were beaten at Friedland last June, twenty thousand men killed or wounded! Czar Alexander and Napoleon signed a treaty of peace July seventh at a place called Tilsit! I must reach Pahlavi and get this news to the Shah. Perhaps he can arrange an audience as well!"

Avakian soon brought back the word that Pahlavi would meet Percy at nine. So Merewether and Percy had a ceremonious drink and then dined at leisure. Percy was still elated. He had the news he had predicted and was convinced that the Shah would now not only refuse to send the message of invitation, but would renounce the Treaty of Finkenstein instanter.

He was gone two hours, and when he returned, his face was mottled red and white with anger. Percy threw his hat on the floor and exploded.

"God damn the man!"

"What?"

"Yes, my old, dear friend, Ricky Pahlavi! He refuses to convey the news of Tilsit to the Shah. Says he cannot act upon a mere dispatch to me! What in Heaven's name does he expect, a personally inscribed copy from Bonaparte? And after I saw to it that he received a hundred thousand guineas—guineas, mind you—last year as the fee for his services!" It was the first time Merewether had seen Percy lose his poise, and it was frightening.

"Surely if you have the news by way of the Overland Mail, and only ten days from Bushire too, the Shah should have it soon enough?"

"Possibly, if his ministers think to send it along, and Pahlavi doesn't suppress it. I'm damned if I'll wait for that. I'll seek an audience directly with the Shah, or get the news to him otherwise, and to hell with Pahlavi!"

Merewether listened to another two hours of fulmination, while he and Percy finished off a bottle of French brandy.

The routine continued next day, another meeting with the Minister of Trade, at which Percy was evidently hard-pressed to contain his impatience. Merewether came out and encountered Beziat again. He had found himself liking the bald, witty officer more with each meeting. Beziat's conversation was stimulating, and his stock of droll, often salacious stories, was entertaining. They stopped to chat, and then Beziat said casually, "Why don't you come over to my house and have a drink? These Moslem affairs are too dry for my taste." Merewether considered the alternatives—return to the house of Avakian and the bitter comments of Percy for the rest of the afternoon, or the stimulating conversation of Beziat over a pleasant drink.

"I'd be delighted," Merewether told him. "Just let me tell His Nibs." Percy voiced no objection—obviously his mind was on other matters—and Merewether came back to join the Frenchman for the short walk to his quarters.

The place was constructed of the usual brick, but the interior was richly furnished and carpeted. A young servant brought in a bucket of ice in which were immersed two dark bottles whose corks were secured with wire. Merewether had heard of the sparkling French wine but had never tasted champagne. He resolved to be cautious.

"Ah," said Beziat, using a heavy knife blade to unfasten the wire. The cork popped out with a report like a pistol, and he poured the foaming wine into two glasses. "Your health!" he concluded, touching Merewether's glass.

"And yours!" Merewether drank, and immediately decided the stuff was vastly overrated: the fabled wine tasted like nothing more than cider!

"This is the last of my stock," said Beziat. "I've been out here nearly two years, and I'm ready for home again." Merewether pricked up his ears. It was a casual comment, but it sounded as though the mission of the French in Persia might be near completion.

"I certainly hope our business is over in less time."

"It is not too bad, once you become accustomed to the ways out here. Of course, native women, except for the very low classes, are almost inaccessible, but a few women manage to come down from Russia, mostly Circassians, and some of them are beauties!" Beziat drank off his wine and poured another glass. "I kept one such for several months here, but lately she has found another protector and visits me only occasionally."

Merewether was startled.

It would never have occurred to him to discuss such a liaison so casually, even with an old friend. The conversation veered into other fields, while he had two more glasses of the sparkling champagne, feeling only a slight glow of exhilaration. He looked at the clock, past mid-afternoon, and decided he must go.

"It's been most enjoyable, Colonel, but I really should be about my duties. You shall be my guest next time at the House of Avakian. I haven't champagne, but we do have some excellent Madeira and brandy."

"I doubt I'll have the opportunity, Captain. I depart tomorrow for Paris. But, I think we have proved that Frenchmen and Englishmen can be civilized gentlemen together, and I find myself liking you immensely!" Beziat rose, and took Merewether's hand before he turned to the door. He opened it, and there stood a woman in the act of knocking. She wore a combination of European and Persian dress, with a caftan draped about her shoulders, and held a veil in her hand, her face exposed.

Merewether recognized her instantly. She was the woman he had seen through the window at Pahlavi's house last week. He saw her second glance of recognition and almost simultaneously remembered who she was.

"Why, Sally, this is an unexpected pleasure," said Beziat easily in English. "Come in and meet Captain Merewether." The woman stepped inside, her eyes green in this light, boring into his, and Merewether felt the warning implicit in the unwinking gaze. "This is my *chère amie*, Captain, I call her 'Sally,' because her real name is so long and Russian."

"Enchanted," said Merewether, bowing.

"And I, Captain," said the woman in the harsh, throaty voice he remembered from last year in Calcutta. "But you were leaving, and I'll not delay you. Au'voir!" She evidently had no desire that he linger.

"Well, goodbye again, Colonel," Merewether told Beziat, bowing to the pair, and went out into the street. He forced himself not to hurry or look back until he had turned a corner, when he increased his pace. At least a small portion of the pieces of the puzzle had just fallen into place, he told himself, as he pressed on toward the house of Avakian.

"Yes, sir," said Merewether, feeling the flush of embarrassment in his face. "I'm certain, though I only met her the one time. She called herself 'Madame Salcedo' in Calcutta as late as last July and had a troupe of prostitutes, though I'm told she was somewhat selective in selling her own favors." Percy continued to stare at him, his face perfectly impassive. He remembered that hot night last year at the bungalow when Flora Dean had led him on to passion and then rejected him. In his frustrated frenzy, he had sought out the house of which he had heard, paid his five guineas, and chosen this woman to quench his fires. "There is no doubt that she is the woman I saw at Pahlavi's house, though I did not place her until this afternoon, and I am sure she recognized me at the same time, not that it matters. Beziat called her his *'chère amie,'* which commonly means mistress, I think."

"Yes," said Percy. "Quite right, and I begin to understand Ricky's ambiguous behavior now. He is infatuated with the woman, and she is a French agent!" He paused, staring into space. "See if young Avakian is about."

In an hour, Avakian was back. "He was not in his chambers or at his house, sir. Shall I try the house of Mossadegh?"

Percy considered a moment. "No, I'll step around there myself." He waited a moment until Avakian closed the door. "Though if his mistress is off on a frolic of her own, I doubt I'll find him there," Percy went on. "Now, Merewether, in order that you may be fully informed, I put certain matters in motion this morning through other channels to make sure the Shah has the news of Tilsit today, Ricky and his mistress notwithstanding. It may destroy Pahlavi to have it reach the Shah that way, but it also should give pause to any immediate issuance of an invitation to Bonaparte. I think it only good faith to warn him." He clapped on his hat and went out into the late afternoon heat.

It was nearly an hour—Merewether had read through an act of *The Tempest,* trying to find for himself the symbols and imagery that Caroline professed to see in the play—when he heard a commotion, the sound of horses and jingle of arms at the front of the house. In a moment, young Avakian burst in.

"Come at once!"

Merewether followed him to the front courtyard. There were half a dozen shaven-headed, fiercely mustachioed men on horseback, dressed in livery of purple and gold, outside the door. The elder Avakian stood in the doorway, speaking loudly in Persian, as Merewether pushed past him.

Percy was on foot between two of the horsemen, hatless, his coat ripped open, and a livid bruise on the side of his face. There were two nooses about his neck, the ends of the cords held by the riders on either side, and his hands were bound behind him. When Merewether appeared, he started to say something. Then one of the men leaned down to clap his hand over Percy's mouth, while the other twitched his line meaningfully.

"What is it, Avakian?"

"Sir, these are some of the Grand Vizier's Royal Guard of Teheran. They say they were sent to the house of Mossadegh, and there found Pahlavi, one of the Shah's ministers, murdered, stabbed in the throat, and this man in the house!"

"Do they accuse Mister Percy?"

"Yes. One of them speaks a little French, and Percy managed to induce them to bring him here to prove his innocence, but the Vizier's adjutant has been sent for."

"Ask them to let him speak."

Avakian made the request, and it was grudgingly granted.

Percy attempted to speak, but merely croaked two or three times, then cleared his throat and coughed painfully.

"Just a moment," said Avakian. "Here comes the adjutant." The officer rode up to the group, ignoring Percy, Avakian and

Merewether, and spoke with the leader of the guard briefly, then turned to them and spoke in Persian. Avakian replied, several sentences, it seemed, and turned to Percy.

"All right, now make your statement, sir."

"Tell these men," said Percy hoarsely, "I left here less than an hour ago and found Pahlavi's door open. I entered and found him dead, lying in a pool of blood."

Avakian repeated the statement to the adjutant, listened to a question, and asked Percy. "Was the body cold, the blood dried?"

"I do not know; I did not touch either. Ask these men." Avakian spoke in Persian again, and the adjutant turned to the leader, spoke briefly, then asked Avakian another question.

"How long had Mister Percy been gone when these men brought him back?"

"About three quarters of an hour, and before that he had been with the Minister of Trade."

Avakian replied to the adjutant, who then asked young Avakian a question, and received an answer in Persian. The adjutant barked out an order, and one of the men holding the ends of the nooses slid off his horse, untied the cords securing Percy's wrists, and lifted the nooses over his head. The man remounted, and the party reined their horses about and galloped out of the gate, leaving Percy standing.

"Fortunately for you, sir, the leader said the blood was dried, and the body cold," explained Avakian. "The adjutant therefore ordered your release, since he believed our testimony."

"God!" said Percy, back in their apartment. "I was never so frightened in my life! I had just gone into the room and saw Ricky lying over by one of the chairs. I went over to look at him, heard someone come in behind me, and as I turned, the bugger hit me across the face with the flat of his sword. I was half stunned, but all I could think of was that under Persian law the authorities may execute an offender taken in the act on the spot. I was sure that was what they were going to do when they put those cords around my neck, and I started shouting in French. Luckily, the leader understood a little, and I was able to persuade him to bring me here."

"No one else in the house?" Merewether harked back to his encounter with Madame Salcedo two hours ago.

"No, not even the maid." Percy removed his torn coat and stock, and undid his collar. Two angry welts circled his throat. He poured a glass of brandy with hands that shook, drank half of it, then got out his kit of medicines and applied unguents to his face and neck.

Merewether sat abstractly watching Percy minister to his wounds. Pahlavi last night had determined to suppress the news of Tilsit. Percy had this morning, he said, put in motion some other means of conveying the news to the throne, and Pahlavi had to reach the Shah first with the news or be destroyed. It was possible there was another agent for the French in the chain interested in preventing its receipt by the Shah, either from Pahlavi, or Percy, and had killed the man. Beziat had said he was leaving tomorrow, and then the woman had appeared at his door at a time when Pahlavi obviously was already dead. Was it possible she had murdered the man? Some other agency had then sent the guard to the house, arriving in time to intercept Percy. The matter was in confusion, and he wondered where Percy and his mission stood at this moment, now that his agent was dead. He joined Percy in another drink, and then they dined.

"I'm bushed," said Percy, at last breaking the silence. "This afternoon seems to have taken all the starch out of me, and I shall retire."

It smelled late. Darkness and silence hung in the air like a canopy through which the raps on the door echoed with startling authority. Merewether rolled to his feet and picked up the robe laid across the foot of his bed as he groped toward the door. He managed to turn the key, and it swung open to reveal Avakian holding a lamp.

"Sir, there's a woman at the outer gate demanding to see you."

Merewether was in some confusion, but at last responded. "Well, all right, send her in, and what time is it?" The time was close to three.

Avakian came in, lighted a lamp, and then shuffled off down the corridor toward the front of the house, while Merewether splashed water on his face and eyes. His mind felt blank, without curiosity or apprehension in these moments as he waited for the visitor.

The taps came again, not so startling with the lamp lit, and he opened the door. As he had expected, it was the Salcedo woman, a bit mussed and dishevelled. She looked directly into his eyes as she entered, then closed the door and stood leaning back against it for a moment with her eyes closed.

"Madame Salcedo?"

"Yes, I was sure you recognised me this afternoon, Captain. It has been a long while and a great distance from Calcutta." She closed her eyes again for a moment, then continued in the harsh, vibrant voice with its overlay of accent that made *v* of *w* and *y* of *j,* "I regret coming to you at this hour, but I just escaped . . ."

"Escaped?"

"I was locked in the house of Beziat about six o'clock tonight. I had no place else to go. Pahlavi is dead . . . You and your diplomat did not know of my liaison with Pahlavi? I was actually beginning to fall in love with the man, me, who never loved anyone! And then that stinking DuFur killed him this morning."

"Why . . ." commenced Merewether.

"They left with their precious document tonight as soon as the chamberlain brought it," she interposed. "I spent three months persuading Pahlavi to have the Shah sign it, and then your Percy comes with his news of the other treaty and betrays my man by sending the news past him to the Shah. Pahlavi had to protect himself by going to the Shah before Percy's news reached him, and they killed him . . ." The woman was on the border of hysteria, Merewether realized.

"Please, come have a seat, and will you have a drink?" He led her over to a chair, and she seated herself.

"Only water," she said, draining off the glass he brought her and holding it out to be refilled.

"DuFur wished to kill me, too," she said dispassionately, "but Beziat would not hear of it, so they only locked me up."

"Where are they going?"

"Oh, back to France. Once I would have jumped at the chance to see Paris, but not with DuFur. Beziat is kind, in his way, but

303

DuFur loves to inflict pain, and he would have made me pay my passage in the only coin I possess, since he stole back the gold they had paid me for my services with Pahlavi."

It was an interesting commentary, but Merewether required specifics. "I mean, how did they leave Teheran, and in what direction?"

"Why, over the mountains and down to Chalus on the sea. There they will take a ship for Baku and ride overland to the Black Sea. I do not know how they may travel from there."

"And when did they leave?"

"It must have been seven o'clock when I heard their train go out of the gate."

"Eight hours!" said Merewether. "And they had that document with them?"

"Yes, it must have come two hours before they left."

Merewether found Percy's map. It appeared to be only seventy or so miles, as the crow flies, to the shore of the huge, landlocked inland sea, but there were mountains to be traversed on horseback, and it would take at least two days, he estimated, to reach the Caspian Sea. Eight hours start now, and probably ten by the time he could get his train moving. Merewether went to wake Percy.

Percy's tongue was thick and his eyes bleary. Evidently he still felt the effects of the ordeal of the previous afternoon. But his mind grasped the situation instantly. "Rouse out Keef and Ali, get the baggage packed. There is yet a chance we may catch them before they embark!"

Not much, Merewether considered, if they kept moving with a ten-hour start.

It was growing light when he found Keef and gave the orders. Avakian, senior and junior, dashed off to the opening bazaar to buy fresh supplies, and Merewether came back to put his effects in the chests. Madame Salcedo was still in the chair in the sitting room, her head back, mouth open, asleep, her face guileless as a child's. She woke at the closing of the door.

"You pursue them?" she said. "And what do you do if you catch them?"

"Take away the document,'" said Merewether. "And now, what do we do with you?"

The woman presented a problem that he had not had a chance to consider or to consult with Percy about. Presumably, she could make her way if he left her here in Teheran, though she had said she was penniless. Yet he felt some obligation for the information she had brought.

"I should prefer to go with you," she said with a sidewise glance. "If I can reach Baku, it is only a short distance to my home, and I have been many years away. I have a child there, if she is still alive." It was difficult to think of this woman of the world longing to return to a home somewhere beyond the Caucasus and a child she had not seen for years.

"I must consult with Percy," said Merewether, turning to go into his room.

"Wait," she said. "I ride like a man. I will not delay you, and I can make a camp like a nomad."

Merewether went on into the room, closed the door, and dressed in the cavalry outfit, pulling on the boots, now stiff from disuse these past few days. He took out the pair of pistols, saw that they were loaded, and reprimed them with fresh powder from the brass flask MacLellan had furnished, then put one in either pocket of his cloak. The few personal items in the room he placed in the drawers of the campaign chests and locked them. He was ready to move.

When Merewether came back out, Percy was in the room, dressed, and looking his usual self. "The lady went to the privy," said Percy. "Quite an attractive and intelligent person. I see no reason that she should not ride with us. She knows the risks." Well, that solved the matter, Merewether decided, making no reply. In a moment, the drivers came to carry out the chests and strap them on the packsaddles, and young Avakian came up with two of his servants carrying another chest.

"The lady's," he explained. "It had been left at the house of Colonel Beziat." In a few moments, the party was mounted and headed north through Teheran, just now beginning to come awake.

CHAPTER TWENTY-NINE

It was a long, hard day over winding, narrow trails, climbing ever upward, it seemed. Percy kept the party at a fast pace, changing horses at intervals, but not stopping even to eat. By nightfall, they were halfway to Chalus, by Ali's estimate, and it was much too dangerous to continue along the rough track through these lofty mountains.

"I don't think these Frenchmen can see any better in the dark than we can," decided Percy, as they reached a grassy glade with a clear brook tumbling along one border. "We may as well stop here." Merewether dismounted, feeling sore and raw again, and wet with sweat. Madame Salcedo swung off her horse lightly and moved to assist Ali with the fire. She was a small woman, but she had managed her mount with perfect assurance and skill all day.

Merewether saw his chests unloaded, a ground cloth spread, and his bedroll laid out, then wandered in the dusk toward the babbling sound of the little stream. A stretch of rapids poured into a quiet pool with a sandy bottom. The prospect was irresistible to a sore and sweat-chafed man, and he was taking off his shirt as he went down the bank. The water was ice cold, not quite waist deep, and he squatted down in it to his chin, feeling the salt rime dissolve from his skin and the smart of the chafing ease. He ducked his head under to rinse his hair, and when he raised his eyes above water, he saw Madame Salcedo stepping into the pool.

"I hope you do not mind company, Captain," she said, "but I am sore and sweaty, too." Merewether found himself unable to avert his gaze until the small, perfect body had disappeared under the surface of the pool ten feet away.

At first light, the party moved off. Before long, the trail began to tilt downward, and finally they came to a gap where far off in the distance Merewether could see sunlight glinting on the sea. It was an anomaly, he thought, a huge salt sea a hundred feet below the Indian Ocean here between Persia and Russia, and no entrance to it from any other ocean. He wondered for a moment if seafarers plied it in the same manner as in the Persian Gulf and the Arabian Sea and what hazards they faced that might be different from the seas he knew. Unaccountably, it was comforting to him to gaze upon salt water again, landlocked though this Caspian Sea might be.

His thoughts turned to the curious episode last night in the pool. The woman had joined him, entirely naked, but there had been a barrier between them that was almost tangible, though no more than the cold water of a mountain stream separated them, man and woman, each chin deep, and ten feet apart, but perfectly at ease. She had ducked her head under the surface, her fingers combing through the curls, finally emerging with the water streaming down her face in the dim light to push the mass of wet hair back from her forehead. She took a deep breath, and spoke.

"You've married since I last saw you."

"Yes, almost three months now."

"Not the woman who drove you to me?"

"No, she married another."

"You were a nine-day wonder that summer."

"More like three days."

"I almost turned you away that night, you were so angry, and with that scarred face! I was afraid you might try to hurt me."

"I never would."

"And are you happy?"

"Quite."

"Would I know your bride? I left Calcutta last December when I was sure the hard-riding Wellesley crowd was through, what with the appointment of Minto. He's religious and very moral."

"She was the Acting Governor-General's niece."

"Oh, the red-haired widow!" she pronounced it "vidder." "She was a beautiful woman."

"Thank you."

"But she is thousands of miles away."

"At least."

Madame Salcedo had laughed deep in her throat. "I like you, Merewether; you are direct. I do not seek to seduce you, that part

307

of me is gone for a while, I think. I told you I was beginning to fall in love with Pahlavi, and now he is dead. I believe I am carrying his child, and I shall go back to the shore of the Black Sea to bear it, taking no more with me than I left with thirteen years ago." She paused to splash water on her face, then continued almost in a whisper, "Though, if you asked me nicely, I might yet accommodate you."

Merewether had stood up resolutely, the vision of Caroline clear in his mind, and waded toward the bank. "I'm really most flattered . . ." he began, as he dried himself off with his shirt. It was almost black dark now, the glow of the fire fifty yards away beyond the scrub not sufficient to cast light enough to find his shoes when he felt the wet body press against him and lips seek his.

"Oh, you're not nearly so disinterested as you pretend!" laughed Madame Salcedo, proving the case with a flick of her fingers as she moved away. He dressed in haste and rejoined Percy, who looked narrowly at him. The woman appeared a few minutes later, her wet hair rolled high on her head, and they dined in silence on the provender Avakian had bought in the bazaar this morning.

Now, descending to the Caspian plain, moving through increasing forests where scarlet wild-pomegranate blossoms lighted the way, he regretted his constancy. Caroline was a long distance away, the vision of her that had been so vivid last night had blurred again, and the woman riding ahead of him, carrying on a steady conversation with Percy, with the caftan draped about her shoulders, her sandaled feet under the tied bottoms of her pantaloons thrust into stirrups, was very near and desirable. He saw her again, stepping into the pool, and then felt her wet, naked body pressed against his for that brief instant that had aroused him, to her amusement. He decided that he was a complete cad, without morals or principles, unfaithful in thought, if not in deed, and tried to think what he should do if they managed to come up with the French party.

This side of the mountains evidently enjoyed adequate rainfall; the forests and occasional fields were green; and the road became smoother and wider. Percy pushed the horses into their tireless canter. Merewether touching his mount's belly with his crop at every stride, as he had been instructed, to make him hold the gait. They stopped only to exchange a sweating horse for a fresh one, and by late afternoon had Chalus in sight. It was hazy out over the sea, there was little breeze, and the heat was humid and oppressive. Now, close to the autumnal equinox, the weather promised to be unsettled, with squalls, possibly thunderstorms, or even a full gale. Percy reined up at the edge of the village.

"Keef, I don't want to ride in there blind and stumble over those fellows. Send Ali in to see what he can learn." They waited in the shade of plane trees a quarter of an hour until he returned.

"Sah, the party arrived an hour before noon and boarded a ship. There was a breeze blowing then, and it sailed off that way." He pointed westward.

"Only about six hours behind them now, and almost a dead calm," said Percy. "How many were in the party?"

"Two Europeans and four servants. Twelve horses, including the pack animals. They all embarked."

"Come on," said Percy. "We must find a ship."

As they rode through the mud-walled village, Merewether was having sober second thoughts. "Do you intend to follow them across the sea, sir?" he inquired.

"Not only follow them, but catch them!" replied Percy.

"But if we come up with them at sea and use force, it may be accounted piracy for all hands, sir."

"What of it! I'll take my chances, Merewether." You also are taking the chances for the rest of us, Merewether thought bitterly, wondering if Russia and Persia hanged pirates in proper English fashion or employed some more exotic mode of execution.

They came to the beach, and Merewether was amazed to see a half dozen respectable ships anchored off the village. There were three brigantines of possibly two hundred tons burden each, two ketch-rigged vessels, a bit smaller, and what appeared to be a topsail schooner. Percy was already giving Keef and Ali instructions when he intervened.

"Now, sir, don't you think this is my department?" Percy stopped in mid-sentence, mouth open, and looked at him. "I mean, the selection of a ship."

"I hadn't considered. . . . Certainly, go ahead."

"And how much are you prepared to pay, and when, and with what?"

"Gold guineas, as many as necessary, and now!" Merewether turned to Keef and Ali, motioning them to follow him. They went down the strand as he looked at the various vessels.

Here there was no proper harbor; the ships anchored out and evidently were served by lighters moored at small jetties in shallow water. What breeze was stirring was now right out of the north, and the haze had deepened in that direction as the sun set. The vessels were painted in various combinations of black, buff and white, with a touch of crimson or gold on beak and transom. His critical eye immediately discarded the brigantines, deep-bellied cargo freighters and too slow. The ketches were under-sparred, he decided, incapable of carrying enough sail for real speed, but the schooner was not too bad. It lacked the lines of *Comet,* or the Salem-built privateer he had brought back from Mauritius, but evidently it could carry almost the same amount of sail.

"Find the captains, and bring them here," he told Keef, and Ali went off toward a teahouse. It was almost half an hour before he came back with four men. Keef explained.

"The captains of one of the ketches and the black brigantine are with their wives in the harem, sor."

"Very well. Ask these gentlemen if they are available for a charter to Baku." Ali put the question, and there seemed to be some difference of opinion. He listened to speeches from each of the men, asked a question or so, and finally turned to Merewether.

"Sah, none of them is anxious for the voyage. There is a festival two days hence, and they would rather stay here."

"Ask them how much money will make up for the festival."

Ali put the question, and after several more speeches, accompanied by vivid gestures, reported. "Sah, only one of them is willing to go, and he wants one hundred pieces of gold for each day."

"Which ship?" The man pointed, and Merewether saw it was the schooner.

Merewether turned to Keef. "How much are we talking about in British money?"

"Fifty pounds a day, near enough." It sounded like an atrocious price to pay, but Merewether considered, it paid the passage of some fifteen persons and double that number of horses.

"Take it," he decided. "And we'll want to go aboard at once and get under way as soon as the wind turns fair." He looked at the schooner captain, a squat, powerfully muscled man, with almond eyes and straight black hair betraying his Mongol ancestry. "And if he will come with me, I will give him a token of his pay."

He walked with the captain back to where Percy was sitting in the shade conversing with Madame Salcedo. "Fifty pounds a day for the schooner, sir. It's the best of the lot, and the captain wants a hundred pounds as earnest money."

"Gad, Merewether, isn't that a bit steep?"

"Not for the ship, and it's that or ride back to Teheran. The others prefer to attend a festival." Percy rose and went back to the pack train, where he ordered his campaign chest unbuckled and set on the ground. He looked about, then unlocked and opened one of the top drawers.

"I didn't exactly tell the whole truth to Legg," he grumbled. "I don't have a bag of gold to carry around this heathen country, but I do have a thousand guineas here." The coin was packed in paper-wrapped rolls in a compartment of the drawer. "Twenty-five to the roll," said Percy. "Four should be the down payment." He fitted the drawer into the chest, locked and strapped it, then called for the driver to put it back on the saddle.

Merewether took the rolls and went back to Ali and the captain. "Be sure you tell him these coins are worth two of his," he warned the Persian. He looked out to sea; the sun was down, and gloom had descended, with lightning flashes in the distance to the north. "And we'll want the horses and baggage on deck at once. We may as well eat before we board."

It was another two hours before the train was loaded, and Percy, Madame Salcedo, Merewether and Keef came on board. It made no difference. The rain had come with a few gusts of wind, but it was out of the north, and the schooner remained at anchor.

Percy and Merewether shared a small, cramped cabin with two bunks, one over the other. He could find no sign of infestation and thankfully laid his bed roll on the planks of the upper bunk. Madame Salcedo had a cubbyhole inside, across the passage. He came back on deck and inspected the topside in the flickering yellow light from lanterns hung in the rigging. There was a villainous-looking crew with shaven heads and bristling beards lounging about the deck once the rain had ceased. The ship steered with a long tiller, but it had a compass in a binnacle that appeared to be operative. Midships, at the break of the poop, was a short brass swivel gun, encrusted with verdigris, that appeared to be about a one pounder. Not much armament, he decided, *Rapid*'s boat gun was a more effective weapon. He saw stars between scudding clouds moving west and then felt the breeze coming out of the east.

Just forward in the waist, the drivers had tethered the horses to ringbolts in a double row down the center of the deck and given them their nosebags of grain. There were tubs of fresh water ranged along the line, and each horse was watered after it was fed. Merewether chuckled at the thought of the rage and consternation Boatswain Tompkins would have displayed at finding his decks in *Rapid* fouled with heaps of manure and yellow streams of urine draining sluggishly into the scuppers. The drivers had spread their rug pallets under the break of the forecastle, set up charcoal braziers, and reclined at ease, drinking steaming glasses of tea. The easterly breeze freshened a bit and promised constancy. He went below to find the captain, and Keef to interpret for him.

He set a course north-northwest, taking the direct route to Baku, rather than coasting to the west as the other ship was reported to have done. Keef had identified her as one of the fat-bellied brigantines, and with the wind now favorable, he guessed the Frenchmen would also change course. The night passed quietly, the schooner apparently making good between five and six knots. Merewether came below into darkness after midnight and slept uneasily, awakening to go on deck at dawn when he felt

312

the increased motion of the ship and the shouts and clump of feet on deck as the hands shortened sail. As he went out, he saw Percy's berth was empty, and behind the door to Madame Salcedo's cubicle, there was a low murmur of voices. He felt an unreasoning surge of jealousy that Percy was enjoying the woman's favors and then told himself that he had all the instincts of a dog in the manger.

On deck, he found the wind had drawn southeast, and had freshened to almost half-gale force. The schooner was plunging ahead under reefed foresail and mainsail, but still making at least seven knots. The sea was beginning to make up, the sky overcast, clouds low, but no rain. He looked around the horizon in the gray light but could see nothing. At the rate the ship was going, it might very well have overtaken and passed the brigantine in the night and now be drawing ahead of that slower vessel. According to Percy's map, it was a little less than three hundred miles across to Baku, and by tonight they should be well over halfway. He considered shortening sail still more, then decided against it, better to be ahead than behind at this juncture.

Keef came up looking pale and green. "I can ride any horse in the world, but the motion of this ship is more than I can bear! Ali and most of the drivers are sick."

Merewether was sympathetic. He had never suffered seasickness in his life but had observed the agonies of hundreds of others. "The only remedy for the malady is to lie down in the grass under a tree," he told Keef gravely, and then saw the flush of indignation make the man forget his distress for the moment.

Below, he found tea freshly brewed in the captain's quarters, and a dish of hard pastries, evidently intended for breakfast. As he poured his second glass, Madame Salcedo came in, her face appearing older in the illumination from the skylight.

"Good morning. I trust you rested well," he said maliciously.

She glanced at him with a tired look. "He is a very fit man for his age!" They sat in companionable silence until Percy came in, his face expressionless.

"Good morning, sir," Merewether offered. "A bit fresh and rough topside, but we're making good progress."

"I'm afraid," said Percy, pouring tea, "that we may have run by the other ship in the night." Merewether wondered irrelevantly if the man's face showed emotion even in the throes of passion.

"Better to be ahead than behind, sir. By night, we should be halfway there, if the wind holds." He had deferred to Percy at every step along the Persian road and in Teheran, but once at sea, he realized he had unconsciously assumed command of the expedition. He went back on deck, leaving the pair sitting silently over their tea.

The day wore on, the weather remained stable, though the sea was still up enough to cause the ship to pitch and roll. She was entirely seaworthy, he concluded, and the captain and crew knew their trade. He spent most of the day on deck in the fresh breeze, now pacing the weather side of the quarterdeck, and again pausing to sweep the horizon with the ancient, half-fogged brass telescope he had found inside the after companion. Percy and Madame Salcedo came on deck at noon, but soon disappeared below again, and Merewether tried to visualize their contortions in a narrow, rolling, pitching berth.

In the late afternoon, he sighted a sail to the west and felt a thrill of anticipation, but by the end of the hour, it was apparent that the vessel was a ketch, not a brigantine, and on an eastwardly course. He passed up cold roast mutton for dinner and contented himself with thin crisp bread, still fresh, dried beef, and the fruit that Avakian had bought in the bazaar. Percy was asleep in his berth as he went back on deck to amuse himself for a half hour in the twilight by exercising the little brass swivel gun, with its long curved pistol grip extending from the breech, until it moved easily, then cleaning the verdigris and old powder residue from the touchhold with a bit of wire until it was clear. A last sweep of the horizon with the glass revealed no targets, and he went aft to sit on the transom to windward of the tillerman, feeling at peace for the moment in the cool of the evening.

"Oh, there you are." Merewether jumped and opened his eyes. Madame Salcedo was dimly visible in the darkness. She seated herself on the transom beside him and leaned back.

"Did Mister Percy strike his colors?"

"I think he was justified. But nine times from midnight to noon! The man was starved; he lost his wife last year, he said."

"But you stayed with him."

"Of course, it is much easier for a woman. I had a girl who accommodated forty-three soldiers in four hours the day General Monck's division paid off in Calcutta."

"She must have been exhausted."

"Oh no, she went home and entertained her husband. Of course, she was a whore."

"Incredible! What's your record?" He felt, rather than saw her stiffen with anger, and her voice was hard.

"Merewether, I am not a whore!"

"But I paid five guineas . . ."

"For the choice of the house, but not me! I took you because I was only curious as to what you might be like. I had seen you deliver the pirate, Abercrombie, to Barlow in a barrel of rum."

"I was mad, entirely mad that night."

"I know, I almost gave you to the Cameroon girl. She had already enough scars that a few more would not matter."

"I'd never hurt a woman!"

"Sometimes you don't know your own self."

"But you said the other night you were with child."

"I think I am, but it is too soon to be sure."

"And you have another child?"

"Yes, if she did not die in the plague last year. Thirteen now, the same age I was when I bore her."

"At thirteen?"

"Yes, her father was the count, the ruler of our district. My aunt was childless, she took the girl, and since there was no longer a bride price for me, my father sold me into a harem in Constantinople."

"Good lord!"

"It was not bad. The Turk chose me only five times the four years I was there; I was not fat enough for his taste. And I learned English and French from the other women."

"How did you leave?"

"I ran away one night and exchanged pleasure with a sea captain for my passage to Cairo."

"Oh."

"I met a Greek there, he became my protector, and we came to

Calcutta five years ago to establish a brothel for the European community and officers. I only managed it; I did not work there. I am not a whore!" She leaned over and punched her finger into his chest for emphasis. She subsided again on the transom.

"Spyro died three years ago, and I had no protector. Wellesley asked me to become his mistress, but he was too hard a man, cold inside and outside, for my taste, and I refused him, but he allowed me to continue to operate. When I knew Gibby Elliot was coming, I sold the property, deposited the money with the Company, and started on a visit to my family."

"Then you are not penniless?"

"Only temporarily. DuFur stole back the two thousand gold francs they paid me to influence Pahlavi."

"How did you happen to meet that pair?"

"They joined the caravan a hundred miles from Teheran as I was coming from Bushire. I was the only one who spoke French."

"And they recruited you for that purpose?"

"Oh no. Beziat is a good, kind man. He asked me to live with him awhile, and I liked him enough that I did. He is not very demanding. Sometimes I thought that he did not actually like women very much . . . But DuFur—ptah!" she appeared to spit into the darkness. "He cornered me one day when Beziat was absent, and I could not escape him. He tried to make me take him in an unnatural way!" She spat again into the darkness. "Such is permissible as a byway of love, but not with him!"

"But how did you meet Pahlavi?"

"Beziat introduced us. Ricky was a guest in his house. I saw the man was taken with me, and so did Beziat. He was trying to obtain the invitation for the Emperor from the Shah, and Pahlavi had advised against it. We made a bargain, Beziat and I, two thousand francs for three months as Pahlavi's mistress, and change his mind. And then I fell in love with the man . . ."

"You knew Pahlavi and Percy were old schoolmates and close friends?"

"Oh yes. I blamed Percy for Ricky's murder at first, but now I see he had no choice but to try to send word to the Shah by other means. The other French agent at the court had blocked it, but Pahlavi did not know that. He thought he must go to the Shah first to save himself, and DuFur killed him to prevent that. Then the chamberlain delivered the invitation to Beziat that night before the news of the other treaty could reach the Shah."

Merewether became aware that the breeze had dropped; the sails were slatting, and the ship was almost dead in the water. He rose and took a turn around the quarterdeck in the darkness; the tiller was lashed midships, the helmsman squatting on his heels against the bulwarks; and he came back to sit beside Madame Salcedo.

"Your Percy is hard on the outside, as hard as Wellesley, but inside he is warm and good, and very like you." Merewether was surprised at her statement. He had seen little of Percy's inner nature, but here was another person comparing him to the man.

"I was surprised at how quickly you two became such dear friends," Merewether said.

She laughed. "He is most persuasive; I saw his need, and I like the man, as I like you!"

"Thank you."

"I have used sex to make my way when it was necessary, but, your five guineas nothwithstanding, I am not a whore!" She punched him in the chest again, and a voice spoke in the darkness.

"There you are!" Percy walked from the companionway and seated himself on the other side of Madame Salcedo. "We are becalmed, I take it?"

"Yes, sir, for about an hour now, and it feels as though a fog is settling."

"I hope a breeze is not still blowing those Frenchmen along."

"Not likely."

"Well, Sally, we don't want you to take a cold in the fog. Shall we go below?" He took her hand and pulled her easily to her feet. "Au'voir."

Merewether settled back again. He evidently had touched a nerve with his flippant inquiry of the woman, but it had inspired an interesting colloquy and revealed some of her history. She might not be a whore according to her lights—courtesan was perhaps a more polite term—but it was only a matter of semantics.

He had slept with her once, and they had bathed in the same pool, but only now was he beginning to feel that he knew and understood her. She, not unlike many a wife, was willing to use her sex to make her way, but she possessed a curious morality, a set of principles of her own, and the fees paid her were never direct. He rose to go below. He envied Percy.

Chapter Thirty

Daylight came late and slowly, the ship enveloped in dense fog, visibility a scant one hundred feet. The deck was wet and slippery, trickles of condensation dripping from the rigging to make their way slowly into the scuppers. The horses were being fed and watered, and the waist smelled like a stable as Merewether came on deck to look about. The captain was on the quarterdeck, peering out and then aloft, sniffing the moist air. He made a comment in Persian, and Ali, close by, interpreted.

"He says clear and a breeze before noon."

"Good. Are you feeling better?"

"All over, sah. Some are still sick." The motion of the ship was much easier than it had been last night, and most of the drivers appeared to be ambulatory, scraping and shoveling up the manure, and then flushing the deck and scuppers with buckets of sea water.

He went below for tea, and the captain joined him. They drank in silence, and Merewether ate two of the hard cakes, and then had another glass of tea after the captain left. Half an hour later, Madame Salcedo came in yawning.

"Good morning, Sally, and what's the score now?"

"I think you are impertinent again, Merewether. It is entirely our business. I talked too much last night, and now I shall be more discreet."

Merewether chuckled and said, 'Oh, I quite agree. It is purely scientific curiosity, to determine the capacity of a man at forty-five. I shall be that age myself in a few years, and I should like to know what to expect."

"Humph!" She poured a glass of tea and looked up at Merewether, a tear glistening on her cheek. "If you must know, the score remains the same. I became unwell, and I am not carrying Pahlavi's child!"

"Oh, I'm sorry."

"No, no reason to be sorry. I wanted Pahlavi's child at the time, but now that I have Percy, it is better this way." Merewether looked at the woman with astonishment. "He wants me to go back to England with him."

"As his wife?"

"I think."

The thing was astounding. He had characterized the woman to Percy in Teheran as a selective harlot, and of course, he might only be playing a game, assuring himself of the continued use of her for the time by means of a pleasant lie. But such tactics did not fit the shrewd, worldly character of the man. He would have remained silent; there was no motive to tell a lie, when he already possessed the woman without the necessity of any commitment.

"I wish you much happiness."

"Thank you. Percy knows all about me, and he agrees, I am not a whore!"

"I never said you were."

"But you thought it, you asked me how many men . . . Oh, I owe you five guineas, and I shall pay you!"

"I'd rather have you owe me."

"No, it is the one time in my life I actually took money. I was only curious, and you were so angry. I would have given it back then, except you slipped out while I slept."

"Do please forget it. I am delighted for you." Merewether put on his hat and went on deck. For some reason, he did not want to face Percy just now.

By mid-morning, the fog had burned away, and the easterly breeze had sprung up, moving the ship at a brisk rate. But they had lost twelve hours, and it would be tomorrow before they reached Baku. Merewether patrolled the deck, maintaining a constant lookout, but there were no sightings. He did not see either of the pair again that day; the woman apparently was in her room, and Keef reported Percy was in the captain's quarters. It had been a surprising turn of events, and he still did not know what to make of it. He retired in total darkness during the midwatch, uncertain whether Percy was in the cabin, and slept until dawn.

An hour after sunrise, a casual sweep of the horizon revealed a sail dead ahead. It might mean nothing; they were squarely in the shipping lanes to Baku, and it was a busy port. The schooner gained, and it was soon apparent that the vessel was a brigantine, but it was a common enough rig in this inland sea. Finally, Merewether called the captain over, and handed him the glass, pointing to the ship ahead.

"Ask him if that is the ship the Frenchmen boarded," he told Ali. The captain took down the glass and turned, nodding.

"Ask him how far to Baku."

"He says about ten miles, it should be in sight soon."

"Let's set more sail, I would like to come up with her before she reaches the port." Ali relayed the request; the captain turned and looked at Merewether, then roared out the orders. In a short time, there was a flying jib and a staysail set; and speed increased appreciably.

Merewether went below and found Percy in the captain's quarters drinking tea with Madame Salcedo. "Sir, we have the ship in sight, about four miles now, and ten miles off Baku. We have all sail set and should overhaul her before she reaches the port."

"Good! I shall be on deck shortly."

Merewether picked up his pistols, the powder flask and bullet pouch and went above. The brigantine was measurably closer, and the coast was now in sight. Percy joined him after a few minutes, and they stood watching the quarry as the schooner ran her down.

"Now, what are your plans, sir?"

"Come up with them and cry halt. If they don't, we grapple, board, whatever is necessary to take the men and document. You know these details, Merewether!"

"I need more than that. How much force may I employ? I don't think Beziat will surrender tamely."

"Oh, you'll just have to use your judgment. Whatever is necessary to take them." It was unsatisfactory, but perhaps it was as much as one could expect from a diplomat unfamiliar with war at sea. He went forward to find Keef.

"You know why we are here. Have the men load their jinghals and stand ready to fire or board or whatever, but make sure they act only on my command."

Keef and Ali assembled the drivers, and Ali made a speech. The men began pulling their firelocks from under their pallets before he was half through, and then burst into a jabber of excited conversation as he ended.

Back on the quarterdeck, Merewether put the glass to his eye again. The schooner was only a mile behind by now, and he could see the tower at the port of Baku. The beach was less than two miles to port, but the harbor entrance was still some distance ahead, and they would surely come up with the brigantine before it could enter. In the glass, he saw two men on the stern of the vessel, one with a glass to his eye. He recognized Beziat and DuFur and realized they had an equally good view of Percy and him. Indeed, the brigantine was already wearing about to port, heading for the sandy beach.

"Damnation! They are going to try to land here!" Merewether turned to Keef. "Ask him how close we can come to the beach."

"Three hundred yards," reported Keef.

"Tell him to follow that ship in!" The schooner turned and squared away before the wind to follow in the wake of the brigantine. "If they make it to the beach, we've lost," he told Percy.

Merewether picked up the glass, and could see a boat—it looked about a pinnace—being cleared and falls hooked on preparatory to its being hoisted out. He swept the glass along the deserted beach, and then caught a flicker of movement beyond on top of a rise. He swung the glass back and saw it was a squadron of cavalry, lancers, sitting their horses, with pennons of scarlet and gold flying from the shafts, the points flashing in the sunlight. Off behind them, another column was moving to meet them.

"Ask the captain whose those forces are," he told Keef.

"He says troops of the Cossack regiment quartered in this province. They hold maneuvers along here every morning."

Another complication. If Beziat and DuFur reached the beach and he pursued them ashore, surely these Russian officers would intervene on the side of the Frenchmen.

Merewether turned to Percy to acquaint him with this new development, and as he turned back, saw the brigantine swing to starboard and let go her anchor. Just beyond her, he could see the discoloration of the water marking the shallows. The schooner continued her approach, only a hundred and fifty yards separated the ships now, when he felt the grating of her keel on sand, and she stopped abruptly, throwing half the hands and horses to the deck. The captain roared out a string of oaths and imprecations, his Mongol face contorted with alarm, and ran to look over the side.

Damnation! The ship was hard aground short of her target. "Tell them to get that boat over!" Merewether shouted to Keef.

He looked over to the brigantine. Evidently she was of shallower draft than the schooner, for she rode easily to her anchor. There was a clump of horses and men at her port gangway, and the drivers were urging the horses over the side into the sea, then jumping after them to cling to their manes to be swum ashore. A procession of bobbing heads appeared astern of the ship, as the animals and men made their way toward the beach. Forward in the ship, the pinnace was in the air, being lowered over the side, Beziat and DuFur, each with a portfolio in hand, and their baggage stacked beside them, waiting at the gangway. They were going to get clean away!

The last of the horses went over, and Merewether guessed the boat was pulling down to the gangway. He shouted to Ali, "Can you hit those two men?"

Ali shook his head, "It's a long range, but we try." He spoke to the drivers, and they clustered along the side of the ship, resting the long barrels of their jinghals on the bulwark, then fired a ragged volley. At this range, Merewether realized, even Gunny and his marines would have been ineffective. Beziat and DuFur merely moved a few steps, out of sight behind the deckhouse. He saw seamen passing the baggage down into the boat from the gangway, and a moment later the two Frenchmen scuttled from their shelter across the deck to drop out of sight into the boat.

The drivers had gotten off two or three more wild shots with no visible results.

Forward, the schooner's boat was suspended in mid-air, a tangled mass of cordage choking the block. Some fool had fouled the tackle, and it would not move up or down. The pinnace emerged astern of the brigantine, two men pulling briskly at her oars. Beziat and DuFur were hunched well down below the gunwales. A burst of fire erupted from the drivers forward, most of the shots splashing well short of the pinnace, and the men began the tedious process of reloading the weapons with loose powder and ball. Hellfire and damnation!

The sudden inspiration struck home. "Ali, bring me all the bullets the men have!" Merewether twisted the corroded plug from the muzzle of the little brass one pounder, then unscrewed the top of his powder flask and poured half its contents down the barrel. Percy was forward raging at the sweating seamen trying to unsnarl the boat falls. He looked about for something to serve as wadding and saw Madame Salcedo standing by, a long linen cloth tied over her head and under her chin. "Give me that!" he snapped, seizing the piece and tearing it in half.

Ali came running up, carrying a double handful of musket balls. "This is all they have left, lead being so dear." He rammed down the cloth and tamped it as a wad on the powder with the butt of a wooden fid, dumped the balls in, then seated them with the other half of the linen. A pinch of powder in the touchhole, and he was ready. Ali came up with a lighted spill from the charcoal brazier as Merewether took the curved pistol-grip handle in his hand and swung the gun about to aim at the pinnace with the target clearly visible along the barrel.

"Fire!" he told Ali. The man pressed the spill to the touchhole, and the little gun roared out. The brass handle of the gun was jerked from Merewether's grip instantly with violent force by the recoil, and the barrel pointed straight up. The charge of musket balls plowed up the water a hundred yards beyond the boat.

Merewether stood looking at the gun, his hand and fingers tingling, then realized his mistake. The long, curved, pistol-like handle was not designed to be held in the hand, but to fit over the shoulder of the gunner, thereby utilizing his body as a buffer to

323

absorb part of the recoil that had thrown his shot high over the boat.

He fell to again, dumping the rest of the powder down the bore, saving only enough for the priming. "More balls, Ali," he shouted.

"There are no more; the men fired the rest."

"What!" Merewether looked about for something, anything that would serve as a missile, even a handful of stones or nails would be better than nothing, then thought of his pouch of pistol balls. He ran over and snatched it up. Its mouth gaped open, empty, its contents somehow spilled and lost. He knew complete despair and failure.

Percy came back shouting that the boat was now being lowered into the water. It was far too late. They could never catch the pinnace before it reached the beach. He stood there staring stupidly at the scene. Percy's mission had failed, and by the narrowest of margins. Merewether turned aside and saw a bearded seaman looking up at him with one eye, the other covered by a black patch. A vision of another man with one eye, the garrulous old prize agent he had bought the desk from at George Town, Penang, last March, flashed across his mind, with his rambling anecdote of how Captain Francis Light had induced the clearing of the site for George Town.

"Percy, bring me your gold!" The man looked at him incredulously. "I said, bring me your gold! Gold, man, gold!"

Percy stared a moment more, then ran for the companionway. He was back in a moment carrying the whole drawer from his campaign chest. Merewether seized three of the rolls of coin and inserted them in the muzzle of the gun. The three, in a trefoil cluster, were almost an exact fit in the bore. He shoved three more, another three, and still three more down the barrel, then drove them solidly home on top of the powder with the butt of the fid and primed the touchhole.

"Stand by!" Ali brought another lighted spill; Merewether ducked under the curved handle, set his left shoulder firmly in it, took a tight hold on the breech, and pointed the one pounder at the pinnace.

"Fire!"

The gun roared again, there was a numbing impact on his shoulder, but the muzzle did not kick up as it had the first time. Percy let out a whoop. "Hit!" he shouted.

Merewether's left arm was still numb, but he managed to drop into the boat behind Percy and pull toward the shattered pin-pinnace.

Both oarsmen were dead, as was DuFur, the whole top of his head taken off, apparently by a roll of coins that had carried intact to its target. The paper-wrapped rolls seemed to have performed much like canister, holding together during the early part of their flight, then disintegrating to cut a widening swathe as they reached the target.

Beziat was alive, lying in the bottom of the boat with gaping wounds in both arms. "Ah, Merewether, Merewether," he said. "The gold guineas of outrageous fortune have struck me down! I knew King George had money to burn, but not that he fired it at his enemies!"

Merewether picked up the two blood-spattered portfolios and passed them over to Percy. "Make sure they contain what you seek." He turned back to Beziat, tore strips of cloth, staunched the bleeding, and bound up the wounds, then moved him to a more comfortable position. "I shall signal the beach to come out for you," he told the Frenchman. "I am truly sorry it had to end this way, for I like you. Perhaps we shall see one another when this war is over and we may be friends." He stood up and waved to the party of drivers on the strand, then beckoned to them. He saw one urge his horse into the water and commence swimming towards the pinnace. There were a dozen or so blackened and bent gold pieces in the bottom of the boat, but he let them lie.

Five minutes later, they were back in the schooner. One of the Cossack squadrons had moved down to the beach, and the men sat their horses idly watching the curious events of the past few minutes. It was certain they could never have pursued that party ashore.

CHAPTER THIRTY-ONE

Merewether took charge of the boat that carried the anchor out
to seaward; he was anxious to be gone, since the cavalry squadron
still lingered on the beach; the brigantine had hauled up its anchor and gotten under way for Baku almost before they had
reached the pinnace. He could visualize a Russian man-of-war
coming down to investigate the affair, and he had no desire to be
present when that occurred.

He positioned the boat so as to give the anchor the maximum
advantage in aiding the vessel to pull itself off the bar, then cut
the line that suspended the anchor under the boat's keel. Relieved of the enormous weight, the boat almost leaped clear of
the water and then subsided, rocking violently. He signaled the
captain and saw the hands begin pushing the capstan bars around
to wind in the heavy cable.

The slack gradually came out, the cable stiffened, finally becoming rigid, extending from the fairleads at an angle into the
water. Streams of water spurted from the cable as the pressure
tightened, and finally the capstan came to a dead halt. The captain shouted to the drivers standing idly about the deck, and they
joined the seamen to double-bank the bars. A drive forward, and
a click of the pawl, another drive, another click, then an immense
concerted surge of the men against the bars, and the capstan suddenly turned easily, tumbling the men to sprawl on the deck, as
the ship slid off the bar. Merewether came back on board in the
dusk, drenched with sweat and utterly exhausted, as they set sail
south.

Percy was elated as he displayed the invitation, engraved in
French upon a thin, flexible sheet of pure gold that rolled into a
scroll with a diamond-studded band to secure it and bore the personal cypher of the Shah and the Great Seal of Persia impressed
in purple wax.

"An invitation from one Emperor to another, Merewether!

Once this crisis is over, I must present it to a suitable museum for display. I have never seen a better example of the art." They were on their second drink in the cabin, the captain and Keef present, preparatory to dining. "But you could probably have delivered a dozen broadsides from a hundred-gun ship for three hundred guineas, and how I shall ever explain the matter to Fawshaw, the Foreign Office Treasurer, is beyond my imagination!" Percy laughed and slapped his knee.

Merewether tasted the colorless liquid in his glass again. The captain, no Moslem, with a benevolent grin on his oriental face, had brought out a squat bottle bearing Russian markings, and Keef had explained it was called "vodka," distilled from potatoes. Whatever its source, the stuff was liquid fire, and he bit hastily into his half lemon. Madame Salcedo, seated beside Percy, was subdued, sipping Madeira, and looking from Merewether to Keef, to Percy, to the captain, as the conversation veered to each quarter. Possibly she still felt unwell and regretted the loss of the putative child.

Percy was speaking again, "Grenville told me when I left if I pulled this off, blocked Boney's march through Persia, there would be a barony for me in the New Year's Honours List." He chuckled and went on, "The family title is now enjoyed by my nephew, as insufferable a prig as I ever encountered! If I become his peer, and by my own accomplishments, his nose will be permanently out of joint!" He laughed again.

The veneer that had masked Percy's nature ever since Merewether had known him, had cracked, then slid entirely off tonight. He was, as Madame Salcedo had told Merewether, warm and very human, inside. As for himself, Merewether was suffering ominous misgivings. He had worked like a Trojan this afternoon to refloat the ship and had insisted on getting under way immediately south under all sail. Insofar as Beziat and DuFur were concerned, they were belligerents in the territorial waters of their ally, and he had a legalistic defense: they had merely suffered the misfortunes of war. The two Persian crewmen of the pinnace were a different matter; their deaths might be accounted murder or piracy, or both. The brigantine had headed for Baku, and a complaint by her captain, or a courier from the Cossack squadrons on the beach, would bring a Russian naval vessel hurrying to the scene, and one might very well be in pursuit of the schooner tonight. He intended to reach Persian territory and disembark at the earliest possible moment. Even a Russian naval commander would hesitate to follow them ashore into the sovereignty of the Peacock Throne. He had no intention of going to a Russian prison, or facing Russian justice.

"By the way, sir," he said during a pause. "I think the captain here is entitled to a statement exonerating him from responsibility for our actions today."

"Quite right. Draft it, and I will sign it," said Percy. "I am delighted to take full responsibility!" They moved over to the table for dinner—pork, not mutton, thank God.

In spite of the exhaustion of the night before, Merewether was on deck at dawn with the old telescope. It was clear enough to the east, but northwardly, haze hung low over the water. Several times, he thought he could see a sail, then decided tendrils of mist had deceived him. He gave up for the time and turned to go forward.

"Good morning." Madame Salcedo was sitting on the starboard side of the transom, huddled into her caftan, with a shawl tied over her head.

"Why, good morning, Sally, when did you come on deck?"

"Oh, I have been here quite some time. Dawn is when you see things most clearly." She appeared depressed, wearing an expression of sadness and speaking almost in a whisper.

"No," she said slowly, "It would never succeed. . . ."

"What?"

She ignored him. "I have heard them talk, those men, officers, Company, politicians, visitors, in my House of All Nations, of your England. It must be a very proper place." He started to make another inquiry, but she went on, "Of course, Percy was determined to seduce me the moment he saw me in Teheran that morning. I did not mind, I wanted to reach Baku; but I made him work a bit for the privilege!" she smiled at Merewether, her eyes sea-green in the early light.

"Nearly everyone in the European community knew of me in

Calcutta, but not so many had actually seen me. When Welles-ley commenced his campaign to make me his mistress, women actually sneaked into my quarters to try to discover what I looked like! I simply took to wearing a veil, like a Moslem woman, even when I took my siesta." She laughed harshly. "But there must be many hundreds in England now who know all too well what I look like and would recognize me instantly.

"Oh, I thought it was the same old story when we first went to bed together; I performed well, and he not so good—he was anxious and much too quick. I did not care, I thought I was car-rying Pahlavi's child at the time, and I was buying passage to Baku. I would have accorded you the same entertainment, but you did not ask, though you were ready enough that night in the pool!

"But then, he came back to me, and I again performed well, but he was magnificent. I thought, 'This man, he really likes me,' and he pleasured me in spite of my reserve for Pahlavi and his child!" The woman was talking in riddles, Merewether thought; he could not see the direction she was taking.

"And after a bit, a few more ecstasies, I saw he was not infatu-ated, but actually in love with me! You know, Merewether," she touched his hand, "if a person loves you, it is hard not to love him back!" Merewether admitted to himself the truth of the state-ment; it was his own experience.

"And I do love Percy, he is good, and kind, and warm, and honest inside, behind that hard face! But it could never succeed; I realized that last night, when he said he would become a baron back in England."

Merewether at last caught the drift of her conversation. If Percy actually took her to England, there were all too many per-sons who might recognize her from her days in Calcutta, and whether whore or not, take pleasure in branding her as one. An irrelevant thought crossed his mind. If Percy did marry Madame Salcedo, would she become his stepmother? He looked back at her and discovered she had covered her eyes with her hands and tears were trickling down her cheeks.

"I think you are making too much of the matter," he told her matter of factly. "Percy is a man who knows his own mind; he knows your history, and if he loves you, Hell and King George himself will not stop him from marrying you and taking you as his wife to England! Why, the two of you may spit in the eye of London society if you truly love one another!" She continued to sob for a moment or so, then took the end of the scarf and wiped her eyes.

"Merewether, you are good! I begin to believe you. I shall see what comes, but you give me courage!" She arose and went forward to the companion.

Merewether sat a moment. The woman was very human, warm and honest, full of fears and doubts as to her own adequacy after a lifetime of making her way through a harsh world and apprehensive that she might injure Percy by her past; but he believed her, she did love the man, enough to deny herself the honor of becoming his wife if it might damage him. He picked up the telescope and went to the rail again.

It was not until afternoon that he was able to identify a pursuer, still far astern. The captain took the glass away from his eye, and said something to Keef, his swarthy face showing an expression of concern.

"He says he thinks it is the *Volga*, twenty guns, stationed at Baku. He also thinks his ship is the swifter of the two." They must be a little more than halfway to Hasan Kiadeh, near the mouth of the Kysyi Usen River, at the northern terminus of the old caravan trail south to the juncture of the Tigris and Euphrates rivers, and on to Shatt al Arab and the Persian Gulf.

"Can he carry a little more sail?"

"No, he says he has everything set now."

Merewether remained anxious, as they plunged through the night, but at dawn, when he picked up the speck in the glass, its position apparently was unchanged.

Percy and Madame Salcedo had been on deck for most of the day. She appeared much happier than she had at dawn, strolling arm in arm with the man or sitting on the transom, for all the world like a newly married pair on a summer cruise, her fears apparently banished for the time.

By morning, the Russian ship was appreciably closer, almost hull up; and the wind had dropped. She had set studding and skysails and had what appeared to be a driver rigged above her spanker. Merewether spoke to the captain through Keef.

"Tell him I want those sails wet down."

The captain was reluctant, but Merewether persisted, and the hands went aloft to pour bucket after bucket of seawater down the canvas, shrinking and stiffening it, and causing the breeze to be contained more effectively. The rate of gain of the *Volga* tapered off, and the schooner began almost to hold her own.

By noon, they were as close in to Hasan Kiadeh as the captain dared approach. There was no time to load the horses into lighters; the man-o'-war was almost within cannon range of them. Merewether took a leaf from Beziat's book, urging the horses over the side at the gangways, the drivers and Keef leaping in after them, to be swum ashore holding on to mane or tail.

The baggage was a different matter. They could not hope to make the long overland journey down the Persian Road to the Gulf without their gear. Merewether had it already loaded in the pinnace and hoisted the boat over the side even as a ball from the *Volga*'s bow chaser howled over his head. Percy, Madame Salcedo and Merewether dropped into the boat, and the hands leaned into their oars to pull double time for the beach.

They had paid the captain his fee in gold, with a bonus, left the document absolving him of their piracies, and—as window dressing—tied him in his chair to be found in that condition by the Russians. Even so, he might yet have some anxious moments.

The *Volga* was rounding to, just beyond the schooner, her ports open to expose ten menacing muzzles. They were in a more precarious position under the guns of the battery than Beziat and DuFur had been risking a tiny one pounder. Merewether could hear the faint commands coming over the water, and then the battery exploded. The balls ploughed up the sea all around the pinnace, drenching the passengers and crew with spray, and one ball ricocheted so close over their heads, they could feel the wind of its passage. Merewether prayed that the gunners would not make good practice of reloading: grape or canister at this range could not miss.

The boat had grated its keel on the sand, and the hands were pulling it up on the beach when he saw the guns run out again.

"All down!" he shouted, setting the example. They had the hull between them and the battery, a flimsy enough shelter.

It was grapeshot this time. The boat was shattered and two seamen killed; but Percy and Madame Salcedo were untouched, and they ran up the beach as the surviving seamen and Merewether dragged the baggage clear. Keef and the drivers galloped the horses down to meet them. Merewether saw the chests strapped on; Percy and Madame Salcedo mounted and cantered off; and the drivers urged the pack animals toward a fold in the terrain that would afford shelter. Percy was just disappearing into shelter and Merewether was beside his horse preparing to mount when the guns peered out of the ports again and the broadside exploded.

He heard the solid "thunk" as the grapeshot struck, the horse screamed, reared, and then plunged head first into the sand. Canister or even gold guineas would have wiped out the party, Merewether thought, but they had slipped through the sparser pattern made by the larger shot.

Merewether stripped the saddle from the dead horse, seeing that the *Volga* had a boat in the water pulling for shore, and ran to join the rest of the party. They moved out at a canter, heading up through the valley of the river where it cut past the Elburz Mountains northwest of Teheran. A half mile from the beach, they topped a rise that gave a view of the sea. The Russian boat was on the beach, her crew gathered about it, and a considerable number of Persians attracted by the gunfire close by. An officer appeared to be addressing the crowd. Ali laughed.

"They will get nothing from those people," he said. "In this province, they hate all Russians!"

Merewether took no chances. They kept going as long as they could see the trail and then turned aside to make a fireless camp well off the track. They were up and moving at dawn, on the way to Takestan. The train fell into the routine of the journey to Teheran, trying to maintain fifty miles a day, but Merewether no longer shared a tent with Percy.

In three days, they passed Razan, where Keef replenished their supplies and bought powder and balls for the jinghals before they headed for Hamadan, the provincial capital. They passed Kermanshah, crossed the old caravan route from Baghdad to Teheran and were now approaching the village of Dizful. The camp was set up that night by the side of a pleasant stream. A party of nomads was already encamped on the other bank.

"Parthians," Keef identified them with a sniff. "And I don't like their looks, sor. They have no flocks or women along and are a long way west of Teheran. The Shah last year waged a war of extermination on the brigand bands over there, and these fellows must have escaped." There appeared to be only eight of them, wearing long sheepskin cloaks and riding sturdy, shaggy ponies.

"Well, post an extra night watch," decided Merewether, and put the matter out of his mind. Three more days, he estimated, would bring them to the coast, and they should easily find a boat there to give them passage down to Bushire and *Comet*.

Before dinner, Percy came over to join Merewether outside Keef's tent. He had two bottles of vodka, the parting gift of the schooner captain, and was still trying to accustom himself to the fiery liquid. It certainly possessed authority and imparted an almost instant glow of well-being. Percy had tasted the stuff and decided he would stay with his brandy. Madame Salcedo was overseeing the preparation of the evening meal by the fire fifty feet away.

"Merewether," said Percy, breaking the silence. "I assume you've formed a rather low opinion of my morals these past few days."

"Why . . ."

"Oh, I don't mind, but I'd rather be in your good graces. You know, I lost my wife last year; my daughter is married; and my son comes down from Oxford this year. I've been quite alone for the time, and it is not a happy estate when you have lived with a woman nearly twenty-five years." He sipped his brandy. "And once you're a widower, you seem to become fair game for every horse-faced spinster and plump widow in the countryside. They think they only need signal their availability with a simpering smile, and you'll fall right into bed—after you've visited the vicar, of course." Merewether smiled to himself. Percy's complaint was almost the counterpart of that voiced by Lady Caroline last New Year's. Except for the vicar.

"I had been lucky. My wife and I were quite happy the whole of our marriage, and when she died, I concluded I would not tempt fate by marrying again. I became the extra man at social affairs, constantly on my guard against the extra woman, and particularly wary of the matchmakers, their number is legion!" Merewether nodded in agreement, rememberering Livie Raffles and her friend Kate Hartley, last winter at Penang.

"And then I came out here, with no intention of changing my situation, and met Sally. Of course, my immediate reaction was . . ." Percy shook his head, looking into the distance. "I was never more mistaken in my life! I discovered a woman with a depth of character, philosophy, and intelligence I had rarely encountered. To make my tedious story brief, I have fallen irretrievably in love with Sally and shall marry her at the soonest possible opportunity!" The man looked directly at Merewether.

"Many congratulations, sir. She is all you say, and a beauty with it."

"I thank you, Merewether, for the advice you gave her last week. She was about to refuse my offer in deference to my career!"

He laughed. "I know her whole past, including you, and it does not trouble me, nor does the prospect of some nabob recognizing her in London and spreading nasty tales."

The air was cleared. Merewether had felt a slight discomfort, some tension, at the situation, but apparently Percy had felt more. They went to dine with Madame Salcedo and Keef on fresh beef, vegetables, and sheep's milk cheese from the village.

The train moved out at daylight, leaving the sullen Parthians still encamped across the stream. There had been no incidents during the night and apparently the nomads intended to remain awhile beside the water. It was late afternoon. The party was traversing a narrow, rocky defile, opening into a flat plateau, when the ragged volley exploded. Ali and two of the drivers fell from their mounts, and a cluster of men on foot dashed into the midst of the train, shrieking like banshees and flourishing scimitars, to seize the lead lines of the pack horses.

Merewether was completely taken by surprise. His pistols were in his saddlebag, and he was still fumbling with the buckle when he heard pistols pop close beside him and saw Percy aiming again, with smoke still rising from a small pistol in the hand of Madame Salcedo. He managed to get his weapons free and shot a bandit in the back as he tried to ride off on the lead pack horse. He saw another in the act of swinging his scimitar to slash Percy's knee and shot him in the face. Jinghals were now banging all along the train as the drivers recovered from their surprise, and in a moment, three surviving brigands ran to mount ponies tethered behind the rocks and retreated toward the plain, empty-handed. Keef dived into the tangled melee of rearing, plunging horses and established order again.

"Those very damned Parthians we left this morning!" shouted Keef, pushing and pulling the train back into some sort of formation. "And Ali is dead and three more hurt!" Two wounded bandits were trying to crawl away into the rocks, and the drivers casually crushed their heads with stones.

Merewether reloaded his pistols and then the tiny Scots pocket pistol that Madame Salcedo had fired, watching the three men out on the plain, gathered in a group on their ponies, shading their eyes to look back.

"Let's get out of here," he suggested, and the train moved out into the flat ground, Ali's body draped over the back of his horse. As the train emerged, the drivers fired two or three long-range shots at the survivors. Two of them turned and trotted away, but the third sat defiantly on his horse to display his contempt for the marksmanship.

"Well," said Percy. "That could have been much more serious . . ."

The lone man out on the plain suddenly gave a great shout, raised and shook his gun in the air, then fired wildly and whirled to gallop off after his fellows.

Merewether heard the solid thwack of the ball as it struck and penetrated leather, flesh, and then bone, even before he heard the sound of the shot.

"The bugger hit me!" said Percy in a surprised tone. He was perfectly white, sitting rigidly in his saddle.

"Where?"

"Right ankle, I think, the whole leg's numb." Madame Salcedo was already off her horse, her face a mask of pale concern.

"Can you hold on until we reach that grove ahead?" asked Merewether. "This is no place to try to dress a wound."

They rode on, Percy holding to his saddle, eyes closed, and Madame Salcedo close beside him with her hand on his shoulder to steady him. For nearly a mile they rode, until they reached the grove. There was a spring bubbling out of a rock outcropping, and it was a good enough place to make a camp.

Madame Salcedo spread a blanket, while Merewether and Keef lifted the man out of the saddle. There was a three-quarter-inch hole punched cleanly through the boot just above the ankle, and blood was dribbling out over the instep. Merewether slit the leather down the seam to the heel, and they peeled it off, spilling a quantity of blood from the foot.

"The ball is still in there, and probably a bit of leather and cotton, too." Disagreeable as the prospect was, Merewether decided it would be necessary to probe for the ball without delay. Percy lay relaxed now on the cot, a compress over the wound, and he had drunk off four ounces of brandy. Merewether and Keef approached him with improvised surgical instruments in hand.

"It will hurt," Merewether told him as he bent over to remove the compress. His hands began to tremble as he remembered that Company surgeon, reeking of rum, last year at Vellore, fishing the ball out of M'sieur Lally's leg in the dawn. He felt himself gently pushed aside.

"I do this better, I think," said Madame Salcedo, taking the knife and spoon into her small, steady hands.

Merewether and Keef stood at head and foot, to hold Percy, but it was not necessary. He saw the man tense as Madame Salcedo inserted the point of the knife into the wound.

"It is not deep," she said, "but it is partly in the bone." She moved the knife blade gently from side to side as it slid in, then pressed sidewise. The lead ball, now lopsided, popped out and fell on the blanket, followed by a gush of blood. She went in again and came out with a leather disc and a bloody piece of cotton sock. "I think that is all," she said, watching the hemorrhage with a professional air. Merewether remembered Buttram's statement last year, "Blood's the best cleanser and healer." Finally satisfied, she clapped a compress soaked in vodka over the wound and lightly bandaged it.

"All over, Rob," she said.

Merewether and Keef attended brief Moslem rites for Ali, and the drivers piled a considerable cairn of stone over his grave. Merewether was sorry to lose the man. He had had a fair command of English, was energetic, intelligent, and had served the Company at Bushire, they said, for more than twenty years. When he came back, he found Percy seated in his folding chair in front of the tent, leg supported by a pillow on a chest, Madame Salcedo beside him, holding his hand.

"How do you feel, sir?"

"A bit weak and tipsy, what with that tremendous dollop of brandy you gave me, but otherwise quite fit." Percy ate sparingly and retired without assistance from Merewether and Keef.

The next morning, the wound was stiff, intensely painful, and the ankle and foot swollen. Merewether could not detect any evidence of infection, but it was clear the man could not ride. He took Keef, two drivers, and two extra horses, and rode five miles to a hamlet. He located a litter, a "takht-e-ravan," young Avakian had called it back in Teheran, but much less ornate than the ones he had seen there. It was owned by the headman of the village, but could not be rented or borrowed. He ended up buying the vehicle for ten guineas.

The contraption was adequate. Percy could lie in it at full length comfortably, and the horses soon achieved a matching gait that did not jar his leg. It halved the speed of the train, however, and during the rest of the day, they travelled less than twenty miles.

By the time they camped for the night, Percy was flushed and feverish. Madame Salcedo had kept the compresses on the wound soaked in vodka, but it was angrier looking, inflamed, more swollen, and there was now a bit of discharge. Percy declined a drink, barely ate, and went to sleep immediately after dinner.

Madame Salcedo emerged from the tent in the dusk and came to sit beside Merewether as Keef discreetly moved off into the middle distance. There were two vertical lines of worry pinched

337

between her brows, and she was subdued, sitting silently for a time.

"It is worse than I expected," she said, breaking the silence. "I believe the infection has commenced!"

"Quite likely," agreed Merewether. "It's almost impossible to avoid it with an open wound." He remembered last year, his own flush of fever, and the throbbing ache in the arm that Tipu Sultan's sword had pierced, as he waited by the beacon on the wall of the old fort for the French frigate to make its signal. "And we don't have the drugs or the skill to treat it as a surgeon would. We must press on, regardless of his suffering. Possibly there is a doctor in the port."

The woman sat silent a while longer, dry-eyed, but filled with concern, staring out at nothing. He tried to think of something he could say that would cheer her, but failed. Finally, she spoke again, but in a different tone of voice.

"He says he confessed to you the other night and cleared his conscience. He feared you thought we were merely fornicating."

"He did, but it was not necessary. I do not pass judgments on what people do with their lives. I am not a missionary." The vision of last summer's Sister Jeanne with her pale, clenched lips and bright hair came to mind, the woman so suddenly and uselessly dead in the night. That woman had expressed an interest in his soul and salvation, but she had also been interested in his body. He wished he might forget her, his conscience troubled him still.

"Rob was happy you gave me such sound advice. Sometimes, you are too close to a thing to see it clearly . . . I went straight to Rob to wake and tell him I would marry him! It came clear to me then it is only the two of us that matters. And you know, we talked all that day, walking or sitting on the deck, while you kept peering through that brass telescope and worrying about the Russian ship!" She laughed deep in her throat. "And then, all night . . . I was still unwell then. We must have told one another every single thing we had ever done or thought in our whole lives, how I left home in disgrace after my child and how my brother came back and castrated the count with his sabre, but too late for me!"

338

The tone of her voice changed again. "And Rob told me something. . . . You could never guess . . ."

Merewether tried to see the expression on her face in the darkness but could not. After a few minutes of silence, she rose. "Good night, Merewether," she said in her usual tone. He sat there thinking of the woman and her happiness, with the prospect of a life with Percy now marred and imperiled by his wound, but he still felt glad for her.

By morning, Percy's whole foot was discolored, and there was a noxious discharge with an evil odor. Merewether's heart sank as he recognized the setting in of gangrene. While the blood vessels had not been visibly damaged, the circulation must have been impaired to some extent, possibly by displacement of a bone fragment, and heaven only knew what corruption the Parthian bullet might have been soaked in. Percy felt less pain and insisted they push on.

"The sooner a surgeon can cut away that proud flesh, the sooner it will heal," he told Madame Salcedo and Merewether. The man did not yet fully comprehend the seriousness of his condition.

They harnessed the horses to the litter, fastened straps in loops to the sides that Percy might hold to, and set off at the tireless canter the horses were bred to hold. Merewether estimated they had made a good forty-five miles by the time they made camp, and it must not be more than a day and a half to the coast by Keef's reckoning.

The foot and ankle were now a dark maroon, almost black, and the odor was nauseous. Percy's fever was higher, but his mind was clear, indeed hyperactive. They did what they could, and he slept the night. The next day was a repetition, but when they camped at nightfall, Merewether was sure he could smell salt water, and they had descended almost to sea level.

By morning, the foot and ankle were a shapeless, stinking lump, and angry streaks had extended almost to the knee. The man was light-headed, but not irrational, as they got under way. Just before noon, they reached the village of Babdur, almost at the mouth of the Karun River at the head of the Persian Gulf.

"See if there's a surgeon of any sort here," he told Keef.

Keef came back an hour later to report, "There are two herbalists who are willing to poultice the wound, and a butcher who claims to have performed many amputations, but no proper physician or surgeon." He looked at Madame Salcedo. Somehow, he had come to understand that she was the person most concerned with Percy. "Do you want to chance him?"

Before she could reply, Merewether said, "I think not. An amputation is a very serious matter, all the blood vessels to be tied off, and then stitch a flap of muscle over to cushion the bone. And Buttram says you must be most careful not to spread the infection to the stump." There were tears trickling down the woman's cheeks as she went over to Percy in the litter.

Keef was speaking again. "The butcher had two bullocks hung up he was working on and said he couldn't do the job this afternoon anyway. He's expecting a boat from some Bombay ship anchored downstream to pick up the fresh provisions."

They went through the town to the abattoir on the edge of a little tributary creek emptying into the river. The butcher and his assistants were stacking quarters of beef into a wooden-wheeled cart drawn by donkeys. The man's hands and nails were caked black and his apron was stiff as a sheet of parchment with dried blood. A cloud of flies buzzed about the place, settling on the exposed surfaces of the meat to cover it like a blue-green wrapper. Merewether shuddered at the thought of this man with his filthy hands and encrusted saws undertaking an amputation of a man's leg.

Keef came back and said, "The landing is right down at the end of the lane." They walked on down to a rickety jetty extending out into the river and stood a moment looking at the small craft moving by or moored along the banks. Far downstream, Merewether could see a boat being rowed up the river, and they moved over under a tree to wait. He tried to guess what Bombay cruiser could be out there, whether it was large enough to carry a surgeon or, more likely, was one of the small gunboats patrolling the head of the Gulf against the endemic Arab pirates who lurked in the creeks and inlets to dash out and plunder unsuspecting merchantmen. Still, two bullocks was a substantial amount of fresh meat to be consumed before it could spoil.

"Hot as Hell," said Keef, fanning himself with his broad felt hat. "Worse than Bushire in July!" Merewether went into the sun, and squinted against the glare to make out the boat. It was a launch, of the type usually carried by sloops of more than fourteen guns. He came back to the shade and waited.

The launch finally pulled into view, the oars moving in rhythmic precision. He heard the coxswain's order, "Way enough," then, "In oars," and saw the bow hook poised with his boat hook, the painter coiled ready over his arm. The man hooked on to the jetty, pulled the bow in, and stepped easily ashore to make the painter fast. The boat officer, a master's mate, was standing up in the sternsheets.

"Eldridge! Eldridge, I need you!"

Chapter Thirty-two

The boatswain hoisted Percy, litter and all, on board with a whip rove through a block at the end of the main yardarm and deposited him lightly as a feather on deck. Merewether was chatting with a tall, pleasant young man in the uniform of an assistant surgeon in *Viper's* waist. He looked aloft and remembered every stay and halyard from the two years he had served in her as a second lieutenant under Captain Kersey at the outset of his Marine career.

"Yes," the surgeon—Bell was his name—was saying, "Buttram and I served our apprenticeships under the same surgeon, Captain, though he was just leaving as I arrived. I have been out here seven months now, and I'm beginning to learn my way about." Four loblolly attendants moved forward to take the litter to the cockpit.

"Just a minute," said Percy unexpectedly. "Do you have a chaplain on board?" Madame Salcedo was kneeling by his side as Doctor Bell moved forward.

"Why, Mister Percy," he said easily, "you are not *in extremis*.

341

Painful, but I have no fear but you'll survive. Anyway, we have no chaplain as such on board, though I am told that Mister Wiley, the carpenter, has been ordained as a Wesleyan preacher."

"Fetch him."

"At the moment, he is ashore buying timber, but he should return before long; and in the meantime, I should like to look at that leg and give you a dosage of laudanum in preparation for the surgery."

"I'll wait here until he returns." The man was adamant, and seeing no sign of the boat returning, Merewether went aft to pay his respects to Captain Dickens. They had been commissioned the same day at Bombay Castle nine years ago and had served together in this ship. He left Percy with Madame Salcedo beside him in the waist, Doctor Bell hovering helplessly to one side and the loblolly attendants lounging against the bulwarks.

Dickens, a short, square man, and Merewether were just pouring their second glasses of gin in the cabin. "Merewether," his opening comment had been, "you are thin and brown as an Arab! How do you manage it?"

"Ride a horse from Bushire to Teheran, to the Caspian Sea, and back across Persia to Babdur. I warrant, Dick, you'll be down to twelve stone again, as you were in 'ninety-eight!"

Dickens laughed. "Last I heard," he said, "you had hoisted a broad command pennant over the Bengal Squadron, and then someone said you had been lost in the Indian Ocean."

"Well, both reports contain some truth, but I managed to survive."

"And have you seen Norman MacLeod of late?"

"Last September, in Macao. The happy Hebridean has not changed a hair."

"What ever happened to Toby. . . ." There was a knock on the door, and then Doctor Bell stuck his head in.

"Sir, Captain Merewether, Mister Percy requests that you come on deck."

"Very well. Come along, Dick, this bloke is at the top of the Foreign Office list, and you never know when you might re-

342

quire a friend in those quarters." They both laughed and went on deck. Merewether felt an intense sense of relief. At least he had the man in the hands of what appeared to be a competent surgeon, and he had relaxed accordingly.

There was a heavy-set man, wearing the expression of a benevolent sheep, standing beside the litter. Percy was looking at a greasy, many-times-folded parchment that bore a large, red seal. "Yes, sir, I heard my call in 'ninety-four, and I studied and read the Bible, and everything John or Charles Wesley ever wrote. I passed the examination before a board of clergy at Dulwich in 'ninety-six and was ordained on Whitsunday that year. Of course, I never got a call to a church, I had to make a living for my family, but I've preached in forecastles, and barracks, and brush arbors, and I guess I've brought some souls to salvation! Yes, I've performed some marriages, but I've read a deal more burial services, mostly at sea."

"Well, your credentials appear authentic enough, Mister Wiley. Of course, I'm Church of England, but John and Charles Wesley started there, too, and I'll not quibble. What are you, Sally?"

"I was confirmed in the Eastern Rite."

"All right, you say you even have some printed marriage certificates, Mister Wiley. . . . Madame Salcedo and I desire to be united in the rites of Holy Matrimony. Here. Now! And, Merewether will you stand up with me?" He strove to rise and, with Merewether on one side and Doctor Bell on the other, stood swaying on one foot. Madame Salcedo moved beside him, and Bell stepped back, the man supported on either side by his bride and best man, the black, lifted, bandaged foot dribbling pus on the deck. "Go ahead, Mister Wiley," said Percy in a strong voice.

The carpenter was surprisingly impressive, reading the ceremony from a dog-eared prayer book he pulled from his coat pocket, Percy swaying a little on one foot between Sally and Merewether. When the minister demanded, "Who giveth this woman?" Captain Dickens had the presence of mind to speak up. Percy's responses were steady, and Wiley pronounced them man and wife, then gave the benediction as the sun set over Persia. Merewether and Dickens signed the certificate as witnesses.

"That is the first wedding ever performed in this old ship," said Dickens.

Percy kissed the new Lady Percy, and said, "Well, Sally, as the preacher said, you took me for better or worse. I'm a whole man now, but I'll be worse soon, when that sawbones finishes with me. And now, I'd better lie down again!" Sally, tears streaming down her cheeks, kissed Merewether, Captain Dickens, Doctor Bell, and Mister Wiley as the loblolly attendants moved forward to take the litter below. Dickens delayed the move again, while his servant brought glasses and a bottle of Madeira from the pantry for the bridal toasts.

They sat in the cabin after dinner, scarcely touched by Sally, for another hour, before Bell came in. He had washed his hands and put on a clean shirt, and his manner was entirely impersonal and professional.

"He stood it very well, off just above the knee, and a splendid stump; he'll be able to walk on a peg in three months, and even ride again! I'll let him sleep off the effects of the laudanum in the Flag Cabin with one of my assistants to watch over him for a couple of hours. Then you may go in with him."

"I'll go now," said Madame Percy, rising.

Viper remained at anchor two more days. She had a landing force of seamen and marines ashore up one of the creeks in a search for the base of operations of an especially enterprising crew of pirates. Merewether called on Percy in the flag cabin two bells into the forenoon watch next morning. *Viper* was nearly the oldest ship on the active list in the Marine, laid down at Surat in 1781, and built as a flagship, though it must be years since a commodore had actually sailed in her. She appeared to be still as sound as the day she was launched; the teak planking was almost impervious to decay.

Percy was propped up in a handsome brass bed, a half basket of wicker supporting the covers over the stump. He looked pale and drawn under his tan, but was alert and cheerful. Sally sat beside him, and there was a tray of tea things, including a bottle of Madeira, at his elbow.

"That young doctor told me to have a glass of wine with every meal," he explained. "He says it helps to replace the blood I lost yesterday." He laughed. "Earliest I ever remember having a drink, the sun not yet over the yardarm, as you navy chaps say!"

"We shall be under way day after tomorrow," Merewether told him. "Captain Dickens has orders to Bombay to refit, but he will drop us off at Bushire. The landing force should be back aboard by tomorrow."

Merewether went out to go down to the warrant officers' mess and find Eldridge. He still wanted to hear in detail an account of the voyage to Columbo in the *Duchy of Lancaster* last winter. As he crossed the open deck, he glanced forward and saw the row of horses tethered along the starboard battery, the drivers squatting in a group against the deckhouse. Already, there was a substantial accumulation of manure, and yellow streams flowed sluggishly toward the scuppers. The boatswain and two of his mates stood at the break of the poop, hands on hips, staring in disbelief. Merewether chuckled to himself as he went down the ladder.

The landing force came back on board the following afternoon, drenched with sweat, torn and scratched by thorns, and covered with insect bites, but they had twenty-six sullen Arab pirates in tow, and the cutter was loaded to the gunwales with recovered booty. Merewether sat with Dickens in the cabin while Throgmorton, the first lieutenant, Fry, the third lieutenant, and Hussain, Jemadar commanding the Marine detachment, made their reports.

"Yes, sir," concluded Throgmorton, a huge hulking man. "We burned the village, and destroyed all the small craft. Nothing big enough to be accounted a prize, worse luck!" Dickens congratulated them, served a drink, and dismissed the officers.

"There's a fair breeze and nothing to keep us here," he told Merewether. "I shall weigh within the hour."

Viper came in to Bushire the next afternoon to greet *Comet*, riding patiently to her anchor in the harbor. Merewether became involved in helping Keef get his horses and drivers ashore, then came back to the flag cabin to see Percy and learn his plans.

"Merewether, Captain Dickens has suggested I stay aboard this ship to Bombay. I'll keep the services of the surgeon, and these are much more comfortable quarters for a married couple. We did not intend to return to Calcutta in any event, and I fear Gibby Elliott might try to steal the Emperor's invitation away from me for his own museum!

"I am depositing my report to London in the Overland Mail here, and the copy for him in your care will reach him as quickly as I could. This is a Foreign Office project, not Company, and I am under no further obligation to Minto. There will be India-men calling at Bombay within the next few weeks, and Sally and I shall take passage to England in one of them." Percy paused and appeared to consider a moment.

"Now, two things: Keef added up the reckoning of the expenses of the journey, and here is the bill of exchange for the balance. Please deliver it to Legg and relieve his mind. Second I want your itemized affidavit as to how you managed to expend three hundred gold guineas at Baku.

"One other thing, Merewether, not Government or Company business now. Full of triumph, and a bit in my cups that night as we escaped from Baku, I bragged that I expected a barony out of this. I still do, but I realize that I had said nothing, given no credit for your services, without which the mission would have failed. Please be advised that I have recognized my oversight, and I shall see that you receive all proper recognition for your endeavors. I am well enough connected with the powers at the Court of Saint James to make this promise. And now, goodbye, good fortune, remember me to Caroline, and thank you!"

"It was a privilege, an honor and a pleasure to serve you, sir," said Merewether stiffly. "Goodbye, Mister Percy, and goodbye, Sally!" He turned and marched out wondering if he would ever see the man he had concluded was his father again.

Halfway down the passage, he heard a light step behind him. "Merewether!" Madame Salcedo took his arm and led him out on the tiny stern gallery that had already been out of fashion when this ship was built.

"Merewether, the other night . . . I almost told you something, and then decided not to." She looked up at him, her green eyes glistening with concern. "Now you are going away, back to your wife, possibly you will have a child of your own someday, and it may be important for you to know"—she looked away across the harbor—"and I may never see you again. . . ." She looked up into his eyes again. "You are Percy's son!"

Merewether laughed and saw her startled expression. "I had come to that conclusion myself last spring, the first time I ever met the man. It does not embarrass me. He did a wrong to my mother, but not to me. I am proud that the blood of Percy runs in my veins."

"You knew?"

"I was sure, as sure as he can ever be."

The woman pondered the thing for a moment, then said wonderingly, "Each of you knowing all this time, but neither knowing the other knew!" She thought a moment more and threw back her head to laugh in the tone she had that night on the edge of the pool when she discovered him ready in spite of himself. "Merewether, I am now your stepmother, and it is proper that you kiss me!" The kiss was not entirely motherly, and it was not until the next day that he discovered the five gold guineas in his jacket pocket.

CHAPTER THIRTY-THREE

Merewether stood on the grating at the gangway, waiting for *Comet*'s boat, and watched the proceedings on deck. The boatswain had turned up all hands, the watch below, holders, idlers and artisans, and turned them to, flushing, scrubbing and holystoning the deck to remove the last traces of the sojourn of the horses. He was still snorting and stomping indignantly back and forth, flanked by his mates, as they oversaw the task. Merewether chuckled to see the sight, making his way down the ladder.

MacRae piped the side and greeted him with full honors.

"Welcome aboard, Captain. Why ye're scrawny and swart as a ghillie!"

Comet made a fast passage to Bombay Castle, and then lay at anchor three days while a draft of seamen and marines was assembled for transport to Calcutta. Commodore Waldron was expected back momentarily from his reconnaissance of Java, so *Rapid* should be at Calcutta by now. Merewether improved the time by renewing old acquaintances around the Castle and dockyard. It suddenly occurred to him that he had crossed Persia twice but had never had the time to stop in a bazaar and buy a gift for Caroline. He went over into Bombay and bought a thick rug from Persia, a selection of Kashmir shawls, and a few knick-knacks of silver, porcelain and brass, but nothing that pleased him.

He was leaving the bazaar when a furtive man accosted him. "Sahib, will you buy a gem—cheap?" The man looked about, hunched over, and opened his hand slowly, almost under his chin. In the cupped palm glittered a green stone, oblong in shape, nearly the size of his fingernail and cut and polished in the eastern fashion. "Please, Sahib, only ten of your pounds?"

"Is it stolen?"

"Oh, no, Sahib!" said the man, rolling his eyes and then looking about again. Either it was glass, or stolen, or both, Merewether concluded, starting to pass on. He heard coins jingle and remembered the five guineas Madame Salcedo had deposited in his pocket to regain her amateur standing as she kissed him goodbye. On an impulse, he fished them out, displaying them to the man.

"I'll give five guineas, and if it's glass or stolen, I will find you!" The man looked about once more, then snatched the coins, dropped the stone in his hand, and scuttled off between two stalls.

It looked genuine enough, felt heavy, and sparkled in the sunlight. It might be anything, glass, jade, agate, or some other variety of semiprecious stone, but it was a pretty bauble. He went back to the shop of the goldsmith he had seen and commissioned him to make a ring for the stone. The goldsmith held the stone to the light, then weighed it in his delicate balance scale.

"Almost six carats, sahib, and about as good a color as I've seen in an emerald this year." Merewether looked about himself in some apprehension, lest the true owner should come up, shouting, "Thief!" He waited, still feeling conspicuous, as the man fashioned a graceful ring with his tools and charcoal forge, then mounted the stone.

Back in *Comet*, he looked at the ring again and thought of the curious train of events that had culminated in this beautiful gift for Caroline. Last summer, Flora Dean had aroused him to passion, then sent him away. Mad with lust, he had sought a prostitute in the House of All Nations, paid his five guineas for the choice of the house, then impetuously chose the proprietress, Madame Salcedo, to quench his fires. She had accepted him, she said, only out of curiosity, to learn what a "nine-day wonder" was like, had insisted she was not a whore, then surreptitiously refunded his fee as they parted last week. Now, he had spent the fee he had paid because of Flora Dean on a gift for his wife. He tried to distill some moral or precept from the transaction, but failed.

It was a magnificent bit of jewelry, he decided, putting it back in its box.

Comet weighed anchor the next day, and as she dropped the pilot, *Viper* was hove to half a mile away, waiting to take him on board. Through the glass he could see Percy sitting in a canvas chair on the quarterdeck, Sally by his side. He waved to them, but they evidently could not see him, as the two ships drew apart. They were an oddly assorted pair, he thought, a harem girl and a Percy, going home, crippled now, to live quietly in that proper place. He hoped that no loud-mouthed nabob would hurt the woman. Percy loved her, and she apparently Percy and he wished them good fortune.

It was a long, hard beat to windward almost all the way against the northeast monsoon, and they sailed eastward to within sight of Sumatra before going about for the run to the Hooghly. With no duties to occupy him, Merewether turned to reconstructing a journal of his service in the Marine the past nine years. Some dates and events were now hazy, but it might amuse Caroline.

Comet came to anchor at dusk off the Sandheads, with Christmas only a week away. There was no pilot boat on station, and they waited until noon the next day before the pilot came aboard. Two days later, they came to anchor off the dockyard. There was a familiar ship anchored upstream, but her yards and upper masts had been sent down; the standing rigging looked frayed, weathered almost white; and her paint was worn dull and lusterless. *Rapid* must have endured an arduous service since he left her off Mauritius eight months ago, and a lump almost rose in his throat to see her now.

Merewether was the only person to disembark from *Comet* that night; it was past liberty hours for the crew in Calcutta, and none of her officers had their families there. He came to the dockyard gate with his baggage, and the duty officer, a second lieutenant, new since last he had been there, was brusque and impatient, suspicious of a man in civilian dress who claimed to be a captain in the Marine. The tonga was not available, and he finally found a porter with a barrow large enough to transport his chests. They came at last to the lodgings Caroline had taken, half a bungalow, the other half occupied by an elderly widow and her spinster daughter. The entrance was at the side of the house, and as they went along the brick wall, he could see yellow lamplight through chinks in the blinds. The door was latched, and he had to knock as the porter stood behind him.

"Who is it?"

"Your husband!"

The door swung open, and Caroline stood against the lamplight. There was something different about her, but he did not hesitate, as he stepped across the threshold, to gather her in his arms.

Three hours later, he ducked under the mosquito net and slid beneath the sheet in their bed. Almost by the time he had entered, the old widow and her daughter had come anxiously inquiring as to the commotion made as the porter brought in the baggage. Merewether had had to be introduced, and then a bit of claret brought out as a reward for their concern. When they departed, he had seen them around the house to their door. When he returned, he found Caroline in tears.

"Oh, Percival, and, thou are lean and dusky as a Moor!"

Caroline's narrow waist had vanished; she was gloriously pregnant, but uncertain of his reaction to her condition.

He had been uncertain himself. It was something to be reckoned with, risked, as a peril of those delightful moments of dalliance last summer; but now that the thing was here, he doubted his readiness, his capacity to be a father.

"You and your 'lover, sighing.'"

"That was your line. Mine was, '. . . the justice . . .'"

"Oh, Percival, and we shall have a child!"

They had drunk a toast to the unborn, then eaten a bite, and now to bed. She would not let him see her, blowing out the lamp, but when she came to the bed, she was naked, and she pressed against him, kissing his lips while tears ran down her cheeks. He stroked her flanks, then ventured to the firm bulge in her middle. Something struck against the taut skin, and he realized that the unborn child had shifted position and kicked out a tiny foot in protest against the confining belly.

He accepted the fact. He would be a father, and he was glad.

THE BEST HISTORICAL AND WAR NOVELS ARE
IN CORONET BOOKS

Ellis K. Meacham
☐ 12360 5 THE EAST INDIAMAN   35p
Airey Neave
☐ 10524 0 THEY HAVE THEIR EXITS   30p
☐ 17406 4 LITTLE CYCLONE   35p
☐ 12749 X SATURDAY AT M.I.9   45p
P. R. Reid
☐ 02406 2 THE COLDITZ STORY   30p
☐ 01180 7 THE LATTER DAYS AT COLDITZ   35p

Nigel Tranter
ROBERT THE BRUCE:
☐ 15098 X   THE STEPS TO THE EMPTY THRONE   40p
☐ 16222 8   THE PATH OF THE HERO KING   40p
☐ 16324 0   THE PRICE OF THE KING'S PEACE   40p
☐ 16466 2 BLACK DOUGLAS   45p
David Weiss
☐ 12803 8 SACRED AND PROFANE   75p
☐ 15134 X NAKED CAME I   50p
☐ 15913 8 THE ASSASSINATION OF MOZART   50p

R. F. Delderfield
A HORSEMAN RIDING BY:
☐ 04360 1   Book 1 – LONG SUMMER DAY   50p
☐ 04361 X   Book 2 – POST OF HONOUR   50p
☐ 12971 9   Book 3 – THE GREEN GAUNTLET   50p
☐ 15092 0 THE DREAMING SUBURB   50p
☐ 15093 9 THE AVENUE GOES TO WAR   50p
☐ 15623 6 GOD IS AN ENGLISHMAN   60p
☐ 16225 2 THEIRS WAS THE KINGDOM   60p
☐ 02787 8 FAREWELL THE TRANQUIL MIND   35p

*All these books are available at your bookshop or newsagent, or
can be ordered direct from the publisher. Just tick the titles you want
and fill in the form below.*

CORONET BOOKS, Cash Sales Department, Kernick Industrial
Estate, Penryn, Cornwall.

Please send cheque or postal order, no currency, and allow 7p per
book (6p per book on orders of five copies and over) to cover the
cost of postage and packing in U.K., 7p per copy overseas.

Name...

Address...

....